Lyn Andrews was born in Liverpool in September 1943. Her father was killed on D-Day in 1944 when Lyn was just nine months old. When Lyn was three her mother Monica married Frank Moore, who became 'Dad' to the little girl. Lyn was brought up in Liverpool and became a secretary before marrying policeman Bob Andrews. In 1970 Lyn gave birth to triplets – two sons and a daughter – who kept her busy for the next few years. Once they'd gone to school Lyn began writing, and her first novel was quickly accepted for publication.

Lyn lived for eleven years in Ireland and is now resident on the Isle of Man, but spends as much time as possible back on Merseyside, seeing her children and four grandchildren.

Praise for Lyn Andrews' compelling Merseyside novels:

'The Catherine Cookson of Liverpool' *Northern Echo*

'An outstanding storyteller' *Woman's Weekly*

'A compelling read' *Woman's Own*

'A vivid portrayal of life' *Best*

'Gutsy . . . A vivid picture of a hard-up hard-working community . . . will keep the pages turning' *Daily Express*

Lyn Andrews

Love and a Promise

HEADLINE

Copyright © 2002 Lyn Andrews

The right of Lyn Andrews to be identified as the Author of
the Work has been asserted by her in accordance with the
Copyright, Designs and Patents Act 1988.

First published in 2002 by
HEADLINE BOOK PUBLISHING

First published in paperback in 2002 by
HEADLINE BOOK PUBLISHING

First published in this paperback edition in 2017 by
HEADLINE PUBLISHING GROUP

1

Cataloguing in Publication Data is available from the British Library

ISBN 978 1 4722 5351 4

Offset in Janson by Avon DataSet Ltd, Bidford-on-Avon, Warwickshire

Printed and bound by CPI Group (UK) Ltd, Croydon, CR0 4YY

Headline's policy is to use papers that are natural, renewable and recyclable
products and made from wood grown in well-managed forests and other
controlled sources. The logging and manufacturing processes are expected
to conform to the environmental regulations of the country of origin.

HEADLINE PUBLISHING GROUP
An Hachette UK Company
Carmelite House
50 Victoria Embankment
London EC4Y 0DZ

www.headline.co.uk
www.hachette.co.uk

For my Canadian friend, Margo Giavedoni, with thanks

Chapter One

Tullamore, County Offaly, Eire, November 1847

'Well, will he pay her for her work or not?' Maddy Kiernan's voice was both strident and questioning, and the frown that creased her normally smooth forehead was accompanied by an angry light in her pretty green eyes. She stopped kneading the oat bread then automatically shaped it into a circle, cut a cross on its top with a knife and deftly transferred it to a griddle pan. Sighing, she wiped her sticky hands on her apron, the unbleached calico one she wore all day, now creased and stained from all the jobs she had to do.

'I'm waiting on you,' she pressed. 'You *did* ask him?' Her voice had an edge of harshness.

'Of course I asked him,' her brother Thomas answered irritably, taking the kettle from the range and carrying it over to the square earthenware sink. He pushed up the sleeves of his black frieze jacket.

'Why don't you take that off and get a proper wash?' she nagged.

Thomas glared at his sister but nevertheless pulled his jacket off, revealing the coarse flannel shirt underneath, its collarless neck unbuttoned, the sleeves rolled up. He poured the water into the enamel washing-up bowl and plunged his hands in it, wincing as the hot water brought the feeling back to his cold, callused hands.

He allowed himself the luxury of soaking his hands for a few moments as he looked out of the window and across the yard to the single-storeyed stone outhouse. Three geese waddled toward the turf shed, dispersing the chickens scratching in the soil between the flags. The light was going already, even though it was only the middle of the afternoon.

His younger sister's voice broke through his reverie. 'Is it anything at all that I'm going to get?' she asked timidly.

At fourteen, Carmel Kiernan was almost a grown woman, but she was as shy and quiet as she'd always been. She never sought conversation with the local people. She blushed at the slightest question or comment from the members of the Mitchell family, her employers. She was really only at ease with her brother and sister. There was not a particle of boldness in her, as Maddy often remarked thankfully.

'Will the pair of youse give a man time to wash and warm himself at the fire?'

'We'll be waiting all afternoon then,' Maddy said sharply, handing him a piece of old towelling to dry his hands on. Although at twenty he was only a year older than herself, since the death of their parents five years ago in the cholera epidemic which had swept with devastating speed throughout the country, Tom Kiernan had become the official guardian of both herself and Carmel.

Maddy began to pluck and draw the chicken that he'd killed earlier that day.

'Chicken, is it? With half the country starving to death, she's having chicken for the dinner!' she'd retorted on her return to the kitchen after Mrs Mitchell had informed her that company was expected for the evening meal.

'Carmel is to be paid in kind, so himself told me,' Tom announced finally.

Maddy stopped her work. 'In kind? What sort of kind?'

'She's to have two laying hens.'

'Is that all? She does as much around this place as I do myself – the cleaning, the baking, the washing and ironing – and she's to have only two laying hens? Where's the use in that? She'd be better off with the money, and that wouldn't amount to much.'

'She'll have eggs to sell on Market Day in town, the same as the mistress and yourself.'

The sale of eggs, butter and cheese had always provided a source of income for the women of country households and the men never objected to it.

Maddy laughed derisively. 'Won't it take her months to get together a dozen, and by then they won't be fresh at all.'

'I don't mind, honestly, Maddy. It's better than nothing,' Carmel interrupted.

'Well, *I* mind. It's high time you were paid properly for your work. It's worth more than two laying hens!'

'But where else would Carmel find work of any kind?' Thomas growled. 'The blight has killed off all the potatoes and people can't pay their rent, never mind be employing others.'

Colour rose in Maddy's cheeks. 'And isn't that a living disgrace? The gentry, all of them back in England and having their agents taking the crops and animals to pay the rent money. In good times there's never much left over for food, and now the blight is on the potatoes again, our people have nothing to eat at all! They're dying in the ditches beside the road. Ragbags of bones they've become, and famine fever raging again.'

'It should make you think yourself fortunate that we have jobs here, money, a roof over our heads, a fire in the hearth and food in our bellies. There's men who would kill for all that.'

Maddy glared at her brother although in her heart she knew he was right. As Canal Agent, Mr James Mitchell's position was one of responsibility: he dealt with all the barges that came into the 30th Lock on the Grand Canal which ran from Dublin to the Shannon. He was well paid and the house was very substantial, as was the small outbuilding in the yard, which was where the two Kiernan girls slept. Thomas, as befitting his status as unofficial assistant and general handyman, slept in the house on the 'outshot' bed in the kitchen. This was really only a piece of heavy wood jammed into the space between the fireplace and the corner of the wall. It was covered with a straw-stuffed mattress and pillow and had a blanket and a quilt.

The whole thing was hidden from view during the day-time by a pair of long curtains drawn across it.

Thomas poured himself a mug of buttermilk and watched his sister preparing the fowl. He and Maddy were very alike in looks. Both were tall, of slim build and with green eyes and dark hair, but there the similarity ended. By nature they were as different as chalk and cheese. Tom had ambitions. He wasn't going to be a nobody all his life, bowing and scraping, and thankful for any bit of a job that might come his way. Nor would he descend to the level of the poorer class who scratched out a living and in desperation so often ended up crossing the water to Liverpool. No, he wanted to be a man like his master, James Mitchell, well-respected and well-paid – and Thomas didn't care what he had to do to get there. As long as he stayed in this house he knew he could one day rise above the rank of labourer. It was fortunate that his employer both liked and trusted him.

'Shouldn't you be out doing . . . something?' Maddy asked. Although it was a large kitchen by the standards of other houses in the parish of Rahan, whenever they were all in it, it felt overcrowded.

'No. There's a barge due but I won't be needed.'

'Why not?'

'It's carrying barrels of porter – and you know what that means.'

Maddy had finished her task and was trussing the fowl with string. Yes, she knew what that meant – they all did. The bargee would stop and quite willingly allow the agent to tap into the barrels, drawing off at least a half-gallon for

5

his own use. Nothing was ever said, nor did it need to be, Thomas thought. Quite a few commodities came into the house this way and everyone ignored the fact.

The canal was well used; sometimes as many as thirty barges a day went through the lock. The heavy horses that plodded along the towpath, pulling the barges, were unhitched and allowed to graze while the water in the lock was raised or lowered by the official lock-keeper who lived in the house just across the narrow stone bridge. Nine times out of ten Thomas himself would do the job, as old Ollie O'Hagan, the official encumbent, was nearly always drunk – a condition Thomas considered a disgrace for a man with so responsible a job when others like himself were denied such positions.

'Well, if you've nothing to do go into the yard and refill those water buckets for me,' Maddy said. 'I've got better things to do than stand arguing with you. Carmel, go outside and see if the washing's anywhere near dry. I doubt it – the wind's from the east and it would perish the crows.'

They both rose, her sister willingly, her brother with a very bad grace.

'You can also bring me in some more turf from the shed,' Maddy called after him, 'or I'll have the fire dying on me – and sure, wouldn't that be desperate with all the cooking that's to be done for the evening!'

There was no piped water to the house so a row of buckets stood on a low shelf by the back door, and these were filled with water from a well behind the turf shed. The canal water was fit only for scrubbing the floors, the mistress had told

Maddy when she'd taken them all in. Their father, Patrick Kiernan, had been on friendly terms with James Mitchell although he could never have been classed as an equal.

Gathering an armful of vegetables from the wicker hoppers in which they were kept, Maddy tipped them straight into the sink, removing the enamel basin, and poured half the contents of a bucket of water over them. Of course there were no potatoes – the entire crop had withered in a day. Green healthy leaves had turned black and the stench from the small 'pratie gardens' was terrible. Like the smell of death spreading across the land.

Maddy began to scrub, ignoring her brother as he carted turf buckets and water buckets into the kitchen.

'Ah, God, would you look at the state of the washing.' Carmel came in, her arms full of clothes. 'It's frozen stiff.'

'Then you'd better lower the rack and put everything on it, hadn't you?' Maddy said impatiently. 'Now we'll look like a laundry with it all draped around the place.'

'What's the matter, Maddy?' Carmel asked. 'You've been as cross as a bag of weasels all day and it's not like you.'

Maddy stopped and sighed. 'I don't know. I just . . . it seems as though everything is so unfair.'

'But you heard what Thomas said. We're the really lucky ones.' Carmel didn't like to see her sister in a bad mood, it unsettled her.

'Isn't that all the more reason for helping everyone else? Herself back there has no conscience. She just ignores what's going on, pretends the poor starving souls don't exist. The only time she has ever mentioned them was to tell me I was to give nothing to anyone who came to the door begging – but how can I refuse them? Women and children and babies, all thrown out in the road, with nothing to cover them and weak and dying of hunger. Sure, the yard dogs are better off.'

Carmel looked sadly out of the kitchen window at the neat rows of vegetables and herbs and shook her head. The light caught her hair which was a pale strawberry blonde.

Maddy glanced at her sister. Carmel was growing into a beauty, a real beauty, even though she had no fancy clothes or hats like seventeen-year-old Florence Mitchell. No amount of finery was needed to enhance Carmel's natural good looks.

'I'm sorry for giving out to you,' she said ruefully. 'It's not your fault.'

'It's not yours either, nor Thomas's.'

But Maddy hadn't finished her tirade against Eliza Mitchell. 'I don't know where she gets the brass neck to go to church or call herself a Christian woman. Is it being a Christian woman to ignore what she can see with the eyes in her head?'

'Oh, it's different for *them* and it always will be.'

Maddy nodded her agreement. It was true – nearly all the important, well-paid jobs went to the ruling Protestant classes.

'Anyway, I heard some news today,' Carmel went on. 'The mistress was talking to Mrs Hayes about Miss Florence.'

'What about her?'

'The mistress was saying she's going to send her up to the Big House for a year or two.'

Maddy nodded. The mistress herself had already spoken to her about it and the importance of the dinner this evening.

'Why is she going?' Carmel wanted to know.

'She's to learn all she can about being a lady and running a house full of staff, for when she's married – and she *has* to marry well. She's going to be a parlourmaid.'

Carmel was confused. 'A maid?'

'Yes, a parlourmaid. It's very different from just living here. Up at the Big House they are the real gentry. Florence couldn't go as a companion or anything like that to the young ladies of the house, she's too lowborn for that, but being a parlourmaid is the next best thing. It's their house-keeper and one of the manservants who are coming to dinner tonight to see if she's suitable. Myself, I can't see Florence Mitchell as a maid of any kind. She doesn't know one end of a brush from the other.'

'I don't want her to go away,' Carmel said. 'I like her. She's always kind and saying nice things to me.'

'Well, I know of another person who isn't very pleased about it either.'

'Who?'

'Haven't you eyes in your head? And for God's sake, will you mind those clothes!' Maddy snapped. 'You'll have them covered in soot from the range if you're not careful, and I'm not washing them again!'

'Thomas?' Carmel queried.

9

'Yes, Thomas. That's why he's had a face like thunder all week. He thinks he's in love with her and she with him.'

Carmel's eyes misted and she clutched a damp sheet to her chest. 'I'd no idea. Oh, isn't that sad? It's sort of . . . tragic.'

'It's sort of stupid. The eejits both know they can never get married. They are of different religions and Florence is of a higher class than us.'

'Not that much higher,' Carmel protested. 'I mean, it's not as though we were desperate, living in a dark, damp cabin with only one room.'

'That *is* the difference. If it wasn't for them, that's exactly where we would be – and we'd be starving too, like thousands of others. And here she is, putting a dinner on the table that would feed a parish. It's a sin, so it is. Now will you fold that sheet properly, Carmel, or it won't be fit to put on a tinker's horse, never mind a bed.'

'Well, I still think it's sad.'

Maddy gazed despairingly up at the ceiling. Her younger sister was so innocent and romantic. That attitude would do her no favours, Maddy knew, in this hard life.

Thomas shaved silently and changed into his best black suit, white shirt and black necktie. He hated the stiff white collar that was worn without a turndown or a crease. Outwardly, since he'd heard the news, he'd been as respectful as he always was, but inside he was fuming. Florence was his only means of achieving his ambition to go up in the world, to be a man like Florence's father and eventually to become a Canal Agent himself. Sure, what else could James Mitchell do for his son-in-law but try to ensure that the daughter he doted on had every comfort and great respect from Tullamore society, such as it was.

He'd managed to catch a few minutes alone with Florence; she'd wept and said she loved him, but she had no choice but to go. She just couldn't flout her father and mother. It didn't matter how much he pleaded with her, she wouldn't take a stand. So, he had had to come up with something she couldn't refuse.

'It looks very grand, doesn't it?' Maddy's voice broke his reverie. He stared around the room.

'Tom, I'm sorry she's having to go away,' she went on. 'I know you're . . . well, fond of her.'

He just nodded.

'It could never have come to anything, but I'm truly sorry.'

'I don't need your pity,' he said tersely.

'Suit yourself,' she replied, stung. She wished she'd never mentioned it, if that was his attitude. She shrugged. He'd accept it in time, and the room *did* look lovely. There was only one room that had to serve as both dining room and living room, but the table had been pushed to one end and a folding tapestry screen served as a room divider. The oil lamps with their frosted glass mantles and candles in brass candlesticks gave a soft warm light. The white damask tablecloth and napkins were just perfect for the china, glass and cutlery set out on it. A good turf fire blazed in the hearth, which added to the comfortable glow; its fragrant smell was one they hardly noticed.

Thomas turned back to his task of decanting a bottle of port. The Mitchells were full of airs and graces, he thought, and both Florence and eleven-year-old William, who was now away at school in Dublin, were drilled in the manners of their betters, as Carmel called the middle and upper classes.

'Oh, it *does* look grand, Maddy! You've done a wonderful job,' gushed a voice.

Maddy and Thomas turned to see Eliza Mitchell standing in the doorway, filling it with the sheer width of her black bombazine crinoline with its white lace fichu at the low neckline. A plain, short, plump woman with sallow skin, the colour and style did nothing for her.

'Thank you, ma'am,' Maddy replied. She and Carmel had polished every stick of furniture, and Thomas had cleaned all the brass and the few pieces of silver the Mitchells possessed.

Eliza sighed and raised a hand to check that her hair was in no danger of escaping from its pins. 'Oh, it's such a pity only having the one room. I asked Mr Mitchell if we couldn't use his office, just for this evening, but he said it was out of the question. If the authorities heard about it, he would be severely reprimanded. At the very least I would have liked a separate room in which the gentlemen could smoke and take their port.'

Maddy looked down at her polished boots. Sometimes she thought the woman was mad. It was only a housekeeper and a manservant who were coming for dinner; you would have thought it was Queen Victoria herself. And all this just for Florence to become a parlourmaid. A bloody parlourmaid, not even a lady's maid. The Mitchells had notions of grandeur all right. They couldn't see how ridiculous the situation was. Florence would hardly set eyes on the young ladies of the house, let alone learn manners from them.

'Will it be yourself or will it be Thomas taking the guests' coats?' Eliza asked.

'It will be Thomas, ma'am. I have to keep my eye on things in the kitchen,' Maddy replied quickly.

'Of course. I *hate* cold soup and it would be an insult to serve it to guests.'

'Then I'll go back to the kitchen, ma'am, and make sure it stays hot.'

They were all exhausted when finally the hall clock struck midnight and the guests had departed. Maddy and Thomas had served the sour-faced servants from the Big House, while Mr and Mrs Mitchell had been over-talkative and obliging to say the least. Unfortunately, there had still been long awkward silences. Florence had looked terrified and had hardly opened her mouth. She said yes and no where appropriate, but had made no contribution to the conversation. Now Maddy was faced with a kitchen that had the look of a battlefield about it. At least Carmel had made a start on the washing up.

'Well, thank God that's over,' she said, taking off her best apron and cap and rolling up her sleeves. 'Better get this lot cleaned up as I couldn't face it in the morning.'

'It'll be morning soon,' Carmel pointed out. She too had found it a long evening.

Thomas removed his jacket and draped it over the back of a chair. Now he loosened his necktie and the shirt collar. 'Oh, for God's sake leave it, Maddy,' he said. 'All this fuss and palaver, scrubbing and cleaning and dressing up to impress that miserable pair.'

'I didn't notice you doing much in the way of scrubbing or cleaning and we'll have it done in no time.'

'You know I can't get to my bed until you've finished,' he said irritably, draining half a glass of port that had been left by one of the men. The one high spot of the evening was that he'd managed to whisper a few words to Florence while refilling her wine glass, with the result that, when everyone was asleep, she had agreed to come down to the kitchen.

'Make yourself useful then,' Maddy told him. 'Bring in more turf. That range is nearly dead and you'll freeze, and I'll have to be up even earlier to light it if it does go dying on me.'

He was about to grumble and then shrugged. At least it would get his sisters out of the kitchen sooner rather than later, so he stoked up the range until the fire roared.

Chapter Two

At last Maddy and Carmel had taken an oil lamp and left the kitchen. Thomas closed the door behind them with relief.

Florence had said she would sit by her window, and when she saw the light and the girls crossing the yard to go to bed, she would come down. His brain hummed with the plans he'd made; all it needed now was for Florence to agree.

The kitchen door opened slowly and he turned.

'Florence? Is it yourself?' he whispered.

She came into the room holding a candlestick in which a long white candle burned. It illuminated her naturally pale skin and her large hazel eyes. The girl's light brown hair was loose; it curled around her shoulders over the pink dressing gown that covered her white nightdress.

'Oh Tom, are you sure it's safe? If I was caught like this, in my nightclothes, I'd be killed.'

He took the candlestick from her and then folded her into his arms.

'Of course it's safe. Do you think I'd put you in a position like this if it wasn't?'

She raised her head from his shoulder and kissed his cheek gently. 'Oh Tom, I do love you and I don't want to go away, no matter what Mammy says.' She was a gentle girl who often forgot her mother's instructions not to call her 'Mammy' any more now she was grown up.

'You know how much I love you, Florence, and we don't have to be parted. I've got a plan.'

She drew away and looked up at him, her expression puzzled and yet hopeful and trusting. 'A plan?'

'Yes – it's our only chance. Do you love me enough to marry me?'

'You know I do, Tom, but—'

He placed a finger on her lips. 'Never mind the "buts". Will you hear me out?'

She nodded.

'Then that's what we'll do. Get married. It will have to be just a civil ceremony, away from here.'

'But where . . . How . . . ?'

'Trust me, Florence, please, please trust me!'

'I do!'

He held her tightly. 'Tomorrow night we'll go to Dublin. There's a man I know with a small barge who'll take us there. We'll get married and then come back. There won't be anything they can do. It will be all legal. Mr and Mrs Thomas Kiernan.' He clutched her hands. 'They'll accept us, Florence – you know how much your Da thinks of you. You won't have to go to the house above and be cleaning and polishing and having to take your meals in the servants' hall and be stuck up in some cold attic room. You're much too refined for that way of carrying on.'

He was voicing her own fears. She dreaded going. She'd never had to do much in the way of housework at home and she'd heard that the servants up there were terrible snobs. If tonight's dinner was anything to go by, then she certainly wouldn't relish having to take orders from the housekeeper, who was the most forbidding, tight-lipped woman she'd ever met.

'Where will we live?' she asked.

'Here, of course.'

'Of course. We . . . we'll have my room. It's big enough for a double bed.'

'And I'll still go on helping your Da until we can maybe get a small house of our own.'

'I'd like a place with my own things around me and Mammy not being able to go giving out to me all the time.'

He embraced her tenderly. 'You'll see, Florence, acoushla, we'll be so happy.'

She reached up to kiss him and he knew he'd won. All his dreams and ambitions were now within his grasp.

'Go back upstairs now before you catch your death of cold, but come down here at midnight tomorrow and bring a small bag with you. Be dressed warmly. I'll be waiting. I'll have arranged everything.'

The girl looked up at Tom admiringly. He made such quick decisions, he didn't ponder on things for weeks like her father did. He was so handsome and at times very romantic. The more she thought about his plan, the more elated she began to feel. There was something very exciting about eloping, running away with the man you loved. She would be so happy, she just *knew* she would. Her father would be furious at first but he wouldn't turn them out on the road or see her in shabby dresses with hardly a shoe to her foot. And a civil ceremony would be all legal and binding. Her future seemed decided.

Even though she was bone weary, Maddy couldn't sleep. Carmel was curled up in the bed beside her, dead to the world. In the dim light from the small fire, which was a necessity rather than a luxury, she could just make out the shapes of their pieces of furniture. The bed took up most of the space, then there was a big old press for their few clothes. A battered chest of drawers held their underwear and stockings. The floor was flagged but threadbare rugs covered most of it. The two small windows either side of the hearth had curtains, although the green and pink pattern of roses and leaves had faded so much that Mrs Mitchell had been on the point of throwing them out before Maddy had begged them for the windows. They were of good quality, chintz lined with cotton, and they helped to keep the cold out. In summer she kept geraniums in pots on the windowsills which brightened the look of the drab room. A chipped jug and basin which had come to them in the same way as the curtains stood on the top of a dilapidated wash-stand, above which hung a mirror so the two girls could see to brush and tidy their hair. Beside the hearth was a black pot full of water which they heated to use for washing.

They were very fortunate, Maddy thought, very fortunate indeed, to have so many comforts – luxuries as many hundreds of people would call them. It broke her heart to see the numbers of destitute people, sitting or lying beside the road, too weak to go on. Women who were little more than walking skeletons carried babies with distended stomachs and eyes that looked huge in their small wizened faces. For the second time the terrible blight had come in a dust-like form and had settled on the potato fields. It was in the early morning when they'd first noticed the haze, and then, as it passed over, they literally saw the potato plants turn brown and wither before their eyes. It was as if God had turned His back on them. She sighed heavily. She would never get to sleep if she started thinking too deeply about the suffering of her country. If there was anything she could have done to help, she would have done it, but there wasn't.

Maddy got up and took her shawl from the hook on the back of the door and wrapped it tightly around her. She went to the window and pulled aside the curtain. The yard was almost as bright as day, bathed in the light of a full moon. There'd be a heavy frost tonight. There was also a light in the kitchen that came from the candle placed in the window; it burned every night in the winter. She'd go over and get a drink, she decided. She'd be very quiet so as not to disturb her brother although he always slept heavily.

Maddy covered the short distance across the yard in her icy bare feet and eased the door open an inch or two. Then she paused, hearing her brother's voice. 'Oh damnation,' she said to herself. Why was he still up, and who was he talking to? Her questions were answered when she heard Florence Mitchell speaking. Maddy drew in her breath sharply. She knew she should return to her bed but she just couldn't. She was transfixed – and the more she overheard, of the murmured conversation, the more shocked she became. She stood there shivering, her feet numb with cold, while above her thousands of stars twinkled and moonlight bathed the house and yard and the canal.

When the voices had fallen silent, Maddy ran back across the yard and opened the door to the outhouse as silently as possible. Carmel was still asleep so she piled more turf on the bedroom fire and pulled the three-legged wooden stool close to it, placing her frozen feet on the hearth. She shook her head in disbelief. They were going to elope. She knew her brother was sweet on Florence, but this was madness. If they thought that James Mitchell would welcome them back with open arms then they were fools. Of course, he wouldn't turn his precious daughter out on the road however much convention would demand it. After all, she would be legally married and not some foolish girl who had let a man take advantage of her and was pregnant. There would be an almighty row, followed by some kind of punishment, but Florence would be forgiven, in time. Tom would not. He would be thrown out, as they all would be, without a job, without money, without a roof over their heads.

Fear and worry enveloped her. They had always had more than the basics in life, even as children. Like everyone else, her parents Patrick and Aoife Kiernan had leased their cottage and bit of land. The couple had worked hard and been prudent, but when they died, the three children had been forced to sell what they could, including the few pigs and sheep, to pay for a decent burial. They'd tried to make a go of it, but crops took time to grow and without animals to fatten and sell they soon fell behind with the rent. If the Mitchells hadn't taken them in, they'd have been evicted. And ever since, they'd grown used to the comforts of good food and decent clothes on their backs. Yet now, it seemed, Tom was willing to risk everything they had because of his love for Florence.

Maddy poked at the blazing pieces of turf then passed a hand over her aching forehead. *Was* it love – or was there another motive on her brother's part? Oh, she knew he had ambitions, he'd told her, but she'd never given them much thought. She was too much of a realist. Now she was forced to face the frightening truth. If he married Florence Mitchell they would all be thrown out. No matter how much they begged and pleaded, and protested their innocence, remarks would be passed about 'one bad apple in the barrel.' To satisfy moral convention they would *all* have to go and that didn't bear thinking about.

Carmel stirred, then sat up rubbing her eyes.

'What's the matter, Maddy?'

'Nothing. Go back to sleep or you won't be able for your work in the morning.'

Her sister drew the quilt around her and snuggled down

21

again. Carmel was so childlike in many ways, Maddy thought, and her health wasn't as robust as her own. She'd never survive the kind of vagrant life that Thomas's thoughtless, selfish act would reduce them to.

There would be no sleep for her now, she thought, gazing into the fire. She sat there until the feeble light of dawn filtered into the room through a chink in the curtains. By then she had made up her mind. She wasn't going to let Thomas wreck their lives. She was going to tell James Mitchell of her brother's plans.

'Aren't you very quiet this morning, Maddy. Is something wrong?' Carmel asked as Maddy tidied away the breakfast dishes and she had begun to peel the vegetables for the next meal.

'No, nothing is wrong.'

'But you sat up all night?'

Maddy sighed. 'I did so, but it was only because I'd been thirsty and gone over to the kitchen for a drink. After that I didn't feel sleepy.'

'If you don't feel well I can do your work.'

Maddy smiled. Her sister was so guileless and obliging. 'I'm not that bad. I'll have an early night tonight.'

'Tom seems very happy with himself this morning, I wonder why? He's been whistling for ages and he hardly ever does that.'

Maddy felt a pang of guilt. He was her brother and she did love him, but she was angry that he didn't seem to care about either of them to the same extent.

'Perhaps the master is going to give him a shilling more in his wages,' she replied, without much conviction. The day any of them got a rise in their pay, pigs would fly.

'Do you really think so?'

Maddy grinned at her sister. 'No, I don't.'

Before she served lunch and before Florence appeared, she asked Mr Mitchell if she could have a few words with him after the meal was over.

He looked startled. 'What is so important?'

Maddy looked down at her clasped hands. 'It is a private matter, sir.'

'Very well. Before you clear away, come into my Office.'

Mitchell picked up his napkin with a flourish. He'd always admired Maddy Kiernan. Such a lovely complexion, unlike Eliza's putty-coloured skin. And a good figure too, tall and slim, but rounded in the places where a woman was meant to be round. Eliza was small and fat. She'd got beyond the stage of being just 'pleasantly plump'; in fact, in her underwear she disgusted him. He'd look forward to his chat with young Maddy.

'Thank you, sir.'

As she served the meal Maddy had to will her hands from shaking and struggle not to bite her lip.

'Are you quite all right, my dear? You seem a little tense,' Eliza Mitchell remarked halfway through lunch.

'Perfectly, thank you, ma'am.' Maddy even managed a smile. God, she must look terrible if the mistress commented on it.

'You're very quiet,' Eliza persisted.

'It's her place to be quiet. Good God, Eliza, would you have her talking fifteen to the dozen while she puts the meal on our plates?' James Mitchell said irascibly.

His wife flushed slightly. He had no right to speak to her like that in front of a servant.

Maddy too felt the colour rising in her cheeks. She knew he was a busy man but that didn't excuse him from being impolite to his wife in front of her, and her mistress had only been concerned for her welfare. She knew that both she and Mrs Mitchell would be glad when lunch was over.

'Right, young woman, leave those dishes and follow me,' James commanded, getting up from the table.

Maddy smoothed down her apron and followed him into the hall, leaving Eliza and Florence looking at each other in mystification.

'Shut the door behind you, Maddy,' he instructed as he sat down in the big brown leather chair behind a desk littered with papers, lists and pens.

Maddy came in here to clean but she never touched anything on his desk. It was a dark room; the small window gave little light and the small turf fire flickering in the hearth did not add greatly to the cheer.

'Now, what is all this about?'

She twisted her hands nervously. 'It's about Thomas and . . . and . . . Miss Florence.'

The benign look was instantly wiped from his face. 'What about them?' he demanded.

'I heard them, sir, in the kitchen last night.'

'Florence was in the kitchen?'

'She was so, sir, and . . . and . . .'

'For heaven's sake, girl, spit it out! I can't stand shilly-shallying.'

'They're going to run away and get married – tonight. At least they're going to go to Dublin by barge and then . . .' She spread her hands.

His face changed colour until it was puce with anger. He stood up, knocking the chair over. *'They're what?'* he bellowed.

She shrank back but she repeated it.

'By God, it won't be to Dublin they'll go, it's to hell that the pair of them will be sent packing if I have any more of this . . . this nonsense!' he spluttered in rage.

'What will you do, sir? I mean about Thomas and myself and Carmel. Carmel and me had no part in any of it, I swear. I'd only gone back to the kitchen for a drink and I . . . I overheard them. I was shocked and upset. I've had no sleep all the night, worrying about it,' she pleaded.

He had calmed down a little. 'I believe you, girl. Go and send Mrs Mitchell in to me.'

'Mrs Mitchell?' she queried, still shaking with fear.

'A mother has the right to know what her daughter is after doing, if she doesn't already know.'

'Oh, I'm sure she doesn't, sir! I really am sure.'

'Go and find her, then.'

'Then what, sir?'

'Then we will both talk to Florence and I will deal with that impudent young pup!'

'Oh sir, please don't throw us all out, please, I beg you.'

His manner softened a little. 'If you swear you didn't know, then I'll consider keeping you and your sister on. Consider, mind, no promises.'

So their future still hung in the balance. 'I swear to God, on the graves of my mother and father, and you knew them well, sir, that neither Carmel nor myself knew anything about this.'

James nodded slowly. He'd never known the girl to lie, he'd never known her parents to lie – but he hadn't been as well acquainted with them as she believed he had.

'I accept your story,' he said gruffly. 'You will both stay on. Now go back and inform my wife that I need to see her.'

'I will so, sir. Thank you, thank you so much. We'll both work hard – extra hard.'

'Get off with you then.'

When she went back into the living room, both Eliza and Florence were still there, waiting to find out what was going on.

'Ma'am, himself is asking to see you now.'

'Oh really? Just what is all this secrecy about? If you have a complaint, Maddy, you come to *me*!' Eliza snapped, still disgruntled about the way her husband had treated her.

'I . . . I'm sorry, ma'am, but—'

Before she could finish, Eliza had bustled from the room.

'Maddy, what's the matter?' Florence asked nervously.

Maddy shook her head. 'I . . . I can't tell you, but your mother will soon let you know.'

She liked Florence Mitchell. The young girl was far too

good for her brother Tom – and that fact had nothing at all to do with class.

'I'm so sorry, miss, I really am,' she said in a low voice, stacking the dishes quickly and almost running out of the room.

Back in the kitchen she dumped the plates in the sink and leaned on the table.

'Maddy! Maddy, you *are* ill!' Carmel cried in alarm.

'No, I'm not, truly. I'll have a cup of tea and then I'll be as right as rain. Where's Thomas?'

'He said he had to go into town for some things and to see someone. He took the trap.'

His absence would only cause her more worry, Maddy fretted, sinking down on to a chair. She wanted it to be all over and done with.

Chapter Three

They could both hear the raised voices that came from the office, but it was impossible to make out the exact words, the walls were too thick.

'Whatever's going on?' Carmel asked anxiously. 'I've never heard the master so angry.'

'It's Miss Florence and Tom,' her sister said dully.

'Our Tom? What's he done?'

'The eejit was planning to elope tonight with Miss Florence and get married in Dublin.'

'*Married!* Our Tom and Miss Florence? But they're so different! Miss Florence is almost a lady *and* she's a Protestant.'

'I know. It was madness. I heard them planning it last night, that's why I couldn't sleep. I had to tell the master or we'd both have been flung out with Tom.'

The colour drained from her sister's face. 'Oh Maddy . . . what will happen to us?'

'Don't be worrying now. Mr Mitchell has almost

promised that we can stay on here, but Tom will have to go. Oh, he's such a fool! I could kill him, I really could. Put the kettle on, Carmel. We both need a cup of strong tea. There'll be murder when Tom arrives home.'

Carmel went about her work quietly, outwardly calm but inwardly a seething mass of nerves. She hated rows, with all the shouting and the insults and the tears. Everything had been fine when her parents were alive. Of course, she'd always been the quiet one, the 'little peacemaker' as Mammy used to call her, for if there was an argument between Thomas and Maddy she would try to calm them down. Oh, how she missed Mammy. She had only been nine years old when Mammy and then Da had died, and it had been so sudden. Even now she could still hear the doctor's words: 'I'm sorry, but she won't get better – neither of them will.' Her safe little world had collapsed that day. Then they had come to the Canal Agent's house to live and work, but now the peace and security she'd found here were being threatened.

It was dusk by the time Thomas arrived back. It had taken much longer than he'd anticipated to find the man who would take them to Dublin, and he'd demanded far more money than Tom had anticipated, but he was in no position to argue. At least things were settled. There would be no more barges through the 30th Lock today, but just in case, he'd hidden the key to the lock gates and would make sure that O'Hagan the lock-keeper was well and truly drunk by the time they were ready to go. The only thing that caused him worry was the noise of the water running through the lock gates when he let in their barge. At this time of year the water in the canal was always at high level and the noise could be very loud indeed. In the stillness of the night it often sounded like distant thunder. Then Tom pulled himself together. He was a fool. The Mitchells were used to the sound; it wouldn't disturb them. And he still had a fair amount of his savings left. That would see him and Florence through until they came back and things were settled.

'What's wrong with you two?' he asked his sisters airily as he strode into the kitchen. 'Don't the pair of you look as though you've had a fright.'

'We've every right to be afraid. There's been the mother and father of a row here while you were off in town.'

'Why so?'

Maddy looked at him squarely. 'About this eejit plan of yours to marry Florence.'

There was a small knot of fear in his stomach. 'How the hell do you know about that?'

'I heard you talking last night,' Maddy answered defiantly.

'But how does the master know? How, Maddy?' he demanded.

'He knows because I told him.'

Maddy took a step backwards thinking he was going to hit her but she stuck to her guns. 'I *had* to tell him or we'd all be thrown out on the road. You never gave us a thought, did you?'

'You interfering bitch!' he yelled.

Carmel gave a frightened little cry and clutched the edge of the sink.

'I wouldn't have had to interfere if you'd told me. If you'd have given *us* a bit of thought. Look at her, look at your poor terrified little sister – how the hell did you think she'd survive? It was your ambition to be something you're not and never will be. All you thought about was yourself. I don't think you really love Florence at all,' she yelled back.

'I'll swing for you, Maddy Kiernan! All this had nothing to do with you. It's *my* future at stake here!'

Maddy laughed cuttingly. 'Did you really think he'd have you back here and raise you up to sit with them, take your meals with them, introduce you as a respectable son-in-law? You fool! You stupid, selfish, arrogant fool!'

He struck out blindly, catching her across her cheek, and she staggered backwards. Carmel screamed but Maddy had regained her composure and snatched up the heavy basting ladle from the table.

'Hit me again and I'll give you a clattering you'll remember all your life.'

Thomas was so furious that he could only splutter. 'You . . . you sneaky, tell-tale, informing little bitch!'

She took a step towards him, her arm raised. 'I mean it – I'll belt you.'

'I'll never forgive you! I'll get the better of you one day, just wait and see! I won't let you stand in the way of my plans again – I'll kill you first!'

Carmel was hysterical. She'd never been subjected to anything like this before and she was scared witless.

'For God's sake, shut her up!' he growled.

'Shut her up, is it? She's your sister and she's bloody terrified.'

Thomas turned to his younger sister. 'She's terrified of bloody everything! For Christ's sake, Carmel, shut up that bloody racket!'

'I thought from all the noise it was yourself come back, you impudent pup!'

Silence descended as they all saw James Mitchell standing in the doorway, his face set in angry, unyielding lines.

'It's all right, sir, it's all over now. You won't be disturbed again,' Maddy said grimly.

'By God, you never spoke a truer word, girl.' Mitchell walked across to Thomas and jabbed him in the chest with his forefinger. 'Get out of my house and my sight before I take a horsewhip to you! Taking advantage of a young girl's innocence, promising her a life she could never have had with you. Where would the likes of you be getting the money to give her a decent home? She's not used to a cabin with a dirt floor and a thatched roof and backbreaking work, and that's all you can offer her! I'll not have her suffer poverty and humiliation for a young scoundrel like you! Now get out! Get your things together and be out in half an hour!'

The door slammed and every dish on the dresser rattled.

Maddy looked at her brother. She didn't like what she had done, but she had Carmel to think of. 'You heard what he said. Half an hour.'

'I won't need no bloody half hour. There's not much to get together – I'll be away in ten minutes.'

Maddy rubbed her cheek. 'And not one single word of regret? No message for poor Florence? You *were* only using her, weren't you? You don't care that she's upstairs crying her eyes out over you.'

'No, I don't bloody care. She's a stupid spoiled brat without a brain in her head. She's a simpering brainless eejit of a girl and she's not even halfway pretty.'

Carmel had calmed down and was sobbing quietly while Maddy, still shaking with anger, watched him hastily gather his few clothes and possessions and stuff them into an old leather bag that he kept under the outshot bed.

When he'd finished he looked around the room. 'I can't even say I'm sorry to leave this house, let alone you two or any of *that* lot! Canal Agent!' He laughed mockingly. 'Nothing but a bloody jumped-up clerk. I'll finish up better off than that.'

'Just get out! Oh, go to hell, Thomas Kiernan!' Maddy shouted.

'Oh Tom, Tom, where will you go?' Carmel pleaded, catching hold of his sleeve, her face pale and her eyes full of tears.

'To somewhere I can get on in life.'

'But where?' Carmel persisted. She at least wanted to know where he was going.

'Liverpool. There's all kinds of work there, so I heard. It's a big, wealthy place where no one asks you what bloody religion you are if you go to seek work.' He turned at the door. 'I'll never forgive you, Maddy. I mean it – and I'll get even somehow.'

He stormed out into the darkness, leaving the door wide open.

Maddy closed it and sank down on a kitchen chair. Carmel came and sat at her feet, her head resting in her sister's lap.

'What will we do now, Maddy?'

'We'll go on doing what we've always done, our chores in the house and the yard and the garden.' She was still shaking with emotion. 'I *had* to do it, Carmel. It was Tom or us.'

'He said he'll never forgive us and he'll get even.'

'Take no notice of that, he'll come round. You wait and see – one day he'll turn up at the door, either clad in rags or in a good suit, with an overcoat and maybe even a stovepipe hat.'

Carmel looked up at her. 'Do you *really* think so?'

'I do. Sure, his bark is worse than his bite. Deep down he does care – he's not *that* bad.' Her words soothed her sister, but held little conviction for herself. Tom had gone and he'd gone for good, and now tears pricked her own eyes.

The atmosphere in the house was strained and tense. When Maddy served the meals it was as though a huge black cloud hung over the dining table. Florence was very pale and withdrawn and Eliza's mouth was set in a thin tight line. Already Carmel had begun to miss her brother and Maddy twice found her in tears. There was extra work for them too – most of the jobs that Tom had used to do except for the work with the lock gates and the barges.

Maddy was surprised when one morning James Mitchell himself came into the kitchen. She straightened up after closing the oven door on the pie she'd made for supper.

'Oh sir, you startled me.'

'I'm sorry, I had no wish to frighten you.'

Maddy pushed her hair more firmly under her cap.

'No, I wasn't frightened, sir. Is there something you require?'

Usually if there was anything urgent or important to discuss it was Eliza Mitchell who came to the kitchen, or she would send for Maddy.

'I expect you are finding it hard without your brother to help.'

'Oh, it's not too bad, sir. Carmel has taken over some of my chores and I see to the ones Thomas used to do, apart from assisting you.'

'Well, you'll be glad to know that I've engaged a lad from the village to take over his duties.'

'Oh, thank you, sir. I have to do the heavier ones as Carmel is . . . delicate.'

James Mitchell looked across the room to where Carmel was standing at the sink scrubbing pans. She did have a delicate air about her. She was a very pretty girl, much better-looking than Florence, he thought ruefully. The weak winter sunlight came in through the window and caught the girl's hair, turning it into a halo around her face. They were both beautiful girls in their own ways and deserved a better life than the one they now had. But of course they were well off compared to half the country.

'Have you had word from your brother?'

'No, sir, and I don't wish to hear from him either.'

He nodded. Young Maddy Kiernan had spirit. Maybe he'd give them both a few shillings extra, seeing as he was only paying the lad he'd hired half of what he'd paid Thomas Kiernan.

Maddy was surprised and embarrassed when first Eliza Mitchell and then Florence summoned her later that day to give her the same news.

'You will be pleased to hear that my husband has found a suitable replacement for your brother,' Mrs Mitchell informed her.

'I *am* very pleased and grateful, ma'am. Mr Mitchell has already told me.'

'Indeed!' Eliza's cheeks had two red spots on them and her tone was very sharp. 'And when did he tell you this?'

'Only an hour ago, ma'am. He came into the kitchen.'

'He did?'

'Yes, ma'am. I was very . . . surprised.'

'Indeed, quite so. Very well, you may go.'

Inwardly Eliza was seething. How *dare* James go down to the kitchen! Domestic arrangements were *her* domain and he'd never interfered before. She would speak to him. He had no right to humiliate her. She'd had enough of that over the past few days. He had blamed her for Florence's behaviour, accused her of not keeping a close enough eye on their daughter. When William was older, James had told her in no uncertain terms, he himself would supervise their son's activities and his friends. Everything was so annoying. Florence had behaved like a ninny – and look at the trouble she had caused. Eliza was forced to admit that maybe she should have kept a closer watch on her daughter, but she hadn't suspected a liaison with Thomas Kiernan. He was just a servant, for heaven's sake. Whoever would have thought he'd have dared to have designs upon his employer's daughter?

Maddy had only just seen Eliza go out, driving the trap, when young William Mitchell appeared in the kitchen and told her that his sister wanted to see her.

'What for?' she asked apprehensively. Florence had been ignoring her, or giving her black looks, from the day of 'the discovery'. Maddy looked at William and her heart lightened. She liked the lad, who had arrived home for the Christmas holidays from his school in Dublin only yesterday. He was a bit of a harum-scarum, always in trouble for tearing some article of clothing he was wearing and minor damage to the wall or fence he'd been climbing. Maddy knew that Florence had often spoken up for him to ward off the worst of his father's anger and his mother's despair.

'That lad will end his days on the gallows!' was a frequent remark passed by James Mitchell.

'How would I know?' the lad answered now. 'They tell me nothing. Half of the time they treat me as if I was a baby and the other half as if I was an eejit.'

Maddy managed a smile. 'Is your father out?'

'He is, at some meeting or another – in Heggarty's pub probably.'

'You're a bold article at times, Willie Mitchell.' Only she, Carmel and of course Thomas called the boy 'Willie' and then only out of earshot of his parents and sister. But he much preferred it.

'How am I expected to keep up with the war that's been going on here? I missed it all. Father as cross as a bag of cats and Mammy and Florence wailing and Tom being given notice . . .'

'Well, where is your sister?' Maddy demanded. She certainly had no wish to try and explain things to an eleven-year-old boy.

'In her room. Where else?'

'Go on, get off with you. You can have one of those little tarts I've made, but just one!'

He grinned, helped himself to two, and disappeared out of the kitchen door.

Maddy sighed. She'd better go upstairs and face the music.

Florence was sitting by her bedroom window in a low-backed chair. Maddy always thought what a lovely room it was when she cleaned it. There was pretty wallpaper, pale blue curtains hung at the windows and the quilt was white and blue patchwork. Beside the bed was a nice rug and on the wash-stand stood a delftware bowl and jug, a dressing-table set and a trinket box. In summer, Florence kept wild flowers in a vase on the broad windowsill. She looked pale and thin, Maddy thought, closing the door behind her.

'You wanted to speak to me, miss?'

Florence turned and her eyes were as cold as the Irish Sea. She stood up, her hands clenched.

'It's all *your* fault!' she burst out. 'By now, Tom and I would have been married, but for your interference.'

'Miss, please, please don't be upset,' Maddy implored. 'I *had* to tell and he . . . well, I know my brother.' She paused. 'He was just using you. He thought he would be in a better position if he married you, because of who your father is.'

'He wasn't! You're lying, Maddy Kiernan. You're a low, nasty, jealous girl – and you've ruined my life!' She started to cry.

'No, I haven't, I swear it.'

'You *have*! There is no one interested in you, only those . . . those peasants you see in town hanging around the alehouses and corners.'

Maddy flushed. 'I don't even give those eejits the time of day.'

'You see? There is no one. You aren't good enough to marry into our society and yet you and Carmel give yourselves such airs and graces that you think you're above the lower orders. You'll be a miserable spinster all your life, so you will, and I'll be glad!'

Although hurt by Florence's words, Maddy's heart went out to the wounded girl. She reached out and took hold of her by the shoulders. 'Florence, you're a lovely, kind-hearted, generous and pretty girl,' she said earnestly. 'My brother never loved you. I don't think he loves anyone, except himself. He simply used you, you must believe that.

Please don't waste your tears or your life because of him. He's my brother – I *know* him. You'll soon meet a nice lad, one of your own class, and you'll forget this ever happened.'

At this, Florence's face crumpled and the tears redoubled. Heedless of the class barrier between them, Maddy took the girl into her arms and held her.

'I *am* sorry to have hurt you, acoushla, I really mean that. But if you'd have married him you would have been an outcast. Can you honestly see your father welcoming Tom as your husband with open arms? No. We're lower class and always will be, like you say. We're servants in this house and glad of it – *and* we're Catholic, you know that.'

'I *do* know that. But . . . but we're not grand. We don't fit. We're not the gentry and yet we're not of the lower orders.'

'Florence, there's nothing to stop you marrying someone from the gentry. It's been done before, but for heaven's sake, marry someone worthwhile, someone who'll be good to you.'

'Oh Maddy, I'm so confused and neither Father nor Mother are speaking to me. And poor William's too young to understand.'

'They'll get over it. Your father dotes on you, you know he does. I wish I still had a father, and a mother, however cross they were with me.'

Florence straightened up and rubbed the tears from her cheeks with the back of her hand. 'When you put it like that . . .'

'That's better. Now bathe your face, I'll bring up some fresh water, and tidy your hair. Why don't you go for a walk? It's bright but cold, so wrap up warm.'

Florence shook her head. 'I can't.'

'Why not? Has it been forbidden?'

'Yes and no. I can go, but only along the towpath or up the fields, but I don't want to. I can't bear to see the poor people. Father says they can't pay their rent so it's their own fault that they get evicted and have nothing, but I still can't bear to see them suffering.'

Maddy nodded, her lips pursed. James Mitchell had the same attitude as many of the middle class. The poor were poor because they were feckless – an opinion she didn't share. To her mind, it was absentee landlords and their agents who caused all the trouble.

'I'll go and get the water.'

She sighed as she went downstairs, thanking God once more for their safe home here, which Thomas had put into jeopardy, and adding a very brief prayer for her brother's own future.

Chapter Four

As the days grew shorter the weather became cold and damp. It was a dampness that pervaded every room in the Canal Agent's house, despite all the fires that burned in them. It even got into your bones, Maddy thought as she struggled to rekindle the dying range. They needed it, not only to heat the kitchen, but to provide hot water for the family to wash in. Once she'd done this, it would be time to rake out and relight the fires in the office and living room. She shivered as she drew the heavy chenille curtains in the living room. There was ice on the inside of the windows and the view was dismal. The steep sides of the canal bank were still green but the trees and the hedgerows beyond it were bare, their twisted branches black and bleak-looking through the heavy mist.

The situation in the country was growing worse. Famine fever was wiping out whole communities, and an air of horror and despair hung over everything. Even in the town, shops were closing; there was no custom except from the middle and upper classes, and the traders couldn't survive on just that, especially since their wealthier customers were notorious for not settling their bills until letters were sent reminding them, respectfully, that money was owing.

Mr Mitchell had instructed his wife to inform Maddy that meat was only to be served on four days of the week; the price was sheer extortion, he told her. There was fish to be had though, and eggs aplenty from their own hens, one of which they would kill and eat once a month. If you had money they could be replaced. Then there were the vegetables that had been preserved and dried, and of course, there was plenty of flour and soda for bread.

Maddy often ignored her mistress's instructions to turn away the people who came to the back door. She couldn't refuse them. Surreptitiously she made extra loaves, and sometimes both she and Carmel went without supper so that one of the callers could eat it. It broke her heart to see the food she'd prepared set out on the dining table. Despite the cuts, one of the Mitchells' meals would have fed a whole family for two days. It was going to be a miserable Christmas.

She'd heard nothing from her brother, nor had she expected to. Thanks to Maddy's plain speaking, Florence had got over her heartache and was now 'walking out' with the son of the town's solicitor. Both her mother and father were delighted. He was a very good catch indeed and she would never have met him, had she gone to work in the Big House. Following the discovery of the planned elopement,

James Mithell had written to cancel the arrangement, so painstakingly made, for Florence to join the staff there.

'Oh, it's cold in here!' Carmel complained, clutching her shawl tightly around her.

'It's warmer than out there, but the range has gone out. Will you set the table and take up the hot water when it's ready, which won't be for a while yet.' Maddy was irritated by the failure of the range. She'd be behind with her work all day now, and Danny Murphy, who'd taken her brother's job, was not much help. He never arrived on time except on the morning of pay day.

Her sister sounded hesitant. 'Maddy, can you take up the master's water for me?'

'Why so?' Maddy was stacking turf into the range.

'Well, I'm a bit frightened of him.'

Maddy got up and turned towards her.

'Frightened of him?' She chuckled. 'What's there to be afraid of? Don't you just take in the water, leave it down on the wash-stand and go?'

'I do so, but . . . but . . .'

Maddy became exasperated. 'Oh, for heaven's sake, Carmel, just tell me.'

'Well, for the last couple of days Mrs Mitchell has been out of the room.'

'So? She sometimes gets up earlier than him.'

Carmel twisted her hands nervously. 'I know, but he keeps telling me I'm pretty and other . . . things.'

Maddy stared at her. 'What other things? Are you sure you're not reading too much into what he says?'

'I'm not! He *does* say things and . . . he touches me.'

Maddy put down the poker. 'Touches you? Where?'

'He strokes my hair and my cheek and he says he's never seen such soft hair and skin.'

This was serious. Maddy pushed her sister down onto a chair. 'Carmel, is this really true?'

'I wouldn't lie about something like that.'

'Have you said anything to herself?'

'No. I wouldn't dare!'

Maddy thought hard. If what her sister said was true, and she was sure it was, Carmel was ill-equipped to deal with it. Oh, Maddy knew it went on all the time and had done for years. Pretty young servant girls were easy prey for their well-to-do employers, and if they complained they were sacked and sent home in disgrace. Well, that wasn't going to happen to them. But what could she do? She couldn't tell Mrs Mitchell, the woman would refuse to believe her. Nor could she confront him with it; that certainly would end in them both being thrown out. All she could do was watch, and try to keep Carmel away from him. She herself would take up the water and do the other jobs that brought her into close contact with him. Why, oh why, now? she thought in desperation. They'd been here long enough and he'd made no advances to either of them. But when they'd first come here Carmel had been a child and Thomas would have protected them. In those days he'd taken his position of guardian very seriously.

'Don't worry, I'll take his water up every morning and you stay in here as much as you are able.'

'But what if he comes in here?'

'He never comes into the kitchen, except for that one day. Go on and start laying the table, then do the fires. Do the one in his office first so there's less chance of him finding you on your own in there.'

Carmel wrung her hands in agitation. 'Oh Maddy, I should have told you sooner but I was frightened to in case you didn't believe me or gave out to me.'

'Carmel Kiernan, you are a little eejit! You *know* you can trust me.'

Carmel smiled in relief. She had been so afraid of him. Unshaven and in his nightclothes, she'd found James Mitchell's attentions repugnant and disgusting.

When Maddy knocked and then entered the bedroom, both her employers were in the room. Her mistress looked far from well, she thought, ignoring James Mitchell and setting the water on the wash-stand.

'Will I be after drawing the curtains, ma'am?' she asked quietly.

'What kind of a morning is it, Maddy?'

'It's cold and a bit misty.'

'Then leave them for now. Time enough to be depressed when I go downstairs.'

'If I might make a suggestion, ma'am, would you like me to bring your breakfast up to you here? It won't take long.'

'That's kind of you, Maddy, but no. I have to go into town so James will drive me. Florence and I are going to do some shopping and to see the dressmaker about her gown for the Whites' party.'

Maddy smiled, seeing a little colour come into the older woman's cheeks. Mr Vincent White was having a party the week before Christmas but you would have thought it was a grand occasion up in Dublin Castle, the way they were all carrying on about it. Florence had had Maddy half-demented, demanding her opinion on numerous swatches of material. She had finally settled on a pale turquoise satin. The gown was to have a low neck, small puffed sleeves and the traditional crinoline skirt.

'If I had to go through all that lacing up and worrying about getting into a trap or carriage without showing my underwear, I'd go mad,' Maddy said to Carmel when the final choice and every detail of the embellishment had been decided upon. It was costing her father a small fortune to deck her out, but James apparently thought it was worth it, according to Florence.

'She'll look lovely,' Carmel said wistfully. 'Don't you ever wish you could wear something like that, just once in your life?'

'I do not. Sure, it'd be filthy in no time, trailing in all the dust and dirt of this place.'

'I wish I could.'

Maddy's tone softened. 'Maybe you will wear something like that on your wedding day, if you can find yourself a rich husband like herself did. You're pretty enough. Prettier than her.'

Carmel blushed. 'Oh Maddy, stop teasing.'

'I'm not. Just don't be taken in by anyone like Tom and ruin your life.'

The preparations for the party were more than one man could stand, James Mitchell declared one morning, what with the dressmaking bills, shoes and gloves to buy and not just for Florence. Eliza was taking this too far. And then there was the cost of the Christmas food and gifts. The place was coming down with the bills and his pockets were not *that* deep. There was no endless source of money.

'Do you want to show us up before the Town? Don't you wish our daughter to make a good marriage?' Eliza had demanded when her husband protested.

'Of course I do. Thank God I put a stop to all that nonsense with that young blackguard Kiernan, or no one would have touched her with a bargepole!' James gave a short bark of a laugh at what he considered to be a witty pun.

His wife had just glared at him, still smarting from his advice on her appearance.

'For God's sake, Eliza, wear something other than black, it makes you look like a scald crow,' he'd snapped when Florence had mentioned the colour of her mother's dress. The dress was half made and she wasn't going to alter it now. The older he got, the more cantankerous, rude and insensitive her husband was becoming, she thought, and if she was truthful with herself, the only emotion he aroused in her these days was that of loathing.

Maddy had managed to keep both herself and Carmel out of his way as much as possible. Fortunately, as Christmas and the party approached, James Mitchell made himself increasingly scarce.

Florence insisted on getting ready early. This was to be her début into society and she *had* to look perfect. 'I'm so excited, Maddy,' she burbled. 'Father has even ordered a carriage to bring us into town and fetch us back. Mother said it would look very unfashionable to arrive in either the trap or the outside car. You'd be soaked on the outside car if it rained and frozen in the trap.'

'Isn't that great,' Maddy replied, not very enthusiastically. She carried a burden of guilt on her shoulders these days. She felt guilty that she had food, fire and a roof over her head because, despite the fact that there were now soup kitchens open throughout the country, and destitute men were being employed to build roads and strengthen river-banks and all kinds of other projects devised to put money in their pockets, the country was on its knees with thousands dying and thousands more emigrating. Soon there would be no one left in Ireland.

'If you don't sit still, how can I get these shoes fastened?' Maddy rebuked, shaking her head in wonder at the satin dancing pumps dyed to match the dress, which in Maddy's opinion was far too fussy with flounces and lace and bows all over it.

'Oh, I'm just so excited!'

'You'll be the loveliest girl there.'

Florence smiled at herself in the mirror. 'You don't think this new hairstyle is too severe? It is the latest fashion.'

'Not at all.'

'I wish I had hair like Carmel's. It looks like a field of ripe barley when the breeze flows over it. She doesn't have to do a thing to it, except brush it.'

'Ah, but Carmel hasn't got a beautiful ballgown, silk stockings, satin shoes and a silver necklace and earrings, and she's not likely to get them, either.'

Florence seemed satisfied with the compliment.

'Here, let me help you with your cape,' Maddy said. 'It's freezing outside.'

'Oh, I'm so excited I won't feel the cold.'

'Ah, believe me, you will. Now, there's your mother calling.'

As Maddy helped her down the stairs to the hall where the girl's parents stood waiting, she noted with concern that Eliza Mitchell looked far from well. There were dark circles under her eyes and her skin seemed even more sallow. The black taffeta dress with the silver embroidery around the neck definitely didn't suit her. Now if she were to wear something with a bit of colour in it, it might help, Maddy thought, unaware that her mistress's dress had already been the subject of an argument. But then she was no expert on fashion. She only had her working dresses, one decent dress, jacket and one pair of boots.

She saw them all into the hired carriage and then went indoors and closed the front door firmly behind her. Thank God for that. Peace at last. Now she and Carmel could tidy up, have supper with Willie in the kitchen, spend a couple of hours beside the fire playing cards with him, and then wait up for the others to return. Carmel would help Florence to undress and no doubt hear of every single detail of the evening and Maddy would assist Mrs Mitchell.

Maddy had fallen into a light doze when she was awoken by the sound of voices. William was long since in bed and Carmel was still asleep.

She shook her sister. 'Wake up. Wake up – they've arrived home.'

Florence and her mother were standing in the hall waiting for Mr Mitchell who appeared to be having an argument with the driver.

'Did you have a wonderful evening, miss?' Carmel asked of a very bright-eyed and flushed Florence.

'I did, too, Carmel. It was so grand and everyone seemed to be surprised that I looked so . . . different.'

'They were all probably jealous.'

Florence flashed her a smile. 'And George said he was delighted with me! Imagine, "delighted"! He's taking me to the races at Kilbeggan on St Stephen's Day and his father was so nice to me, although his mother was cool.'

'Ah, take no notice of her,' Carmel advised as Florence went towards the stairs.

'Did you enjoy the evening, ma'am?' Maddy asked, taking Eliza's cape.

'To be honest, my dear, I didn't. Oh, it had nothing to do with Florence and George. I'm very happy about all that. I think I'll see her comfortably settled.'

'Then what, ma'am?' Maddy asked gently. The poor woman looked all in.

'It was so hot and stuffy that at times I felt quite faint. I think these feelings must have something to do with my age.' She sighed. 'And the music seemed to be very loud.'

'A good night's sleep will work wonders.'

Eliza smiled. 'You are always so considerate, Maddy.'

The conversation was curtailed as James Mitchell staggered into the hall, his collar undone, his jacket creased, his face red and his voice loud.

'That thieving blackguard! Tried to overcharge me! What? Does he think I'm some class of an idiot who can't add up? Well, does he?'

Maddy looked sympathetically at her mistress. Having to cope with a drunken husband was now added to the list of Eliza Mitchell's woes. James had gone into the living room.

'Where's the port, girl? Where have you hidden it?' he demanded, returning to the hall.

'James, I think you've had enough,' Eliza said sharply.

'*I'll* decide when I've had enough,' he blustered. 'Not a decent drop of whiskey and table wine like vinegar! That Vincent White's a cheapskate for all his money.'

'I'll help you upstairs, ma'am, then if you've no objection, Carmel and I will go across the yard. Himself will probably fall asleep in the chair in the living room.'

'Himself can sleep in a ditch for all I care!' Eliza snapped back.

Maddy was a little surprised. She'd never heard her mistress make a derogatory remark about her husband in front of servants, no matter how great the provocation.

She met Carmel on the landing. 'Go down and go straight to bed,' she advised her. 'Don't dawdle.'

'Why?' Carmel whispered.

'Himself is as drunk as ten Lords.'

'Oh, God!'

'Put the bolt on the door. I'll knock when I want to come in. Just don't go to sleep and leave me to freeze,' Maddy hissed back.

When she'd helped her mistress to bed, Maddy closed the door behind her and went down the stairs slowly and cautiously, afraid she might step on a creaking board. Thankfully she got past the door of the living room where a lamp still burned. It was one of her duties to see that all the lamps and candles were out before she retired, but tonight she didn't care. She began to untie her apron as she opened the kitchen door and then uttered a sharp cry as she saw her employer sitting at the table, the half-empty decanter of port in front of him, next to an empty glass.

'Oh sir, you startled me! Mrs Mitchell is very tired.'

'She's that, all right. Tired and a bloody misery. A man can't enjoy himself properly.'

'Sir!'

'Where's your sister?'

'Gone to her bed, sir, as I'm going to do now. It's been a long day.'

'So it has, Maddy. So it has. But sure, every day is long and miserable stuck out here.'

Maddy was edging her way towards the door.

'I thought you enjoyed your position, sir.'

'I do except for the iso . . . iso . . .' He gave up.

'Isolation?'

He got to his feet unsteadily. 'That's what I said.'

There was no way she was going to argue.

'Come here to me. Let me look at you properly. Is it your mother you favour or your Da?' He reached out and caught her wrist. 'Is it Pat's eyes you have, or the lovely Aoife's?'

'Sir, please let me go,' she begged, beginning to feel afraid. Drunk as he was, she was no match for him.

'I'd say your mother. Aoife was a good-looking woman.' His face was close to her own and she turned her head away. He reeked of drink.

'Now isn't that a nice way to treat a man like me? Who was it took you in? Who keeps you? I pay you good money so I want a little bit of thanks!'

Now she was both afraid and angry. 'We work hard for that money.'

His face darkened alarmingly. 'And you'll work harder, my girl, and be thankful – *and* give me the things I want. You and that soft-breasted sister of yours.'

Maddy was shocked. Dear God, just what did he mean by that? Then his hands gripped her shoulders tightly and he tried to kiss her.

She began to struggle, shaking off his grip, lashing out at him, trying to claw at his face. Then she stepped backwards and fell over a stool. Sprawled on the floor she felt terribly vulnerable and tried desperately to get up, but then had the wind knocked out of her by the weight of his body.

'Yes, you two young girls will give me everything I want. Just do as I tell you, and you'll enjoy it too!'

His lips were fleshy and moist and Maddy felt sick. He was pulling up her skirt and she twisted away and tried to scream but the sound died as she saw Eliza Mitchell standing in the doorway.

'James Mitchell! Get up and leave that girl alone, you . . . you beast of a man. You drunken sot!' Eliza's voice seemed to penetrate his drink-sodden mind and he got to his knees, spluttering.

'Little bitch! Throwing herself at me! Bitch on heat!'

Maddy pulled down her skirt and got to her feet, shaking all over. 'Ma'am, please, I did nothing wrong, I promise.'

'*Liar*!' he roared. 'She's always putting herself in my way. Her and that whey-faced sister of hers, they've both given me the eye. They both wanted it!'

'Ma'am, we've never done anything like that! He's tried to kiss and stroke Carmel and she's terrified of him. Please, ma'am, it's not true!' Maddy sobbed.

'I think it would be best if everyone went to their beds,' Eliza said coldly.

'*Bed*! There'll be no more bed for those two hussies. Not under my roof! Pack your things and get out. PACK THEM AND GO! I WANT YOU OUT!' James bellowed, his face puce.

Maddy clutched the overmantel for support. Mitchell was throwing them out and neither of them had done anything wrong. *She* was the wronged one. Her stunned gaze went to her mistress's face but Eliza had turned away and was standing in the doorway.

'Ma'am, please don't let this happen. We've nowhere to go. We'll die in the road! Please, please, ma'am.' Tears were falling unheeded down her cheeks.

Eliza still didn't turn around. 'I'm sorry, Maddy, but there is nothing I can do. The law says he is my husband, for better or for worse. Well, from now on it will be for worse!' Her voice was filled with bitterness and hatred. No matter how he treated her, there was no law to protect her – to protect any woman. A wife was just another chattel.

Maddy crossed the yard and knocked on the door of the little outbuilding that had been their home for five years. She heard the bolt being drawn back and then her sister's face appeared in the doorway.

Carmel was shocked when Maddy sat down on the bed. Maddy was pale, trembling and her dress was torn.

'What happened?' she asked. 'I heard the voices and I was going to come, but I was—'

Maddy laid a hand on her arm. 'Mr Mitchell was very drunk, Carmel. He tried to kiss me and . . .'

'Oh Maddy, he didn't – you know?' Carmel's eyes were round with fright.

Maddy shook her head. 'No, he didn't. She came into the kitchen in time.'

'The mistress?'

Maddy nodded. 'I fought as hard as I could but I fell over a stool and then he was lying on top of me, I could hardly move, but she came in and . . . and . . .' Maddy broke down.

Carmel put her arms around her sister. What would he have done if it had been she and not Maddy in the kitchen?

Maddy had tried to fight back but she herself would probably have been paralysed with fear.

Maddy calmed down a little. 'Oh Carmel, it's not just that. It gets worse.'

'Worse?' Carmel's voice was hoarse.

'We've got to leave here. We've both been sacked and now we have to leave. Oh, I begged herself to speak up for us but she said there was nothing she could do. She hates him but she couldn't help.'

'Where will we go? We've no money! We'll starve like everyone else! Oh Maddy, what will we do?' Carmel panicked.

'I've got a bit saved up. Not much though, it won't last long.'

Carmel tried to calm herself; she wasn't being much help to her poor sister. 'Will we look for some other kind of job?'

'There are none, you know that.'

Carmel's resolve disappeared and she began to cry. Why had this happened? Why was James Mitchell such a pig of a man – and why hadn't the mistress spoken up for them? She would miss young Willie, and Miss Florence, come to that. Oh dear Lord, she was frightened, so very frightened. She knew she was not as strong as her sister, nor as clever.

'Hush now. We'll just have to do the best we can. We must try to be brave.' Maddy got to her feet and, taking the candle, went over to the window and scrabbled with her fingers against the wall until she found the stone that was loose. She removed it and drew out the small cotton bag in which she kept her savings. The coins glinted in the candlelight. It had taken her years to save this amount, and it was so paltry – only about four pounds. Still, her mind was made up.

'Pack your things, and dress as warmly as you can,' she told Carmel. 'Put on all your clothes, since the less we have to carry the better. I've enough here for our passage.'

'Passage! To where?'

'Liverpool. Isn't that where everyone is going?'

'Will we look for Tom?' Carmel asked.

'No. We'll manage without him. We'll get work of some kind and this bit of money will see us through our first days.' Maddy managed a smile. 'Come on. Let's get away from Tullamore as soon as we can.'

Chapter Five

'Carmel, don't cry. We're well rid of this place,' Maddy said in a tight little voice. She put her arm around her sister to comfort her and tried to dispel her own mounting trepidation. What did life hold for them now? Pushing the question out of her mind she looked back at the house. Well, that part of their lives was over and strangely, she found she no longer cared. Oh, she'd miss Master William and Miss Florence, but the girl would soon be married and William back to school. That just left Eliza and James Mitchell. Here and now, Maddy Kiernan made a solemn vow to herself: no man would ever treat her the way James Mitchell treated his wife, no matter what material comforts he could give her.

'There'll be a barge along any minute now,' she stated firmly, although it was in the early hours of the morning, and pitch black apart from the moon.

Carmel wiped the tears from her cheeks with the cuff of her coat, one that Florence Mitchell had discarded because it was last year's and no longer fashionable. The few nice things she possessed had been given to her by Florence.

'Maddy, how long will it take us to get to Dublin?'

'I don't know – well, not for certain anyway. It will depend on how many barges are going up and down the canal, but I think I once heard that the ferry to Liverpool sails at about seven o'clock at night.'

They both lapsed into silence, Maddy hoping she was right about the ferry while Carmel was still in a state of bewilderment.

The appearance of a familiar small, rotund figure swathed in coat, muffler, cap and gloves cheered the girls up enormously.

'Mr O'Hagan! Is there a barge coming?' Maddy called to the lock-keeper, who peered at her with bloodshot eyes.

Too hungover to wonder why the two Kiernan girls should be hanging around the lock at this late hour, he answered waspishly, 'There is so. Why would I be dragged from my bed otherwise. Aren't the Grand Canal Company barges always the first?'

Maddy peered downstream and saw the long narrow outline of the barge as it came slowly up the canal, the dark water parting silently, the ripples stirring the frozen remains of the reeds at its edges.

As the boat drew level, Maddy called: 'Would there be any chance of a ride to Dublin? We can pay.'

'Unhitch the horse, girl, and let him graze, though he'll be hard pushed to find a decent bit of grass to eat, for 'tis all frozen,' the bargee instructed.

Maddy did as she was bid as Ollie O'Hagan closed the huge wooden lock gates behind the barge and then began to open their partners, allowing the water level within the lock to rise, lifting the barge with it until it was level with the steep bank.

'Come on then, the pair of youse, but don't fall. Himself will see to the horse.'

The bargee, a slightly stooped man, muffled up against the cold morning air, held out his hand to help the girls aboard.

'It's very kind of you,' said Maddy, very relieved. 'How much do you want?'

'Nothing. The Company don't like us carrying passengers, so you'd better get below and stay there.'

The tiny cabin was cramped and dark, but it was reasonably warm. It appeared to be carrying turf, from the smell that pervaded the atmosphere.

The girls settled themselves as comfortably as they could on the narrow strip of wood that served as a seat and a bed, and as the horse was hitched up again and the barge moved slowly forward towards the next lock they both drifted into sleep.

It was nearly midday when Maddy opened her eyes. For a brief second she wondered where she was and why she felt so stiff.

'Have we arrived?' Carmel asked drowsily.

'I don't think so. Let me get up and see.' Maddy opened the door cautiously. They were in another lock but she couldn't see anything that gave a name to the place.

'Where are we, please?' she asked of the bargee in a loud whisper, thinking of his words about the Company rules.

'About three-quarters of the way to Dublin. You've slept for hours.'

'I know. How much longer will it take?'

'About another four hours. We change horses here.' The bargee was a kindly man and he certainly didn't blame the two of them for running away. He'd seen sights during the past weeks that he never wished to witness again.

'Have ye anything to eat at all?' he asked.

Maddy shook her head. She was starving.

'Have ye money?'

'I have so.'

'Then get off and buy yourselves some food. There's a bit of a huckster's shop here and we'll be another ten minutes yet. But don't ye go attracting attention or talking to everyone.'

'I won't, I promise.'

She went back to Carmel. 'There's a bit of a shop and I'm going to get us something to eat. Stay there. Don't worry, I won't be long and himself says we're nearly in Dublin.'

Before her sister could reply, Maddy had taken a few coins and had gone back outside.

The shop was only small and there didn't seem to be much on offer, but then they couldn't afford much. The bulk of the money was to be kept hidden, to pay for their passage to England.

She bought bread and cheese and tea and sugar. She had hoped to get some milk too, but there was none.

When she got back, Carmel was boiling water on a little paraffin stove.

'Where did you find that?' Maddy asked.

'He brought it in to me and said to boil the water to wet the tea. What did you get?'

'Bread and cheese, tea and sugar. It will have to last us until we get to Dublin when I can buy more food to take with us.'

As they ate the slices of bread and cheese she'd cut and sipped the scalding black tea, Maddy said with false cheerfulness, 'Well, now, isn't this great altogether?'

She'd given a hunk of bread and cheese and a tin mug of tea to the bargee, who had taken a small bottle from his pocket and emptied half of the contents into the steaming drink. 'To keep out the cold,' he'd explained.

'Where are you two ladies headed?' he asked.

Maddy shot a glance at her sister, warning her not to say too much. 'We want to go to Liverpool,' she said. 'Tom, our brother, is there and we've heard there's work.'

But the bargee was shaking his head. 'I wouldn't count on that. From what I've heard, the place is packed out with the poor creatures trying to escape the famine and the fever that has the country destroyed. But maybe you'll be lucky, especially if you've someone there already.'

Maddy nodded slowly. And now, as she sipped what might be their last brew for a while, she hoped with all her heart he was wrong about the jobs.

* * *

Maddy and Carmel both felt much better when they reached Dublin, and after thanking the bargee and insisting he take two shillings for his kindness, they set off for the docks in the early dusk of the winter afternoon.

Along the way Carmel gazed around her in wonderment at the traffic, the crowds of people and the shops, decorated for Christmas.

The two girls stopped in front of a shop that displayed cakes and sweets of all kinds. The sweets were in little dishes, the cakes on paper doilies set out on plates. Snow cake, queen cakes, porter cakes and barm bracks – they all looked so tempting.

'I never knew there were so many kinds of sweets,' Carmel sighed.

'Neither did I.' Maddy smiled at her. 'I think we can afford a pennyworth of something we've never tasted before. It's almost Christmas, so it is.'

Carmel's eyes lit up and Maddy thought once more how childlike she was; the notion troubled her. She would have to look out for them both.

The woman behind the counter was very patient with them. She had the time. Business was far from great, although some people did have money. Usually she got a girl in to help her with the Christmas trade, but not this year.

The sisters finally settled on tuppenceworth of lemon drops and watched while the sweets were weighed and then tipped into a small paper cone. Once outside, they took one each and smiled at the taste of the special treat.

Further along the road, Maddy bought another loaf and some more cheese and wrapped them in the bundle she was carrying. It held, she reflected sadly, everything she had in the world, and it wasn't much.

The docks were busy with ships being loaded and unloaded. Their masts and spars and rigging looked very alien to the Kiernans' country-bred eyes. Maddy thought they looked like tangled spiders' webs, black threads against a gunmetal sky. She also noticed that the crowd had become more dense the nearer they walked to the ferry berth. It was a depressing sight. So many of the people there were in rags, their faces showing the ravages of hunger and cold. Again she felt guilty because beside them, they looked well off. They had warm clothes and money, and she had committed the sin of sheer wastefulness by buying those sweets. She forced herself to ignore their stares, and their plaintive voices begging for money for food.

'Carmel, keep tight hold of your bundle and don't even think about producing the lemon drops,' she whispered.

The tickets cost Maddy more than she had bargained for, but at least she did have the money and hadn't spent too much of her precious savings. She pushed her way ruthlessly through the crowd, dragging Carmel behind her. Her sister was so afraid of getting lost that she clung to Maddy like a limpet.

On board the ferry, the saloon was already crowded, nor were there any places left on the wooden slats that served as seats, so they sat out on the deck, their backs to the bulkhead.

'We'll have to use our bundles as pillows,' Maddy said practically, secretly thinking that it was the safest place for them. There were people here who would steal the boots off your feet, she thought as she tried to get comfortable on the hard planks.

By the time the mainsail had been hoisted, the anchor hauled up and the small barque sailed slowly down the Liffy estuary to the open sea, there was hardly room to move and both girls had been forced to give up part of their original space and now sat with their knees drawn up.

'I never thought it would be like this. We're like cattle, herded and penned in. God help us if the weather turns bad,' Maddy said, biting her bottom lip.

Fortunately, the weather held. The wind was sufficient to carry them along at a fair rate of knots but wasn't strong enough to pitch and toss the ship. Even so, when they left the lee of the land many people were sick and after a couple of hours the stench was almost unbearable.

'I think I'm going to be sick,' Carmel said faintly.

'No, you are *not*! Wrap your scarf around your face – pull it up over your nose. It might help,' Maddy instructed firmly. 'And here – have a sweet,' she finished in a whisper.

As the hours went by the discomfort grew much worse. A few brave souls had ventured up on deck, unable to stand the stench and the racket below any longer. It was impossible to sleep because of the noise and there was no room to stretch cramped and numbed limbs. If you did get up, someone would instantly shove forward to claim the space.

Neither Maddy nor Carmel felt much like eating, but they did manage to doze off from time to time.

At seven o'clock they finally sailed up the Mersey estuary in the murky grey light of dawn. A steady drizzling rain fell from the sky. People started to stir; a murmur of thanks rippled through the crowds of immigrants, when it was learned that Liverpool was in sight.

'Oh, thank the Holy Virgin for that,' Maddy said with deep relief, as she awkwardly got to her feet. 'I never, ever want to do that crossing again. I'd die first. I'm so stiff and cold. I can't feel my feet!'

'Neither can I,' Carmel agreed. They must both look terrible, she thought – grubby, untidy, pale and hollow-eyed. But the damp air, smelling strongly of salt, was a blessed relief as they clung to the rail and peered into the gloom at the line of docks along the waterfront of the city that was to be their new home.

'Would you look at all the ships!' Carmel said in amazement. 'There's hundreds of them.'

'It's even bigger and busier than Dublin,' Maddy answered. Even in the half light the masts and rigging were like a forest. They filled the skyline. She'd never seen anything like this before. It gave her hope. Surely, with all this obvious prosperity, there would be work for them both. There *had* to be.

As they came alongside, there was a fight to get to the gangway. The deckhands flogged the rabble into some sort of order, shouting and swearing. They were well used to this, obviously, Maddy thought as she held tightly to her bundle. The crowd was so dense her arms were pinned to her sides and she prayed that she wouldn't be separated from her sister. At last her feet were on firm ground again and the crowd was dispersing slowly. She looked around. The whole place was jammed with ships of all sizes, and in the yellow gaslight from the street lamps she saw dockers and carters, policemen, carriage and cab drivers, beggars, hordes of ragged street urchins and groups of weak, bewildered immigrants wondering what they would do now as many had no money. Across the road in a small churchyard – a sanctuary of peace in this bedlam – the spire of the Church of St Mary and St Nicholas soared above the tallest of masts.

'Where do we go now, Maddy?'

Maddy looked around her. The sooner they got out of the crowds the better. 'I don't know. I think we should ask.'

'Ask who?'

'That policeman over there.'

Carmel looked across at the burly figure in the navy-blue uniform who stood surveying the scene with shrewd eyes. Well over six feet tall, he had a chest like a barrel and looked far from friendly.

'He looks terrifying,' Carmel gulped.

Undeterred, Maddy made her way over to him.

'Sir, I was wondering if you could help us, please?' she said boldly. 'We don't know where to go to look for lodgings or work.'

He peered down at them. They were nothing special, just another couple of Irish incomers who would probably not survive six months in the overcrowded, disease-ridden fever slums of the city. Even strong men had succumbed to the epidemics: two young and frail-looking girls stood no chance at all.

'Please, sir?' Maddy prompted.

'This is a hell-hole of a city, girl. If you're lucky and have some money, you can look for lodgings around Wapping. It will only be a cellar and you'll probably have to share it, but it's not as rough as some places. Go along the dock road, it's fairly straight, and just ask.' It was still no place for two young girls but it was better than the Scotland Road area, where even police officers dared not venture.

'As for jobs,' he went on, 'try the factories and ropeworks, but I doubt you'll have much luck. Keep your belongings with you at all times and be careful. Trust no one.'

Maddy nodded, wondering had she done the right thing to come here. Maybe he was just exaggerating. But Carmel was clearly terrified. She wasn't used to such crowds, nor to the noise and dirt. She was just a country girl.

'Thank you, sir,' Maddy said. 'We'll be very careful. We have a brother over here but we don't know where.'

'Then I wouldn't bank on finding him. There are more Irishmen over here than in Ireland.'

'I know, it's the famine and the fever.'

'There's plenty of that over here, too. Be off with you now and take care.'

'We will and thank you again, sir.' Maddy took Carmel's arm and they walked away in the direction he'd pointed out.

Two hours later they sat on the doorstep of a church, exhausted and horrified. What they'd seen had left them in a daze of disbelief. Of course they'd seen poverty and sickness and death before – but nothing on a scale like this. The streets were little better than open sewers, the houses ramshackle and overcrowded, with four or five families living in one room. Men stood on street corners or staggered drunkenly from one side of the road to the other, fighting in the filth of the gutters. Tiny children, like little ragged scarecrows, begged for food or farthings or anything they could get. There were obvious ruffians and villains of every kind, and gaudily dressed women, openly flaunting themselves, calling out obscenities and their prices.

Maddy dropped her head in her hands. 'Oh, Holy Mother, what have we come to! What have I done?'

Wandering the roads of Ireland would have been far better than this. At least the air was fresh and clean, there was grass to walk on and the poorest, humblest cabin was a palace compared to these houses that were so crowded together that not a ray of light could penetrate them.

'Maddy, don't cry, please.' Carmel tried to bolster her own courage. 'We'll find somewhere better eventually and there must be some shops.'

'Gin shops and alehouses, that's all we've seen. Oh Carmel, I don't know what to do.'

Carmel had never seen her sister like this. 'Let's rest a bit here and then we'll start again,' she suggested. 'We haven't been down that street yet.' She nodded towards two intersecting main roads.

Carmel's attempts to look on the bright side were not in vain, for they helped Maddy to pull herself together. 'True for you. Let's eat the last of the bread and cheese. We'll definitely feel better then.'

In silence they ate the remains of the now stale bread and cheese, and Maddy wished with all her heart that they could have got some hot water for a cup of tea. There was no use just wandering around for hours; it was getting darker and darker and the thought of spending the night on the streets was terrifying.

She brushed the crumbs from her coat and then pulled her sister to her feet. 'Let's try again. I've got an idea.'

'What?' Carmel asked eagerly.

'I'm going to ask one of those . . . er . . . women if they know anywhere. I don't care what kind of a house it is, as long as it's got a room free or even a bit of a cellar.'

'Maddy! You can't ask one of *them*!'

'Why not? They know the area, and I'm past caring what they do.'

Carmel clutched her arm. 'But—'

'Needs must when the Devil drives, as Mammy used to say.'

She was nervous but determined not to show it as she approached what she thought was a young girl dressed in a faded blue taffeta dress that must have looked very fashionable once. A dirty yellow shawl covered her shoulders. She wore no hat of any kind and her hair was matted. Only when Maddy got within a few yards of her did she realise that it

73

was not a girl at all but a woman. A woman with a face so raddled she looked to be about forty.

Maddy took a deep breath. 'Can you help us, please?' she asked.

' 'Elp yer with what, like? Yer don't look the type fer this game, but . . .' She shrugged.

'We came over on the boat this morning and we need somewhere – anywhere – to stay. It's getting dark and every place we've tried is full to bursting.'

' 'Ave yer gorrany money?'

Maddy looked at her suspiciously. 'What if I have?'

'Yer'll get nowhere without it.'

'I can see that for myself.'

The woman looked her up and down. The girl was far better dressed than anyone around here. It was a wonder she hadn't been robbed.

'Yer not thinkin' of goin' on the streets, are yer?'

'No! All we want is a roof over our heads for tonight at least. Then we intend to find work, any kind of work, except . . .'

The woman threw back her head and laughed. 'Except what I do, yer mean. Well, I'm honest too, in me own way. There's many that'll rob the fellers blind, especially them foreign fellers offen the ships. Strip them naked and pawn or sell the lot.'

'Look, I'm not giving out to you about what you do,' Maddy said desperately. 'I just want a bed. Any kind of bed.'

The woman's gaze was speculative. 'Iffen yer that

desperate, yer can kip down with me for half a crown. I've gorra room up there, but yer'll 'ave ter sling yer hook for a while iffen I get any trade, like.'

The sum was nothing short of extortionate and Maddy knew the woman wouldn't earn that much in a night, but she was too tired and despondent to argue. Her poor Mam would spin in her grave if she could see her now. Thankful for a shared room with a prostitute!

The room was at the top of the house and was reached by a staircase that was rotten and dirty. The floorboards in the hall were all missing, burned for firewood, she supposed. There were all kinds of noises coming from each room. Babies crying, young children squabbling, a man and a woman fighting, a woman screaming in either pain or anger – it was hard to tell which.

'If yer dead beat yer won't take no notice of the row,' their benefactress said as she led the way.

To Maddy's surprise the room was not as small as she'd imagined and, although grubby, it contained a table and two chairs, a small chest on which an oil lamp stood, and even a small fire. She determinedly kept her gaze from the bed.

'Yer can sleep on the floor over there.'

'What are we to call you?'

The woman roared with laughter. 'Anything yer like, girl. Bloody anything! Most people call me Sall, me Mam – the drunken owld bitch may she rot in 'ell – 'ad me baptised Sarah.'

Maddy handed over the money and indicated that Carmel should sit while they both untied their bundles.

'Yer've gorra few nice bits there.'

Carmel looked up with fear in her eyes. The 'nice bits' referred to were the things Florence Mitchell had given her and she was afraid they would be taken from her.

Sall threw a few ragged garments on the floor beside them.

'Use these ter sleep on, or ter cover yer.'

'Thanks. We'll sleep in our clothes,' Maddy replied.

'Yer'll 'ave ter in case yer 'ave ter scarper for a bit, like.'

Both Maddy and Carmel blushed.

'I've got some tea and sugar,' Maddy said. 'Would there be any chance of a bit of hot water?'

'There's an owld kettle over there. Yer can go down an' get some water from the stand-pipe an' boil it on the fire. I wouldn't mind a cup meself. It's a while since I 'ad one.'

'You're very welcome, but would you . . . could you get the water, please? I don't know how one of those stand-pipes works and . . . and—'

'Jesus Christ! Give me the bloody kettle! Where did yer come from anyway? Don't they 'ave bloody water pipes in Ireland?'

Maddy looked down at her feet while Sall dragged out a rusty kettle and disappeared with it.

'Oh Maddy, this is desperate,' Carmel hissed.

'I know, but we've nowhere else to go. Tomorrow we'll find something better. Let's just hope she doesn't have any . . . callers. Fasten up your bundle again. I don't trust her.'

When the kettle had boiled Maddy made the tea but again there was no milk. Still, it was hot and sweet and Sall produced three tin mugs.

'Yer know, yer not bad-lookin', either of yer,' Sall remarked pleasantly, peering at them in the dim glow of the oil lamp. 'God 'elp me, there was a time when I looked just like youse. Yer wouldn't believe it now. This is a bloody tip of a city. What's yer name?'

'I'm Maddy, short for Magdalene, and this is Carmel.'

The information seemed to amuse Sall. 'That name would 'ave suited me better than bloody Sarah. Mary Magdalene was a tart like me, wasn't she?'

'Yes, but she gave it up and became a Saint,' Carmel ventured.

'So she can speak, eh? She's not dumb, after all. I thought she was. Well, there's no point in me givin' it up. I'd bloody starve ter death an' no one would make me a bloody Saint. Right – yer'd better get yer 'eads down, I'm goin' downstairs again ter see if there's any trade.' She screeched with laughter at the expressions on both their faces.

Maddy began to spread out the rags on the floor, looking at them with distaste; she'd have sooner slept on straw. She had never felt so dirty in her life. Her clothes were stained, and neither of them had been able to wash their face and hands since yesterday. Had they really left Ireland just one short day ago? It felt like a lifetime. She gazed up at the dirty, damp-spotted ceiling and remembered that it was Christmas Eve. There would be nowhere open tomorrow, except the pubs.

'Deliver us from evil, Lord,' she prayed before beginning the Lord's Prayer, but she didn't finish it, falling instead into an exhausted sleep.

Chapter Six

It was still dark when Maddy awoke. She was stiff, cold and hungry, and her head was throbbing. Beside her, Carmel lay asleep and she could hear Sall snoring. She sat up and wrinkled her nose. The air smelled of unwashed bodies and clothes and strangely enough, of cats. But there was another smell, the overpowering reek of cheap ale. Sall must have left them and gone out and spent all the money on beer. Two shillings and sixpence of her hard-earned money wasted!

She wondered should she wake Carmel but decided to leave her. Let the blessed oblivion of sleep blot out the horrors of this place for a few more minutes. She lay down again, gritting her teeth at the pain the movement caused, and watched through the fly-speckled, dirty panes of glass in the uncurtained attic window, the first fingers of dawn creep across the sky. They had to find somewhere else today. They *had* to. Then she remembered that it was Christmas morning and at the memories of other, happier Christmases, tears welled up in her eyes. 'Oh Lord, help us, especially today!' she prayed.

Things had happened so quickly. Her world had been turned upside down and she'd not felt so lost and depressed since the death of her parents. Oh, damn Tom and damn Mr Mitchell! But for that pair of selfish men, they wouldn't be in this terrible predicament. Tom would not have been sent packing, he would have been there to protect them, and James Mitchell would have kept his hands off them. But for Tom, she and Carmel would be in a clean, warm kitchen. Carmel would be preparing breakfast while she would have started to pluck the goose. The thought of rashers being fried, of the goose in the oven, the plum pudding boiling on the range, wrapped up in butter muslin, brought tears to Maddy's eyes. Oh, she'd never forgive James Mitchell, the foul lecher that he was, nor her brother and his stupid ambitions! She hoped he was suffering as they were, in some dark, damp, filthy room. That would serve him right for his sins of pride and vanity. At that moment, Carmel stirred beside her.

'Hush! Don't wake her,' Maddy whispered.

'Who?' Carmel asked.

'That woman Sall – don't you remember where we are?'

Carmel rubbed her eyes and looked around. Oh yes, now she remembered.

'Look at the state we're in,' Carmel breathed. 'I'm cold and hungry and I've a headache.'

Maddy gathered her in her arms. 'So have I, it's the air in

this room. I'm cold and hungry too – *and* it's Christmas Day.'

That made Carmel feel worse. 'What will we do? We can't look for work today and there won't be any shops open. Oh Maddy, I wish we hadn't come here.'

'So do I, but we'll have to try to make some kind of a fist of it. We've got a few sweets left – we can have them.' Maddy thought for an instant how ludicrous it was. They had no sustaining food yet they had sweets.

'We can't have them yet,' Carmel objected.

'Why not?'

'We have to go to Mass and Communion.'

Maddy looked at her with disbelief. 'How can we go to church looking like this, and today of all days?'

'It won't matter what we look like, we *have* to go. It's Christ's birthday.'

Maddy nodded. How could she have forgotten that. 'I wonder if there are any churches around here at all?'

'There must be. Phew, she stinks! I don't want to stay here another night – it's desperate and so is she.'

'Well, please God we won't have to. We've got all day to find somewhere else to stay. Get your things together before she wakes up.'

'She won't be doing that for hours, judging by the state of her,' Carmel said scathingly.

There was a little water still in the kettle. It was cold but Maddy tore a piece off her underskirt and soaked it in the water. They both rubbed the cloth over their faces and hands and then Carmel took a hairbrush from her bundle and they tidied their hair.

'Well, at least we look far more presentable now,' Maddy said with a false cheerfulness.

They crept down the rickety stairs. The house was silent but she wondered how long that would last. There was no front door and they stepped straight out into the cold morning air. The area didn't look much better than it had done the night before, although there was no crowd of people now, only a mangy cur and a couple of gaunt starving cats foraging in the ashpits.

'Let's try and make our way back to the church where we sat on the steps,' Maddy suggested.

Carmel was doubtful. 'It didn't look like much of a church.'

'What would, around here? Just watch where you walk and try to avoid the worst of . . . of *it*.'

There were very few people about and it was bitterly cold but at least the rotting filth beneath their feet was half frozen, which diminished the smell.

They seemed to have wandered around for an age, but the air had cleared their heads. Nothing looked familiar but they noticed a few people making their way along the road that led to the Canning Dock.

'Let's follow them. They're all women, so it must be going to church they are. I imagine all the men are abed still,' Maddy said dryly.

They followed at a distance and turned eventually into a wider road that was cobbled and did have a pavement of sorts. Halfway down on the opposite side was a soot-blackened building that did look like a small church.

'Will we go in?' Carmel asked a little fearfully. 'It might be the wrong church.'

'That's what we've come for, isn't it, and we'll soon find out.'

It was a Catholic church but it was devoid of all the statues, pictures and candles of the one they'd attended in Ireland. Except for the red Sanctuary light.

'It looks different,' Carmel whispered as they genuflected, crossed themselves and sat down on a rough bench.

'It's a miracle that it's got anything at all. It would be robbed.'

'But that's sacrilege!' Carmel said.

'I don't think that would matter much to anyone around here.'

The priest was a tall thin man who looked as half-starved and pallid as his parishioners. His soutane was faded, stained and creased, as were the vestments he wore. They should have been of a rich, cream-coloured material and embroidered with gold thread. There was only one boy to attend him and he had no surplice, no boots, only a grubby, greasy jacket that was obviously a 'hand me down' and was too tight and short. Ragged trousers came to just below his knees.

The two sisters prayed as hard as they could for a decent room and a job. Maddy even asked for guidance as to whether they should stay or go back to Ireland if things didn't get any better; she knew Carmel's health would suffer and she was afraid they would both catch typhoid fever.

When Mass ended the priest came down from the altar to

his small congregation to shake them all by the hand and to say a few comforting words. At last he reached them.

'Ah, haven't some of my prayers been answered,' he said genially. 'I am Father Molloy. I see I have two new members of my flock, although it's a small one.'

'You have, Father, and aren't we glad to be here,' Maddy answered.

'Where do you come from, child?'

'The County Offaly, Father. Outside the town of Tullamore.'

'Ah, Offaly – the "Faithful county". I'm not too familiar with it, being a Cork man myself. When did you arrive?'

'Yesterday and oh, Father . . .' Maddy couldn't help herself. She burst into tears.

'Come, child, will you tell me what it is that's so upsetting to you both?' he asked kindly, for Carmel too had dissolved into tears.

'It's . . . it's *everything*, Father,' Maddy gulped.

'Come along with me to the Parish House. It's only small, as I have a very poor parish, but at least I can offer you some bit of hospitality on today of all days.'

They followed Father Molloy up the aisle and through the sacristy to a small door that led directly into the house.

Maddy was calmer now. She had someone older, wiser and with local knowledge to confide in, and it was such a relief. Some of the heavy burden had been lifted from her shoulders. The priest was right, it was a very small house, stark and comfortless compared to the Parish House in Killina, four miles from the Canal House, but in the kitchen it was warm and that in itself was a luxury. A very old woman was stirring a pot of oatmeal on the fire in the range, while a black kettle boiled beside it.

'Sit down at the table. Warm yourselves and Mrs O'Moore will serve out the breakfast.' He smiled. 'She's my housekeeper. She has nowhere else to live, poor soul. But what am I saying, sure there's plenty like her around here and I can only help a few – and when fever strikes, my own health and strength are in God's hands.'

'Father, if I had known, if I had only known what this city is like, I'd never have brought us here,' Maddy said, close to tears again.

'Ah, child, not all of the city is like this. There are fine houses and parks and the docks are booming. Trade is flourishing – but those who have riches turn a blind eye to the plight and suffering of the poor.' He shook his head sadly. 'And they call themselves Christians. I declare to God that they mislead themselves so much that their vicars and ministers cannot shame them, try as they may.'

'All we wanted, Father, was a job of work and a bit of a home for ourselves. I didn't think it would be so hard.'

'That is no simple thing.'

'I see that now.'

'Why did you come?'

Maddy paused and picked her words carefully. 'We were turned out and for no fault of our own.'

'Were you in a comfortable position?'

'We were indeed. It was a small household, but the master

was a man of some standing. There were only two children and the work was not hard.'

'And now, are you alone?'

Maddy nodded. 'The fever took Da and Mammy five years ago and my brother Thomas came to Liverpool not long ago but we don't know where he is or how to go about finding him.'

'I can try to help you with that.'

'No. No, not yet, Father,' she added. A look of surprise passed over his face at her reply but he said nothing.

'Eat up your oatmeal while it's hot and Mrs O'Moore, sit yourself down and join us,' he instructed. Raising his hand, he blessed the food and said a short Grace. The old house-keeper poured the tea and then placed a plate of thickly cut bread on the table. Both Maddy and Carmel tried not to bolt the food but they were so hungry, and tea with sugar *and* milk made this simple meal seem like a banquet.

The priest smiled sadly at them. Theirs was not a new story. They were clearly decent, well brought up girls unused to the depredations of a place like this.

'I'll do all I can to help but it won't be much, I'm afraid.'

'Any place will be better than having to share a room with a fallen woman.'

'Was that where you slept last night?'

'It was so, Father.'

'Then tonight you must sleep here, by the fire with Mrs O'Moore, and tomorrow I will try to find you somewhere else.'

Maddy was so relieved that her eyes were bright with tears again and there was a lump in her throat.

'Father, do you think, I mean can we . . .' Carmel ventured. She too was so relieved.

'Can we wash and clean up our clothes?' Maddy finished for her.

'You can so. Boil up the water and I have some lye soap. There's a sink in the scullery and we keep three buckets of water in there too. It saves Mrs O'Moore going backwards and forwards to the pipe in the street all the time.'

The old woman spoke for the first time, revealing a few rotten teeth. 'Isn't he an Angel of Mercy? I'd be dead these two years but for him.'

'If I could feed and clothe half the parish I would be more than content, but I'd need the help of a hundred Angels to do that. Is the famine bad?'

Maddy put down her cup. 'It is. It's desperate and there's fever raging too. The sights . . . the terrible sights . . .' She shook her head, unable to find the words to describe the sufferings of her country.

'Then there's many thousands more will take the emigrant ship and aren't we crowded out as it is, God help us.' The priest drained his cup and pushed his plate away. 'So now, I have some visiting to do. You settle yourselves here.'

When he'd gone Maddy and Carmel insisted they wash up the dishes and mend the fire, leaving the old woman to doze in a chair by the range. Oh, it was heaven to wash in hot water, to change out of the clothes they'd worn day and night since they'd left Ireland. They rinsed through what clothes they could and draped them all over a bit of a clothes line strung above the range. Then they sponged their coats and scraped the mud off their boots.

'Oh, I feel so much better now. Things will get better soon, won't they?' Carmel said, smiling at her sister.

'I'm sure they will,' Maddy agreed. 'And tomorrow we'll start again.'

The day and the evening passed quickly, or so it seemed. When Father Molloy returned he was cold and looked upset, but they didn't question him. They knew the reasons. There were herrings fried in oatmeal with potatoes for supper and both girls had cleaned everything they could in the kitchen as a means of showing their gratitude. The kitchen floor was flagged but they didn't mind. At least the flagstones were clean.

Father Molloy had gone out again after supper on sick calls but he promised that first thing in the morning, he would set about finding them shelter.

It was raining next morning and looking up at the heavy grey clouds, Maddy longed for the kitchen in the Canal House. Life had been so uncomplicated there, and easy even. Why, oh why had all this had to happen, she asked herself for the hundredth time.

The streets and alleys were once again muddy and filthy. It had been a waste of time cleaning their boots, Maddy thought as they followed the priest down the narrow entries. But at least they *had* boots. Father Molloy was taking them to a house he knew of where there was a room free. He had heard about it last night.

' 'Tis only a basement room but it's not too bad and there's only yourselves to fill it,' he informed them.

One side of the narrow laneway was dominated by the wall of a foundry that rose forty feet into the air, and on the opposite side there were dilapidated houses and dark, stinking courts. They followed Father Molloy into one of them.

'This is known as Gillings Entry and is home – if it can be called that – to sixty-five people.' He sighed. 'It is at times like this that I can't stop myself from falling into the sin of despair.'

'I can see why,' Maddy said quietly. The conditions were dreadful. No light filtered into it at all. There were four ashcans and two stinking earth closets. She felt faint when she thought of what it would be like in summer. Two privies for sixty-five people. But it was no worse than some of the streets they'd travelled through yesterday.

The priest spoke to a man who was hanging around the door of a house and Maddy saw him slip something into the man's pocket. She tugged gently at his sleeve.

'Father, we have money to pay.'

'Nonsense, child.'

'Please, Father? That money you gave him could have gone to feed little children.'

'I know, but it was promised and you have money for the rent from now on?'

'We do.'

'Then come and inspect this grand room with me,' he joked.

They went down the steps and through a small door made of rough planks that were rotting at the bottom. The cellar was only about nine foot square and the ceiling was dark and low. Some light filtered in through the panes of the window that was set high in the wall and from which they could see the feet of the passers-by. On one wall was a fireplace of sorts and the floor was flagged, although many of the flags were cracked and broken and uneven. It wasn't much, but it was better than the alternatives.

'It's grand, Father. We'll manage just fine. A few bits of furniture and it will be great. Thank you. Tomorrow we'll try for work. A policeman suggested factories or ropeworks.'

'The ropeworks employ girls and women but the pay is not much.'

'That won't matter. We'll manage, truly we will, and we have so much compared to most people.'

'You do, and it is a worry to me. But I'll see you on Sunday?'

'You will so.' Maddy smiled up at him. Their prayers had been answered.

When he'd gone, they looked around and then at each other.

'Will I go and see who else lives here and maybe ask where we can buy furniture and things?' Carmel offered.

'No. I'll go. You stay here.'

Carmel was relieved. She'd felt safe in the priest's house

but not any more. She took the piece of cloth they'd used to wash themselves and began to try to clean the window.

Maddy knocked loudly on the first door in the hallway and eventually it was opened by a middle-aged woman who was tidily dressed, although her clothes had obviously been darned and mended and were very faded.

'I'm Maddy Kiernan,' she said. 'My sister and I have come to live in the cellar. Father Molloy found it for us.'

The woman smiled. 'And I'm Mary Shannahan. I have this room with my husband Bernard and my lad John.' She looked away, sadness in her eyes. 'He's the only one I managed to rear.'

Maddy smiled sympathetically. 'Does Mr Shannahan have work?'

The woman's face brightened. 'Thanks be to God he does. At the foundry over there, and John too. I'm the lucky woman. Come on in, girl.'

The room was tidy and clean. There wasn't much furniture but a fire burned in the hearth.

'I've come to ask where can I go for some cheap furniture and things? You see, we have nothing. We've only been in Liverpool since Christmas Eve.'

'If you have the money, go up to Canning Place to one of the pawnshops. You'll get most things there, but keep your hands tightly on your purse. This is a terrible neighbourhood and by the look of you, you're not used to poverty.'

'Not like this. Doesn't anyone *do* anything at all to help people?'

'No. They look away, pretend we don't exist. There are some who think we even prefer to live like this.' Her tone was bitter. 'Would you like me to come with you, you being so newly arrived?'

'I'd be very grateful. I feel so out of my depth.'

'Do you come from the country? I know you're Irish, like me, but from where?'

'From a small town in County Offaly.'

'I've heard tell of it. Ourselves are from County Clare. We've been here ten years or more. No wonder you're confused. This must seem like hell on earth.'

Maddy nodded.

'Wait while I get my shawl. Is it still raining?'

'Yes.'

'Then God help them in Paradise Street and those other streets around there. The basements in those houses flood.'

Maddy shook her head in disbelief. She thought she'd seen the worst areas of this city, but obviously she hadn't. 'Paradise Street', eh? It was like some kind of hellish joke.

Carmel was almost in tears by the time Maddy came back.

'I was so afraid for you,' she said shakily. 'I didn't know whether to go and look for you.'

'I'm sorry, Carmel, I was thoughtless.' She nodded at the smiling woman next to her. 'This is our neighbour, Mrs Shannahan. She's going to come with me to get some furniture. Do you want to come too or will you stay here?'

Carmel bit her lip but Mary Shannahan resolved the matter.

'Come with us, my dear. At least you won't be worrying yourself to death down here.'

Carmel was relieved that a decision had been made for her, although she didn't relish going through those terrible streets again.

As the two girls readied themselves to leave, Mary Shannahan looked at Carmel speculatively. The younger girl was pretty, very pretty and clearly also very timid. That combination wouldn't work in her favour, not in a neighbourhood like this. The older one seemed more confident, more sensible, and she was a good-looking girl too. She'd have to have a long talk with Maddy Kiernan later on about how to take care of her beautiful younger sister.

Chapter Seven

Puffing and panting slightly, the two Kiernan sisters lugged some of the things they'd purchased back to their new home in Gillings Entry. Mrs Shannahan said that her husband and son would collect the rest after work. Maddy had been so glad of the woman's help. Mary Shannahan knew all the pawnbrokers by name and had bargained with them over the prices, so not too much of her money had been spent. Still, an alarming amount seemed to have gone since they'd left Dublin.

Gratefully, the girls put their parcels down on the floor. 'There's not much we can do until the furniture arrives,' Carmel said, looking around helplessly.

'You can get a fire going and clean the place up a bit, then come up to me and we'll have a bite to eat,' Mary suggested.

'Oh, I forgot to get any food!' Maddy exclaimed. 'I was so intent on the things we've bought that I completely forgot we've nothing in the house.'

'Go after dinner to Ma Healey, she's better than the rest. She'll put it on the slate for you. Just say I sent you. In the meantime, I can give you bread and dripping and a cup of tea.'

'I'll go now,' Maddy said hastily. 'We mustn't take from you.'

'Of course you can, girl. When I'm short I'll come and ask you. That's how things work in this neighbourhood. Now I'd better get back to my own jobs.'

Maddy took off the shawl she was wearing. She had exchanged her decent coat for pans, a kettle and some dishes, and two shawls – one for herself and one for Carmel. For her sister's coat she'd got two grey blankets and a very faded quilt.

'Right, let's light the fire,' she decided. 'We have wood and some coal. I hope I did the right thing trading in my good boots for these and that bit of firing.' She looked down at the well worn, heavy boots. Still, they were more sensible for life here than her others had been.

The sisters worked in silence, washing the walls and re-doing the window and door and scrubbing the flags. Earlier on, Mrs Shannahan had taken them to the stand-pipe and Maddy had queued with other women and girls who had all kinds of receptacles for that precious commodity – water. She'd thought back then to the ease of the well at Canal House and the more than abundant supply of canal water, no matter how dirty Eliza Mitchell said it was. She could have scrubbed out this place every single day with the canal water. Now each drop had to be queued for and carried in.

To her alarm, Mary had advised her to speak to no one else in the house.

'There's things that go on here that would turn your hair grey. I keep myself to myself and I don't lend *anything* – only to those I like and trust and who would do the same thing for me and mine. The trollop who has the backroom is always sending one of her kids to beg or borrow, but take no notice. She sends them hoping you'll take pity on them. Don't. They're a set of thieving pickpockets – she has them well trained.'

'Does she have a husband?'

'Of sorts, though I don't think they've ever set foot in a church. Living "over the brush" they are, if you ask me. He's always drunk. Spends every penny he can get his hands on, on drink. You'll not be so bad down there. At least you won't have to step over him in what passes for a hall. As for the rest of them that live here . . . When we first came here Bernie put down boards on the hall floor. Next day they were gone – ripped up and burned so we didn't bother after that. No point in wasting money, is there?' She sighed and then shrugged.

'Will our things be safe while we're out?' Maddy asked, concerned.

'I'll get Bernie to put a good strong lock on the door for you, like the one he put on ours, and I don't think that window opens, which is a good thing in summer. It would let in some air but the stink and the flies would drive you mad and besides, the sun never reaches down here to the Entry.'

* * *

'It's going to be a much harder life than we're used to, isn't it, Maddy?' Carmel said, looking around at the results of their hard work.

'It is so. There's all the water to carry and boil. I'll get a couple more buckets and keep them filled, like I used to do at . . .' She was about to say 'home' but this was their home now. 'These walls could really do with lime-washing.'

'Tomorrow, will we go to find work?'

'We will. We'll try the ropeworks on the corner, like Mrs Shannahan suggested. It's very near to here so at the end of the day we won't have miles to walk home.'

'I saw some girls hanging around the gates at the ropeworks, and they didn't look very nice.' Carmel looked scared.

Maddy sat back on her heels. She was tired and irritable. 'Sometimes I could shake you!' she told her sister. 'You'll have to learn how to cope with things. You're grown up now. You can't hang on to my skirt for ever. I know things are desperate, that we've never lived like this, but at least now we do have a home and a good neighbour, which is more than we had yesterday. The new year is nearly with us, and we must try to make the best of it. You'll have to harden yourself, you really will.'

Carmel nodded slowly and then her pale cheeks became flushed. 'Oh, I *hate* Thomas! I really *hate* him!'

'Well, at least that's something we share. *I'll* never forgive him for doing this to us, either. Never.'

* * *

98

Bernie and John Shannahan were both big, amiable men, and Carmel and Maddy liked them as soon as they met them. The pair had brought the furniture back to Gillings Entry on a handcart, as promised.

'We had to fight off a few thieving blackguards to get this lot here in one piece,' Bernie said solemnly, but his eyes were twinkling.

Maddy smiled back. They looked well able for any thieves.

'I see you've already been busy,' he went on, indicating with his head the cleaner walls, window and floor.

'We have, and I intend to give the place a coat of limewash. I know how to do it.'

'So you may, young lady, but this great lump here can do it. It'll only take a couple of hours.'

'And I'll be glad to,' the lad said, smiling at Carmel.

His father grinned. 'I can see how the land lies there.'

Carmel blushed and Maddy thought how pretty her sister was. As usual, the knowledge made her uneasy, but John Shannahan looked a decent enough lad.

'Well, we'll leave you to it,' Bernie said, turning to go.

'Thank you, thank you so much for everything you've all done for us. I think our prayers have been answered,' Maddy said fervently. 'We were getting really desperate.'

'Well, just remember you've a job to find yet,' Bernie Shannahan cautioned as he and his son left.

When the girls had finished arranging things they stood back to admire their work. There was now a table and two chairs, where they could sit and have meals. The bottom half of an old dresser that had drawers and cupboards held their belongings tidily. A mattress stuffed with straw and covered with the blankets and quilt filled the alcove by the fireplace, making a snug bed. The few pots and the kettle stood in the hearth, and in a metal box on the mantel were stored some items of food that Maddy had bought from Ma Healey's shop and for which she'd paid cash. She didn't want to get into debt just yet, she'd explained to the surprised shopkeeper. Mrs Shannahan had advised them to buy the box to keep the food safe from the vermin that infested all the houses, despite the tribes of mangy cats that stalked the alleys and houses in search of prey. A couple of nails hammered into the wall served as a wardrobe until times got better.

'It looks grand,' Carmel sighed. 'I feel so much easier and comfortable now.'

'So do I,' Maddy agreed. 'At least we've somewhere of our own, we can cook and wash and clean, and Mrs Shannahan has been goodness itself!'

'I liked Mr Shannahan too.'

'And John?'

Carmel blushed.

'Oh, you like him, I can tell that.' Maddy laughed and put her arm around her sister. 'Come on, let's get some sleep. First thing in the morning we'll go across the road and try for work.'

They had both slept well and by half past seven they were washed, dressed and had swallowed a meagre breakfast of oatmeal and bread. Wrapping the heavy shawls around them, they pulled the door shut.

'I'll feel better when there's a proper lock on that door,' Maddy said, a little concerned.

'Sure, didn't herself above promise to keep her eye on the place for us, and if we get any kind of a break it's not far to run and check things,' Carmel said.

They were first to arrive and stood outside the gates of McPherson's Ropeworks. Neither of them had any experience or even an idea of what a job here would entail, but they were determined to learn and learn quickly. Girls and women soon began to arrive, in twos and threes, all huddled in shawls against the cold and damp of the winter morning.

'What time do they start, please?' Maddy asked of two women whose faces were almost completely hidden by the shawls pulled over their heads.

'Eight o'clock. I 'aven't seen youse two 'ere before.'

'No. It's our first time. Do you think we'll get a job?'

' 'Ave yer ever picked oakum before?'

'No. What is it?'

'It's the stuff they make the ropes from. We 'as ter pull it apart, like, so it can be twisted inter lengths. Yer'd better be quick learners.'

'We will. If you do get a job, is it steady work?'

'As steady as any other bloody job. Just turn up each mornin', work 'ard, keep yer 'ead down an' yer gob shut and yer might get kept on. If yer don't turn up, iffen yer sick, like, then that's yer lot. No work.'

'Who're yer talkin' to, Ada?' shouted a big, brassy-looking girl from behind them.

'These two 'ere. They've never done work like this before.'

'What kind of work did yer do?' the girl wanted to know.

'Housework, cooking, things like that,' Maddy answered.

'Housework! Bloody cookin' – an' yer want ter work 'ere! Bloody Irish, comin' an' takin' our jobs. Takin' the food out of our mouths!'

'Shurrup, Peggy Spencer,' the woman called Ada told her. 'Cookin' an' housework's somethin' yer don't know nothin' about.'

'That's because there's nothin' ter bloody cook in our 'ouse most of the time, an' me Mam does what she can with the midden we 'as ter live in!'

This didn't bode well, Maddy thought, so she kept quiet. Carmel simply looked cowed.

At eight o'clock sharp the gates were opened by an old man who sat in a ramshackle hut behind them. Beside him stood the tall figure of the foreman who picked out the women and girls he'd use for the day. He began to point at women who pushed through the crowd and went into the yard.

'Sir. Sir, please, can we have work?' Maddy shouted.

'Who the hell are you? I can't see you.'

Dragging Carmel with her Maddy stepped forward.

'I'm Maddy Kiernan and this is my sister and we need work desperately, sir! We'll work hard, I promise.'

He looked down at them. The younger one didn't look as though she would last a morning. 'Why should I take you on? Everyone needs a job, otherwise they wouldn't be here.'

Maddy thought quickly. 'Because . . . because you are a knowledgeable man, sir. You can pick out a good worker and we . . . we're good workers.'

A smile lifted the corners of his mouth. 'You've a quick tongue, and a sharp mind, girl. Just for that I'll give the pair of you a try. Give your names to old Joe here and go on inside.'

'Oh Maddy, I wish I could be as quick as you,' Carmel said thankfully.

'Come on, let's show him that we are as good as our word.'

They followed the others into a large room. It was cold and damp and there was nothing in it except rows of small stone bollards and huge piles of what looked like brown straw. A thick dust covered everything.

'What do we have to do, please?' Maddy asked the woman called Ada.

'Go and grab as big a hunk of that stuff as yer can, then watch me.'

They did as they were told and came back to stand beside the older woman, watching as she began to pluck and tear at the matting, teasing it out into long strands that she coiled around the stone bollard at her feet and which they learned was called a 'stoop'.

'Do we ever get to sit down?' Carmel asked timidly.

Just then, Peggy Spencer went past her with her arms full.

Overhearing the question, she scoffed, 'The only time yer get ter bleedin' sit down is in the few bloody minutes they give yer for a dinner break.'

The morning seemed endless. It was tiring standing up and Maddy was sure the work could have been done sitting down, but maybe that wasn't allowed in case the workers became slower. The dust got up your nose, in your hair and you could taste it in your mouth. The skin on their hands soon became dry, and where it was stretched over the knuckles it was really sore. Maddy knew that eventually it would crack and be painful. She resolved to get them to rub a bit of dripping on their hands before they went to bed. Untreated cuts and cracks often became infected and the dripping would act as a barrier.

'You'd better nip down to the house and see if everything is all right,' Maddy tiredly instructed her sister as the girls looked for something to sit on for the fifteen minutes they were allowed for a break.

'Will I bring back something to eat?'

'Yes, grab a bit of bread and cheese. I don't think I could go the whole afternoon without anything.'

Carmel began to walk briskly towards the gate.

'Where's she goin'?' Peggy Spencer asked, sitting down beside Maddy on the bit of a low crumbling stone wall that made for a precarious seat.

'Home. We didn't bring anything to eat.'

'Then she won't be let back in. Old Joe shuts the gate dead on time.'

'She'll be back well before then.'

'Where do yer live then?'

'Just across the road and down a piece.'

'Dead 'andy, then. Do yer share?'

'No. We have the cellar.'

Peggy eyed her with interest and Maddy felt uneasy. The girl was only fishing for information.

'Well, she won't last a bloody week 'ere. She looks as if the wind would blow her over.'

'She's stronger than she looks. We both are.'

'Oh, aye? When did yer come over on them cattle boats?'

'Two days ago. Liverpool isn't . . . isn't the place I thought it would be.'

'So, go 'ome iffen it don't suit yer.'

'No. There's famine and fever there.'

'Well, yer don't look like yer starved.'

'That's because we weren't and we chose to come here.'

'Well, I'm tellin' yer, iffen yer don't 'ave enough stoops done by the end of the day, yer'll get no work termorrer.'

'We will have. Don't you go worrying your head about that.'

When Carmel came back with two sandwiches wrapped in a bit of brown paper Peggy looked her up and down with pale grey, protruding eyes. The Kiernan sisters' clothes were far better than anyone else's. Their hair was clean, shiny and brushed up tidily, and they both were attractive. The young one could be said to be beautiful. The pair of them would find themselves fellers to marry and keep them with no trouble at all, while she and *her* sisters would be left on the shelf. Beside these two slight, fine-boned girls, the other women there looked big, awkward, and plain. They made Peggy feel downright ugly.

'She hasn't got much ter say for 'erself, 'as she?' she commented nastily.

'And isn't that a good thing too, seeing as we're not supposed to talk,' Maddy shot back quickly.

'Oh, bloody 'ard-faced, aren't yer?'

'I've had to be,' Maddy said coldly.

Peggy looked at her through narrowed eyes. She'd begun to hate the pair of them and she knew how to deal with the likes of these brass-faced little madams. Everyone in the neighbourhood gave Peggy and her three sisters a wide berth, and she'd soon show these Irish bitches why.

Maddy and Carmel were both too tired to talk as they walked the short distance home. Maddy opened the door and was thankful that everything was as they'd left it. The room was freezing so they kept their shawls on. Maddy lit the oil lamp and the fire and Carmel fetched water for the big kettle.

'It won't take long to get sorted out. We'll have a cup of tea and then we'll feel better and I'll make something to eat,' Maddy said briskly. Tired as she was, she was determined to be positive about things.

The fire did warm up the room quickly and there was even a bit of cheerfulness in its glow. Carmel set out the plates and mugs and cutlery they'd bought while the kettle was boiling.

'I don't think Peggy Spencer likes me,' she said.

'She doesn't like either of us. She's jealous. I saw the way she looked at us, taking in everything we were wearing, but don't worry. Just ignore her and she'll get fed up and find someone else to pick on.'

They were sitting by the fire, after their meal. Maddy had cooked some bacon and boiled some potatoes, and there was bread too and a mug of tea. The few dishes had been washed and put away. Carmel had made two sandwiches for tomorrow's lunch and they were now wrapped in paper and in the tin box. Maddy had taken their clothes and given them a good shaking to remove the worst of the dust and she'd washed their stockings and they now hung from the mantel. They'd be dry by morning. With the remains of the water they'd both had a good wash.

'This isn't too bad now, is it?' she said, looking around the tiny room.

'It's grand and I'm so glad we're on our own.'

No sooner had Carmel said these words than there was a loud knocking on the door. When Maddy opened it, Mary Shannahan was standing in the doorway.

'I've come down to see how you are,' she said pleasantly.

'Oh, come in, please. Take a chair – Carmel will sit on the bed.'

Carmel got up instantly and indicated that their guest should sit on the chair by the fire.

'So how did you get on then?' Mary asked.

'Not too bad. We were given a day's trial. It's tiring standing all day, but we both managed to do enough stoops as they're called, so I hope we'll be taken on again tomorrow.

We'll get there early again to be first in line. We don't mind waiting.'

'Good. Hard work never killed anyone yet. Bernie told me to ask you when you want the place limewashed?'

'Oh, whenever he has time. It's very good of him.'

'It will be our John who'll be slapping it on, and I declare to God that that lad makes more mess than a horde of kids. Don't worry – I'll have a few words with him. Bernie has a good bolt and padlock and he'll be down later to put it on.'

'I'll feel better when we can lock the door behind us,' Maddy said with relief.

'Aye, there's some that would steal the eyes out of your head if you so much as blink.'

'Will John want us to get the limewash?' Carmel asked.

'No, Bernie will get it. He knows someone who'll charge half of nothing for it and John will mix it with the water.' The older woman smiled at Carmel. The girl was definitely a cut above most of the lassies around here. A bit timid, mind, but that was no bad thing. She'd have no objections at all if John and young Carmel Kiernan took to 'walking out'.

'Will Saturday be a good day?' Maddy asked.

'They both work until dinner-time so it can be done in the afternoon.'

'Then I'll put all the furniture in the middle of the room,' Maddy said, then she laughed. 'Sure, there's not much of it to move.'

'It's more than most have. Well, I'll go back up now. They'll have finished their meal. I'll send our John down to see how much lime he'll think he needs, and then his Da can have it for Saturday.'

Both girls got up.

'Mrs Shannahan, thank you. We're very grateful to have such good neighbours,' Maddy said sincerely.

'That's all right, girl. Decent people stick together and help each other. You have to in this Godforsaken neighbourhood.'

When the woman had gone, Carmel took her hairbrush from the mantelshelf and removed the pins that held the coils of red-gold hair. It fell around her shoulders and she began to brush it.

Maddy laughed. 'Carmel Kiernan, I do believe you've set your cap at John Shannahan.'

Carmel turned pink. 'What if I have? He's nice. He's good-looking and kind and decent.'

'Don't you think you're a bit young for that kind of thing?'

Carmel was indignant. 'I'll be fifteen next month, and you know as well as I do, that back home across the water there's girls who are wives and mothers at sixteen.'

'Oh, I'm not giving out to you. I agree. He *is* nice and it's a decent family he comes from.'

'Then what is there to complain about?'

Maddy laughed again. 'Nothing. Nothing at all.' At least her sister was showing some spirit at last.

'Here, let me help you,' she said. 'We can't have him coming in on us and seeing you with your hair down your back like a child.'

And Carmel, just like a child, obediently held out the hairbrush and allowed her sister to take charge.

Chapter Eight

The foreman at McPherson's Ropeworks took on the Kiernan girls for the next two days, and also for the Saturday morning – something that Carmel wasn't too happy about although she said nothing to her sister. On Saturday she'd intended to make sure the place was tidy and that she herself looked as attractive as she could, despite their limited resources. She'd planned to iron the white blouse Florence Mitchell had given her and which she only wore on special occasions. Now she'd have to do it on Friday night after work. Already Maddy had been teasing her, asking her why she wanted to dress up when young John Shannahan was coming to throw limewash all over the place, and probably splash them too. Her good blouse would be ruined.

Carmel didn't really mind Maddy's teasing. It wasn't malicious, unlike Peggy Spencer's endless digs at them. She was afraid of the girl and never answered back, although Maddy gave as good as she got. Carmel was also beginning to hate the job. It was hard, standing all day, and she loathed the ever-present blanket-like dust which got everywhere. She wondered if she should suggest to her sister that they look for something else. Somewhere where the air was cleaner. Somewhere where there were no girls like Peggy Spencer.

As soon as they got in on the Saturday dinner-time, Carmel put the kettle on while Maddy lit the fire.

'When that's boiled, wet the tea and then help me pull all this stuff into the middle of the room,' Maddy said. 'And then, if there's time, you can smarten yourself up.'

'Fine. I'd like to look halfway decent.'

'Oh, put on the blouse if it will please you.' Maddy laughed, not unkindly. 'But . . .'

'But what?'

'It's Sunday tomorrow. What if he asks you out?'

'Asks me out! Oh, I never thought . . . I mean . . .'

'Don't start getting in a state about it, it was just a suggestion.'

As she made the tea Carmel thought about it. Maddy was right. If John did ask her out, and she sincerely wished that he would, she'd have nothing fresh and a little bit stylish to wear. Maddy had said they would go to early Mass on Sunday, which would give them a whole day free.

They had hardly finished their tea when John knocked on the door, his father behind him.

'We're not stopping,' Bernie said. 'I just came to see if you needed a hand with anything before Meladdo here gets started.'

'No, thanks, we've done everything.'

112

'Right then, lad, pull yourself up by your boot straps and get going. Goodbye, ladies,' Bernie said, and disappeared.

'Will you have a cup of tea before you start?' Maddy asked the boy, smiling with amusement at the way he was gazing at Carmel.

'There's plenty left in the pot, Mr Shannahan,' Carmel said archly.

Maddy raised her eyes to the ceiling.

'Well, if you've a cup to spare I won't say no – and would you call me John? I don't want to be calling you "Miss Kiernan".'

'All right, John. Call me Carmel.' She ducked her head and busied herself with the tea.

Later on, Mrs Shannahan came in to see what progress had been made and to ask Maddy if she wanted to go with her to the market in Great Homer Street, where there were great bargains to be had.

'I'd like to, but I've got the washing to do. I've no time to do it on Monday and I can't do it tomorrow, not on the Lord's Day.'

'Maybe next week then?' The older woman glanced quickly from her son to Carmel, understanding why Maddy wanted to stay. She was going to be a chaperone – and of that Mary definitely approved. It showed the girls had been well brought up.

'Is there anything I can get you? How about some salt fish? Everyone in Liverpool who can afford it has it for breakfast on Sundays.'

'Yes, that would be great. Wait while I get my purse.'

Maddy handed the coppers to her neighbour and they both smiled.

The limewashing took longer than the couple of hours Bernie had predicted because Carmel insisted on making another cup of tea halfway through, just so that John could stop work and she could have the chance to speak to him. She did hope Maddy was right. She really wanted him to ask her out. Maybe she was a bit young, but it didn't matter. John knew how old she was and it didn't seem to bother him.

His mother called in on her return from the market with the fish.

'Good God, is that lad still not finished!' she exclaimed to Maddy, who shrugged. 'Shift yourself, John Shannahan, or you'll still be here at midnight.'

She turned to Maddy. 'Now this will have to be soaked in cold water all night; at the moment it's like a piece of leather. Then you can either boil it or fry it. Have you a bowl big enough to soak it in?'

'I've a pan big enough, but . . .'

'I'll get John to bring you down a bowl, when he gets finished – which at the rate he's going won't be soon. I'd ask Bernie to come and give a hand but he's gone for a couple of pints. It's his weekly treat and he earns it.'

Carmel felt downcast at the thought that John would soon be finished and away home.

'I'll come up with you for the bowl,' Maddy said. It would leave Carmel and John alone for a short time – enough time for him to make a move, if he intended to at all. She hadn't really given much thought to the future, but if Carmel and John became close then she would have no objections. In fact, it would be a relief to her to see her sister settled in a relationship with a decent lad who had work and didn't drink or gamble. She was sure that Mary Shannahan felt the same way.

When John could delay the moment no longer, he stopped and looked at his handiwork without much pleasure. 'I think that's about done,' he told Carmel.

All afternoon he'd watched her and he'd never seen anyone so lovely, so fresh, so slight and delicately boned. The girls around here were a product of their upbringing. They couldn't be blamed for that, but beside Carmel they all seemed awkward, coarse, and rowdy.

'It looks so much better now, John,' she said shyly.

'Do you really think so?'

'I do. You're very good to give up your time for us.'

'Oh, it's nothing. I was pleased to do it, because . . .'

'Because what?'

'Because it was for you.'

'That's a nice thing to say. I mean it.' She couldn't look at him.

'Will you . . .' He coughed. 'Will you . . .'

Carmel's heart began to flutter. He was going to ask her, he *was*.

'Will you be at Mass tomorrow?'

She felt deflated. 'Early Mass, so Maddy says, so we can have a day's rest.'

'Carmel, would you . . . I mean, will you . . . would you like to take a bit of a walk with me tomorrow afternoon?' John blurted out. 'It's a great day for seeing all the ships.' He would have liked to have taken her somewhere special, somewhere indoors. It was winter, after all, and the wind coming in from the Mersey estuary could be bitter.

She smiled at him and his embarrassment faded.

'I'd like that, John, I really would. We did see some of them, from the ferry boat, but . . .'

'Then will I call for you after dinner?'

'Yes.'

'Wrap up warm, it could be freezing.'

'I will.'

'I'd better go up now before Mam comes down looking for me. I'll see you tomorrow, Carmel.'

'You will so and thanks, John, for everything.'

He tried to think of a plausible excuse to linger but couldn't, so picking up the bucket and brush he smiled at her and left.

Carmel hugged herself. He *did* like her. He really *did*. She felt as though she was floating on air and her insides were all in a knot, but it was a pleasant feeling.

'I can see by your face that he asked you,' Maddy said, smiling. She'd passed the lad in the hall. In fact, he'd helped her to step across the exposed joists, and he too had been grinning all over his face.

'He did. He's taking me to see all the ships after dinner tomorrow. You don't mind, do you? I mean, I do like him a lot and if his Mam doesn't mind either . . .'

116

'Oh Carmel, neither of us mind at all. I'm delighted for you and I'm sure Mrs Shannahan is too. Come here to me.'

She embraced her sister and smiled at the radiance in her face. Carmel was so beautiful, and that beauty and innocence needed someone like John Shannahan to protect it.

They'd cleaned up and put everything back, and the little room looked and smelled infinitely better. Maddy thought about getting a bit of cheap material for curtains, to make their cellar room look even more of a home.

Carmel spent ages with the flat iron, pressing out the creases in her white blouse and even gave her skirt a bit of a press. 'I wish I still had my coat,' she said wistfully.

'Well, there was nothing I could do about that and besides, everyone wears a shawl round here. They're far more practical than a coat. You'll look just grand.'

Neither of them got much sleep. Carmel was restless and that kept Maddy awake, so they were up, washed and dressed and in plenty of time for early Mass. Despite being hungry after fasting before Communion, Maddy insisted they stay behind and thank Father Molloy for his kindness and inform him that they now had jobs.

He was, of course, delighted. 'I've remembered you in my prayers every day and they appear to have been answered. Would that some of my other requests had been successful, but "the Lord works in mysterious ways, His wonders to perform," as they say. I never give up hope and you both look very well.'

'We are, Father. Thanks to you we've a decent bit of a home and good neighbours.'

'Ah, Mr and Mrs Shannahan. A good family and they've known trouble in their lives.'

Maddy passed him a silver florin.

'What's this for, child?'

'To help someone else. We've been so fortunate that we feel we need to give something in return. Something practical.'

'God bless you. Now get off home and have your breakfasts.'

Back at Gillings Entry, Maddy decided to fry the fish as it would be quicker and they were both famished.

Carmel set the table, cut the bread and made the tea.

'Isn't this a feast? And just think – I'll have a few hours to myself later on,' Maddy said.

'Oh, I never thought about you being on your own.'

'Pay it no mind. It will be heaven just to sit here and do a bit of mending.'

'If you're sure?'

'Of course I'm sure.'

Carmel was ready half an hour before John came to call. She had redone her hair twice and had no intention of putting her shawl up around her head unless it rained.

'Will you sit down? You're making me tired, just looking at you pacing up and down the floor,' Maddy chided her. 'Did John not say what time he would come for you?'

'No. He just said "after dinner".'

'Well, sit down and calm yourself.'

'I can't!'

Maddy picked up the mending and was halfway through darning one of her stockings when John finally knocked on the door.

He looked so different in his grey frieze jacket, black trousers and boots, a stiff collar to his shirt and a 'Canadian' hat as they were called, being low-crowned and wide-brimmed and made of soft black felt. It was quickly removed.

'For heaven's sake, John, take her away,' Maddy joked. 'She's that restless, she's driving me mad!'

He grinned at Maddy. 'I wanted to come earlier, but Mam said to wait while you got ready. You look lovely, Carmel.'

'Thank you, John,' she said formally but then smiled as he offered her his arm.

Maddy looked fondly after them and returned to her darning.

John and Carmel walked along the dock road towards the Canning, then the Salthouse and Albert Docks. It was cold but the sky was bright and for that Carmel was thankful. There was no wind to speak of, another reason to be grateful as her hair wouldn't blow about and get untidy.

'I'm glad Father Molloy found that cellar for you,' John told her.

'So am I. It's the first bit of luck we had since we arrived, and then we both got jobs, and . . .'

'And?'

She looked up at him. He was very tall and well-built, and she felt perfectly safe with him. 'And I met you.'

'And I met you – and from the first time I saw you, I wanted to get to know you better.'

'And I wanted you to like me. I don't normally act like this, I'm usually terrified of people I don't know, but you're different. I knew that, the minute I set eyes on you.'

'And I feel exactly the same about you, Carmel. I've never felt anything for any of the girls around here. You're so different. I'm really glad you left Ireland.'

'I am too, now. I was in despair the day we arrived and even Maddy wasn't sure we'd stay.'

'Thank heavens you did. By the way, I have steady work. I'm very fortunate. I work in the foundry with Da.'

'Yes, I think your mother told us that.'

'I know that you're only young,' he went on hurriedly. 'I'm nineteen and Mam says—'

'I'm nearly fifteen, John. I'm grown up and I know my own mind,' Carmel interrupted quietly. She was amazed with herself. Never had she been so sure and confident.

'Then could you . . . would you . . . think about us walking out together, getting to know each other properly?'

She gazed up at him adoringly. It was as if wine was flowing through her veins and making her light-headed and so very, very happy.

He bent and kissed her gently on the cheek and then took her hand and held it tightly as they resumed their walk and she felt so safe and deliriously happy.

It was nearly dark when they got back an hour or so later, and John kissed Carmel once more before she knocked on the door.

'Well, did you enjoy yourself?' Maddy asked.

'I did – and oh Maddy, guess what?'

'I don't know. What's the big secret?'

'It's not a secret, it's a surprise. John has asked me to walk out with him and I said I would. I think I'm falling in love with him Maddy. I know it must seem so quick, but I can't help how I feel.'

Maddy stared at her dumbstruck.

'You don't mind, do you?' Carmel was horrified. 'Oh Maddy, please don't be vexed with me.'

Maddy recovered her composure. 'I'm not, it's just that it's a bit sudden. You only met him recently and you've only been out with him for a few hours and—'

'But I feel as if I've known him always and he's so . . . so . . . *wonderful*!'

Maddy placed her hands on her sister's shoulders.

'Is it really what you want? Really and truly? Because if you do walk out with him, it may well lead to an engagement and then marriage. It's a huge commitment, my love. Marriage is for life, Carmel, and you're so young.' For a moment, Maddy looked careworn and very young herself.

'I know all that, but I think I love him, Maddy. I'll never want anyone else but him. It's strange – but I realised that as soon as I met him.'

'Then I'm happy for you, I really am and I don't think you'll have any problems from his Mam either. You're a good girl, she knows that.'

Maddy went to fill the kettle and make them a welcome cup of tea. The day was drawing in and it would be good to have an early night after their disturbed one the night before. Picking oakum on a cold Monday morning was not a job to be done on half a night's sleep!

Chapter Nine

Both sisters were happy as they waited at McPherson's Ropeworks for the gates to open on Monday morning. Carmel had spent the previous evening in a dreamlike trance while Maddy watched her, yet pleased at the change in her sister.

Mrs Shannahan had made a brief visit, her expression similar to Maddy's, to ask if what her son had just told her was true – that the two youngsters had fallen in love.

'It is. I can't take it in myself. They seem to have made up their minds very quickly,' Maddy said. 'Have you any objections?'

'Not really, but Carmel is a bit young.'

'She is, but I've never seen her so determined, or so full of confidence.'

'Well, it will take them a while to get to really know each other before they can think of taking matters further,' the older woman pronounced. 'Although they do make a lovely pair, and I would be glad to see my John settled.'

Maddy had nodded. 'I feel the same way about Carmel. You know, Mary, I'm nineteen myself – the same age as your John – yet sometimes I feel much older than I actually am.' Maddy looked pensive.

'It's the daily grind that does that,' Mary said sagely. 'Women like us don't stay young for very long, my love, and once you've had kids, they only add to the worry.'

'Well, at least when the time comes I'll make sure she'll have some sort of a wedding. I owe her that much. Mam would have wanted it. Your John is a good lad.'

'Although he's my own, I agree with you there. He *is* a good lad and will make a fine husband and, in time, father,' Mrs Shannahan had added.

Most of the other women at McPherson's had now become friendly to them both, and Carmel could hardly contain herself as they waited for the gates to be opened.

'Will I tell people that I'm courting? I feel so happy I could burst and I want to tell *everyone*.'

Maddy smiled at her. 'I suppose you do. Falling in love is one of the most exciting times in your life, but if I were you I'd wait until dinner-time, otherwise you'll be shouting to people and your pay'll be docked. You know the rules on talking.'

Carmel sighed. 'I suppose it would be and that's something I can't afford now. I have to save every penny I can from now on. I want to know I've got something put by for the future. Each week I'm going to give John as much as I can afford. He says his Mam keeps the money in a tin box with a lock on it, and when she goes out she takes it with her. It'll be as safe as houses.'

'Not the houses round here,' Maddy joked. 'One good gale and they'd all go down like a pack of cards.'

At dinner-time when they went out, the wind was bitterly cold and everyone drew their shawls tightly around them.

'We must be mad sitting out here. It's so cold it would perish the crows,' Maddy said, unwrapping her sandwich.

'It's the only bit of fresh air we ever get. The cold doesn't bother me. It's as cold as charity in our house these mornings,' Ada Barnes put in.

'Can I tell them now?' Carmel said in a low voice.

'Ah, go on, then maybe I'll get some peace. Carmel has something to tell you all.'

A row of curious faces were turned towards her.

'What?' Ada asked.

'I . . . I started to walk out with someone on Sunday,' Carmel said proudly. 'If everything goes well, we might get engaged.'

'Engaged! Who to?' Ada demanded.

'John Shannahan – he lives in the room above ours.'

'Well, fancy that. I've known Mary all my life,' Ada said. 'They lived next door to us when we were kids.'

'There won't be a wedding for quite a while, we've got to save up.'

'Aren't yer a bit young, like?'

'I suppose I am, but by the time we have enough saved I'll be older,' Carmel replied confidently.

'Well, that didn't take yer long, did it?' Peggy Spencer said nastily. The news had brought a flush of anger to her pallid cheeks and she was filled with a jealous rage. The stuck-up Irish bitches had only been here five minutes and they had a decent place to live and a job – and now that whey-faced little miss Carmel Kiernan had got her claws into one of the best-looking and most steady lads in the neighbourhood. All that 'shy little thing' pose was an act; she was a scheming brass-faced little madam. Well, she'd soon learn that she couldn't have everything.

'Just what do you mean by that, Peggy Spencer?' Maddy asked, staring at the girl through narrowed eyes. She'd watched her face closely after Carmel's announcement and she didn't like what she saw.

'She's a bloody fast worker, is what I mean,' Peggy shot back. 'I wonder 'ow free she was with 'er favours ter get him running after her like a dog with two tails?'

Maddy's eyes blazed at the implication and she got up off the wall and stood in front of Peggy. Everyone else fell silent.

'Say that again, Peggy Spencer!' she demanded.

'I'll say more than that. She's a bloody little whore – how else would she get a feller so soon, an' her only a birrof a kid.'

Maddy slapped the young woman hard across her cheek and Peggy was so stunned that for a few seconds she did nothing. Then with a shriek of rage she got to her feet and caught Maddy by her hair.

Before things could deteriorate, some of the other women pulled them apart.

'You and yer bloody big dirty gob, Peggy!' Ada Barnes yelled.

'Yer deserved that. I think yer just jealous!' another woman said.

'Geroff me! Jealous, am I? Jealous of 'er? I wouldn't bloody spit on 'er!'

The sound of the whistle that marked the end of dinnertime prevented any further arguments.

Carmel looked at Maddy with fear in her eyes.

'Don't worry about her,' her sister flamed, furious. 'She's a bully, and if you stand up to bullies they always back down. Come on inside.'

Peggy glared at them both. She'd been humiliated and scorned, and that cow Maddy Kiernan would pay dearly for belting her.

Maddy told Mary Shannahan of the incident that evening.

'There's not one of them in that family that is any good at all,' was Mary's reply. 'Her father is always in jail, her mother's always in the alehouse, those lads have the people in the street they live in terrified of them, and those three girls are no better. If anyone's a whore it's Peggy Spencer, although I've heard it said that she has to pay *them*, she's that flaming ugly.' She laughed grimly. 'I'm amazed she even bothers to go to work; the rest of them don't. They live by their wits and by what they can thieve and sell. Stay well clear of them all, Maddy, they're bad through and through.'

'I will.' Maddy grimaced. 'There's nothing more I'd like better.'

'If she gives you any more trouble, you tell me and I'll sort her out,' John said angrily.

Maddy nodded. Yes, Carmel needed someone just like him. She couldn't stand up to the likes of Peggy Spencer alone.

'Just ignore her completely,' Maddy advised as they went to work next day.

'I will. At least I work at the other end of the room to her,' Carmel said nervously.

But they didn't have to ignore Peggy for she didn't turn up for work.

'I wonder what's up with 'er?' Ada remarked. 'She'll be lucky ter get took on termorrer.'

'Well, I couldn't care less if she doesn't,' Maddy replied, feeling more than a little relieved at the respite.

It was the sound of the whistle announcing the lunch-break that made Carmel cry out.

'What's the matter?' Maddy asked.

'I forgot to pick up our sandwiches. I left them on top of the dresser.'

'Oh, honestly, Carmel. Ever since you met John Shannahan your head's been in the clouds. Run down and get them, I'm starving.'

'I'm sorry, Maddy. I'll be as quick as I can.'

'Ferget 'er head iffen it wasn't screwed on,' Ada said with a grin.

'I just hope she's not going to be like this from now on or I'll be demented altogether,' Maddy replied. To keep herself warm, she marched up and down, hugging her shawl around her. Her tummy rumbled and she thought longingly of the cold bacon sandwich that was on its way.

The minutes went by and there was no sign of Carmel.

'What *is* she doing? At this rate we'll have to go back and be hungry all afternoon,' Maddy said irritably. She just hoped her sister wasn't dawdling around, thinking of John.

Two minutes later the whistle sounded.

'Well, that's it. No food fer you,' Ada remarked as Maddy walked back into the picking room.

Maddy was annoyed. This could cost Carmel her job.

When Carmel still wasn't back at two o'clock, Maddy's annoyance turned to worry and then fear. She put down her work and picked up her shawl.

'Where are yer going?' Ada asked.

'Home. I'm really worried, Ada – this isn't like Carmel. She wants to save so she certainly wouldn't risk her job. I'm going home.'

'What about yer own job?'

'I'll explain when I get back.'

It was such a short distance but with every hurried step Maddy felt more and more afraid. Her heart was hammering in her chest when she pushed open the cellar door. She looked around in horror. All the furniture had been thrown around the room, the few dishes they had had been smashed, the clothes that had been hanging on the makeshift hooks were thrown around and the box with the food was empty.

'Oh, Jesus, Mary and Joseph! Carmel! Carmel, where are you?'

A groan came from beneath the upended dresser and she shoved it to one side. Carmel was lying on the floor, her clothes torn and her face covered in blood. Her beautiful hair had been hacked off in vicious clumps. Tufts of it stood up at all angles.

'Oh, God! Carmel! Carmel, are you badly hurt? Who did this? Who was it?' She gathered her sister gently in her arms.

'Maddy, oh Maddy . . . they were in here when I got home, breaking our things, and then . . .' She began to cry.

Maddy wiped her face with the hem of her skirt. 'Is anything broken?'

'I don't think so, but I'm hurting all over.'

'I'm going up for Mrs Shannahan. Lie still now, I won't be long.'

'Don't leave me, Maddy!' Carmel panicked.

'I have to get help. I promise I'll only be two minutes.'

She raced up the cellar steps into the hall and hammered on her neighbour's door.

'Maddy! Mother of God! What's the matter?'

'It's Carmel. She's hurt. Oh, please come quickly.'

She almost dragged the older woman down the steps. When Mary Shannahan saw the state of the cellar room and the beaten and bloodied girl lying on the floor, she cried out, 'Merciful God! What happened?' She fell to her knees beside Maddy.

'She says she's hurting all over but that she doesn't think anything is broken.'

The older woman moved each limb of the now sobbing Carmel. Then she pressed her hands gently over the girl's stomach and ribs. Carmel cried out in pain.

'It's her ribs. They must be cracked. Let's try and move her.'

'Where to?'

'The mattress, what's left of it. Gently now.' The mattress cover had been ripped open and the straw stuffing strewn around, but Maddy gathered some of it and stuffed it back in before helping to lift her sister.

'Will I go for a doctor?'

'Let's get her cleaned up and see how bad she is first. There's no good getting a doctor out, if one would come at all, if it's just minor things. Boil up some water and go up and bring down the bits of cloth I keep on the window-ledge.'

They bathed Carmel's face, arms and hands.

'She'll have some terrible bruises and two black eyes, but at least that gash on her cheek has stopped bleeding and there doesn't seem to be anything seriously wrong. We can bind up her ribs, that's all a doctor would do.'

'Who did this to you, girl?'

'Peggy Spencer and two other girls.' Carmel gasped with the pain as the two women strapped up her chest.

'Her sisters,' Mary said grimly. 'Real hard cases, the lot of them. I didn't hear a thing. They must have slipped in when I went out for water. Oh, just wait until our John and Bernie come home – they'll sort those three trollops out, by God they will! Look at the mess they've made of her face, and her beautiful, beautiful hair. They did that on purpose. The three of them are as ugly as sin!'

The initial shock was wearing off and now Maddy felt only anger. She wished she'd broken Peggy Spencer's nose instead of just slapping her face. She looked around at the mess and then she jumped to her feet.

'What is it now?'

'The money! Where's the little tin I keep our bit of money in?' Maddy began feverishly to search around and Mary joined her, to no avail.

'Look's like it's gone, Maddy,' Mary said sadly. 'I'm so sorry. I should have come down here, just to check. I never even noticed that the door was broken into.'

'How could you? It's dark at the bottom of the steps.'

'But I never heard a thing and they must have made some noise chucking all this stuff around. I wish to God I'd never stopped and chatted to that woman from further down.'

'Don't be blaming yourself. What could you have done anyway, against three of them?'

The woman shook her head and Maddy sank down on the bottom of the mattress. They had nothing now. Nothing. Every penny they'd brought with them and their wages had gone. Carmel wouldn't be able to work and would need looking after. She herself probably wouldn't be taken on either, not after the way she'd just run out with no explanation. What on earth were they to do now?

'I'll go for the police,' she said, getting to her feet.

'There's little point in that,' Mary told her. 'You've no hard evidence it was them. Don't forget it will be their word against Carmel's – and there's three of them, and the rest will back them up, plus the police won't do anything to anyone around here, unless there's a murder. Meself, I think they're afraid of the Spencers. Why else would those hooligans be allowed to terrorise everyone? No, leave it to Bernie and John. I'll go up and make us some tea. I think we all need a cup.'

Carmel was asleep and Maddy was sitting staring at the wall in shock when Bernie and John Shannahan came down.

'Mary told us all about it, Maddy,' Bernie said grimly.

'Oh God, Carmel! Carmel, what have those bitches done to you! My God! Your hair!' John cried, kneeling down beside the mattress.

The young girl opened her eyes and started to cry, but the pain of her cracked ribs turned the sob into a whimper of pain.

John took her hand. It bore a deep, livid scratch. A rage such as he'd never known before coursed through his veins. 'I'll kill them!' he choked. 'I'll kill the whole bloody lot of them. The low, dirty, pig-ugly three of them! I'll more than cut their hair. I'll bloody scalp them!'

'They took the money?' his father said.

Maddy nodded. 'And they've destroyed our clothes and the few bits of plates and things, and thrown the ashes from the fire over everything. Look at the mess they've made of the walls you've just painted, John.'

Bernie caught hold of his son's shoulder and pulled him to his feet.

'Right, lad, let's get this sorted, and when we're finished with them they won't know what bloody day of the week it is! Mary will be down, Maddy. She's made a bit of scouse. See if you can get some down Carmel.'

Maddy could only nod. She still couldn't take it all in.

Mary came in, a bowl in her hands. 'They've gone and I don't think I've ever seen Bernie so mad. I told him to take care, them Spencers are as tough as old boots. Now, let's try and get some of this down her and you. You look terrible, Maddy, but then who wouldn't. A bowl of this will work wonders though.'

Carmel did feel better after the hot meal. Mary and Maddy took it in turns to spoon-feed her, breaking down the potatoes and carrots so the stew would pass easily through her swollen lips. Mary Shannahan started to tidy up, her own lips compressed in a tight line at this needless, wanton destruction. All this because they were jealous and Maddy had slapped Peggy's face. Well, they'd get more than they'd bargained for. Normally Bernie would never raise a hand against a girl or woman, but you couldn't put those three in the same class as anyone around here. Not by any means.

Carmel was again sleeping, Maddy had pulled herself together and was helping Mary to try to put the room to rights when the door was forced open. They both turned and then cried out in horror. Bernie Shannahan was leaning against the wall; there was blood on his face, his clothes were torn and dirty and in his arms he carried the limp body of his son.

'They were waiting,' he gasped out. 'All of them. The three lads and that jailbird.'

Mary crossed herself before rushing to his side.

'We left them a few broken bones and bruises to nurse, I'm just bruised but he's bad, Mary. One of those bastards kicked him when he went down, kept kicking him – and it was all I could do to get him out. One of the fellers in the street helped me get him to the top of the road.'

'Oh Bernie, no! What's the matter with him?' Mary pleaded, her voice cracked with fear.

'I think it's his back that's the worst. I'm going to take him to the parish hospital.'

'I'll get my shawl. I'm coming with you! Oh, God help him and he so strong and tall and . . .' She broke down as she fled from the room.

'Mr Shannahan, I'm so, so sorry,' Maddy said. A stone seemed to be blocking her throat.

He just nodded before turning and leaving her alone with Carmel.

Oh God, why had it all gone so wrong? What had they done to deserve all this? she begged through her tears. But there was no answer and she huddled beside the form of her prostrate sister and began to sob.

Chapter Ten

Maddy had never expected anything like this to happen. All they'd both wanted was to escape the famine and fever that raged back home. Why, oh why, Maddy thought as she clung to a weeping Carmel, had Peggy Spencer taken such a strong dislike to them? They'd done her no harm.

It seemed an age since the Shannahans had gone to the hospital. She lit the lamp, the only one that hadn't suffered at the hands of the Spencers and looked around at the room that only this morning had been so tidy and comfortable.

They were both cold, for she needed to conserve the coal. At last she heard footsteps outside and went to open the door. Only Mary and Bernie stood there, Bernie with the dried blood still on his cheeks.

'Where's John?' Maddy asked fearfully.

'They've kept him in. The doctor said he was badly hurt. It's his back. They said he'll never . . . be able . . .' Mary couldn't finish. She started to cry.

'Oh God!' Maddy's hand went to her throat.

'He'll never be able to walk again,' Bernie said hoarsely. 'He'll be a cripple for the rest of his life.'

'No! *No!*' Carmel screamed.

'Oh, I'm so sorry, so very sorry,' Maddy said with tears in her eyes. Poor, poor John. He would never work again or be able to help Mary out. He'd need constant care when he came home.

'When will he be able to come out?'

'At the end of the week,' Bernie replied.

'You have to go to the police. You *have* to!' she urged.

'It won't do no good, girl. What could they do?'

'Arrest the Spencers, all of them. They've half killed John, so they'd be sent down for years of hard labour, and good riddance!'

'It'd take the entire police force of this city to arrest that lot,' Mary said bitterly.

'What's wrong with the police here? Are they afraid?'

'They are, Maddy. There are certain parts of this city that they won't go near. It's always been their policy to leave things alone. To let us fight our own battles. They see us as scum, not worth the risk of getting themselves injured for.' Bernie was exhausted. Apart from his own injuries, he was in a state of shock as the doctor's words about John's condition had sunk in.

Maddy looked at him with despair. 'So people like the Spencers can get away with murder, and if John dies it *will* be murder – and no one will lift a finger? In the name of God, what kind of a city have we come to?'

'It's worse than a bloody jungle. Wild animals behave better than some people around here. My cuts and bruises will heal quickly and I can get back to work, but our poor son . . .' His voice died away and he gripped his wife's hand fiercely.

'Oh, I'm so sorry, so truly sorry. We've brought nothing but trouble upon you.' Maddy was desperately contrite.

Mary had regained some of her composure. 'It's beginning to look that way.'

A cold fear gripped Maddy's heart. Her neighbour was turning against them.

'What's going to happen to us now?' Carmel whimpered. 'Oh, John! John! It's all my fault but I love him.'

'You'd better think hard about that, Carmel. Think what's best for *him*,' Mary said grimly. Six children she'd borne, only John had survived and now . . .

'He'd have been better off if he'd never met me! At least he would still be fit and able to work.'

'I know,' Mary agreed curtly. 'Well, we'll be going upstairs. I'll have to see to Bernie.'

'Will you let us know how John is, please?' Maddy begged.

Mary nodded quickly and left.

When they'd gone, Carmel broke down.

'Maddy, we're cursed, that's what we are. That's why so many bad things have happened to us, and I hate myself, I *do*! I wish I was as ugly as sin because then none of this would have happened!'

'Don't be an eejit! There's no such thing as being cursed,' Maddy said tiredly, but her words lacked conviction. 'We'll manage,' she went on, rallying. 'We've still got a few things to pawn, the furniture mostly. That should tide us over until we're both able to work again.'

'Work at what, Maddy? We'll never get our jobs back and I don't ever want to see that place again.'

'We'll find somewhere else. We've a bit of experience now.'

'Do you think we should try and find Tom? I know I said I hated him, but things were different then.'

Maddy was indignant. 'What could he do to help?'

'I don't know. He might have found steady work.'

'He might, but he'd not spend his money on us. He ran off and left us.' She refused to even contemplate Carmel's suggestion. It was *his* fault they were in this predicament.

The next day, Maddy took anything that wasn't too badly damaged to the pawnshop. The money she got would last only a week and then they would have nothing, but she determinedly pushed the matter to the back of her mind.

Twice she went up to enquire about John's health and progress.

'There'll be no progress,' Mary had replied on the second occasion. 'He's a cripple. A fine big lad he was, with his life before him and now, all that's gone.' Maddy didn't call again but she heard the sound of wheels, then voices and knew that John was home from hospital.

When Carmel was a bit better and able to manage the stairs, she begged Maddy to ask if she could see John.

Maddy had serious misgivings, but she went upstairs and knocked.

Mary's face was set when she opened the door.

'I'm sorry to trouble you, but . . . but . . .'

'For God's sake, spit it out, girl!'

'It's Carmel. She's begging me to ask you could she see John, just for a few minutes. She feels terrible about what's happened – we both do.'

'Well, I don't know if he even wants to see her.'

'Please, could you ask him? You know I wouldn't be here unless . . .' She threw out her hands in a gesture of appeal.

Mary nodded slowly. 'All right. I'll ask him.'

'Will I wait?'

Mary gave a curt nod.

Maddy stood and bent her head and prayed that the lad would see her sister. Carmel was in a bad enough state as it was, and if he refused . . .

'He'll see her. Bring her up, but it can only be for a couple of minutes.'

'Thank you. I really do appreciate it.'

Mary turned away, leaving the door open slightly.

'Oh Maddy, what did she say?' Carmel begged.

'She said just for a few minutes. Come on, I'll help you.'

'Oh Maddy, thanks.'

It was a slow and painful ascent and Carmel bit her bottom lip hard as each step sent a knife-like pain through her ribs, but she had to go on. She *had* to see him. She'd been so miserable all week.

He was lying on a mattress in the corner of the room and Bernie had rigged up a bit of a curtain to give him some privacy.

Mary held it aside. 'Go on.' She turned to Maddy. 'I'd offer you a cup of tea, if I had any to spare.'

'I know you would. Do you think that in time you might be able to forgive us?'

Mary pondered this. 'Maybe, in time. I don't know. It's a heavy cross to bear.'

'But would you think about it?'

Mary didn't reply.

Carmel with considerable pain eased herself down until she was kneeling beside the mattress. She reached out for his hand, her sight blurred with tears.

'John. Oh John, I know words are cheap, but . . .'

He gripped her hand tightly and she looked into his eyes.

'Carmel. I'm sorry.'

'But it's me that should be sorry. I've caused all this.'

'No, you haven't. I'd do it again – they really hurt you.'

'Do you still love me, John?' she asked pitifully.

'Of course I do, I can't help it, and when I'm back on my feet again we'll get married.'

Carmel took his hand. 'Oh John! I love you so much, but . . .'

'But what?'

She couldn't tell him, she just *couldn't*. She took a deep breath. 'Nothing. We'll get married when you're better.'

Maddy felt Mary's hostile gaze boring into her back. The curtain hid them from view but they could hear everything that was said. Carmel shouldn't have made that promise but Maddy could understand why she had.

'I think it's time to let John get some rest,' she said to Mary, who pulled aside the curtain. Maddy helped her sister to her feet.

'Thank you,' Carmel managed to say to Mary.

Once back in their room Carmel turned to Maddy. 'What else could I say? I couldn't tell him that he isn't going to get better – that he'll never walk again. I just *couldn't.*'

'I know, but you have to realise that as much as you love him, there's no way he'll ever be able to marry you, or anyone else. The poor lad will need nursing for the rest of his life. He won't be able to father children, to work, to lead any kind of a normal life. I'm sorry, love, but you simply must face the truth.'

On hearing this, Carmel covered her face with her hands and sobbed. In her heart of hearts she knew that Maddy was right. But she would never love anyone else the way she loved him.

That night, the worst night since both their parents died, Maddy lay awake watching the pale shadow of light that filtered through the window panes. What was she going to do? They would have to leave here. The longer they stayed, the worse it would be for Carmel and John, and she had no money to pay the rent. Carmel couldn't work and whatever class of a job Maddy would get, it wouldn't cover the bare essentials of living. Much as she hated it, she knew she would have to go and look for Tom to see what help, if any, he could give them. But where should she start? She decided that tomorrow she would go and see Father Molloy.

The priest was helpful, as usual. He had already heard all the details from a bitter and broken-hearted Mary. He suggested that Maddy start with the docks and he drew a map for her.

'I've put in all the names, and if you ask to see the foreman it will be quicker. He'll know who is working for him, well enough. But be careful, child. Is there no one at all to go with you?'

'No, Father. Is . . . is it very rough?'

He sighed. It was. 'Look, I'll do my best to accompany you.'

'That's so good of you. I know you have little time to spare.'

'At least I can give you a couple of hours a day. How are the Shannahans doing this day?'

'Well, I think, under the circumstances. But we can't go on living there. Apart from having no money for the rent, it would raise John's hopes and Carmel's,' she replied sadly.

They set out that afternoon, threading their way along the buzzing, bustling dockside. Maddy was glad she hadn't come alone. It was frightening. They had no luck, and she thought that, had she been alone, she would have been treated far less deferentially. The priest at least was shown some respect.

'I'm sorry, Maddy, but there's a lot of ground to cover.'

'I know, and without your help I'd have got nowhere at all. I'd have been ignored.'

'We'll try again tomorrow,' Father Molloy promised her.

'It's all we can do,' Maddy replied with a depressed note in her voice.

By Thursday they still hadn't found any trace of Tom, and Maddy was close to despair. The rent was due, there was no money left and Carmel still wasn't able for work. Maddy would either have to give up this search and get a job, or face eviction. There was nothing to pawn now. Soon it would be the shawls off their backs and the boots off their feet – and they'd never been so poor that they'd had to go barefoot.

When Friday dawned, they had covered all the docks without success. Then Father Molloy said they should give the Salthouse Dock one more try. They walked along the dockside asking foreman after foreman, but no one had heard of Tom Kiernan.

At last Maddy turned away, her spirits very low. Her despairing gaze went idly over a group of men shovelling coal into sacks, then, her hand going to her throat, she cried out: 'Father! That's our Tom, I'm sure of it even though his face is black with the coal dust! He's over there.'

As they hurried towards the group, the men stopped to puzzle over the unusual couple, an old priest and a young, attractive girl.

'Tom! Tom!' Maddy called out. As they drew closer he turned towards her.

'Oh, thank God I've found you!' she burst out. 'We've spent the whole week searching.'

'What in the name of God are *you* doing here?' Tom asked in astonishment.

'Oh, it's a long story,' Maddy cried, all past animosity forgotten, 'but we've found you and that's the main thing.'

'Well, I'll leave you two to talk things over,' Father Molloy said, his voice full of relief. It had been like seeking a needle in a haystack, but they had been lucky.

'I can't talk to you now. You'll have to wait until I've finished my shift,' Tom said, glancing towards the driver of a coal cart.

'How long will that be?'

'Another hour.'

'I'll stand over there, out of the way.'

'There's a bit of a shack that's supposed to be a café further down where you can get a cup of tea. Have you the money?'

'I have so. I'll wait for you there,' she replied before hurrying away.

She spent the next hour with her hands clasped around a mug of tea, thinking about what she would say to him, and hoping he could suggest something that would help them. At last she saw him approaching.

'So, how did you get here?' Tom asked as he sat opposite her. He looked very odd, she thought, his face black and the whites of his eyes very white in contrast to the coal dust.

Now she had found him she felt awkward. 'We were thrown out. Himself tried to . . . to molest me. He was drunk and the mistress came in and he accused me of leading him on. He'd already made advances to Carmel. He denied it and then threw us out, there and then, in the middle of the night. We came to Liverpool and we weren't doing too bad – we had jobs and a home in a cellar that was dry and comfortable – but then there was trouble between us, the Shannahans who live above us, and a crowd of blackguards called the Spencers. John Shannahan and Carmel were walking out, they might even have been going to get married—'

'Married!' he interrupted. 'But she's just a child.'

'I know, but she and John suited each other. Then she was attacked and beaten up, and John and Bernie, his father, went to punish the family who did it. They were set upon and outnumbered, because the Spencers were waiting for them. Carmel's in a terrible state, Tom. Her eyes are blackened, her lips swollen, her ribs are cracked and they hacked off her hair. She looks awful! *And* they wrecked our room and stole all our savings.' Maddy's voice was trembling. 'The worst thing of all is that poor John will be a cripple now. The Spencers beat him so savagely that he'll never walk or be able to work ever again.'

Her brother looked grave as he pondered her words. 'Carmel is trouble, Maddy. Her looks will cause trouble wherever she goes. Her injuries will heal, that blonde hair of hers will grow again.'

'That's not fair! She can't help it if she's so much prettier than other girls.'

'I still say she's trouble.'

Maddy drank the rest of the now cold tea, wondering what she should say next. 'Florence was courting George White, the solicitor's son.'

'I don't give a tinker's curse about bloody Florence. He's welcome to her.'

Maddy decided not to go down this road.

'So, where are you living?' she asked. 'Have you a place?'

'I do. A couple of rooms in a house in Grayson Street. I've got a wife too.'

'A wife! You've only been here two months.' It was her turn to be astonished.

'So, there's no law against it, is there?' he replied indignantly.

When he'd first arrived he'd lived in a room with four other men, so when the daughter of a widow who lived further down the street had smiled and flirted with him, he decided it would be prudent to marry Johanna Doyle before someone else did. She was a good catch. She lived with her elderly mother in two rooms, and had a trade, so he'd courted her with enthusiasm and all the charm he could muster. To his surprise she'd more than eagerly promised she'd marry him. Two rooms, even if he had to put up with his mother-in-law, were far better than one – and that full of working men and no comforts. Now an idea was forming in his mind. If Maddy and Carmel came to live with them and helped out with the expenses, life would be even easier. His sisters could both work and he'd have more money in his pocket. He got to his feet.

'Come on then, take me to this cellar. We'll collect your belongings and you can live with Johanna and me and the Mammy, who's as deaf as a doorpost and hardly utters a word so isn't much trouble.'

Maddy breathed a sigh of relief. Maybe Johanna's Mammy would look after Carmel until she was fit enough for work.

'Oh thanks, Tom,' she said gratefully. 'I feel as though a burden has been lifted from my shoulders. There's not much to collect.'

He just nodded and Maddy followed him, wondering what her new sister-in-law was like.

Carmel greeted her brother with joy. She held out her arms and gave him a hug at which he stiffened awkwardly. 'Oh, you found him! Tom! Tom, I'm so happy to see you!'

'A nice mess you've got yourself into,' he replied tersely as she released him.

Maddy, although relieved herself, thought her sister was overdoing the welcome, particularly since she'd denounced him so often since he left Ireland.

'I suppose your hair will grow back,' he said, shocked despite himself at her appearance. She'd obviously taken a real beating and had probably done nothing to try to save herself.

'I'll keep my shawl over my head,' she replied, embarrassed.

The few things the girls had left were bundled together, then Carmel turned to Maddy.

'Do you think I could just go and see John, to say goodbye?'

'No. You'd only upset him. You have to forget him.'

Carmel looked at her with determination in her eyes. 'I'll never *ever* forget him.'

Maddy knew they were doing what was known as 'a flit' but she didn't care. She was leaving no debts. She'd paid the last week's rent. Their life here was over.

Grayson Street looked very much the same as the street they'd only just left, but as she helped her sister up the cracked and worn steps of the house Tom led them into, Maddy thought that anything would be better than a cellar.

'Tom, you're late, love. I was getting . . .' Johanna greeted her husband, then her voice trailed off as she caught sight of the two girls behind him.

'My sisters. They too were thrown out on the road and came looking for me.' Tom's tone was very bitter.

Johanna was a kind young woman. She loved her husband but there were times when she feared him a little, even though they should have been in the first flush of their marriage.

Maddy smiled shyly at the plump, auburn-haired girl.

'I've told them they can stay with us,' Tom went on, not asking her permission but stating a fact. 'They were living in a cellar, see, and there was some trouble with the neighbours. Carmel was beaten and every penny they had was stolen.'

'Oh, you poor things. How terrible! Of course you must stay with us, we've plenty of room.'

'Aren't you the kind one,' Maddy said with sincerity. It was all a bit of a surprise, but she went on: 'We're so glad to meet you, Johanna. We're related now.'

'Indeed we are. Oh, isn't this wonderful, Tom? The family united.' She hugged both girls, Carmel carefully because of her ribs. 'Take off your shawls and sit down and have a cup of tea. We can get to know each other better, then we shall sort out beds for you.'

Carmel looked at Maddy and bit her lip. Hesitantly, she lowered her shawl and saw the look of pity in Johanna's eyes. Maddy spoke to ease Carmel's plight.

'I'm afraid our sister looks a bit of a mess. Normally she has beautiful red-gold hair, but they cut it off.'

'How cruel of them, but please – take your shawl off. There's only family here now.'

'I wondered if you or Tom knew of any places where we can get jobs,' Maddy said. 'Do you work?'

Johanna smiled. 'Yes, I'm a seamstress but I work from home. That's why we have two rooms and I can look after my Mam.'

Maddy glanced quickly at her brother and wondered if the rooms were the reason why he had married Johanna Doyle. She liked her new sister-in-law, who seemed kind and generous. There weren't many young wives who would welcome two complete strangers the way Johanna had done. She hoped that Tom was treating her well.

When they were all seated around the table, Johanna smiled at them all.

'Isn't this nice?' she said gaily. 'I feel as though we're a proper family now.'

Chapter Eleven

It was still hot, Maddy thought as she leaned against the stone parapet of the dock wall. The slight breeze coming in from the Mersey estuary did nothing to cool down the air. The ships out in the river were becalmed, their sails hardly moving, and the odours of the dockside were far from pleasant.

Still, it was better than being cooped up as they had been in the cellar in Gillings Entry. That episode in their lives now seemed a long time ago. Things were considerably better in some ways, Maddy mused. Both she and Carmel had jobs. Tom had managed to get a slightly better job working as a carter for one of the bigger coal merchants, although the hours he worked were long. Johanna worked hard too. She did all the housework, looked after her now increasingly frail and silent mother, and always had some piece of sewing in her hands. One corner of the living room had been turned into what she laughingly called her 'work room'.

Maddy turned away. It was getting late and she took care never to be near the waterfront at night even though it didn't get dark until nearly ten o'clock these summer evenings. She'd have to be up early for work and it was so stifling in the house that she slept badly.

When she arrived home she nodded to the women sitting on the doorstep trying to get a bit of relief from the sultry heat.

'God, it ain't 'alf hot!'

'It is so, Mrs Mannion,' Maddy agreed.

'Where 'ave yer been, girl?'

'Down to the waterfront but it's not much cooler there.'

'I've 'ad a bloody 'eadache fer two days an' I can't get shut of it.'

'What we need is a bloody good thunderstorm. That'll clear the air,' Flossie McBride said.

'It might clear some of the bloody rubbish in the road too,' her neighbour said tartly.

The living room was airless. Johanna was sitting by the open window and Maddy thought she didn't look too well. She prayed that there'd be no cases of fever, remembering how swiftly the epidemic that had killed her mother and father had spread.

'Where's Carmel?' she asked.

'In the bedroom. You know what she's like.'

Maddy nodded and dragged a chair over to the window. There was complete openness between them and Carmel's moods were a constant concern to both of them. 'She's not got over him,' Maddy said. 'I thought that by now she'd have at least started to take an interest in other lads.' She looked more closely at her sister-in-law. 'You really don't look well, Jo.'

'I don't feel too good, but it's nothing to worry about. It's not a fever,' she added, catching the quick glimpse of fear in Maddy's eyes.

'You work too hard.'

'No, I don't. Tom works much harder than I do. He's so tired when he gets home that I feel guilty.'

'Guilty! What for?'

'For not working hard enough. I could take on far more sewing.'

'You'll ruin your eyesight.'

'I want to help Tom as much as I can. He doesn't want to be just a labourer all his life.'

'What does he want to do?' Maddy asked, taking more notice.

'It's not very clear, but he wants us to live a better life than this.'

Maddy remained silent. So he hadn't given up his ambitions.

'You understand that, don't you, Maddy?'

'Oh, I do so.'

'The thing is, well . . .'

'What?' Maddy realised her sister-in-law was trying to tell her something. She hoped it wasn't bad. 'What is it, Jo?'

'I suppose I should wait and tell Tom first, but I'm so excited. I'm going to have a baby. It's been four months since – you know.'

Maddy's face lit up. 'Oh, that's great! Can I tell Carmel? We won't say a word until you've told him, and then we'll act surprised.'

'Yes, of course you can.' Johanna paused. 'I'm so happy and yet . . .'

'What?'

'I know Tom would want something better than this for his children.'

'Ah, won't you get somewhere decent one day. Don't worry, Johanna. It may give him the push to try for a better job.'

'Or make him work even harder and be out later and later, and Mam's getting so frail.'

'She is, and I know what it's like to have your Mam die.'

Johanna nodded, remembering how her husband's parents had died. At least her Mam was older than they'd been. Mam had had more time to live.

The sound of heavy boots on bare wood came to their ears and Johanna got up. 'He's home at last.'

Maddy too rose. 'I'll be taking myself off into the bedroom to give you more privacy.'

Her sister-in-law nodded her thanks.

The bedroom Maddy shared with Carmel and the old lady seemed even hotter, although the window was wide open. It was so small and crowded. There was a double bed, covered by a clean but old quilt that she and Carmel shared, a single bed in which the old lady slept, and a cupboard that fitted into the corner of the room and on which stood a jug and bowl set. Behind the door Tom had put up a row of pegs for their clothes. What underwear they had was in a chest. A small mirror hung on one wall next to a large painting of a young girl in her wedding dress, surrounded by her female relations, in the kitchen of her home. It dominated the room and looked out of place. Carmel had bought it for the sum of three shillings from a neighbour who'd been left it by her late employer, and there had been an argument subsequently between Tom and Carmel over 'wasting money on rubbish' as her brother called it. With more insight than her brother, Maddy had told Carmel she was only torturing herself every time she looked at it, but the girl had borne all the objections in stubborn silence.

Carmel was sitting on the chest which she'd pulled across to the window, her thoughts, as always, on John Shannahan.

Maddy sat down on the edge of the bed. 'Phew! It's like a furnace in here,' she whispered so as not to wake old Mrs Doyle.

Carmel sat up. 'I know. I'll never be able to sleep.'

'You might have a better chance if you turned that painting to face the wall.' Maddy's voice held no note of sarcasm. 'Tom's only just got in and guess what?'

Carmel looked faintly interested. 'What?'

'Johanna's going to have a baby. It's due in November.'

Carmel's eyes widened. 'Oh Maddy, isn't that great!'

'She's telling him now, that's why I came in here.'

They both fell silent, listening to the murmur of voices in the other room where Tom and Johanna slept. They were both startled when the murmuring turned to shouting.

Maddy scrambled off the bed and hurried to their door, followed closely by Carmel.

As Maddy tapped and opened it, she stared in astonishment. Her brother's face was red with anger and Johanna was deathly pale, tears trickling down her cheeks.

'What's wrong?' Maddy asked, crossing to her sister-in-law and putting a comforting arm around her shaking shoulder.

'What's wrong? She's pregnant, that's what's bloody wrong! I won't have any son of mine born into a midden like this!'

Maddy rounded on him. 'Stop swearing at her! And lower your voice – you'll frighten poor Mrs Doyle. This place is no midden – it's as clean as a new pin. Doesn't Johanna spend hours scrubbing and cleaning. She does all the washing and ironing so we all have clean clothes to wear – and that's not easy – *and* she works! I'm ashamed to call you my brother. What do you think Da and Mammy would say? You should be delighted, Thomas Kiernan! On top of the world!' She paused. 'And what makes you so sure the baby will be a boy, I'm asking?'

Tom was still angry. 'I wanted my children to be born in a house of our own, with decent furniture in a respectable neighbourhood. Not now and not in this street.'

'Well, it's not all her fault! It takes two, in case you've forgotten, and there's nothing you can do about it, so try and be thankful. See how upset Jo is? You're cruel, that's what you are!'

'Why don't you mind your own business, Maddy? You're always poking your nose into what doesn't concern you.

And while we're at it, you'll have to look for somewhere else. We're cramped as it is, without the addition of a baby.'

'Oh no, no, Tom! There's no need for them to go!' Johanna protested, clinging to Maddy.

'Yes, there is. We've no room and we'll get no peace with her interfering, bold brass-necked article that she is!'

'We know when we've worn out our welcome. We'll look for somewhere else,' Maddy said icily, trying to keep her temper under control. She didn't want to upset Johanna even more. Foolishly, she had thought her brother had changed. Well, he obviously hadn't. His ambitions seemingly took precedence over everything else, his wife's feelings included.

'And now do you think a man could have a bit of peace to eat his meal in?' he asked scathingly. With a pat on Johanna's shoulder, Maddy steered her sister out of the room.

'Oh Maddy, what's wrong with him? Poor Johanna's so upset – and what about us?' Carmel said in a whisper when they had shut the bedroom door. Thank the Lord Mrs Doyle was still deeply asleep.

'All that's wrong with *him* is that he hasn't changed,' Maddy said shortly. 'He's still selfish, still hard-hearted, still wants to become something he's not and never will be.'

'Now we'll have to find somewhere else to live. Life is always changing and I hate it. I wish it was like it was in Ireland before Tom and Florence ruined everything.'

Maddy sighed. 'So do I, Carmel, but never mind. He's not going to get rid of us that quickly. Johanna will need help until the baby is born.'

'But he wants us to go soon.'

'Then he can just want, can't he? I'll keep saying I can't find anywhere. Now let's try and get some rest.'

Next morning, when they came into the living room, Thomas had already gone out to work. Johanna looked pale and worried. Maddy went and put her arms around her.

'Don't worry about us. We're not going to desert you. We've decided to stay. I don't care what *he* said, we're not leaving you to cope all alone with the housework, your Mam and your work.'

'Oh Maddy, I just don't know what came over him. I've never seen him like that before. I was so sure he would be happy, and now . . .'

'Oh, take no notice of him. He will be happy when the baby arrives. You wait and see. He *will*.' Her voice was full of a certainty she didn't feel.

Johanna wiped her eyes on her apron. 'I wanted him to be really, really happy.'

'He will be!' Even if I have to nail a smile to his face, Maddy added to herself.

When Thomas returned from work that evening his mood had softened a little. With Maddy and Carmel gone there would be more room, and if his mother-in-law were to conveniently die, the place wouldn't be too bad at all. If only he could find some way of earning more money without having to put in long hours and be out in all weathers. Working down on the docks, he'd heard men talking. Many of the ships were owned by shipping companies, but some were owned by as many as four or five people who all took a cut of the profits. If only he could get enough money together he could become part-owner of a ship and after that, well, the sky would be the limit. He would have the kind of life he'd always wanted. He could laugh now at his former pathetic ambition of becoming a Canal Agent in a backwater of a country decimated by starvation and disease.

'So, you're still here,' he remarked tersely on seeing his sisters.

'We are so. It will take time to find somewhere where we can live decently and that we can afford,' Maddy replied just as tersely.

'Tom, sit at the table, your meal is ready,' Johanna instructed quietly.

He was glad she seemed to have reverted to her old self. Pliable and respectful. It did no harm at all to put a wife in her place now and then.

The meal was eaten in a strained silence, and after Maddy and Carmel had helped to clear and wash the dishes, they both went into the bedroom. The old lady was dozing; she went to bed for a nap mid-afternoon.

'Well, he didn't rant and rave so I suppose we must be thankful for small mercies,' Maddy said.

'What will we do? It's so hot in here again.'

'I suppose we could go out for a walk or maybe just sit on the step. We'd not get any cooler, though.'

'I don't think I've got the energy to walk anywhere so it will have to be the doorstep. I wonder if Johanna would teach me how to sew, then maybe I could get home work and not have to go to a dirty factory filling sugar sacks every day. The place is alive with rats and mice.' Carmel shuddered.

'Isn't everywhere alive with them, and it's a job, after all. Ah, I'll give you it's not a nice place to work, but it pays our wages,' Maddy said more kindly as they went down the stairs to join the women on the steps.

'Isn't it good news about Tom and Johanna?' Mo Mannion said, tucking her long skirt around her legs to make room for them.

Maddy was surprised. 'News travels fast.'

'There's nothin' much goes on 'ere that we don't know about, is there, Flossie?'

'Not with the walls like paper. When 'er next door ter me 'as a row with 'im, yer might as well be in the same room. An' iffen I was, I'd be on 'er side. 'E's nothin' but a bloody drunken sod, an' 'er with five kids ter feed. It's no wonder they never 'ave no boots. You tell Johanna from me, ter stop at one or two otherwise she'll never 'ave no money an' she'll be wore out.'

'I know 'e's yer brother,' Flossie said gruffly, 'but Tom Kiernan's a cold fish. Never speaks to yer unless 'e 'as to. No offence, Maddy.'

'None taken, Mrs McBride. He is a cold fish. I suppose you know he's told Carmel and me that we've got to find somewhere else to live because he says they'll be crowded and that I interfere,' she added as an afterthought.

'*Crowded*?' Flossie McBride jeered. 'There's only five of yer in two rooms. He doesn't know what bloody crowded is. Where will yer go, like?'

'Nowhere. Jo needs help and she won't get any from him. I'll just keep putting it off. I'm not afraid of him, even if Johanna is.'

'She's a nice, quiet girl. A credit to 'er Mam an' Da, God rest him. It was 'er Mam who got 'er a place in Brown's work rooms. She says ter me, before she went funny in the head like, "Maureen" – she always gave me me full title – "she'll have a trade in her fingertips, so she'll never go 'ungry".'

'When did Mrs Doyle go funny in the head?' Maddy asked. Nothing like this had been mentioned; she just assumed that the old lady was a victim of a life of drudgery.

'About a year ago. She was fine. Yer could 'ave a great laugh with 'er, then she 'ad a fall and banged 'er 'ead an' from that she got worser and worser. She's not that old either, Maddy. She's only forty-eight.'

Maddy was incredulous. 'Forty-eight! I thought she was at least seventy.'

'There's not many round 'ere who live ter be sixty, never mind seventy. Bloody wore out with all the kids an' no money an' drunken fellers. When yer do go, Maddy, make sure it's ter somewhere better than this dump.'

'I'll bear that in mind and try to save a bit although we turn up most of our wages for our keep.'

'She'll miss yer birrof money.'

'I know, that's another reason why I'm staying.'

Mo leaned towards her. 'Isn't it about time yer both started lookin' fer 'usbands? Your Carmel shouldn't 'ave much trouble. She's gorra face like a picture of Our Lady.'

'Well, I wouldn't go that far. I don't think our priest Father Molloy would be very pleased if he heard that, but I know what you mean. There's only one lad she'll ever love, so she says, and she can't have him,' Maddy whispered.

'She's young, she'll forget, an' iffen she were to come out of that 'ouse more, the fellers would be round 'er like bees round a honey-pot. Not that I've ever tasted honey and not likely to either, iffen yer know what I mean.'

'I know. I keep urging her.'

'Then urge 'arder, girl.'

'I think I'll have to,' Maddy replied, wondering for a moment if she would ever meet someone herself.

Chapter Twelve

One morning at the end of September, Maddy was awoken by the sound of weeping. She sat up in bed, rubbing the sleep from her eyes, and found Johanna in their room, kneeling beside her mother's bed, sobbing into the quilt.

'What's wrong?' Maddy asked, swinging her legs over the side of the bed. The movement woke Carmel.

Johanna couldn't speak. Maddy knelt beside her and took her into her arms. The baby was due in four weeks and she shouldn't be upset.

'What is it?' she asked again but her sister-in-law still couldn't reply. 'Carmel, will you go and get Tom,' Maddy requested.

Carmel was properly awake now and her eyes were wide with fear. 'Is she . . .? Has she . . .?'

'Go and get Tom!' Maddy interrupted.

Tom was still half asleep and none too pleased at being dragged from his bed by an almost hysterical Carmel.

'Just what the hell is going on?' he demanded irritably, then followed his sister into the second bedroom.

Tom bent over his mother-in-law and tried to find a pulse. There was none. She was dead and all he could feel was relief.

'She's gone,' he said gruffly, 'but at least she died peacefully. She must have passed away in her sleep. Why were you in here, Johanna? Did you hear something?'

Johanna raised her head from Maddy's shoulder. 'I woke up and I knew, I just *knew* something was wrong.'

Maddy drew her to her feet. 'Tom's right. Your Mam went peacefully and that's something to be thankful for. We all knew she wasn't going to get any better.'

Johanna took a deep, shuddering breath. She was more in control of herself now. 'I'll go for the priest,' she said. 'Mammy must have the Last Sacrament even though she's gone.'

'I'll do that on my way to work,' Tom offered.

'Thanks, love, it's just the shock. I'll be fine in a few minutes. There's things to organise.' Johanna was making a real effort.

'I'll help you,' said Maddy. 'Carmel, you'd better get ready for work and you too, Tom. Go on, I'll see to things. There's no use us all staying and losing a day's pay.'

The mundane chores of getting washed and dressed and cooking breakfast seemed to calm her sister-in-law, Maddy thought with relief. Poor Johanna had nothing to reproach herself with. She'd done everything she could for her mother.

When Tom and Carmel had gone and the dishes had been

washed and the beds made, Maddy made a fresh pot of tea; they both needed it.

'Who does the laying out?'

'Mrs O'Keefe from round the corner in Hurst Street.'

'I'll go and get her, then I'll go and see Father Molloy. It's awful to be asking at a time like this, but do you have money put by or are you in a burial club?'

'A burial club. Everyone is.'

Maddy nodded. She'd have to go and see whoever it was who held the money. 'Don't worry, the Mammy will have a decent funeral. I'll make sure of it.'

Johanna wiped her eyes again. 'Maddy, you're so good, so considerate.'

'I am not. Isn't it just the way anyone in the family would act? I'll finish my tea and then I'll be off. You take care that you rest. All this isn't good for you.'

Although pale, Johanna seemed relieved.

Maddy seemed to have run around all morning.

'Ah, God love poor Johanna. She were devoted to 'er Mam,' Mo Mannion said with regret.

'She's nothing to be guilty about at all,' Maddy replied.

'Then you'll be wantin' the few bob from the burial club. I'll take yer round ter Vi Harding ter collect it.'

'Thanks. I have to go to the Parish House now and see Father Molloy.'

'An' yer'll 'ave ter go an' speak to Maggie O'Keefe – or do yer want me ter go, luv?'

'I'll go, but thank you. Do any of you have white sheets or candlesticks?'

'No one 'as sheets or candlesticks round 'ere, but ask Father Molloy. He always lends them out.'

'When will they bring her to the church for the Removal?'

'What Removal? I never 'eard of anythin' like that.'

'The friends and neighbours come to see the dead person, to pay their respects, and then the dead person,' she couldn't bring herself to say 'corpse', 'is removed to the church and stays there all night, and then there's the funeral and burial next day.'

'We don't do nothin' like that 'ere, luv. We come an' pay our respects like, ter the 'ouse, an' then it's straight off ter the church.'

'Things are different in England.'

'Will yer be 'avin' a wake, like?'

'I don't know. That depends on Tom – and knowing him, he won't be after providing much.'

'We don't expect much round 'ere. No one's got the money fer it. I don't know from day ter day what my feller will bring 'ome, and Mary Kennedy from the corner 'ouse meets her feller ter make sure she gets a few pennies before he drinks the bloody lot.'

'Well, I'll be off. Thank you so much, for everything.'

'Isn't that what neighbours are for, girl? Keep your eye on Johanna – this could start 'er off. Go on, geroff with yer now, Maddy.'

Everything was arranged and Maddy soon learned that she had been right in her prediction that Tom would spend as little on the funeral as he could.

'Is there to be a wake?' she asked when he returned home.

'And where would I get the money for that?'

'It's customary.'

'Not over here it's not. We're not back in the Old Country, remember. I've been speaking to some other carters and there's no such thing as a Removal even.'

'I know.'

'So there'll be no wake – and apart from that, I'm not breaking my back to provide food and drink for half the street. They'll have to make do with a cup of tea and be thankful for it.'

Maddy had glanced at her sister-in-law to judge her reaction to his words, but Johanna shook her head so Maddy didn't press the point.

Tom wasn't very happy about the neighbours who came to call and pay their respects. He was tired, and the last thing he wanted was a houseful of people, even though they did speak deferentially and quietly. He just wished they would all clear off so he could get some sleep. The sleeping arrangements didn't please him either but he was resigned to the fact that his deceased mother-in-law's body had to lie in the single bed in a room on its own. It would only be for one night.

Now Mrs Doyle had gone, he'd concentrate on saving for his 'ship money' as he thought of it. Johanna was a good manager. She didn't waste money; she worked hard too and passed over her wages to him without a word of complaint. She'd even be able to go on working after the baby was born

– and that was something most of the women they lived amongst couldn't do. Apart from taking in washing, for which they broke their backs for a pittance, they had to go outside the home, and with small children that was impossible. Oh, he'd chosen a wife very well indeed. He just had to get rid of his sisters, despite what they contributed to the housekeeping. He'd weighed that matter up carefully. He was certain Johanna could keep the same amount of food on the table and he could save a few shillings extra. Maddy irritated him so much that he found he was constantly having to keep a rein on his temper, and by his reckoning a man shouldn't have to do that in his own home. She was a thorn in his side and always had been; she had far too much to say on things that didn't concern her. No, the pair of them were more trouble than they were worth.

Maddy felt sorry for Johanna even though she was bearing up under the strain. She got little comfort from Tom who seemed almost glad the old lady had died. Well, she'd take care of Johanna and the baby too.

A bare week after the funeral, Tom began to refer to their moving out.

'Have you started looking for somewhere?' he asked one morning.

'Isn't that a nice way of going on and the Mammy hardly cold.'

'We've got more room now, Tom,' Johanna said haltingly.

'And where will the baby sleep?'

'With us.'

'But not for ever. He should have his own room.'

'He? And I've never heard of a baby having its own room.'

'Well, you have now and there may well be others in the future.'

'But Tom, that's a long time away.'

'Johanna, I've told you what I want,' he stated curtly.

'All right, we'll start looking. There's no need to take it out on her,' Maddy said acidly.

With the nights drawing in and the weather getting colder, Maddy realised that Johanna would need her help and the money both she and Carmel contributed, and she had no wish to come home from work to some freezing cold, barely furnished room or cellar. She and Carmel had moved out of the one bedroom, so that Tom and Johanna could have it, and they now slept in the bed in the corner of the living room.

In early October, Maddy and Carmel had come in from work and had barely taken off their shawls when Johanna clutched the back of a chair and cried out in pain.

'Oh Maddy, I think I've started,' she gasped when the pain had subsided. 'I haven't felt well all day. The baby's not really due for another month, but maybe I got the dates wrong.'

'Will I go for Mrs O'Keefe?' Carmel asked, feeling little flutters of apprehension in her stomach. Maggie O'Keefe was also the local midwife.

'Yes, go on, I'll start boiling some water.'

'Maddy, there are a pile of old newspapers and clean bits of cloth in the chest by the bed. Mrs Mannion said I'd be wise to keep them clean and handy. I don't know what they're for.'

'Neither do I, but I think we're going to find out soon.' She gently led the girl into the marital bedroom and helped her up on to the bed.

'Will you give Tom his tea?' Johanna asked tearfully.

'Don't be worrying about him. I'll see to him and there'll be none of this wetting the baby's head in the pub with the men in the street, although I don't think he'd part with the money.'

Maddy was secretly apprehensive. She didn't remember Carmel being born and had no idea what the boiling water and other things were for.

Johanna's screams of pain brought both Mo Mannion and Flossie McBride down.

' 'Ave yer sent fer Maggie O'Keefe, Maddy?'

'Carmel went about ten minutes ago.'

' 'Ave yer gorreverythin' ready like I told yer, Johanna?'

The young woman nodded. 'Tom will be in soon wanting his tea,' she said again, fretting.

'Tea? He can go an' whistle fer 'is bloody tea!'

'I'll see to him, Johanna, I've already told you that,' Maddy's voice was soothing.

Johanna turned fearful eyes on her neighbours. 'How long will it take?'

'Hard ter tell, girl. Could be an hour, could be ten.'

'Fer God's sake, Flossie, don't be tellin' the girl that! Put the fear of God in 'er, that would. You take no notice, pet. Try an' rest between the pains.'

Johanna screamed again and the two older women exchanged glances. There'd be no ten hours here.

'Come on, luv, gerrinto bed. Maddy, bring them things an' let's 'ope Carmel doesn't dally along ter Mrs O'Keefe.'

Before they could help Johanna, Carmel almost fell in through the door.

'Where's the midwife then?' Flossie demanded.

'She's on her way. I ran back to tell you.'

At the sight of her sister-in-law's contorted features, Carmel went pale.

'Go and set the table. We'll have Tom in on top of us soon,' Maddy instructed.

'The pair of you stay in there,' Mo Mannion ordered. 'This is no place fer young unwed girls,' she added to Flossie in a mutter.

Maddy was glad. She went into the kitchen, where she began to peel some potatoes.

'Oh Maddy, it must hurt terribly!' Carmel whispered as Johanna's howls of agony continued.

'I think you're right, and I think it is messy too.'

Johanna's cries made Tom hasten up the steps.

'What's going on? Has it started?' he asked as soon as took in what was going on.

'Yes. The midwife and Mrs Mannion and Mrs McBride are in with her. You stay put and eat your meal, when it's ready.'

'That'll be hours I'm thinking,' he said sulkily, 'with the potatoes not even cooked.'

'You're lucky we're here to cook them at all! You'd go

173

hungry to bed for she's in no fit state to be preparing meals!'
Maddy snapped. Even now he was thinking only of himself.

They were all silent, tense and uneasy until at last, a
couple of hours later, they heard the wail of a new baby.

Flossie opened the door, a smile all over her face.

'There yer are, all over an' yer've gorra fine, healthy
son.'

Tom stood up and Maddy and Carmel hugged each other.

'We're aunties now! Oh, I'm dying to see him!' Maddy
exclaimed.

'Give us a few minutes ter clean the place up a bit and
give 'im a wash, then yer can come in.'

'Is she all right?' Tom asked.

'Fine. Worn out, but yer always are. 'Ave yer decided on
a name fer 'im?'

'Yes. Ronan Michael.'

'Ronan Michael Kiernan,' Maddy repeated. It had a nice
ring to it, she thought.

Johanna was still confined to bed so Maddy and Carmel
and the neighbours took charge of the running of the
household. Little Ronan thrived but Tom soon began to
mention that the child needed his own room, which everyone
thought ridiculous. It led to rows which Carmel hated.

She didn't want to move from the comparative security
of her brother's home to a cellar like the one in Gillings
Entry. She missed John terribly. Oh, she knew that her sister,
brother and sister-in-law thought she'd get over him, but she
wouldn't, ever; nor could she forgive herself for bringing ill

fortune on his family and ruining his life completely.

Now that her injuries had healed and her hair was growing again, Carmel was aware of the admiring looks cast in her direction by many of the lads who lived in the surrounding streets as she walked home from work. Sometimes she just ducked her head and kept her eyes on the pavement. At others she smiled shyly back. The whistles and cat-calls she ignored totally.

Over the last few weeks she'd noticed that two lads followed her, whether she was with Maddy or not. She knew both of them slightly. Johnnie Fearon lived in their street and David Evans just around the corner.

It was a dry, mild evening in mid-October when David Evans appeared beside her and asked could he walk her home. Maddy smiled when she realised what was happening and walked quickly ahead. Maybe now Carmel would be finally over John Shannahan enough to go out with another lad, and Davie wasn't too bad. She was glad it was him and not Johnnie Fearon, who was far too bold in her reckoning.

'Do you ever go out, Carmel?' Davie asked.

'Sometimes, not often.'

'Do you go with your sister?'

'Most of the time.'

'There's no other lad then?'

'No. No, there isn't.' Not now, she said sadly to herself.

'Where do you like going when you do go out?'

'Just for walks. Down to the riverside or occasionally to a park. I like going to the parks best. You see, we lived in the country in Ireland.'

'And the parks remind you of that?'

She nodded. 'But there are some memories of home I'd sooner forget.'

'The famine?'

'Yes. It was terrible, terrible!'

'Would you like to go to the park on Sunday, with me?'

She looked up at him. He was quite a handsome lad although he was in his rough working clothes.

'Well, I . . .'

'Will I call for you, say at two o'clock?'

She nodded again. 'What if it's raining?'

'We'll just think of somewhere else to go. I know, we'll go to Sefton Park. That's got a Palm House – we wouldn't get wet there.'

'I've never seen a Palm House.'

'It's a sort of a house made of panes of glass and it's very warm so there's all kinds of tropical plants and things. We'll go there anyway.'

She smiled up at him as they parted company at the house he lived in and she hurried on to catch up with Maddy.

'Well?' her sister questioned with an amused look on her face.

'Well what?'

'Did he ask you out?'

'He did so and I said I'd go with him to see the Palm House in Sefton Park on Sunday afternoon.'

Maddy's smile became wider. Thank God for small mercies, she thought. 'What will you do if Johnnie asks you out too? He seems pretty keen.'

'I don't know. I'll wait and see. He might not ask me.'

'I think he will, especially as you've said yes to Davie. Flossie says you'll have the lads flocking round you like bees around a honey-pot.'

'Oh, she's desperate sometimes, she really is. I'm not like that.'

'I hope not, but you're going to have to learn how to cope with them. You are a real beauty, Carmel. I know I shouldn't say that kind of thing, I don't want you getting ideas, but it's true.'

'Oh Maddy, stop it!' Carmel had gone pink. 'You say some desperate things yourself.'

'I'm just speaking the truth. Home at last,' she remarked as they reached the open front door.

The following evening, Johnnie Fearon was waiting for Carmel at the factory gates. He was leaning on the wall and trying to look nonchalant.

'Right, you can deal with this one yourself,' Maddy said as she spotted him.

'No, stay with me, please?'

'No! I told you yesterday you'll have to learn how to deal with it yourself, but I don't agree with two-timing. Choose one or the other.'

'How will I know which one I like best if I don't go out with Johnnie too?'

Maddy was exasperated. 'Oh, Carmel Kiernan, make up your own mind!'

'Where's Davie tonight?' the lad asked, falling into step beside her.

'I don't know. Perhaps he's not finished his work yet. Aren't you finished early?'

'I *had* finished my work,' he said emphatically. He'd managed to slip out of the gate ten minutes before the whistle sounded. 'I'll walk home with you if you like,' he offered.

'You only live around the corner, so it's not really walking me home,' Carmel pointed out.

'Well, will you walk out with me on Sunday?'

She didn't reply. She was thinking about Maddy's words about two-timing and her reply to them. She liked them both equally. She could never love them though.

'Not this Sunday, but the next one.'

'Oh, I see. You're going out with Davie this Sunday?'

She didn't know what to say and became flustered and flushed. 'I'm not going anywhere on Sunday, except for Mass. I have to help Johanna.' The lie had popped out before she had realised it. Now what was she going to do?

'Are you really going to help her?'

'I am so!'

He looked at her quizzically, trying to decide if she was telling him the truth or just stringing him along. 'All right, a week on Sunday. I'll call at half past two. I'll see you before then though.'

'When?'

'Walking home. You said it yourself – I only live around the corner.'

Back at home, Maddy approached her. 'Well, did you decide?' she asked.

'I did,' she replied, her heart dropping like a stone. What

kind of a mess had she got herself into now? Maddy would be no help, nor would Johanna, but only because she had her hands full with the baby and Tom. Oh Lord, what would Tom say? Well, she'd made her bed, now she must lie on it.

When Sunday came, Carmel kept her good clothes on after Mass. Normally her one good blouse and skirt were taken off and hung up when she got home.

'What's she still dressed up for?' Tom asked.

'She's going out this afternoon,' Maddy answered.

'Who with and where to?' he demanded.

'Sefton Park with Davie Evans.'

'Just see that you're home before it's dark – and behave yourself,' Tom said in his bullying way.

'I will, Tom, I promise.'

'I'll get the meal ready, not that it's much. Johanna, you rest,' Maddy instructed. They always managed to have meat on Sundays and Johanna made it last until Tuesday. There was scouse on Mondays as it was wash day, and cold cuts with potatoes on Tuesdays. The rest of the week they had herrings or eggs. On Saturday night they had spare ribs, or pigs' trotters and cabbage.

Maddy insisted that she wash up.

'At least I can dry the dishes,' Johanna said.

'Carmel can do them. She won't get messed up – you sit there.'

Tom gave her a malevolent look and Maddy sighed. He was going to start on them moving out again and she was running out of excuses and time.

They were all startled when there was a loud knock on the door at a quarter to two.

'Can a man get no peace on his one day off!' Tom said irritably.

'Davie's not due yet,' Carmel said, her gaze going to her sister's face.

'He might be early. Go and open it.'

Carmel gave a startled cry as she opened the door and found Johnnie Fearon standing there.

'You weren't supposed to call this week.'

'I know, but I thought, on the off-chance, like.'

She didn't know what to do. If she had been wearing her old clothes she could have sent him away, telling him she was too busy, but he could see she wasn't.

Should she invite him in? Should she go out with him now before Davie arrived? Carmel looked around at the faces of her family.

Johanna looked mildly concerned, Tom was scowling and Maddy wasn't going to be any help. Oh God, why had she ever agreed to see him?

'Perhaps . . . perhaps you should come in for a minute while I get my things.'

He stepped into the room and into the gaze of its occupants, and as Carmel began to get her shawl there was another knock on the door. She froze. Davie was early. Oh God above, what was she to do now?

Maddy looked perturbed. Trust Carmel to get herself into a mess like this. She went to open the door as Tom got to his feet.

'Davie, hello. Look, I'm afraid Carmel's not well, she can't go out,' Maddy lied, but it was too late; Davie had caught sight of his rival as Tom opened the door wider.

'Then what's *he* doing here?' the young man demanded, pointing to Johnnie.

'You told me you weren't going out. You're a little liar, Carmel Kiernan!' Johnnie shouted.

'Don't you call her a liar! You forced yourself on her. I asked her first,' Davie shouted back.

'Oh, please, please stop,' Carmel begged of the two lads who were glowering at each other.

Tom leapt up from his chair. 'That's it! Out, the pair of you! Clear the hell out of my home, disturbing my peace and quiet! Go on, the two of you! If you want to half kill each other over her then do it in the bloody street,' Tom roared.

The silence that descended after his last words held everyone in its grip until Tom caught Davie and Johnnie by the shoulder and pushed them out, slamming the door on both lads.

'This is the last straw, Maddy,' he told her viciously. 'I've had enough of the pair of you! I told you she was trouble and she always will be, and I'm not having her carrying on like this under my roof. The pair of you have five days to find a place of your own. I want you out by Friday or I'll personally throw you out, bag and baggage! As for you, you bold article, get those clothes off and change. You're going nowhere today!'

Carmel began to whimper and it angered Maddy. 'For heaven's sake, stop that noise! We'll go, Tom. We'll be gone by next weekend. We won't stay where we're not wanted.'

'Good. Now at least can I get a bit of bloody peace?'

Chapter Thirteen

'Oh Maddy, what will we do?' Carmel asked tearfully as they went out for a short walk, there being nowhere private in their brother's home.

'Isn't this a nice mess. I told you, no two-timing! It was just the excuse Tom was looking for, and will you stop saying, "Oh Maddy, what will we do?" You said it when we left Ireland and when we left Gillings Entry. Things will work out – they always have done before. The only thing that upsets me is that now Johanna will be on her own with the baby, and don't start crying, Carmel, it's more than I could stand.'

Carmel sniffed. It *was* her fault. It had been her fault too, having to leave Gillings Entry and John. The thought of him brought back the tears.

'Are we just going for a walk or . . .?' she ventured.

'We're going to see Father Molloy. He helped us last time. Let's hope he can help us now.'

When they arrived, the priest had just finished his meagre lunch and was debating whether he should go visiting the poor of his parish before or after Benediction.

'Didn't I just see the two of you a few hours ago at Mass? Come on in. I was going to call round tonight, about Ronan's baptism.'

'We're in trouble – again, Father.'

His brow furrowed and the smile left his eyes.

'And what kind of trouble is it now, child?'

'Tom has thrown us out. At least, he's given us until Friday to find somewhere else to live.'

'Why so? What happened?'

'He wants to get rid of us, Father,' Maddy explained. 'He says I interfere too much. We never really got on well, although I tried – he is my brother, after all is said and done. Now he wants more room for Ronan.'

Carmel felt she needed to confess her part in it all. 'Father, it wasn't just that. I had agreed to go for an outing with Davie Evans, and then,' her voice faltered, 'with Johnnie Fearon too.'

'The both of them?'

She nodded.

'Ah, the impetuousness of youth,' Father Molloy said gently, hiding a smile. 'I gather your brother objected, though they're not half bad for around here anyway.'

'He did so, Father. You see, they both turned up at the same time. There was a row and Tom threw both of them out,' she finished apologetically.

'We have jobs, but no savings. We paid for our keep – Tom didn't have to put a hand in his pocket,' Maddy said.

The priest shook his head thoughtfully. 'Would you like me to have a word with your brother?'

'Father, we couldn't stay there now. He really means it.'

'Perhaps he would agree to extend your departure date, then?'

'He might do that,' Maggie sighed. 'It's going to be very hard on poor Johanna. She has to side with Tom.'

'Indeed she must. Right or wrong he's her husband. But will you let me try?'

Maddy nodded gratefully.

'Why don't the two of you stay here while I go and see him.'

'We didn't expect you to go right away, Father. You must have so little time to yourself.'

'And what would I need time to myself for? The souls and bodies of my flock need my time far more than I do.'

'We're very grateful,' Maddy said.

'I'll ask herself to give you a cup of tea.'

'He's so kind,' Carmel said when he'd gone. 'Do you really think he can talk to Tom?'

'He can talk – whether it will do any good is another matter,' Maddy said tersely.

Father Molloy returned in a quarter of an hour and the girls looked at him questioningly.

'He has some fierce notions – notions of pride,' the old priest said thoughtfully, 'but sure doesn't every father want the very best for his son. He's agreed to let you stay until the end of the month. 'Tis the best I could do. He wouldn't move on that. Thomas Kiernan is a fierce stubborn man.'

'Oh, he's that all right,' Maddy said. 'But thank you so much. Where we would be without you I don't know.'

'Ah, 'tis little enough, child. Go home and see if you can at least be reconciled.'

But Maddy knew there would be no reconciliation, and as she'd told her sister earlier, the thing she regretted most was leaving Johanna and the baby.

'Don't think you've won, Maddy,' Tom greeted them when they arrived back. Johanna bit her lip. She was very fond of her sisters-in-law but she was also a dutiful wife and mother.

'We didn't ask Father Molloy to come here to fight our battles. He offered to and we accepted the chance of more time, that's all. Don't worry, we'll be out every night from now on, looking for somewhere else,' Maddy snapped and the subject was dropped. The atmosphere would be terrible for the next few weeks and Carmel would hate it but there was nothing she could do. If it hadn't been for her indecision they wouldn't be in this situation.

The sisters went out after their meal every night, hunting for accommodation but decent housing was very scarce, especially as they couldn't afford much.

'Oh, it's hopeless, Maddy!' Carmel said, close to despair as they'd turned down the offer of sharing a room in a filthy old house with three other women.

'Let's go down to the waterfront to get away from the stink of these houses,' Maddy suggested tiredly.

Although the docks and the river were always crowded, the air smelled strongly of the sea, with the promise of cleaner, fresher air just beyond Formby Point.

'Follow me,' Maddy instructed her sister as she made her way towards the dockside. A group of ragged urchins seemed to be blocking the way and at their centre was an elderly man, dressed in dark and rather formal clothes. He was looking about him in a bewildered fashion.

'Just what are those little hooligans up to?' Maddy said impatiently.

Suddenly, as if at a given signal, they all ran off, in different directions, leaving the old man alone.

'Are you all right, sir?' Maddy asked him.

He was patting his pockets and looking very troubled.

'Is anything the matter?' Maddy persisted.

'My wallet has gone! They've robbed me!'

'I thought they were up to no good, the shower of little villains. Can we help? Where do you live?'

He seemed to be lost in a world of his own. 'I have to get the police. I must go to the police.' He was still patting his pockets.

'It won't do any good, sir, they'll never catch them. They all ran off in different directions and sure, don't they all look the same?' She tugged at his sleeve and he peered at her.

'Who are you, miss? Do you live here? Do you know them?'

'I'm Maddy Kiernan and this is my sister Carmel. We do live nearby but no, we don't know them. Can we see you home?'

He looked a little confused. 'Home. Home,' he repeated.

'Yes. Tell us where you live and we'll help you there.'

'In Faulkner Square. My name is Benjamin Frazer.'

'We'd better get a horse tram, then. That's too far for you to walk. You've had a nasty shock. Why were you down here at all?'

He seemed more at ease now. 'I came on an errand for the mistress. She told me not to but I came just the same. She doesn't always know what's best, you see. I couldn't send someone else to see Captain Sparling with an important message like that.'

'Were you going to one of the ships?'

'Yes. I gave the letter to Captain Sparling and then, as I was walking back, those boys appeared from no-where.'

'They're hooligans but they steal because they're half starved and have probably been abandoned by their parents, so they have to learn to live on the streets.'

'Oh well, that puts it into perspective. Thank you, Miss Kiernan, I am much obliged to you. Now, have you the money for a Hackney cab? I'll repay you. I feel too shaken up for the tram.' He ran his fingers through his thick white hair which made it stand up in spikes.

Maddy did have just enough money, but it was supposed to last all the week. 'We'll take a cab, sir,' she nodded.

Carmel had said nothing but she felt sorry for the old

man. He was well-spoken and well-bred, and he should never have come down here alone.

When they arrived at the address the old man gave both girls were astounded by the size of the house. They had never known that there were such elegant little squares with their own private parks in the centre, confined and protected with iron railings. All the houses were the same – three storeys high, with long sash windows and a glass fanlight over the imposing front door that was reached by a short flight of steps. They also had iron railings.

'This house is like a mansion,' Carmel marvelled as she helped the old man down and Maddy paid the cab driver.

'Come inside, young ladies, while I get the money to repay you.'

They followed Benjamin Frazer in and stood in the hallway. The sheer size of the place and its furnishings stunned the sisters into silence.

'Oh Maddy, isn't it *huge*!'

'It is so.' Maddy was looking around. The floor was of black and white chequered tiles. All the wide doors were of highly polished wood. The pictures on the walls showed a selection of dour-looking men and women, some in very old-fashioned clothes. There was a huge hallstand with a brass tub for umbrellas, a large plant in a decorative jardinière and on the half-moon table stood a marble bust of a very handsome young man.

Mr Frazer appeared and handed over the money.

'Thank you, sir,' Maddy said politely.

'Frazer, where have you been?' A loud, imperious, feminine voice came down to them over the banisters.

They all looked up but Maddy and Carmel could see no one.

'I've been robbed!' Frazer shouted back.

The girls were taken aback. They'd had no idea he could speak so loudly or clearly.

'I told you to send the damned thing with the kitchen boy! I told you! I don't know when I've ever been so vexed! You're a fool, Frazer,' shouted the voice from above.

'I'm no worse a fool than you, sending down notes to sea captains instead of summoning them up here. You wouldn't have done it in the master's time!'

'To hell with the master! Who have you there with you?'

'The two young girls who have looked after me. They need the money they spent on getting me home.'

'Well, don't leave them standing there. Send them up to me!'

During this rapid exchange, that had been conducted in voices that would have raised the dead, both Maddy and Carmel had been amazed and amused. But now, at the prospect of meeting the owner of the voice, they felt very apprehensive.

'Go on up to her or I'll get no peace.' Benjamin gave them a little shove in the direction of the stairs and Maddy and Carmel made their way up them slowly. They'd never been in a house that had carpet on the stairs; not even Eliza Mitchell had been that well off.

To their surprise a very small, wizened old lady was waiting for them. She looked like a walking rag bag, Maddy thought. She wore a bonnet like the Queen's and her fingers were adorned with diamond rings.

'Come in. I'm much too old to be standing here shouting at daft old fools who will never do as they're told. I'm always fighting with the staff here. They give me no peace.'

Maddy wondered how many servants there were.

The room they were led into was huge and lit by scores of candles. The Persian rugs that covered the floor were faded and a little threadbare, Maddy noted. The brocade furniture was also faded, the once bright colours diminished. She saw too that the gilding on chairs and tables was dulled with dust and age. A big fire burned in the huge marble fireplace; on the mantlepiece above were displayed a large, intricately decorated clock and two matching figurines. The walls were covered with pictures.

'Sit down,' the little woman said imperiously. 'Will you have some tea?'

Maddy was taken aback but surely it would be very bad manners to refuse. 'Thank you, ma'am. Will I ring?' She looked pointedly at a well-used tapestry bell-pull.

'You can, but it won't do any good. It's been broken these last two years. Wait now.'

She shuffled back out of the room and then leaned over the banisters.

'Frazer, will you kindly bring up some tea!' she shouted.

Maddy was fascinated by this odd behaviour.

191

'Where was the old fool when you found him?' their hostess puffed, sitting down again.

'Just standing by the dock wall surrounded by a crowd of street urchins. He was rather upset and seemed not to know where he was.'

'That doesn't surprise me. He often doesn't know where he is!' came the terse reply. 'What are your names?'

'I'm Maddy – er, Magdalene – Kiernan and this is my sister, Carmel.'

'I'm Mrs Buckley.' They were both scrutinised by small, dark, beady eyes and Maddy wondered just how old this seemingly indomitable little person was.

'Where do you live? Now, I mean. You're Irish, I can tell. My late husband was Irish – a great gambler. He'd bet on two cockroaches walking across the floor. That way, he went through a small fortune. He drank, rode, shot and was by far the best man I ever knew!'

'Is he dead long, ma'am?'

'These eighteen years. Fell off a horse and like a fool broke his neck.'

Carmel tried to hide a smile.

'Have you any children?' Maddy felt relaxed enough now to ask this question.

'None. The Lord in His wisdom saw fit not to bless us with children. Where did you say you lived?'

'In Grayson Street, near the Wapping Dock. Well, we do until the end of the month.'

'And what is happening at the end of the month?'

'My brother is throwing us out.'

The old lady cackled. 'Ah, brothers! Brothers! I have three left and I fight with them all the time, *and* their wives. Impudent, under-bred creatures the lot of them. So, where will you go?'

'I don't know, ma'am, and that's the truth. That's why we were out tonight, looking.'

'Did you see anything?'

'Nothing that's decent and that we can afford.'

The old lady peered at Carmel. 'She's a real beauty, but can't she speak?'

'Oh, I can indeed, ma'am,' Carmel replied.

To their amusement their hostess again got to her feet, went to the banister rail and roared over it, demanding to know how long it took to make a cup of tea. Shortly after this, an elderly woman wearing a black dress, white apron and cap appeared carrying a tray of china cups along with a silver teapot, sugar basin and milk jug.

'I can't get up the stairs as quickly as I used to, ma'am. You should know that. Hasn't Frazer told you often enough,' the newcomer said querulously.

The tray was set on a low table and Mrs Buckley indicated with a scrawny bejewelled hand that the tea was to be poured.

Both girls were handed china cups and saucers which they were terrified of dropping.

'Do you both work?' Mrs Buckley asked.

'Yes. We work at Cupples, a sugar factory.'

'And is it interesting, working there, or is it extremely boring?'

'It is so, ma'am, boring I mean, and it's dirty work too, filling sugar sacks.'

'And how much do they pay you for this dirty, boring job?'

'Four and sixpence a week.'

Their hostess raised her eyebrows. 'They expect you to live on that?'

Maddy nodded, holding the cup gingerly. The old lady noticed her wariness.

'China is remarkably strong,' she trumpeted. 'It doesn't break as easily as one would think, although those fools downstairs contrive all the time to wreak havoc with my Crown Derby!'

Again they were scrutinised very closely and both dropped their eyes. Mrs Buckley was the most peculiar person they'd ever met. Here they were, drinking tea from expensive china cups and being treated as if they were the gentry, when all the time, they were strangers off the street!

'It's about time I pensioned them all off,' the old lady concluded. 'A fearful crowd of incapables, fearful. Why is your brother throwing you out?'

'He wants more space now that they have a baby. He thinks little Ronan should have his own room. They have two rooms, you see. A living room, where we sleep, and one bedroom, which they have.'

'Two rooms! You all live in two rooms? Upon my word that must be inconvenient.'

'He also says I interfere but I try not to. We really didn't get on very well after our parents died of the fever five years ago.'

'I don't get on with my brothers, either – I've told you that, and I *always* interfere when I can. Seeing that I have more money than any of them, despite the late Mr Buckley's gambling, they're obliged to put up with it.' She laughed drily. 'Do you get along with your sister-in-law?'

'Oh, yes. She's a lovely person. She keeps everywhere so clean and she's a seamstress by profession.'

'Indeed. Quite a paragon.'

They had never heard the word before but took it to be a compliment.

Mrs Buckley leaned back in her chair. 'I've come to a decision. I like you, Maddy Kiernan; you have spirit even if others don't.' Her gaze settled briefly on Carmel. 'So, you will come and live here with me and those incompetents downstairs. There is more than enough work here for another pair of hands. She can come too, although I'm not prepared to pay her anything. If she can't speak up for herself then she doesn't need money. You look after her and she should be grateful.' Mrs Buckley turned to Carmel. 'You can't go through life being a shy retiring violet, girl. The world doesn't owe you a living. Very well. I'll expect you both here on Friday evening. Tell Frazer before you leave.'

Maddy was astounded and Carmel didn't know whether to laugh or cry.

'You mean you'll give us a home with you, and let us work here? But we're complete strangers, ma'am. We could murder you in your bed.'

'I'd like to see you try. Well, do you accept?'

'Oh, yes! Yes, indeed, ma'am.'

'Then that's settled.' She suddenly seemed weary. 'Off with you now and tell your brother you no longer need his roof over your heads.'

'Will I call into the kitchen?'

'Suit yourself. That nincompoop is probably in there.'

'Then we'll see you on Friday evening, and thank you. Thank you so very much, ma'am.' The girls both rose and left the room, closing the door quietly.

On the way down the thickly carpeted stairs, Maddy hissed, 'If you dare say "What will we do now?" I'll strangle you, Carmel Kiernan.'

Carmel giggled nervously. 'Do you think she's *mad*?' she whispered.

'No. Not at all. A bit odd, that's all. She wouldn't have offered us a home if she didn't like us. She seems to please herself on everything she does. I think we'd better go into the kitchen. I can't stand here in the hall and yell, even if they all do it. Did you ever hear the like?' Maddy chortled. '*And* she fights with her brothers, so it's not just me.'

She pushed at a green-baize-covered door and found it opened onto a large kitchen. Seated at the table in the middle of the room drinking tea were Frazer and the woman who had brought up the tray, along with one other woman and a young boy.

'Mr Frazer,' Maddy began somewhat nervously, 'we thought we should come and tell you that Mrs Buckley has very, very generously offered us a place here. I'm not quite sure what she wants us to do – in the way of work, I mean. She didn't explain.'

'She never does, Miss Kiernan,' he replied heavily. 'Just do as the meddlesome old creature tells you, and you'll find it can be anything from cooking and serving dinner in the formal dining room to scrubbing the kitchen floor. Maybe that's what she wants you to do. We're all more than a bit long in the tooth here, apart from young Freddy, or we wouldn't put up with her.'

'Ah, I see,' Maddy replied, although she still didn't really understand. 'We'll be moving in on Friday evening.'

'Did she say which rooms you were to have?'

'No.'

'Typical. Don't worry, I'll sort something out. There's too many bedrooms in this house, all unoccupied.'

'Does she live here alone entirely? I mean, she told us she's a widow and she argues with her brothers, but—'

'On her own it is because she fights with everyone in time. The secret is to shout back at her.'

'Well, thank you,' she said, and both girls murmured their goodbyes.

'What do you think Tom will say?' Carmel asked when they were in the street.

Maddy smiled. 'He'll be as cross as a bag of cats! Let's hurry home and tell him.'

The baby was asleep, Johanna was sitting sewing and Tom was dozing in his chair.

He sat up as they came in.

'Any luck?' Johanna asked. She hated the atmosphere but didn't want them to leave.

197

'Yes. New house, new jobs.' Maddy grinned.

'How so?' Tom demanded.

'We helped an old man after he was robbed,' Carmel said.

'He's the butler up at a house in Faulkner Square and the mistress, Mrs Buckley, took a liking to us, so we're going to live there and work there. We're to be there with our things on Friday evening. So we won't be a burden to you for much longer.'

Maddy smiled sweetly at her brother, not one bit surprised when it was returned with a glower.

Chapter Fourteen

Maddy promised Johanna that she would visit as often as she could.

'Don't be thinking I'm abandoning you,' she said gently. 'We must get time off. I don't know the goings-on of being in service, but we must be entitled to a couple of hours to ourselves, surely.'

Johanna wrapped Ronan in a shawl, nursing him until his fretful whimpering stopped. 'It sounds a very peculiar household,' she said. 'Are you sure you're going to be all right – safe, I mean?'

'Of course we are. But I agree, it is a very strange arrangement.'

'Tom was very surprised.'

'Oh, I'll bet he was. But don't go worrying yourself about him,' Maddy said with some satisfaction.

They had very little to pack so on Friday evening the sisters stood on the steps of the house that was to be their new home with only one carpet bag between them.

'In future you will come and go by the back door. I'm too old to be answering the door to the junior domestics, and it's not fitting either,' Frazer grumbled.

'We will. Where is the back door?' The fronts of the houses all faced the square little park.

Fraser pointed to an archway that they had failed to notice.

'Through there. It leads to the stables and coach-houses. The mistress has a carriage mouldering away but no horses. She never goes over the doorstep.'

'I see, and is that what we're to be? Junior domestics?'

'The Lord bless us, I don't know what you'll be, she didn't see fit to tell me. But you young girls are always called "junior domestics" – in this house anyway. Freddy, the boot boy, will show you up to your rooms – my rheumatics are playing me up again. It'll be raining by morning, I know it will.'

The other occupants of the kitchen looked up as the girls walked in.

'Freddy, show the young ladies up to their rooms. Your legs are younger than mine and you don't pull your weight. Now, this is Mrs Appleton – she's the cook.'

'And the housekeeper,' interrupted the woman who'd served them tea.

'This is Ada Miller,' Frazer continued.

'Maid of all work, according to the whims of her upstairs,' grinned this woman.

'I'm Maddy Kiernan and this is my sister Carmel,' Maddy said, a little shyly. 'We'll do anything, we don't mind.'

'You'll not have to – she's the divil of a temper on her. No one stays very long, servants I mean,' Ada informed them darkly.

'She throws things sometimes, too. Then accuses us of breaking her best china when it's herself that hurls it around in temper,' Mrs Appleton added. 'Oh, don't look so worried, pet,' she chuckled to Carmel. 'You'll soon get used to her.'

Carmel was not convinced that she would get used to her new mistress and her temper, but she said nothing.

Freddy led them up a narrow, dimly lit back staircase until they reached the top storey of the house. 'These two are yours,' he said with not much grace, flinging open the doors of two adjacent rooms.

'Thanks,' Maddy said.

'Can you find your own way down, like?'

'I'm sure we can. Isn't it just a matter of using the back stairs? Look, Carmel – a room each.'

'Oh Maddy, would you look at the style, and these are servants' bedrooms!'

Maddy was looking around her own small room. A skylight in the roof let in plenty of light. There was a carpet on the floor, albeit faded and threadbare, and a single bed covered with a pristine white bedspread. The furniture and wash-stand were of good quality and only needed a good polishing. Towels were hanging ready on the rail at the side of the wash-stand. Carmel's room was the same. In fact, they had every comfort there was, including a fireplace.

'We've never had a room to ourselves, nor a bed either. Oh, isn't it grand,' Carmel said excitedly.

'Let's just hope we can put up with her. Do you think I should go and see her and say that we've moved in? I should really ask her what she wants us to do, and what she will pay me.'

Carmel hesitated. She didn't want to confront the old lady again yet. 'You go, Maddy. She's not paying me, but I don't mind. I'm getting free board and lodging, which is grand. I never got paid in Ireland.'

'Except the offer of two laying hens, remember?' How long ago it seemed. 'All right, I'll go and see her, but I'll take you back to the kitchen first.'

A pot of tea and a plate of sandwiches and Dundee cake was waiting for them on the table. Only Frazer was there, dozing in a chair.

Maddy looked around. This kitchen was far bigger than the one in Canal House. There was a large pantry too, and through its half-open door they glimpsed the shelves and the marble-topped chest that had dozens of little drawers which later she learned contained spices in various stages of decay.

The room itself was below street-level, but wasn't dark or dingy thanks to the window set high in the wall. The whole place was spotless. The range had been black-leaded, the pans shone, the furniture was old-fashioned but clean. All the utensils hung from a rack above the range.

'Mrs Appleton left you these. I don't suppose you've eaten?'

'We haven't, thank you. I was thinking of going up to see herself regarding our position.'

'You can if you like, but she might be asleep and if she's woken she'll be in no fit mood to discuss anything.'

'Then I'll go now, just in case.' Maddy thought it was very early for Mrs Buckley to be asleep, but then she remembered that she was old and had some very odd ways of going on.

The door to the drawing room, as she must learn to call it, was slightly ajar. Maddy pushed it gently until it was open enough for her to see clearly into the room. The frill of a black bonnet was just visible over the top of a winged chair so she knocked loudly on the door.

'Now what's the matter Frazer, you old fool, disturbing me at this hour when I'm having a nap?'

'It's not Frazer, ma'am, it's Maddy. May I come in?'

'Of course you can, girl. Have you been shown your rooms?'

'We have so and they're grand.'

'Well, I wouldn't call the attic rooms "grand".'

'I meant they were fine, lovely, great.'

'All right, that's quite enough description. Have you eaten?'

'Mr Frazer and Mrs Appleton have kindly seen to that, thank you.'

'Well, Maddy, what is it you want now?' The old lady peered up at her through a pair of lorgnettes.

'I'd like to know what my duties and Carmel's are, ma'am, if you please, and . . . and how much . . .'

'I see. You want to know what you're worth?'

'Please.'

203

'Your duties first. Both of you will help out with such tasks that require doing, and if the mood takes me, I should like to have you read to me, since my eyesight is poor.' She gestured at the lorgnettes to emphasise her point. 'You *can* read, I presume?'

'Oh yes, ma'am,' Maddy replied, noticing a newspaper folded up beside the old lady's chair.

'And you will be paid accordingly.'

Maddy waited. Did she mean she would pay her just to read to her?

'Six shillings a week and your keep. You will have Tuesday and Sunday afternoons off, unless one of those incompetents below stairs objects, then I expect you to fall in with their arrangements.'

'Thank you, that's very generous of you.'

'It's not. It's what I can afford to pay you.'

'Oh . . . er . . . I see.'

'Go back downstairs. Frazer will enlighten you on our daily routine; it isn't too taxing. If it were, I'd be having to bury them by the end of the week. Tell Frazer I'll have my cocoa now and not too much sugar. You can bring it up to me.'

'I will so, ma'am.' Maddy retreated, closing the door behind her.

Six shillings wasn't too bad. They didn't have to pay rent or buy food or coal.

'Mr Frazer has told me how the household is run,' Carmel informed her when she entered the kitchen.

'I'm glad one of us knows,' Maddy answered, pouring

herself a cup of tea and helping herself to the ham sandwiches. 'Mr Frazer, she wants her cocoa now – I'm to take it up. Can I ask you what it is? I've never seen it or even heard of it.'

'It's a drink. A sort of thick chocolate that you mix with hot milk. It's sweet, too sweet. I wouldn't touch the stuff myself but it's what she always has before she retires for the night and we all get some peace.'

'It's up at seven,' Carmel continued. 'Rake out and relight the fires. Tidy the kitchen. Then one of us will take up the mistress's breakfast. We'll clean the house and help Mrs Appleton as much as we can.'

'I'm to read to her as well, since her sight is poor,' Maddy added through the ham sandwich.

'She can see well enough when she wants to,' Frazer remarked.

'Do you think that it would be possible to get the bells fixed?' Maddy asked suddenly. 'I can't go yelling at the top of my voice all day.'

'We can get them mended but she won't use them. We've tried before. Mr Richard even had a talk to her but it did no good. I declare she enjoys it.'

'Mr Richard is her brother?' Maddy queried as she watched the cocoa being made.

'One of them. She doesn't like him much.'

'I gather she doesn't like any of them.'

'She doesn't. She delights in having furious rows that we can all hear. Oh, you'll get used to it. We have. We've all been here for years, except Freddy. You'd not hear a voice raised in any other normal household but this is far from normal.' He turned to Carmel.

'Go up and make sure the fire in her bedroom is burning. It's the second room on the left at the top of the first flight of stairs. She hates cold rooms. Has fires burning in the middle of summer and we all have to swelter.'

Carmel and Maddy exchanged glances and Maddy raised her eyebrows expressively.

After a couple of weeks the Kiernan sisters had adjusted to the routine, such as it was. They both worked hard and Mrs Appleton said she'd not seen the place look so well for years. Maddy was called upon to sit and read to her mistress after dinner each evening, and came to know and understand her better. They got on well, for Maddy always answered questions directly. She'd already had her first altercation over a missing bookmark, of all things, but as she told Carmel, she'd held her own.

'It's just as they said. Stand up to her, and she respects you more,' Maddy explained.

'Thank God I hardly ever see her,' was Carmel's response. She had no wish to tangle with the fearsome old lady.

Maddy had even got used to shouting questions and answers, though Carmel swore she never would.

A week later, Maddy was standing in the hall, holding a book from the library while Frazer went to open the front door.

'Is it *Pride and Predjudice* you mean, ma'am?' she yelled up the stairs at the top of her voice.

'Isn't that what I asked for!' came the equally loud reply from above.

Maddy turned to see a middle-aged man standing in the hallway.

'Good God! Who are you?' he demanded.

'I'm Maddy Kiernan. I'm a sort of maid.'

'And when was it deemed correct for the lower orders to bellow at their employers?'

'I'm sorry, sir, she . . . Mrs Buckley . . .'

'You know what she's like, Mr Richard,' Frazer said curtly, taking his coat and hat, and Maddy sensed he had as much liking for the visitor as the old lady had.

'Go up and inform your mistress *quietly* that I am here and that I wish to see her. Hurry up, girl!'

Maddy bobbed what she hoped was a curtsey and went quickly up the stairs, still holding the book.

'It's Mr Richard, ma'am. He wishes to see you.'

'Well, I don't wish to see *him*. In fact, I wish he was on the other side of the world, then I would be spared these visits. He only comes for money.'

'Ma'am, what am I to tell him? I mean, sure I'm only a bit of a servant.'

'You are always a "bit" of something. Your grammar is atrocious. Go and tell him I said he can go to perdition.'

'Oh ma'am, I'll be killed!'

'Don't be ridiculous, girl. I am mistress in my own house.'

Maddy left, still clutching the book which had been completely forgotten by them both.

'Well, girl?'

'She said, sir, that you can go to "perdition", whatever that means. I'm sorry, sir, I really am, but what was I to do?'

His face changed colour, the red flush of anger rising in his pallid cheeks. 'I'll show myself up,' he said in a voice like the slam of a door.

'What will I do now?' Maddy asked Frazer who was standing in the hall, taking great pleasure from the other man's discomfort.

'Stand by the front door ready to let him out. He won't be long.'

'Maddy! Bring up that book, girl!' Mrs Buckley shouted over the banister rail.

'Oh, God!' Maddy cried but did as she was bid.

Mrs Buckley's youngest brother was standing leaning against the ornate fireplace, his expression stony.

'The book, ma'am,' Maddy said gingerly.

'See, Richard, she's not a scullion! She's my ... companion.'

'For the love of God, Maud, have you no sense? You pick people up off the street and set them up as a companion!'

'I have more sense than you will ever have or that wife of yours,' his sister said calmly. 'She's an empty-headed, under-bred bore. I suppose she's run up bills that you can't afford to pay again? I warned you. I warned you years ago that Elizabeth would bleed you dry. How much do you want this time?'

Maddy wished the floor would open up and swallow her. This was private family business and shouldn't be witnessed by someone like herself.

'I . . . I'll go and see about some tea,' she said and scuttled to the door before there was some demand from the old lady that would make her stay. Now this man would hate her and it wasn't her fault. Tomorrow she would go and see Johanna, she decided. It would be a break and after tonight she certainly needed one.

'I just hope to God she doesn't call for me any more tonight,' she said to Carmel who was hanging the tea towel above the range to dry.

'Well, you can't say life is ever dull here,' Mrs Appleton said, smiling.

Chapter Fifteen

Carmel was excited by the big box of decorations that had been delivered.

'We never had anything like this for Christmas!' she exclaimed, her eyes shining and her hands clasped together.

'It's some new-fangled idea Prince Albert brought with him from that place I can't pronounce. Sax Co something. Anyway, what's the matter with the normal holly and ivy, that's what I want to know. Never mind decorated trees. If we wanted them, haven't we enough trees of our own? And as for putting candles on them, that's downright dangerous. The house could burn down around you,' Frazer remarked grumpily. He was getting slower and slower and his joints were inflamed as the weather got colder and damper. 'I suppose it was her idea?'

'It was so. She read about it and even cut out a picture for us to follow. It has to be a special tree – a fir tree,' Maddy explained.

'She's done it to spite me and make more work for you. The older she gets, the worse she becomes,' he mumbled.

Carmel and Maddy exchanged amused glances. They were both used to the household now and were happy. Maddy was more of a companion to the old lady than a servant and had learned to treat her cantankerous outbursts either with silence or by shouting back.

'When will Freddy be here with the tree?' Carmel asked, all agog.

'If he gets it home in one piece it will be a miracle. It might be taken from him by some ne'er-do-wells to use as firewood,' Frazer said with some satisfaction before he shuffled away.

'Oh, I hope not!' Carmel cried, her face falling.

'Well, you can't blame them,' Maddy said, remembering their last Christmas. Had they really been in Liverpool for a whole year? It seemed so short a time for all the experiences they'd been through.

When they returned to the kitchen it was to find Mrs Appleton and Ada baking in what seemed like a sea of dishes, bowls and utensils.

'Is herself having company?' Maddy asked.

'No, but we have to go through this performance every year.' Ada stopped and shook her head. 'She did have Mr Richard and his wife for Christmas lunch years ago, but it all ended in a shouting match and her throwing the entire goose, plate and all, at his head. Oh, there was some cleaning up after that, I can tell you.'

'But we can't eat all that,' Maddy protested.

'Of course we can't.'

'Then what happens to it?'

'She gives it away. Usually it's me who has to take it to the workhouse,' Ada answered gloomily.

'She has her lunch in the dining room, on her own, and then we have ours down here.'

'She must be lonely,' Maddy mused.

'She's only herself to blame for that,' Frazer said darkly.

'I've not heard her speak of her other brothers.' Maddy pondered. She had thankfully seen nothing of Mrs Buckley's youngest brother since that unfortunate débâcle.

'She doesn't. She fell out with Mr Harold first, almost five, no six, years ago. Then the following year it was Mr Edmund and his wife.'

'Why?' Maddy asked.

Mrs Appleton stopped rolling out pastry. 'Because she holds the purse strings,' she said simply. 'She's the eldest and like her father, or so I've heard. That's why he left everything to her and not his sons. Of course there was holy murder over it, but the solictor and the court decided her father's Will would stand. There was nothing irregular in it, even if none of them approved of his wishes.'

Frazer took up the story. 'The master, God rest him, went through all his money, and once it was gone she'd not give him a penny piece.'

'She doesn't put her hand in her pocket much at all,' Ada interrupted.

'I thought she wasn't well off. To look at her clothes you'd think she hadn't a penny.'

'She's had them for years, and as for not being well off, there's this house, stocks and bonds, and what's left of the Buckley Line.'

'I don't understand,' Maddy said, her brow creasing in a frown.

'Two ships out of six. That's all that's left. They go to Africa.'

'I remember now – that's how we met you! You'd been to deliver a letter,' Maddy said, recalling that day down at the docks.

'Of course, they're all waiting for her to die, then they'll inherit the lot, as she's childless,' Mrs Appleton finished, and returned once more to rolling out the pastry for her mince pies.

Maddy had been thinking of Johanna and the spartan Christmas they would have, compared to all this. Wouldn't their sister-in-law love to see this new idea, the Christmas Tree, and baby Ronan would like all the coloured decorations and tiny candles, even though he was too young to know what they were. She made up her mind to ask her mistress about it.

'Ma'am, I have a favour to ask of you,' she said, taking in the afternoon tea.

'What is it? If it's got anything to do with money then the answer is no, and will you put more coal on that fire. It's as cold as charity in here.'

Maddy thought of the two ships. 'It has nothing to do with money, ma'am. I was wondering if I could bring my sister-in-law and her little boy to see the decorations, especially the tree.'

The old lady didn't reply.

'Well, if you don't agree you don't agree and that's that,' Maddy said, feeling upset and almost hurling a shovel of coal onto the fire.

'Did I say I don't agree?'

'No.'

'Then don't jump to conclusions, miss! Of course they can come and I'll take a glass of sherry with her. No one can accuse me of not being charitable at Christmas.'

Maddy thought of Mrs Buckley's relations. Old hypocrite, she thought. 'Thank you, ma'am, she'd like that. I'll send Freddy with a note. Shall I pour or would you prefer to do it yourself?' Maddy was never sure of the answer and 'storms in a teacup' had, quite literally, been the outcome.

The visit was arranged for the day before Christmas Eve and both Carmel and Maddy were excited at the prospect of seeing baby Ronan's little face. Mrs Buckley's instructions that they have a sherry with her had brought pursed lips and eyes raised to the ceiling from the rest of the staff.

'She *is* generous,' Maddy had defended her mistress.

'When it suits her,' Frazer had replied.

Johanna came to the back door. Both she and the baby were well wrapped up against the cold.

'Maddy, are you sure she said it was all right to come?' The young woman was nervous.

'I am so. Come in before we all freeze.'

'But the glass of sherry and all that?'

'It's all right, Jo. Mrs Buckley's got some very odd notions but she's quite nice.' When it suits her, she thought, as Frazer had so accurately put it.

Johanna was over-awed by the size, number and furnishings of the rooms as she followed Maddy up the wide staircase.

'Don't get upset if anyone starts shouting. They all do here, myself included.'

'I can't see you yelling at the top of your voice, Maddy.'

'Oh, I do. You'd be very surprised by how loud I can be.'

'Come in, girl, and let me see you and the baby,' came the imperious demand from the depths of a Queen Anne chair. For the occasion Mrs Buckley had worn over her dress a very old, hand-painted silk shawl with long fringed ends. The colours of the flowers had once been fresh and bright; now they were faded and grubby.

Johanna didn't know what to say to the old lady.

'Well, Maddy, don't just stand there, get the glasses and the decanter. Sit down, girl. Your name is Johanna, I believe?'

'It is, ma'am, and thank you for allowing me to —'

'There's no need to be so effusive. Maddy asked and I agreed. As simple as that.'

'But the sherry . . .'

'It pleases me. So, how do you like our Christmas Tree?'

Johanna followed her gaze to the corner of the room where the fir tree stood decorated with baubles and bows and tiny flickering candles.

'Oh, ma'am, it's beautiful,' she breathed, entranced.

'Take the child closer.'

Johanna did as she was bid while Maddy watched them fondly. The baby reached out a chubby hand towards the shiny objects and gurgled. Johanna gently made sure he didn't go near the candles. All their expressions were noticed by the old lady, and what she saw, she liked. The girl looked neat and tidy, as did the baby.

'Now come over here while you have your drink. Pass the child to me.'

Hesitantly Johanna put Ronan on her lap.

'Don't worry, girl, I won't bite him!'

Maddy passed her sister-in-law a glass and Johanna took a tentative sip. The drink, she found, was a bit too sweet for her liking.

Maddy was watching her mistress and was amazed how well she was getting on with Ronan, who was fascinated by the sparkling of her many rings.

'If you've finished, Maddy, take the child while I have my sherry.'

Maddy put down her glass and lifted her nephew from Mrs Buckley's lap. He put his thumb in his mouth and regarded them all with huge dark eyes.

'What does your husband do?' the old lady asked, adjusting the shawl.

'He's a carter, ma'am, but he can turn his hand to most things.'

Mrs Buckley nodded. 'Then you're fortunate.'

'I know it. There's so many without work of any kind, and he has ambitions ma'am.'

'Indeed. And to what does he aspire?'

'To be something he'll never be. Well-to-do,' Maddy remarked dryly.

'You've a sharp tongue in your head, miss! There's nothing wrong with ambition, although I agree with you. It's better to know your place and stick to it. You may leave me now. I am tired. Go downstairs and they'll give you something to eat.'

'Thank you, ma'am.'

'I have enjoyed your visit, girl. Take care of that child.'

'I will. Thank you so much. Happy Christmas, ma'am.' Johanna bobbed respectfully before leaving the room.

'I was terrified!' she confided to Maddy as they went downstairs.

'She has that effect on a lot of people, but she really took to Ronan.'

'Has she ever had a child?'

'No. Maybe she'd be different if she had.'

'The poor old thing. All this, but never knowing the joy a child can bring.'

'We'll have some tea and I know Mrs Appleton has made mince pies and scones. I'd sooner have tea than sherry. It was desperate, like drinking treacle.'

After Johanna had gone, with a bag full of pies and scones and a jar of jam, the staff never seemed to stop work. The dining table looked magnificent, ready for Christmas dinner the next day, but as Carmel said, 'It's such a shame that she has to dine alone.'

'She doesn't have to,' Frazer said grumpily. 'She has plenty of relations.'

'I thought Christmas was a time for forgiving,' Maddy said.

'I don't think that rule applies to her. Anyway, I'm saying nothing or I'll get my head bitten off,' Frazer replied.

The following morning both Maddy and Carmel went up to the drawing room.

'A deputation, no less. What's the matter now? Have you come to give notice?'

'We have not. Where else would we get such comfort?' Maddy replied with spirit.

'Then what is it?'

'We bought you this. It's from both of us, for Christmas.'

Maud Buckley looked at them with amazement. No one had given her a Christmas present for years. She took the parcel that was wrapped up in plain brown paper and began to untie the knots of the string. Inside was a shawl of soft pale lavender wool, encased in sheets of tissue paper. It had cost Maddy almost a month's wages and had been bought in Bold Street.

'We thought you'd like the colour and that it would be useful,' Maddy explained.

For a few seconds Maud Buckley couldn't speak, but her thin bony fingers stroked the soft wool.

'It's very kind of you both,' she said finally. 'I like it. It *will* suit me. Help me put it around my shoulders, Maddy.'

Maddy did as she was bid and noticed that the old lady's eyes were very bright. 'It's not really much, not when you've given us a safe, good home with all the comforts we've never even dreamed existed.'

'I wouldn't expect you to be going out and paying a small fortune for something I wouldn't use or like. Richard bought me a fan once. A fan! What use would that be in a huge, draughty place like this – and my dancing days are well over!'

'Well, Happy Christmas, ma'am,' they chorused.

'You sound like a pair of parrots. Now get off with you.'

They both smiled. Her bark was far worse than her bite and she had been genuinely surprised and grateful.

'I'm sorry we didn't have enough money to buy something for all of you, too,' Maddy apologised to the rest of the staff, once they were back downstairs.

'I wouldn't worry about it. We never give presents. Her upstairs gives us a sovereign and that's it,' Ada said matter-of-factly.

'It's a wonder she didn't throw it back at you, the way she did with Mr Richard's present a few years ago,' Mrs Appleton remarked.

'She told us he gave her a fan but she said nothing about throwing it at him. She really is desperate at times.'

'She knows she can do and say what she likes and get away with it, if they want any inheritance at all,' Frazer said.

'I can yell all the time then, so I can,' chuckled Maddy. 'Since I'm not in line for the inheritance.'

When things had quietened down Carmel sat brooding, staring into the fire. She wanted to go and see John, but she knew Maddy would only tell her to grow up, and she suspected what kind of a reception she would get from his mother. Nevertheless she was going. How could she stay away, especially at Christmas? She still loved him. She'd go tomorrow night, and take some pies and cakes. She wished she had some small gift to give him, but then he would be embarrassed, having nothing to give her in return.

They duly went with the others to receive their gold sovereigns from their mistress, who very formally wished them Christmas Blessings and Joy, and then reverting to her normal self, told them to go away and have their lunch and not be bringing her to the table until at least three o'clock. Fraser was foolish enough to grumble and got a dressing down for his trouble.

Even though it was a quiet meal, both Maddy and Carmel thoroughly enjoyed it. It was like being with family, Carmel said, and it had never been as sumptuous even when their parents were alive, Maddy added.

That evening Maddy was summoned – in the usual way – to the drawing room where Mrs Buckley gave her a box that contained a silver teething ring.

'Some fool bought it for me years ago,' she said gruffly. 'I never had the need of it. I want you to give this to that sister-in-law of yours.'

'It's beautiful.'

'There is one condition.'

'Which is?'

'That no matter what kind of financial difficulties your brother and his wife find themselves in, they don't sell or pawn it. They come to me for assistance.'

'He'll never do that.'

'But your sister-in-law will.'

'If he lets her.'

The old lady shrugged. 'Get off with you now. All this excitement is wearing me out and that plum pudding is sitting like a lump of lead in my stomach.'

When Carmel heard that Maddy was going to Grayson Street with the gift she was relieved. She'd take the opportunity to go and see John, even if it was only for a few minutes. Putting some pies and cakes into a bag, she donned her coat and hat and left ten minutes after her sister. Everyone assumed she'd gone to catch her up, despite the fact that Maddy had told her not to come, that she'd only get upset if Tom took offence at Mrs Buckley's conditions.

She walked to the corner of the square where she could catch a horse tram, and throughout the cold and bumpy journey tried to think of what she could say to John and Mary Shannahan. Oh, she missed him so much.

Gillings Entry hadn't changed much; if anything, it was worse. Going up the worn steps, she recalled how glad they'd been of the cellar room last year. A dim light shone from down below so obviously someone else lived there now.

Mary herself opened the door, looking tired and thin. A sour expression came over her face when she realised who was at the door.

'I . . . I've come to see John, please?' Carmel burst out. 'I've come all the way from Faulkner Square where Maddy and I are in service and it *is* Christmas.'

She looked well, Mary thought, wondering what she'd done to get into service. It wasn't easy for a factory girl.

'Come in then. I'll ask him, but he's not been well. Bernie's gone for a drink. He deserves it. He works all the hours God sends to keep the roof over our heads.'

Carmel followed her into the room. It was dark and cheerless and there wasn't much in the way of furniture, although a fire burned in the hearth. Times must be bad, she thought, a wave of guilt washing over her.

'I brought you these.' She handed over the bag and Mary looked inside.

'Very nice,' she said flatly, putting the bag on the table. 'Wait while I ask him if he wants to see you.'

Carmel bit her lip as Mary pulled aside the curtain and then let it drop. What if he wouldn't see her?

'Go on, but don't tire him or upset him too much.'

Carmel gingerly held back the curtain and her eyes widened with shock. Even in the dim light of the candle beside his bed she could see a terrible change in him. The tall, healthy young man she had known was little more than a skeleton. His face was lined with suffering and his eyes looked huge, yet seemed to have sunk. There was an unpleasant odour that seemed to surround him.

She knelt on the floor beside him and took a claw-like hand in her own.

'Oh, John! John! What have I done to you? It's my fault and I left you here, like this! I haven't even called to see you.'

There was a hint of animation in his eyes. 'Carmel, don't blame yourself. You couldn't have done anything – and remember what they did to you? You were hurt, too. You

223

meant everything to me. I only did what any man would have done.'

'But if I hadn't come here to live and work, then—'

'But you did and I still love you,' he interrupted. 'I've prayed every day you'd come and see me.'

'Oh John!' Carmel choked, the tears pouring down her cheeks. 'I've always loved you and I'll never, never stop. There is no one else I could love and there never will be, I swear.'

'Don't waste your life, Carmel. Don't waste it because of me. I'm happy now that I've seen you. You look beautiful.'

'I wish I didn't!' she cried. 'I wish I was as ugly as sin, then no one would ever love me.'

'I would. They say beauty is only skin deep. It's *you* I love, Carmel, not just a pretty face. I'm happy now. I really am.'

'I'll come and see you every week, on Sunday afternoons. I'm in service now but I get time off.'

He shook his head. 'No. Don't waste your time off coming here.'

'But I *want* to!'

'No! You must live your life without guilt and without me. Just remember the short but happy time we had together. I do. I go over every word, every single thing we did. It comforts me.'

She was sobbing openly now and he was powerless to help her. He called for his mother.

'Mam, help her! Make her go back.'

'I don't want to go!' Carmel sobbed.

Mary caught her by her shoulders and dragged her up. 'Pull yourself together, Carmel Kiernan! All you're doing is thinking of yourself, as usual. Now stop that carry-on and go back where you belong.'

Carmel let herself be propelled across the room but she turned at the door.

'He said he's happy. He's happy to see me.'

Mary shook her head and her lips twisted into a bitter travesty of a smile. 'What he means is he's happy to die now. You little fool! You empty-headed, thoughtless, selfish little fool! Get out of here and don't ever come back. You killed him. You killed my son!'

Carmel half fell down the steps and ran blindly towards the main road.

Chapter Sixteen

Carmel arrived home at the same time as Maddy, who was startled to see her sister with her hair falling down and tears running down her cheeks.

'What's the matter? Where have you been?' she asked, pushing her sister into the kitchen, which fortunately was empty. The others had gone to bed early, she thought with gratitude.

'Sit there and tell me what's the matter.'

'I . . . I went to see John,' Carmel sobbed. 'Oh God, Maddy, he's . . .'

'Why didn't you tell me you were going?' Maddy interrupted.

'Because you'd say I was an eejit and I am!'

'Maybe I would but at least I'd have gone with you. Although it can't have been a worse evening than the one I've had,' she said gloomily.

'It was. Oh Maddy, he's dying! He looked awful, all skin and bone, but I still love him. I always will and I told him so.

Then she . . . she said he was dying and that I . . . I killed him!' Carmel broke down.

Maddy took her in her arms. Oh dear God, what a night it had been. Tom had insisted she take Mrs Buckley's gift back where it belonged. He wasn't having her imposing conditions. What sort of a gift was that? he'd shouted. Then she'd shouted back, Johanna had dissolved into tears and the baby had woken and added his cries to those of his mother. And now this.

'Don't upset yourself, love,' she soothed. 'Of course she's bitter – life is hard for her at the best of times. But it *isn't* your fault! You couldn't have stopped him. That lot had hurt you badly – it's what any man would have done.'

'That's what he said, but I'll never forgive myself and I'll never stop loving him, even after he's . . . he's . . .' A fresh wave of sobbing gripped her.

'My precious, you're only young, there will be someone else. You *will* get over him.'

Carmel raised her head from Maddy's shoulder and fought to control herself.

'If – when – he dies,' she swallowed hard, 'can I go to the funeral, to say goodbye to him for ever?'

Maddy's heart went out, to her poor sister, and to the Shannahans, too.

'Of course you can,' she said gently. Maybe it would be for the best. Carmel might then start to see life through different eyes. 'Come on to bed now. Sleep is a great healer.'

'I won't be able to sleep.'

'You can't stay down here all night. Will I make us some cocoa?'

Carmel nodded and Maddy got to her feet. There wouldn't be much sleep for her either.

The next day, the household returned to normal. There would be no celebration to welcome in the New Year. 'It only reminds her that she's another year older. And then she wonders if she'll live to see next year,' Mrs Appleton explained.

'Just how old is she?' Maddy asked.

'We don't know for sure, but we think she's eighty-two.'

'Isn't that a great age,' Maddy marvelled. There were few people who lived to be as old, but of course Mrs Buckley had had good food all her life, plus warmth, people to take care of her and decent sanitation.

Ada leaned across the table and dropped her voice. 'Frazer's not far behind her, he'll be eighty this year.'

'Glory be to God! No wonder he's slowing down.'

'We all are, but we're thankful for the roof over us. There's many a one got rid of when they're too old to work.'

'She'd never do that to you.'

'You'd never know, but I don't think she would.'

'She's fond of you all, even if she doesn't show it. Have you any savings?'

'Not much. You don't think about that until suddenly you realise you're heading for seventy, and by then it's a bit too late.'

'Well, I'm sure she wouldn't treat you badly. As you always say, her bark is worse than her bite.'

Ada looked thoughtful. 'You know, Maddy, I've never known her to take to anyone as she's taken to you, and you get away with murder. She'd not have any of *us* lecturing her quite the way you do.'

'I know, and I am fond of her, too,' Maddy said, smiling. She couldn't really explain it either.

It was a late February afternoon when a white-faced and shivering Johanna came to the back door.

'Good grief, you're soaked. Come in and get those wet things off you and that baby. Carmel – go and find a couple of blankets,' Maddy instructed, leading her sister-in-law to the fire.

'I'll make a cup of tea. You look as though you could do with one, lass,' Mrs Appleton said.

It was only when both mother and baby had been stripped of their outer clothes and her nephew given to Carmel to nurse while Johanna sipped the hot drink gratefully, that Maddy asked for the full story.

'It's Tom. He—'

'Now what?' Maddy demanded.

'Let the girl finish, Maddy,' Ada rebuked her.

'He's lost his job. He finished three weeks ago but he wouldn't tell anyone. He's been searching, but there's nothing. Too many men are unemployed.'

'How did he come to lose it?'

'He had an argument with another carter who worked for

the same company. The other man complained, and as Tom had only been with them for a few months, they sacked him. There's plenty looking for work who won't make trouble.' Johanna hung her head in despair. 'Oh Maddy, I don't know what to do. I'm at my wit's end. He doesn't know I've come. He wasn't in so I left him a note saying I'd gone to the market to see what I could get in the way of scraps.'

'He never could keep his temper, the eejit!'

'Maddy, we've no money. I was sure he would have had some savings, but he swears he hasn't and I haven't had much work lately. They say they are cutting down.'

An idea was forming in Maddy's head. It was a serious one and wouldn't just involve her brother and sister-in-law.

'Leave it with me, I'll try to think of something,' she said. 'You'd better take some food home. Will that be all right, Mr Frazer?'

'Aye, and that idle, useless lad Freddy can carry some coal back with you.'

'I'm not idle and useless. I do my fair share!' the lad protested indignantly.

'Your fair share? When I was your age I did twice as much again,' Frazer snapped back. This damp weather was torture for his aches and pains.

'Thank you, sir, thank you so much.'

When mother and baby were warm and dry again, and the food packed in a basket and the coal in a sack, Freddy was sent out to find a Hackney cab.

'You'll get pneumonia if you walk home in the teeming torrents, and then what would you do?' Mrs Appleton said, pressing the money for the fare into Johanna's hand.

'Oh, you're all so kind.' She thought with a shudder of the cold, damp rooms she was going back to.

'I'll come and see you as soon as I can, and don't let him bully you,' Maddy urged, hugging her sister-in-law as she hobbled wearily into the darkening afternoon.

That night, Maddy sat brooding until she'd made up her mind.

'Are you intending to make my cocoa tonight?' Mrs Buckley shouted over the banister rail.

'Nothing can please her today. It's the weather,' Frazer said.

Maddy got up. 'I'll make it and take it up to her.'

Frazer shuffled off into the hall and bellowed at his mistress that it would be up in a few minutes, and did she not have any patience with a poor suffering old man?

They all heard the rude reply, issued in tones that would raise the dead.

'Here's your drink, ma'am. There's no need to be wailing like a banshee. You knew it would be made and brought up,' Maddy chastised when she brought in the tray.

'Later rather than sooner!' the old lady shot back.

Maddy set down the small silver platter.

'I'd like to discuss something with you. It's quite important.'

'At this time of night? Will it wait until morning?'

'No, ma'am, it won't.'

'Oh, very well, persecute a poor, infirm old woman.'

'You are not poor or infirm.'

'That's a matter of opinion. Oh, get on with it then. Spit it out. I hate people beating around the bush.'

Maddy took a deep breath. 'My sister-in-law came to see me this afternoon. She'd walked here in the rain and both she and Ronan were soaked. My brother has lost his job and can't get any work and they have no money. And you told me to tell them that if they were in trouble to come to you.' She didn't mention the teething ring, which was in the drawer under her stockings.

'So?'

'I was thinking, ma'am, that Frazer and Mrs Appleton and Ada have been with you for years and years and they really are getting very slow, and I know Fraser must be in agony with his rheumatics and—'

'And you want me to pension them off and take your brother and sister-in-law to replace them?'

Maddy was so surprised she couldn't answer.

'It certainly makes a change for you to be lost for words. I have eyes in my head,' the old lady said. 'I've been thinking of pensioning them off for a while. Oh, I'll see they are provided for. I might be old but I've still got my wits about me. I liked your sister-in-law, but didn't you tell me she was a seamstress?'

'She is. Unfortunately she doesn't get much work now.'

'And how do you think you'll get on with your brother if you are living under the same roof? I'll have no screaming rows!'

Maddy smiled. She had thought about that. 'There won't be any,' she assured the old lady. 'He'll be obliged to me for a job and a home.'

'Maddy Kiernan, you're a hard-hearted, conniving creature.' Maud Buckley cackled with appreciative laughter. 'Someone after my own heart. Tomorrow I will tell the rest of the staff my plans and then you can go and see your brother. I know you will enjoy informing him that you have persuaded me to give him *a job and a home*.' She paused and grinned wickedly. 'I only wish I could be there to see it. It would be better than any play.'

'Thank you. I only asked on behalf of Johanna and the baby. If it had been just himself, I would have left him to sink or swim,' Maddy replied, and she meant it.

Next morning she said nothing to anyone but raised her eyebrows when everyone except herself and Carmel were called upstairs.

'What's going on?' Carmel demanded.

'You'll find out soon enough.'

'Tell me! I know you had something to do with it. You were up with her for ages last night.'

'She's pensioning them all off and it's about time too.'

'What – poor Frazer and Mrs Appleton and Ada.'

'Carmel, they are not being thrown out on the road. She'll pay them either a lump sum or a monthly amount.'

'So, who is she going to get to replace them? Just you, me and Freddy can't run the house.'

'Tom and Johanna.'

Carmel looked apprehensive. 'I'm glad for Johanna, but Tom?'

Maddy nodded, her face serious. 'I know, we'll have to keep the arguments down.'

'When will you tell them?'

'Now. I shall strike while the iron is hot.' She took her coat and hat from the peg. 'I'll leave you to help with lunch.'

It was a damp and dismal day, Maddy thought as she walked towards Grayson Street, and she doubted her visit would please her brother until he had heard her out.

Johanna opened the door to her. 'Maddy, come in. What's the matter?'

'Nothing.'

Maddy followed her into the room where Tom was sitting by the hearth looking dejected.

'And to what do we owe this visit? More cakes, is it?' he said sarcastically.

'Isn't that a nice way to greet anyone, but I'll take no notice.'

'So, what *have* you come for? To gloat?'

'No. Mrs Buckley sent me.'

'I want no more gifts that come with conditions.'

'It's not a gift. She is pensioning off the staff – they've been with her for years and they're too old.'

'What's that got to do with me?' he demanded.

Maddy gritted her teeth at his tone. Sometimes she really detested him.

'She is willing to give you their jobs,' she said. 'Johanna will see to the running of the house.'

'Oh Maddy, I couldn't do that! I have no idea of how things should be done,' Johanna cried.

'You'll have me and Carmel to help you. Don't you run this home well?'

'And what about me?' Tom said, his face suspicious.

'You'll take over Frazer's duties and do any repairs that need doing. And of course you'll both live in.'

'I'm a working man – what do I know about being a butler?'

'I'm glad you *know* you're a working man. Frazer will tell you what to do and herself doesn't care much about convention.'

Johanna was astounded. 'You mean we will be living in that big house and have all those comforts?'

Maddy nodded.

'Oh Tom, do you remember what I told you about the place?' the young woman said excitedly. 'It will be like living in a palace!'

'A rather rundown and shabby palace, Jo,' Maddy grinned.

'What about wages?' Tom asked.

'I don't know. She didn't mention it to me. She'll probably tell you that herself, but don't expect a fortune. She's very careful with her money.'

'When will we come, Maddy?'

'As soon as you can. You can come back with me, if you want.'

Johanna looked towards her husband for confirmation. She couldn't wait.

'All right, get your things,' he said ungraciously. This offer was far better than anything he had hoped for, except for the disadvantage of being under the same roof as Maddy. He had his 'ship money', but even though they were desperate he hadn't touched a penny of it. Now it looked as if he would be able to save even more. They'd pay no rent and have all the comforts without having to fork out for them. He could save almost all his wages. Johanna could make all her own and the baby's clothes.

When Maddy returned with Tom and his family, it was to a silent kitchen. Frazer, Mrs Appleton and Ada all sat at the table wearing dazed expressions.

'So, she told you?' Maddy enquired.

'She did,' Frazer answered.

'And?'

'We're to receive a more than generous sum of money so we can spend our last years in comfort, and do things or go to places we've only dreamed of,' he told her.

Mrs Appleton dabbed at her eyes with the corner of her apron. 'She can be a tartar at times, but she's done us proud. I'm going to go and live with my sister in Manchester. She's on her own now and the money will help.'

Ada nodded happily. She had her own plans.

'I told you she wouldn't just throw you out,' Maddy said. 'Look – I've brought your replacements.' She nodded towards the silent Tom and Johanna. 'My brother would be very obliged to you, Mr Frazer, if you can teach him what to do over the next few days.'

'And I wonder, could you help me, Mrs Appleton?' Johanna asked shyly. 'I only know how to cook plain food.'

The cook had met Johanna before and liked her. 'Of course I will. The mistress doesn't entertain and only sticks to plain food herself. She has trouble with her stomach if she eats anything rich. As for the rest of it, well, it's just like running your own home. Most of the rooms are closed off. They only need a good clean once or twice a year.' She took the baby out of the girl's arms and gave him a good cuddle.

'I've told Mrs Buckley that Carmel and I will help out, and there's Freddy to give Tom a hand with the odd jobs. Tom might even get some work out of the lazy little bowsie. I'll go and tell herself you're here.'

Tom had already glanced around the room. Johanna was right. The place *was* like a palace, if the kitchen was anything to go by. Whole families lived in rooms half the size of it.

Maddy went into the hall. 'Himself and Johanna are in the kitchen. Shall I bring them up, ma'am?' she bawled, her face turned enquiringly to the first floor.

'Isn't that what you brought them for?' came the reply in equally loud tones.

Ada looked at Tom's shocked face and laughed heartily. 'Oh, you'll get used to that in time. It's the way she carries on. Won't use the bells and you'd never credit the fact that such a small, frail person could make so much noise.'

Johanna smiled timidly. 'It will take me a lifetime to get used to shouting like that.'

'Well, we've had a lifetime of experience,' Mrs Appleton said.

'Maddy hasn't, but then again she was always loud and bold,' Tom replied. Palace it might be, but there'd be no peace and tranquillity in it, not with those two carrying on like that.

Chapter Seventeen

It seemed strange just to have Tom, Johanna and the baby, and of course young Freddy, in the house. The departures had been times of deep regret and tears on both sides. Ada, who was the only one who was staying in Liverpool, promised to visit as often as she could.

'I've got myself a nice room in a house in Walton-on-the-Hill where I'll be well looked after. It's lovely out there. Just the church and school, a couple of shops, a pub and the rest is countryside. I've always wanted to get away from the dirt and noise of the city and now I have. And I'm considered very well off indeed, me that was born and brought up next to the Georges Dock.'

'We'll always be pleased to see you, Ada, and I'm sure herself will too.'

'I'm glad you're staying here with her, Maddy. I'd hate her to be amongst strangers, hate to think that she'd be alone when her time comes.'

'I'll be here until she goes,' Maddy had replied. And she meant it.

Johanna was over the moon at this change in their fortunes, and with the help of both her sisters-in-law, soon had the household running far more smoothly than it had done for years. Although he had certain duties as butler and manservant that he wasn't comfortable with, Tom told himself smugly that he'd fallen on his feet here, all right. The old lady paid him far more than he'd ever earned, and more than he'd been going to ask for. His days were not hard. When he thought of how, as a carter, he'd been up at the crack of dawn and out in all weathers until late evening, he felt even better. His future looked very rosy and his savings were growing. The only fly in the ointment was that he owed it all to Maddy.

In what spare time Johanna had, she mended and darned furnishings and linen, and made clothes for them all, including Mrs Buckley. She'd found some material and trimmings in a chest in the attic.

'They must have been there for years but the thick wood has protected them,' she explained when she brought them down. In no time at all she'd made two short bedjackets, trimmed with lace and ribbons, for her benefactress. Mrs Buckley complained of the cold in the bedroom while Maddy sat and read to her each night, even though an enormous fire roared in the grate.

The old lady had been genuinely pleased.

'I get treated better by my servants than I do by my family,' she'd told Johanna. 'Thank you, dear. When you get

242

to my age you learn to be a good judge of character and I liked you from the day you came to see the Christmas Tree.'

On hearing this, Maddy had smiled to herself.

'And what is so amusing about that, miss?'

'I was thinking of something my Mam used to say: "You can choose your staff and your friends, but you're stuck with your relations". She was in service herself for a time when she was young, you see. I thought how well it suited.'

'I would have liked to have met your mother. She sounds like a person of sense. I could have talked to her with ease.'

'Ah, you would so, ma'am,' Maddy had answered, with a tinge of sorrow in her voice.

Towards the middle of March the weather turned unseasonably warm and the trees and shrubs began to sprout. In the little private parks in the squares, daffodils and tulips began to bloom and Carmel started to carry Ronan across to theirs each afternoon. The mistress had given her a key for this purpose. Laying out a blanket, she set him down on it for a good kick. She especially liked the garden; it reminded her of her childhood in Ireland.

She was tickling the baby's bare feet with a blade of grass which made him laugh and squirm and reach out for the grass when she heard Maddy calling her from the front step.

Picking Ronan up, she went towards her sister; she'd go back for the blanket and lock the gate later.

'Why are you yelling at me like a fishwife from the front step?' she called out jokingly.

'Freddy has brought a note.'

'A note? Who from?' Carmel asked, following her sister into the house and then down the back stairs.

'Give Ronan to me,' Johanna instructed, holding out her arms.

'It's for you. Sit down and read it.' Maddy passed over the piece of paper. It was hardly more than a scrap of brown wrapping paper which had been written on. There was no envelope.

'Who did Freddy get it from?'

'A lad he knows from school. Freddy doesn't come from around here, if you remember.'

Carmel nodded slowly. Freddy came from a house in the neighbourhood of Gillings Entry. She read the scrawled lines with difficulty, and then tears welled up in her eyes.

'He . . . John . . . is dead.'

'I know, I read it. I'm sorry, Carmel, so very, very sorry.'

'I loved him so much, Maddy, and yet in a way I'm glad. It was no life really, being like that.'

Maddy put her arm around her shoulder. 'Mary's got someone to write to us because she's no money for his funeral.'

'Oh no! NO! He *can't* be buried in a pauper's grave!'

'Don't worry, we'll all help out. I've got my sovereign and a few shillings, and I'll get Tom to put his hand in his pocket, and for the rest, well . . .'

'Will you ask herself?'

'I will, but only as a loan. We'll pay it back.'

244

'I wish I had some money, even just a few shillings. It makes it so much worse that I haven't even got a few coppers to help bury him.' Carmel broke down then and Maddy felt her own heart swell with pity. The girl had never got over him. She really *had* loved him, short though their courtship had been. She prayed that now her sister would at last let go.

It took a row with Tom to get him to part with some money. A row that was so bad, Mrs Buckley shouted down to know what was going on, and who or what was disturbing her afternoon nap!

'Now see what you've done, Tom Kiernan!' Maddy hissed furiously. Then: 'Wasn't I only after trying to get Tom to part with some money for a good cause,' she yelled back.

'And what, miss, is this "good cause"? Come up here and tell me, for I'll not be having servants screaming abuse at each other in my house!'

Maddy dismissed the irony of her mistress's objections to screaming and went quickly upstairs.

'And what was all that about?'

'My precious brother won't give a single penny to help bury a poor lad who was more or less engaged to Carmel,' Maddy fumed, pacing the carpet. 'The boy was crippled for life after going to teach a thing or two to a desperate family called the Spencers. Three of them had badly beaten Carmel out of pure jealousy.'

'Stand still, the carpet's almost threadbare as it is! What's all this about Carmel being engaged to a cripple?'

Maddy sat down opposite her mistress and told her the sad little story.

'Could the police do nothing? Isn't it that sort of thing we pay their wages to put a stop to? The whole family should be in prison, permanently!'

'No, ma'am, they'll do nothing to help. Everyone is afraid of that family.'

'That's anarchy and I'll write to the Mayor and demand that he rectify such conduct.'

'It won't do any good, ma'am, and anyway it's all over now.'

'How much does the woman need to bury her son?'

'About three pounds. I've got my sovereign, although I really wanted to keep it, but Tom says he can't help. *Won't*, more like. He could give ten shillings.'

'I'll pay,' Mrs Buckley said crisply. 'I know how I'd feel having to ask for money from my brothers.'

'Thank you, ma'am. It will be paid back. It's only a loan I was going to ask you for.'

'Indeed. If you insist.'

'I do, ma'am. Carmel blames herself, still.'

'Did she really love this boy? She's only a child.'

'I think she did, young as she is. I hope that now he's dead she'll be able to get over him.'

The old lady nodded slowly. Carmel was like a child in so many ways that it amazed her to think the girl could be capable of such strong emotions. 'Fetch my purse, Maddy.'

Maddy did as she was bid; she knew well where her mistress kept it.

The old lady opened it and took out three pound notes. 'I want you to keep that sovereign.'

'Thank you. I'll go round to the Shannahans' with it later on, this evening probably. I'm sorry we disturbed your nap.'

Mrs Buckley nodded mildly. 'That's quite all right, but don't do it again.'

Maddy replaced the purse and went back downstairs with the money.

'I've got three pounds,' she told Carmel. 'That should cover it all.'

'Oh Maddy, I don't know what I'd do without you. Thank you, it means so much to me.'

'I know it does. I'll take it down to Mary this evening.'

'Can I come with you?'

'No. It's best that you don't. She'll be very upset and she's bound to tell you it's your fault again.'

'But I'll *have* to go to the funeral. I just couldn't not turn up.'

'Very well, but not the burial. Church only.'

Carmel nodded slowly. She had no wish to see his poor body being lowered into the ground.

Maddy set out after supper; it was still quite light. The nights were slowly getting longer. She wasn't looking forward to her visit at all but she was better able to cope with it than Carmel.

Bernie Shannahan opened the door to her.

'Could I come in, please, Mr Shannahan? I have something for your wife.'

He looked old and tired, she thought, as she went into the room. Mary and a couple of neighbours were sitting by a small fire.

'Could I see you privately, please,' she asked Mary. 'Just for a few moments.'

Mary got up and the neighbours excused themselves.

'We got your note and I've brought you this to give him a decent burial.' She took out her purse and then handed the three notes over to the woman.

'We'll pay it back. Every penny,' Mary Shannahan said, stiff with pride.

'No, there's no need. We have it, you don't, and besides – it's what Carmel wants.'

Mary sniffed. 'It's the least she can do. It's all her fault.'

'It's not. You can't blame her if your son fell in love with her. She's very upset. She loved John and she's told me that she'll never love anyone else, and I believe her. So, please take it. Will you send word about the funeral? We'll both attend.'

'I will and . . . it's good of you to pay.' The words were very difficult to say but Mary Shannahan managed to do it.

'Good night then, and I'm so very sorry for your trouble. John was a fine boy. At least he's out of all pain now.' With that, Maddy left, thankful when she was out on the street again. It hadn't been too bad. Far better than she'd anticipated. It was a long walk to Faulkner Square and the weather had suddenly turned cold and blustery. She'd walk to the main road and try to catch a tram, she decided. There was a short cut she knew of from when they'd lived in this area.

That should shorten the journey a little. She just wanted to get back now.

She was walking with her head down, thinking about what she was going to say to Carmel, so at first she didn't realise she was being followed. All of a sudden she became aware of it and she turned around quickly.

'Who's there? What do you want? I haven't got any money,' she called loudly in the voice she used when answering her mistress.

There was no reply and she resumed her journey. What came next happened so quickly that it all seemed a blur. She was grabbed from behind, and she screamed before a strong hand across her throat abruptly cut off the sound. She thought she was being choked and began to kick out wildly.

'Watch 'er legs, the little bitch.'

She managed to bite the hand that was now covering her mouth and began to scream again, loudly.

'Shut 'er up! Fer Christ's sake, shut 'er up!' another voice demanded. Maddy renewed her struggles, but she was no match for her attackers. She was being painfully forced to her knees by the grip on her hair, but still she managed to cry for help.

Suddenly the sound of running feet was heard.

'Oh Christ! It's the bleedin' Peelers!' said one of the men.

She was released and she slumped down on the cobbles, shaking with terror and shock. As the figure came closer, she looked up. It wasn't a policeman. She cried out and tried to get up.

'Here, let me help you. Have they hurt you?'

Maddy looked at the outstretched hand and then into the face of a young man who must have been at least six feet tall. He was well built and had very blue eyes and brown hair that curled over his collar, and his face was weatherbeaten. He looked friendly enough, she thought with relief, stretching out her hand.

She was gently pulled to her feet.

'Are you hurt?' he repeated.

'No, just shaken, but I . . . I would have been if you hadn't come along.'

'What's a girl like you doing around here?'

'I used to live in Gillings Entry. I'd been to see a neighbour who'd had a death in the family, and was on my way home.'

'Where do you live now?'

'In Faulkner Square, I'm in service there. What's your name?'

'Martin Brennan. And yours?'

'Maddy Kiernan,'

He smiled. 'Short for Madelaine?'

'No, Magdalene.'

'Well, Maddy Kiernan, I'm seeing you back to Faulkner Square.'

'Oh no, please! I can manage, I'm perfectly all right now,' she protested.

'You are far from all right. You've had a shock and we are still in this neighbourhood. How did you get here?'

'By tram.'

'Then we'll go back by tram. Don't worry, I'm not going to hurt you.'

'Thanks. I suppose I *am* feeling a bit shaken.'

On the journey, Martin told her he was a seaman but not just an ordinary seaman; he'd been studying and had just become a Bosun. It was his ambition to become a Captain one day. She told him of their decision to leave Ireland, life in Gillings Entry and Grayson Street, and finally Faulkner Square.

When they reached the old coach-house she turned to him.

'We've arrived. This is the back way in. I'll be quite safe now.'

'I want to see you go through the door, it's almost pitch dark in here.'

'Really, there's no need.'

'Maddy Kiernan, are you always this stubborn?'

She laughed. 'I hope not.'

'Then will you do as you're told.'

'I will so, just to keep you quiet, Mr Brennan.' She emphasised the 'Mister'.

When they reached the back door, she turned towards him again. 'Would you like to come in for a few minutes?' She felt awkward and shy, something she had never felt before.

'I assume there will be other people in there? I'd hate to be accused of taking advantage.'

'You assume right. There's my sister Carmel, my sister-in-law Johanna and my brother Tom. Oh, and young Freddy – he's the "boots",' she answered, opening the door.

Freddy was the only one who was absent and as all eyes

were turned towards her, Maddy felt the colour rush to her cheeks.

'This is Martin Brennan. I was attacked on the way back and he came to help me.'

'Oh Maddy, are you hurt?' Johanna asked, getting up.

'No, just a few scratches, thank goodness. I was terrified, I'm still shaking.'

'Carmel, put that kettle on and make some sweet tea. Mr Brennan, will you have a cup too?' Johanna asked.

'That's very kind of you, Mrs Kiernan, but I'd better get back to my ship.'

'You're a seaman?' Tom probed. None too politely, still smarting from the fact that Maddy had told the old lady about the row and she was sure to make some sarcastic remark.

'I am. I'm a Bosun.'

'Aren't you a bit young?' Tom was sceptical. Usually it took years before the mast to get to that position.

'I suppose I am, but I made my first trip when I was barely fourteen and I've worked and studied hard. One day I aim to be Master of my own ship. The sea is my life,' Martin replied.

Tom said nothing. He didn't like the look of Martin Brennan. He was everything he himself was not. He obviously had a very good position, with a title, and if he had all the experience he claimed to have he was already halfway up the ladder to success. Tom himself had barely got a toe-hold on it.

In turn Martin scrutinised the other man. He hoped he was a good judge of character and it was seldom he took an instant dislike to anyone, but he didn't like Tom Kiernan. What in Maddy was guts and spirit, in her brother was arrogance.

Maddy thanked him again and led him to the door.

'Can I see you again?' he asked in a low voice.

She looked up at him in surprise. 'But your ship?'

'We don't sail for another five days. We've only just returned home after three months away.'

'Oh, I see.' Again she felt shy and she was blushing. Stop it, you eejit, she said to herself.

'Would you like to go to a Music Hall?'

'I've never been to one.'

'Well, there's singers, dancers, men who do card tricks and all kinds of entertainments.'

'I'd like that.'

'Then we'll go tomorrow evening, if that's all right with you?'

Maddy nodded.

'I'll call for you at a quarter to seven.'

'That'll be grand and thank you again.'

'I was glad to be of help. Good night, Maddy.'

'Good night . . . Martin.'

'He's nice. I liked him,' Carmel said when he'd gone.

'So did I. Maddy, were you really terrified? Are you all right?' Johanna was concerned.

'Truly, I'm not hurt but I *was* scared stiff. There were two of them, you see.' She shuddered.

'Let me take a look at those scratches and then you must have an early night to get over the shock,' Johanna fussed.

'What was all the whispering at the door? Did he ask to see you again?'

'Yes, he did, Carmel. He's taking me to the Music Hall tomorrow.'

'Will you tell madam upstairs?' Tom asked.

'I haven't made up my mind about that. It's all a bit sudden.'

'It certainly is. We don't know what he's really like,' Tom said disparagingly.

'He's only taking me for an evening's entertainment, and he did save me from God knows what.'

'She's right, Tom. He can't be a bad person, otherwise he'd have just left her to her fate. Some men would have been scared to tackle two other fellows,' Johanna stated.

'Well, he seems to me to be too sure of himself, altogether,' Tom said sourly. 'A bit of a chancer, all that talk about him being a Captain.'

Maddy glared at her brother. What Tom really meant was that Martin Brennan's ambitions would become reality in time – while his own did not stand a chance.

Chapter Eighteen

'What will you wear?' Carmel asked, sitting on Maddy's bed. She hoped Martin Brennan was someone special. Maddy deserved to be happy and loved. She herself had begun to love someone and then had lost them, and she never wanted her sister to go through the pain and heartache she had endured. Maddy had told her that Mary Shannahan would let them know the day of the funeral, and she hoped the woman would keep her promise.

'The grey, white and red check dress Johanna made for me. I've got my black jacket and good boots and my grey bonnet.'

'Don't you think it could do with brightening up a bit? It's nice, but it's very . . .'

'Dull?'

'It is not, and I didn't mean that at all.'

'You're right. It's great for going to church, but not much else.'

'I'll lend you my red jacket that Johanna made. Will you tell herself you're going?'

255

'No. I might never see him again.'

'Do you think you'll *want* to see him again?'

'I don't know. From first impressions he seems nice and he did help me, but he'd do that for any woman in trouble.'

'True for you. What exactly is a Bosun?'

'I've no idea and I don't intend to spend the evening learning. I'm going out to enjoy myself.'

'What if herself asks for you? You always read to her and I just *couldn't*. She still frightens me.'

'Johanna will do it; you know she's done it for me once or twice before when I had that heavy cold and herself wouldn't let me near her for fear of catching it.' Maddy glanced in the mirror. Carmel's red jacket *would* look nice, it would set her dark hair off really well. She wished she had a pair of silver earrings, they would have looked very smart. Still she was grateful for what she did have. Things could have been very different, she knew that.

Maddy was ready and waiting half an hour before Martin was due to call for her. Johanna said how well Carmel's jacket looked over the dress and hoped she had a good evening.

'You never go out, Maddy, you deserve some fun,' Johanna said.

'It depends on what that feller classes as fun,' Tom said disparagingly.

Maddy glared at him. 'That's nice, trying to spoil my evening. Well, you won't, Tom Kiernan.'

'If you stare at that clock any longer the hands will fall off,' Carmel teased her.

'Well, wasn't it yourself who said to get ready early?'

'I thought you'd take longer.'

'Stop bickering,' Johanna laughed as there was a loud knock on the kitchen door.

'Go on,' Carmel urged.

Maddy opened the door and smiled up at Martin. He was wearing a frockcoat, straight-legged trousers, a gleaming white shirt and grey silk cravat. In his hand, he carried his black silk top hat.

'I thought you might have some special uniform,' Maddy said shyly.

He grinned. 'Are you disappointed?'

'No. Not at all.'

'I do have a uniform but it's not very comfortable.'

Martin stepped into the kitchen and wished everyone a good evening.

Carmel and Johanna were stunned into silence; the visitor looked every inch a gentleman of means. Tom felt the bile rise in his throat. The man was done up like a bloody toff and they were only going to a Music Hall. Jealousy gnawed at him.

'You look lovely,' Martin said as he opened the yard door for Maddy.

'Thank you. You look very well yourself. Where are we going?'

'To the Olympia Theatre. It's one of the better ones and we'll have good seats.'

'I really am looking forward to it. I've never been to one before.'

'Then prepare to be entertained,' he laughed.

It really was a very nice place, Maddy thought, looking around at the red plush seats, the gold and red décor and the real velvet curtains. He'd bought her a box of pastilles and a box of chocolates which she determined to save for Carmel and Johanna.

Martin watched her face as the entertainment started. She looked amazed, excited and nervous all at the same time. He smiled to himself. She was beautiful, and from the minute he'd helped her to her feet last night he hadn't stopped thinking about her. When she'd opened the door to him tonight, something had fallen into place for him. He knew he loved her.

After it had all finished she was pink-cheeked and bright-eyed and had lost her initial reserve with him.

She clutched his arm and smiled up at him. 'Oh Martin, wasn't it just grand! I've never enjoyed myself so much – and it was so funny when those people started to throw things.'

He laughed. 'You should see the carry-on in some places. They throw eggs, rotten fruit, anything.'

'Really?'

'Yes, really, Miss Kiernan. I'm glad you enjoyed it. I'm also very glad you agreed to come out.' He took her hand and pulled it through his arm.

'I am too, Martin.'

'I thought we could go for some supper?'

'I don't think I could eat a thing, but thank you.'

'Then I'll get you home safe and sound.' He hailed a passing hansom cab.

'For me? A cab for me? Isn't it cheaper to get a tram? You've already spent so much on me.'

'Nothing is too good for you, Maddy. Anyway, I spend months in the most uncomfortable means of transport, so that when I come ashore I always get about by cab.'

She didn't speak much during the journey but he held her hand. She liked him. She liked him a lot, but she'd only just met him and he'd said that the sea was his life and he was away for months at a time.

'How long will you be away next time?' she asked as they walked to the coach-house.

'Two months, approximately. It depends on the weather.'

'Will it be bad?'

'It can be, but at this time of year we're more likely to be becalmed. That can drive you mad. Nothing to do until the breeze picks up. It makes the men restless.'

'I see,' she said in a small voice.

'Maddy, would you come out with me tomorrow and the day after and every night until I sail?'

'Do you really want me to?'

'I wouldn't have said it unless I meant it. I never play games with people's emotions if I can help it.'

'Yes, yes, I'd like that. I . . . I do . . . like you, Martin.'

He took her hand and pressed it to his lips and she felt giddy and faint.

'Oh Maddy, I hardly know you but I've never felt like this before.'

She raised her head and moved closer to him. In seconds she was in his arms and the faint feeling got stronger as she clung to him. She didn't know what love was, but she was sure that this was it.

'I love you, Maddy,' he whispered into her ear and she held him tightly.

'Oh Martin, I think I love you, too. I don't know how you can tell but I've never felt like this before either.'

'Will you wait for me, Maddy? I know it's not fair, I have no right to ask you, but . . .'

'I'll wait for ever, Martin. I mean it. Oh, hold me tightly, I want to stay here all night.'

He did hold her but it couldn't be all night.

'I'll see you safely in and I'll come for you tomorrow night.'

'Yes, yes, please,' she answered shyly.

'You'll have to tell her if you're going to be out with him every night,' Carmel pronounced after Maddy had told her everything. Maddy had crept into her sister's bedroom and they were having a heart-to-heart talk. Maddy and Martin had just spent their second evening together.

'I know, and I'm afraid she'll get upset.'

'Why so?'

'Because I usually spend that time with her.'

Carmel nodded thoughtfully. 'Do you think she'll be jealous?'

'I don't know, but there's only one way to find out. I'll tell her in the morning.'

Later, she lay awake remembering everything Martin had said to her and trying to think of the best way to tell Mrs Buckley.

After a night when she'd tossed and turned, she'd more or less decided what she'd say.

'Maddy, don't forget to tell herself that the sweep is coming this morning and there'll be no fires in the house until he's been. She'll have to have a cold collation for her lunch,' Johanna called as Maddy picked up the old lady's breakfast tray.

As usual her mistress was awake and sitting up in bed.

Maddy drew back the curtains and the spring sunlight streamed in.

'It's a lovely morning. Did you sleep well?'

'I did not.'

Oh God, she was in one of her contrary moods, Maddy thought. 'Perhaps you can have a doze after your breakfast.'

'I'll not be accused of lying in my bed all day.'

'Well, it's your choice. Johanna told me to inform you that the sweep is due this morning so there'll be no fires.'

'Then I might as well stay in bed. I'd freeze without a fire.'

'She also said there will be a cold collation for lunch.'

Suddenly the old lady's temper erupted and she hurled the sugar basin across the room. 'When I want a cold collation I'll ask for it!' she screeched.

Oh, God! Why today? Maddy asked herself.

'Well, isn't that a fine way to be carrying on, ma'am. Just look at this mess and the sugar bowl has a dent in it!'

'Don't lecture me, Maddy Kiernan. I can put as many dents in the silverware as I like.' Maud Buckley lay back, exhausted. Her temper tantrum was over.

Maddy picked up the bowl. Thank God it contained sugar lumps and not the loose variety. Telling her about Martin wasn't going to be easy with the mood she was in. She tried another approach.

'Is there something that's troubling you, ma'am? You're not eating very much, or so Johanna says.'

'I'm old and useless, that's what's troubling me.'

'Oh ma'am, you're not useless,' Maddy said in a conciliatory tone.

'Where have you been for the last two evenings?'

Maddy hated lying. 'I've had a cold.'

'You don't look well. You look feverish,' the old lady replied, her mood changing.

'I didn't sleep very well last night. There's something I have to tell you.'

'What?'

'The night I took the money to Mrs Shannahan I was attacked but a young man came to help me.'

'I *told* you to get a cab there!'

'I know, but I didn't. Anyway, he's asked me to go out with him tonight.'

'And what does this Sir Galahad do for a living?'

'He's a Bosun, ma'am. His name is Martin Brennan.'

'For which shipping line does he work?'

'I've no idea, I didn't ask him but I'm sure it isn't yours, ma'am.'

'How old is he?'

'I don't know.'

'You certainly didn't find out much, did you?'

'I never thought to ask questions like that. I was very shaken.'

'Why didn't you tell me?'

'I didn't want to worry you and I wasn't hurt.'

'And when does he sail?'

'In three days, ma'am.'

'And you want time to go out?'

There was something in her tone that made Maddy uneasy.

'Well go then, don't worry about me, I'm sure I'll manage. Of course I may very well have succumbed to pneumonia by then or maybe I'll be so fortunate they'll have lit a fire by then.'

'Thank you, ma'am.' Maddy got up and walked to the door.

'Maddy, don't tell me any more lies about fictitious colds.'

Maddy turned. 'Oh ma'am, I'm sorry. I hate lying but . . .'

'Oh, get out of here and let me have my breakfast in peace.'

'Did you tell her?' Carmel asked, when Maddy arrived, breathless with nerves, downstairs.

'Yes, but she's in one of her moods. She threw the sugar basin across the room.'

'Glory be to God! I've never known anyone to have a temper like her. And her mood changes so quickly,' Johanna said.

'Neither have I, but I told her off. Carmel, you'll have to go up and clear it all away, after she's dressed,' Maddy added, seeing the look of consternation in her sister's eyes.

'I don't think it's just her temper. I think she's not feeling very well, but you know what she's like. She's complaining about the sweep too.'

'Well, I can't do anything about that,' Johanna said with resignation. 'The chimneys have to be swept and as she doesn't go anywhere, like the rest of us she'll have to put up with it.'

By the end of the week Maddy knew that she had fallen for Martin Brennan and that she didn't want him to go away.

'I know how you feel, Maddy, but I have to go. It's how I earn my living.'

'I know it is, it's just that it's so long and everything is so new to me.'

'Will you write to me?'

'Yes. I'll write every single day, but how will you get the letters though?'

'From the Shipping Agents. All mail is forwarded to them. Your letters might take a while to reach me though and I'll have to wait until we reach port before I can post mine, but don't get upset if you don't hear from me. You know I love you and when I get back we'll be able to see more of each other and talk.'

She clung to him, wanting to stay in the yard all night. She never wanted to let go of him. His was a dangerous occupation at times and she'd be worried about him until he got home safely.

'Are you all right?' Carmel asked, when Maddy finally let herself into the kitchen.

'Yes, I suppose so. It's going to be a long, long time before I see Martin again, but I'll write to him and he's promised to write to me.'

'And pigs might fly,' Tom jeered. 'Once he's past the Bar Lightship he'll have forgotten all about you. There's plenty of girls when they reach port who'll be very free with their favours for a man like him.'

Maddy glared at her brother.

'Oh Tom, that's not a very nice thing to say,' Johanna rebuked.

'By the way, herself said for you to go up when you came in. She wants to talk to you,' Carmel interrupted.

'At this time of night?' Maddy was surprised and a little uneasy. 'Can't it wait until morning?'

'No, she was most insistent.'

'And she's another one who won't be sorry he's gone,' Tom muttered to himself.

The old lady was propped up in her bed by a mound of pillows and looked to be dozing.

'Ma'am, you wanted to see me?' Maddy said quietly.

Mrs Buckley opened her eyes. 'I do. Sit down beside me.'

Maddy did as she was bid.

'I have made up my mind about an important matter.'

'What important matter?'

'I am going to change my will. I am going to leave everything to you, Maddy. My brothers want me dead so they can finally get their hands on the money.' She smiled sardonically. 'I'd love to see their faces when they find out there's nothing for them, no matter how much they create and contest it. It is *my* Will and will be legally drawn up and signed. But there is one condition, dear.'

Maddy was still staring at her with complete shock.

'Ma'am, you can't do that! You can't leave everything to me! I'm only a servant – we all are. They're *family*, ma'am!'

'I know. But I hold the same views as your mother about servants, friends and relations, and as I said, there is a condition.'

Maddy was still stunned. 'What?'

'That you don't marry for ten years or until I'm dead, whichever is the sooner. Me or him? That's what you have to decide.'

Maddy could find no words.

'Think about it,' Maud Buckley urged her. 'Financial comfort and security for all your family or those you choose to help – or marriage. You've only known this man a few days. He's a seaman, there will be long absences, worries over storms, your children to bring up almost alone or to be orphaned. Will he be faithful while he's away, or will he have a girl in every port?'

'I love him,' Maddy said firmly.

'I don't doubt it and I hope he is worthy of it, but you

must decide. Those are my conditions. Go to your bed now.
You must be tired. I am.'

Maddy walked to the door in a daze. She'd get no sleep
tonight or for many nights to come. It was going to be the
hardest decision she would ever have to make.

Chapter Nineteen

After Mrs Buckley's ultimatum, Maddy didn't go back to the kitchen but went up and sat on her bed, staring blankly at the walls. Her mind was racing. Oh God, what was she to do? Like her sister before her, she had fallen in love quickly, but deeply, and for ever. She loved Martin with all her heart and wanted to spend the rest of her life with him, if he asked her to. But what about her mistress?

Mrs Buckley had been more than kind to her and Maddy was very fond of the cantankerous old lady. And then there was the offer of the money and the house and the business. Wealth beyond her wildest dreams. It would provide lifelong security for Carmel and for Johanna and baby Ronan. Only the thought of including Tom in this bounty caused his sister a moment's reservation. But she could pay for Johanna's son to have the finest education money could buy. That would set him up for life, as it would any future children Johanna might have. As for her sister . . . In beautiful clothes and with expensive jewellery, Carmel would be a rare catch.

Half of the eligible young men in the city would beat a path to her door and in that crowd there would be someone special for Carmel. Someone who would love her and cherish her fragile health and beauty, protect her from the brutal realities of life and mend her broken heart.

But what about herself? Maddy covered her face with her hands. She wanted to marry Martin and have children of her own – was that too much to ask? They would manage; he had a good position. Ten years was such a long, long time to wait. She would be thirty-one at least before having her first child. But then again it could be less; her mistress was getting very frail. Martin wanted to be a Captain one day and Mrs Buckley had two ships; he could achieve his ambition if he was willing to wait for her. But would he mind her part in helping him to achieve his dream? He might have too much pride to accept all she offered.

Shaking her head, she got up and began to undress. Perhaps sleeping on it would help, though she doubted that there would be many peaceful hours.

Maddy tossed and turned, her mind in a turmoil that wouldn't be stilled, until at last she sat up. This was useless. A mug of warm milk might help. She shrugged on her dressing gown, opened the door quietly so as not to disturb the rest of the household, then tiptoed down the back stairs. A chink of light showed beneath the kitchen door and she wondered who was up. Just don't let it be Tom, she prayed. Her prayer was answered; it was Johanna who was sitting in a chair by the fire, a mug clasped between her hands.

'Maddy, what's the matter?' her sister-in-law asked.

'Oh, I couldn't sleep.'

'Thinking about Martin?' Johanna smiled.

'Yes, and . . . other things.'

'The milk is still warm in the pan, will I get you a mug?'

'That would be great. Couldn't you sleep either?'

'No,' Johanna answered, pouring the milk into another mug.

'Why so? Are you worried about anything?'

'Not really worried.'

'Then what?'

Johanna pulled her chair a little closer to the dying fire. 'I'm almost certain that I'm going to have another baby. I haven't told Tom yet because—'

'Because what?' Maddy demanded.

'Because he's desperate about his ambition to be someone one day. It's becoming an obsession. He saves every penny he can and another child would mean more expense.'

'Oh Jo, he's not that bad, surely, not wanting to have any more children just because they would cost money? He wants for nothing in this house.'

'I know that and I wish he could just be content with what he has got, and there is a lot. This is a very comfortable house. We have soft beds and a proper bathroom – there's no stinking shared privy. We eat plenty of good food, and we're never cold in winter. But he still wants more – and sometimes I worry what we will do when Mrs Buckley dies. We could all be flung out, her brothers would inherit everything and I suppose they'll sell this house. If Tom wasn't so ambitious with what savings we have, we could

271

manage well and now we have experience, we could get another position in a big household.'

Although her sister-in-law's last words should have been comforting, they only increased Maddy's indecision. It was true – the young couple might well be flung out, and with two young children and no proper references it wouldn't be as easy as Johanna said to get other positions. Why did Tom insist on being so bloody stubborn and greedy? Did he never think back to their days in Ireland when they had had very little, and more recently to the hardships he'd suffered in Liverpool? His dream to be part-owner of a ship was one he seemed prepared to sacrifice his family for, but if she didn't marry Martin he would have his dream and more besides. She would seriously curb his excesses, for she would have a firm grip on the finances, but it would benefit Johanna and the children too if he gained the role and standing in society to which he'd aspired for so long. Maddy sighed deeply. All she could see ahead of her were years of fights and arguments with him if she chose that road. He was ungrateful to his very core.

'Well, I think it's wonderful you're having a brother or a sister for Ronan.'

Johanna stared at her hard. 'Maddy, what's wrong? You look so pale and sort of distraught.'

'I am. Oh Johanna, I am!'

'What is it? The old lady? I wondered why you didn't come back downstairs.'

Maddy nodded.

'Has she upset you? She's been in a temper all day. Let's

hope with the warmer weather to come it will ease her rheumatics and we'll all get some relief.'

'She hasn't really upset me. Oh Johanna, I wish I'd never come home tonight. I wish I could have sailed away with Martin – to the ends of the earth if necessary.'

'Did she want to ask about him? Sometimes I almost think she's jealous of you. You're young, with your life ahead of you, while she . . .'

'Sometimes it's hard to fathom her,' Maddy interrupted. Oh, she was so heartsore and confused, she *had* to tell someone.

'She called me up tonight for a very good reason.'

'The "Important Decision"?'

'Yes. She's given me a choice, Jo. She will leave everything to me if I promise not to get married for ten years or before she dies.'

Johanna's eyes widened. 'You mean . . . you mean . . .' she stuttered.

'Yes. She'll leave me the money, the house, the ships – on condition that *I don't marry Martin*. Oh Johanna! What am I going to do? I can give everyone a real chance of a good future. We'll all have the kind of life beyond our wildest dreams, Tom included.'

'But what about Martin?' Johanna pressed.

Maddy swallowed hard. 'If he asks me to marry him I . . . I'll have to ask him to wait and it's a long, long time. I'll be nearly thirty-one. By then I might not be able to have any children, but I could offer him the ships.'

'Oh, Maddy, what a thing to do to you! Isn't she a

273

tormenting demon of a woman? Why did she do it?'

'I don't know – I didn't ask her. I was too shocked, but as I said, you can't fathom her.'

Johanna got up and put her arms around Maddy.

'It has to be jealousy or fear of being left alone. Don't think of us. Don't go putting our security before your own chance of love in this life. We'll manage, we *will*. We've learned so many things since we've been here, and we've got savings. You can't sacrifice your life, Maddy.'

'She might not live for all that time.'

'No, she might not but she's that contrary she could cling on. Maddy, you can't do it and it's not fair of either her upstairs or us to expect you to.'

'I'm so confused, Jo. I want everyone to be happy.'

'And for that you'd miss out on your own happiness with Martin?'

'Oh, everything has been going round and round in my head. It makes me feel dizzy!'

'Then just try and put it all out of your mind and get some sleep.'

'I wish I could.'

'You can, Maddy. Just think about something else.'

'Like what?'

'Well, I don't want to add to your worries but I'm sure that tomorrow we'll get word about poor John Shannahan's funeral.'

'I'd forgotten about that. Carmel will be so upset.'

'She will, and she'll need your support. Now go to bed and try to sleep.'

Maddy got up, kissed Johanna on the cheek and went back upstairs. She lay staring up at the ceiling. Now that Johanna was pregnant again it had added to her indecision. Her worries over Carmel had also increased. No amount of money could bring John back, but it could compensate in other ways. Mrs Buckley would want an answer soon. Maddy had only what was left of the night to make up her mind.

As she went into the kitchen next morning, Maddy looked pale and tired.

'I can see by just looking at you that you had no sleep at all last night,' Johanna remarked, looking a bit pale herself. This morning she had been sick for the first time and knew she had to tell Tom soon.

'I didn't, but I've made up my mind.'

'What are you two talking about?' Carmel asked, concerned that both women looked so strained.

'We'll tell you later on, maybe after tea. Is her tray ready?' Maddy asked.

'You're going to promise, aren't you?' Johanna said emotionally.

Maddy nodded and picked up the tray, wanting to get out of the room before Carmel could ask any more questions.

'You look dreadful,' Mrs Buckley said as soon as Maddy had placed the tray on the bed and opened the curtains.

'And so would anyone if they'd not had a wink of sleep all night.'

The old lady seemed satisfied. 'Then you've given the matter a lot of thought?'

Maddy felt the tears pricking her eyes and she swallowed hard. She *wouldn't* think of Martin.

'I have, and you'll be glad to know, ma'am, that I will make the promise not to get married for ten years, or until . . .'

'You're a wise girl and I'm glad of it. I will write to Mr Hatfield, my solicitor, today and ask him to visit me as soon as possible. What made you decide? I'm sure it had nothing to do with my precious brothers being passed over and their noses put out of joint?'

'My family – Carmel, Johanna, Ronan and the baby that's on the way.'

'Another little Kiernan, and so soon? Well, I'm glad for her. You didn't mention your brother in that list.'

Maddy's expression became grim. 'Oh, I'll keep a tight rein on things where *he's* concerned.'

'Good.' She picked up her cup of tea and took a sip. 'How old will you be, Maddy, in ten years' time?'

'Thirty-one, ma'am.'

'You'll still be a slip of a thing. Isn't all this worth the wait?' The old lady made a sweeping gesture with her thin, gnarled hands. 'You're a fine girl, Maddy,' she went on. 'Sensible, loyal, selfless, compassionate. Your parents would be pleased and proud of you.'

'Thank you, ma'am, but . . .'

'But what?'

'But I will have missed spending all those years with Martin.'

'If he's honourable and if he truly loves you, he won't mind the wait.'

Maddy could only nod as she left the room.

'What did she say?' Johanna asked as soon as Maddy entered the kitchen, very near to tears.

'She was very happy about my decision.'

'She would be! Selfish old woman!' Johanna raged.

'What decision?' Tom demanded. It was seldom that his wife spoke so forcefully.

Tom was about to start questioning her when Freddy came rushing in.

'It's a letter for you, Maddy.'

'It can't be from Martin, he's only just sailed,' Carmel said, looking confused.

Maddy took the letter from him. It was from Father Molloy. 'John is to be buried tomorrow at ten o'clock, Father Molloy says.' She saw Carmel's eyes fill with tears and went and put her arms around her. 'I know it will be upsetting, but I'll be with you and he wouldn't want you to go on being miserable, would he?'

Carmel shook her head.

'You'd better tell herself about it,' Tom said tersely.

'I will. She won't mind us being gone for an hour in the morning – we're only going to the church,' Maddy replied, more in control of herself now.

'Well, you'd better find her something to wear,' he said moodily. 'She can't go showing us all up by wearing that red jacket thing she wears to Mass every week.'

'She can borrow my black cape,' Johanna said, frowning

at her husband's lack of tact and sensitivity, but heading off an argument. Today she felt too sick to have a row on her hands.

Everyone seemed subdued all day, a fact Freddy remarked upon cheekily, getting a clip around the ear from Tom for his pains. Maddy was tired and preoccupied, Carmel was upset, Johanna felt ill and Tom was trying to work out what his wife and his sister had been talking about.

That night when Maddy had finished reading to her mistress she just put her head around the kitchen door and announced her intention of going to bed.

'At this hour?' Tom demanded.

'I didn't get much sleep last night.'

'I'll go up too. It's going to be a desperate day tomorrow,' Carmel added tearfully.

Tom turned to his wife. 'And I suppose there's some reason for you to go up as well?'

Johanna shook her head. 'No, there isn't. In fact, I have something I want to talk about with you.'

Maddy managed a smile, to try to give her sister-in-law support.

'So, what is this big secret? What's going on with Maddy and herself and "decisions"?'

Johanna sighed. Maddy's promise had made things easy for her, but at what cost? All day she'd prayed that Martin would wait until Maddy was free of that accursed promise.

'Herself upstairs gave Maddy a choice last night. If Maddy agreed not to get married for ten years, or until the mistress dies, whichever is first, then she'd leave everything, *everything* to Maddy, not to her brothers. Money, house, business – the lot.'

The colour heightened in Tom's face and there was disbelief in his eyes. 'Jesus Christ Almighty! Are you sure?'

'Of course I'm sure. Wasn't I down here last night with her. She was nearly demented. It was a terrible, terrible state to put anyone in. The mischievous old madam!'

It was sinking in slowly that Maddy had the chance to be an heiress. 'What did she say? What answer did she give?' He was all eagerness now.

'She promised. She put us all before her own happiness.'

Tom was relieved. He gave no thought to his sister's sacrifice.

'She can afford to wait, and if he's got any bloody sense in his head, Martin Brennan will wait for her.'

Johanna nodded. 'There's something else.'

'What?'

'I . . . we're going to have another baby.'

'Another one!'

'Yes. Is that all you can say? We can well afford another one, Maddy's seen to that. In fact, since Maddy fell on her feet here, she has always looked out for us. It's thanks to her we have a roof over our head and food in our bellies. She got us our jobs here as well, remember.'

'Of course I'm pleased about the baby.' Tom changed his tone quickly.

'You don't seem it.'

'You've just told me two shattering pieces of news. It's hard to take it all in.'

'Well, I'll leave you to think about it then. I'm tired too.'

'Go on up then, get some rest. With those two going to that funeral there'll be more work for you in the morning.'

When his wife had gone, Tom stood up and walked back and forth across the kitchen floor. They'd be wealthy, really wealthy. This house alone must be worth hundreds of pounds, and the stuff in it was all expensive and old. The old lady undoubtedly had money, too – large sums of it, probably, and most of all, there was the business. There was, of course, Martin Brennan to consider, but he'd have himself well established by the time the ten years were up and besides, Brennan might have lost interest by then. Although he'd worked his way up to Bosun, he just might not be patient or greedy enough to wait. He could even find someone else and abandon Maddy.

Tom's excitement grew. He would become a rich and respected man. He'd move in different, more exalted circles, but it would be all Maddy's doing – and that was the fly in the ointment. If it had been Carmel, he'd have had no trouble persuading *her* to give him a free hand, but Maddy was different entirely. She would want to know everything and approve of everything. Still, it was more than he'd ever dreamed of, and just to be on the safe side he'd find a way of getting some extra funds that no one else would know about.

The old lady kept far too much money in the house. He went to the bank for her once a month to cash a cheque. It would be a simple matter to add ten pounds to the amount: he would simply alter her cheques. No one would question it. He would give some excuse – he was trusted at the bank and the old lady would never know. Twenty pounds a month would really increase his 'ship money' as he called it. The future looked rosy indeed. He wouldn't stop at the two ships, he decided. They'd own three and then four; trade was good, the Port of Liverpool was booming. Oh, he had plenty to be happy about. And another child, maybe a girl this time, as beautiful as his mother had been, and he would be able to give her the world.

Oh, he was indeed a happy man this night.

Despite a blue sky and spring sunshine, it was blustery next morning when Maddy and Carmel set out for the church. Maddy could see by her sister's reddened eyes that she had already been crying, probably for half of the night.

'Are you certain you want to go?' she'd asked Carmel before they put on jackets and bonnets.

'Yes. I know it will be awful, but I can bear it,' Carmel had answered with a catch in her voice.

Johanna had kissed them both and had pushed something into Maddy's hand.

'It may help Mrs Shannahan a bit. I asked Tom and he gave it to me.'

Once outside, Maddy had looked at the crumpled-up paper. It was a five-pound note. So something good had come out of her promise already. Obviously Johanna had told him last night. Maddy smiled wryly. It was the promise of a fortune that had made her tight-fisted brother so generous this morning.

There were very few people in the church and the sisters sat near the back. Neither of them wanted to be close to the bereaved family, who all filed in, dressed as best they could in mourning clothes. Mrs Shannahan wore a long black veil that completely hid her face and a black coat, obviously borrowed. Bernie Shannahan had a dark coloured jacket, on the sleeve of which a black mourning band had been sewn, moleskin trousers, a white shirt – also borrowed – and a flat, workman's cap. John's parents followed the coffin, clinging tightly to each other. At least the coffin was of a decent wood with brass handles and crucifix; a single wreath lay on its top. Maddy was so glad to have been able to make sure that the lad had a decent funeral. Both his parents looked old and bowed down with anguish.

Carmel was fighting hard to keep herself from sobbing out loud. The sight of the coffin and the flowers tore at her heart. He was dead because of her. She wished he had never set eyes on her, never loved her. At least he'd be alive and whole, not the weak, pathetic cripple she'd made him. She could picture him when they had first met. Young, handsome, strong and smiling. She would always remember his smile. She would always remember him the way he was. She would never forget him.

As the priest began the prayers for the dead, Carmel couldn't help herself and broke down completely. Maddy put an arm around her. 'Hush. Hush, acoushla, he's at peace now and he wouldn't want you to get into this state.'

'I . . . I know that, but I keep thinking, Oh, I wish it had been me the Spencers had killed, not him. It was *my* fault, Maddy.'

'It wasn't. It just happened. And perhaps that's the way things were meant to happen. Only the good die young, Carmel, and he *was* good. Always try to remember that, for his sake.'

'I'll never, ever forget him, Maddy.'

'I know you won't, but hush now, Mass is starting.'

They both went to Communion and as Carmel passed the coffin, she bent and kissed it. Then she walked on with Maddy's arm to cling to for comfort. She didn't glance in the direction of John's parents, she couldn't, but the priest laid his hand gently on her head after he'd given her the Host.

'It's nearly over now, Carmel. Soon we will go home,' Maddy whispered as she led her sister back to their seats.

Outside the wind had dropped and the spring sunshine was warm. Maddy left Carmel on the church steps and went quickly over to the Shannahans.

'Mrs Shannahan . . . Mary . . . nothing can bring him back and Carmel is devastated as you can see. She says she will always love John, that she'll never forget him and I believe her. It might help in some way for you to know that. This may also help a little. God bless and comfort you both.' She pressed the money into Bernie's hand and turned away.

'Maddy, wait, please.'

She turned around.

'Were the flowers from you?' Mary asked.

'They were. From both of us. I'm taking her home now, she's in a terrible state.'

'You're a good girl, Maddy Kiernan. God bless you,' Bernie said brokenly.

Maddy thought of his words. Mrs Buckley had said those same ones only yesterday. They both meant well, but it wasn't much comfort.

'Take my hand, Carmel,' she said wearily. 'We're going home. It's all over now.'

Chapter Twenty

The weather grew warmer as the long days of summer arrived. Maddy spent them trying not to think of Martin and being as near to her normal, cheerful self as was possible. Johanna's pregnancy was showing and she was tired at the end of the day, so Maddy found some relief in taking on as many of her sister-in-law's responsibilities as she could. After John's funeral Carmel was listless, depressed and often in tears, and Maddy and Johanna worried about her health.

'If she carries on like this she'll make herself really ill,' Johanna said. She was sitting at the kitchen table peeling cooking apples for a big apple and cinnamon tart. 'I never believed that people could die from a broken heart; now I'm not so sure.'

'Don't you think I know all that, Jo?' Maddy was rolling out the pastry. She sprinkled flour on the table. 'She should be happy, she has a good life ahead of her. I thought that in time she'd get over him. God knows what I'm going to do with her.'

'The only time she seems to be happy is when she's looking after Ronan for me. She gets on well with children. Maybe it's because she is so childlike herself in many ways.'

Maddy nodded. She doubted that her sister would ever really grow up. She would always have that childish innocence and naivety.

'How long is it now before Martin's due home?'

'Two days and six hours, if they've had no bad weather and they catch the tide.'

'Oh Maddy, how will you tell him?'

'I don't know. I've been trying so hard to think of the way to put it, but nothing seems right and I get so upset.'

'Who wouldn't? I hoped herself would change her mind, that she'd tested your loyalty enough, but she hasn't. I wonder if she's told the Reverend Owens? I'm sure he wouldn't approve.'

'I don't think she has,' Maddy replied. The Reverend Owens was the Church of England vicar of the parish and he called to see Mrs Buckley every Sunday afternoon.

'Do you think I should tell him, Maddy? I hate to see you like this. I know how hard you try to keep cheerful.'

'No! No, I promised, Jo. It's between me and herself.'

'But ten years is such a very long time. Couldn't I ask her to consider making it five?'

'I know you mean well, but a bargain is a bargain. A promise is a promise. I made my choice.'

'You don't have to do this for us.'

'I do. I considered everything, and it's my decision.'

'I only hope Martin will wait, Maddy. I'm sure he will,' Johanna added stoutly.

Maddy bought a copy of the *Journal of Commerce*, which gave the movements of all shipping in and out of the Port of Liverpool. She scanned the lines and sighed with relief. They were going to be on time. Martin's last letter had been full of cheerful nonsense with a few serious passages, and his now usual ending *My love always, Martin*. She'd found it so hard to write to him, to keep up the pretence that everything was fine. She told him the trivia of her days and weeks, she told him she loved him and would always do so, which was no lie. Now he was only a day's sailing time away and she dreaded the moment of truth.

'Are you all right?' Johanna asked as Maddy came into the kitchen wearing her best dress and a light straw bonnet tied with pale blue ribbons.

'Yes, I'm grand. Don't worry if I'm late getting back.'

'Have you told herself?'

'I have so.'

'And?'

'She said nothing. Nothing at all.'

'Oh Maddy, you should have let me talk to her.'

Maddy shook her head and let herself quietly out.

Even though it was early evening the cobbles and the buildings seemed to have retained the heat of the day. A warm breeze fanned her face and lifted the ends of the ribbons on her bonnet. The dock road was still busy but as she walked to Canning Dock her mind wasn't on either the heat or the wind.

The *Providence of Montrose* was already tied up along-side, her sails furled and lashed down.

'Maddy! Maddy!'

She looked up and saw Martin waving and her heart dropped like a stone. He was so handsome, she thought. His eyes seemed bluer than ever, his face more tanned.

'Wait there,' he called. 'I'll be down. I'm packed and signed off.'

She stood watching the gulls squabbling raucously over a few pieces of black bread that had been cast into the dock, her pulse racing.

Dropping his seabag he took her hands. 'Maddy! Let me look at you!'

She looked up into his face and he swept her into his arms and was kissing her. Tears of relief, love and also despair filled her eyes and rolled down her cheeks, but she didn't care. This moment, this briefest of moments, was hers entirely. She would think of nothing else except him.

At last he pulled away but still held her in the circle of his arms. 'You're crying, my darling. Did you miss me so much?'

'I did, Martin. I love you so much that I missed you every day and night, but . . .'

'But what?' He looked puzzled.

'There is something I have to tell you.'

'Has something happened at home?'

'Yes, but everyone is fine, there's no sickness or any-thing.'

'Then what is it?'

'I can't tell you here. It has to be somewhere private.'

He was thoughtful, then he took her hand.

'It's not the sort of thing I do – in fact, it's forbidden to the crew, but once won't do any harm and I can tell there's something very wrong, Maddy.'

'Where are we going?'

'Back on board, to the cabin I share with the Mate. He's already headed off for home to his wife and family.'

Maddy let him help her down a dark, steep narrow-stepped stairway and along an equally dark low-ceilinged passageway and into a tiny room.

'Now tell me what's wrong,' he said, seating her on a bunk.

'Martin, I . . . I don't know where to start. Do you really love me?'

'Maddy, how can you ask that? You know I do.'

'Would you ever consider marrying me?' She felt her cheeks burning with embarrassment.

He chuckled. 'Is that a proposal? You know the answer to that, too. In fact, I was going to propose to you tonight and buy a ring tomorrow!'

'Oh, Martin!' Maddy broke down and he took her in his arms.

'Why, Maddy, dearest, what is the matter? Aren't you happy, my darling girl?'

'I *can't* marry you, Martin.'

'Why not?' He was bewildered, his smile gone.

'Because I promised . . .'

'Who did you promise?'

Through bouts of sobbing she told him the whole story, and when she'd finished he looked angry; his eyes had turned to the colour of a flinty cold sea.

'That's a monstrous thing to ask of you! Has this woman no scruples, no conscience, no compassion at all?'

'That's the awful thing about it – she *does* care. She'll make me very rich, Martin.'

'Is that supposed to make up for the unhappiness you'll suffer all those years? It's moral blackmail, emotional blackmail. She's a selfish, jealous old woman.'

'Martin, I promised.'

'Under duress and out of consideration for your family. It won't bear scrutiny, Maddy. I love you and I want to marry you. God knows I'll see little enough of you as it is, me being away so much! You can't be responsible for them for ever. Tom can find work and keep his own family. Carmel will eventually get married. She could live with us in the meantime; she would be company for you while I'm away. Maddy, we don't *need* Mrs Buckley's damned money. I'm well paid. You'll never want for anything.'

Maddy's resolve was weakening. 'But what about the ships?' She had explained about Mrs Buckley's business, the Buckley Line, about the benefits to him that could come in the future.

'She can keep her damned ships! I'll make Master on my own, by my own efforts, not because someone like *her* holds me to ransom! Maddy, we don't need her or her money. Let her brothers fight it out; she's only leaving you her inheritance to spite them. Doesn't that show you the kind of person she is? I love you, Maddy, and I want you now, not in ten years' time! Say you'll marry me? Maddy, I'm begging you! Don't turn me away to wait ten long years for happiness. Who knows what could happen in that time? I told you the sea is my life and it is, but the sea can be a cruel mistress. I've seen only too often how she can toss a ship like a piece of matchwood, sending it to the bottom to lie there for ever.'

Maddy wiped away her tears with the back of her hand. 'Martin, I don't *want* to wait! I love you. I love you more than life itself.'

'Then we don't need her. Marry me, Maddy?'

Maddy was torn between her love and a promise, but her love won. 'I . . . I will, Martin, but only after your next trip.'

'Why wait?'

'Because I'll need to warn Johanna. It's only fair that I tell her, so she'll know what to expect. She's going to have another baby, you see, and the only reason Tom is happy about it is the fact that he knows he'll be wealthy. She *has* to know, Martin! She's been such a comfort to me; she begged me to let her tell the vicar about the promise or to ask Mrs Buckley to reduce it to five years.'

'Your brother Tom is as bad as that bloody-minded old bitch! As for reducing it to five years! You've committed no crime for which you have to pay ten or even five years.'

'I know he is, and I also know that if he'd come into money thanks to me there'd be rows all the time because I wouldn't give him a free rein, but I was doing it for Johanna and the children. I love you, Martin, and I promise I'll marry you the day you sail back into Liverpool.'

He was disappointed but he wouldn't upset her still further. She must have gone through agonies of indecision already, torn as she was between her love for him and her love for her family. Her tender-heartedness, generosity and loyalty were the things he loved about her.

'Then I'll wait a few months longer. You won't go back on it?'

'Never. I'd sooner die than do that.'

'Do you know, Maddy, I love you so much it hurts.'

'I feel that too.'

He sighed deeply. 'Well, my love, let's try and enjoy what time we do have.'

'Oh, yes, please.' Her guilt began to fall away from her. They didn't need the old lady's money. He was right about Tom and he'd known instinctively how she worried about her sister. She felt no remorse for her change of mind. It *had* been a monstrous thing to ask of her.

It was late when she returned home. Martin had taken her for an early supper in a hotel where everyone was far better dressed than she was and the battery of cutlery had confused her, until he'd laughed and said it didn't matter to him which knife and fork she used. They'd had champagne, he'd bought her flowers and a beautiful gold crucifix on a chain, promising that next time he was home it would be an engagement ring and a wedding ring they'd be buying. Then they'd taken the ferry across the Mersey to New Brighton, a small town that was just becoming a fashionable resort. They'd walked along the new Promenade and the beach, as far as the fort on Perch Rock where cannons could still be seen, even though the danger of an invasion by the French had ended thirty-five years ago at Waterloo.

By the time he took her back to Faulkner Square, both were drowsily happy.

'Oh Martin, thank you for the happiest day of my life,' Maddy said sincerely.

'Thank *you*, Maddy, for my wonderful day. I still wish you would marry me before I sail again.'

'I know you do, but it's just not practical. And I really need to make it right for Johanna. Tom will be livid with me and he may take it out on her.'

'Maddy, they don't deserve you. You won't change your mind?'

'No! It doesn't matter what they all say, I'll marry you next time you're home. You're everything in the world to me Martin.'

He held her tightly, not wanting to let her go, ever.

'I must go in now,' she told him. 'It's late. I don't want to, but I have to.'

'I'll see you tomorrow?'

'Yes. Will I meet you in town?'

'Can you meet me just before lunch? I have some business to attend to in the morning and then we can have the afternoon together. Will the old battle-axe mind you having another afternoon and evening off?'

'I don't care if she does. Where shall I see you?'

'On the corner of Dale Street and Chapel Street.'

'I'll be there. Good night, my love.'

'Good night, my own darling Maddy.'

He stood and watched her go in, then turned away.

'By the look on your face I can see you didn't tell him,' Tom said nastily as soon as Maddy let herself in. He'd waited up deliberately. Johanna had, too.

'Yes, I did,' she snapped. As usual he always took the shine off everything. 'It didn't spoil the day though.'

'He's crafty, all right. Wants to wait for the money and the ships – is that the way of things?'

Maddy ignored him. 'I've had a wonderful day. Look what he bought me.' She handed Johanna the box containing the cross and chain.

'Oh Maddy, it's beautiful!'

'And the flowers, and we went to the Exchange Station Hotel for supper and then across to New Brighton, for a stroll.'

'Oh, tell me all about it,' Johanna begged.

'If this is going to be the carry-on out of the two of you, I'm going to bed,' Tom said, obviously annoyed.

'Then go!' Maddy retorted.

'Good night,' Johanna added.

'Holy Mother, did he need to take the door off its hinges!' Maddy exclaimed as her brother slammed out.

'Now tell me all about it. I want to know every detail.'

Maddy looked thoughtful. Johanna was so pleased and excited for her, how could she tell her sister-in-law that her future wasn't as rosy as it had been when she'd gone out this morning?

'Maddy?' Johanna pressed.

With false cheerfulness Maddy described her outing, omitting her time spent aboard the *Providence of Montrose*.

'So you told him?' Johanna said, her expression becoming serious.

'I did.'

'And?'

Maddy got up and wrung her hands as she walked up and down the kitchen.

'He said it was a monstrous thing for her to do. Moral blackmail, he called it. He said we didn't need her money. Oh Johanna! I love him so much! I'm so sorry, but—'

Johanna smiled. 'But you promised to marry him?'

'I did. After his next trip. Oh, what is Tom going to say? I'm sorry, so very sorry.'

'Maddy, I told you not to sacrifice your happiness for us. We'll be fine. Leave Tom to me. Are you going to tell herself?'

Maddy sat down again and took Johanna's hands. Thank God her sister-in-law understood.

'I don't know. Maybe not just yet,' she said.

'Then don't tell her until just before he's due home again.'

'She's bound to ask tomorrow.'

'Then tell her all about your day. You've not promised to stop seeing him, have you? Tell her all the details, leave no room for her to question you.'

'The fact is, I don't really want to tell her yet,' Maddy admitted.

'Then don't. Are you afraid her health might suffer? That she'll have a fit, maybe even die of the shock?'

'I suppose that's part of it.'

'Well, I wouldn't worry. She's too pig-headed and stubborn to let something like that send her to her grave.'

Maddy smiled. 'I couldn't wish for a better sister.'

'In-law,' Johanna finished.

'No. Sister – and I mean it. By the way, where is Carmel?'

'She's gone to bed with a dreadful headache. She didn't look at all well. She's obviously still pining over John.'

Maddy sighed. 'I had hoped she was getting a little better. I worry about her so much.'

'I know you do. What will happen to her when you get married?'

'She'll come and live with us. Martin has already settled my mind on that and without any prompting.'

'He's a good man, Maddy, and I'm so pleased for you. Go on up now, I'll be up myself in a few minutes.'

'Thank you, Johanna.' Maddy felt so much happier now that she'd told her sister-in-law. She wouldn't confide in Carmel yet – her sister might let something slip. Maddy would have her work cut out not to tell a downright lie to her mistress, but somehow she'd manage it.

Tom pretended to be asleep when Johanna quietly opened the bedroom door, but in reality he was wide awake and fuming. He'd gone down to get a glass of water, for the night was very hot and humid. He'd only got as far as the kitchen door, but he'd overheard everything. His hand had been shaking with rage as he'd reached out to grasp the door handle, but then he'd pulled back. No, he wouldn't confront them now. It would cause a huge fight and the old lady and Carmel would get up from their beds wanting to know why everyone was shouting. He couldn't believe that Johanna, his own wife, mother of their two children, had condoned what Maddy had done. She must be mad! They both must be, but Johanna knew how much everything meant to him and she'd let him down very badly. She'd thrown away all their futures and for what? So Maddy could marry that jumped-up deckhand! Well, tomorrow he'd find some excuse for them to go out and then he'd give her the telling-off of her life. However, Maddy wasn't going to inform the old lady that she'd changed her mind, and he certainly wasn't going to. You never knew in this life. Fate could intervene and Maddy might not get to marry Martin Brennan after all. Being a seaman was a dangerous occupation.

The atmosphere in the kitchen next morning was strained. There was definitely a coolness in Tom towards his wife, Maddy thought. As for herself, she knew Tom hated the thought of her having any enjoyment. Carmel was pale and preoccupied.

'Is there something the matter?' Maddy asked, concerned.

'No, I'm just feeling a bit faint.'

'Has the headache gone?'

'Almost. I'm sure it's the heat, Maddy.'

'Then this afternoon, why don't you take Ronan down to the riverside. He likes seeing all the ships and it might be a bit cooler. Unless you'd like to lie down?'

'No. I'd sooner go out, if Johanna doesn't mind.'

'Of course I don't mind. I'll have a bit of a rest myself. You know, a good storm would clear the air.'

'It would so,' Carmel agreed.

Tom said nothing. With both his sisters out of the way, there would be no need for him to take Johanna out. He could confront her here in the kitchen. The old lady always had a nap then and anyway, even if she heard them she couldn't make out words, she just heard sounds.

'I'll take up her breakfast,' Maddy said, glancing at Johanna with foreboding.

'Good morning, ma'am,' she greeted her mistress.

'Is it? The heat is good for my old bones but not for a comfortable night's sleep,' Maud Buckley complained.

'Then let's hope we have a storm soon. Now, may I have the afternoon and evening off, ma'am?' There was nothing said about not being able to see Martin.

'You had all of yesterday. Your poor sister-in-law looked very tired.'

'Johanna has said she doesn't mind and Carmel will help out.'

'There's something wrong with that girl. I heard she had a migraine last night?'

'It's the heat. I worry about her too. I told her to take Ronan down to the waterfront this afternoon.'

'That's very dictatorial of you, miss!'

'It will give Johanna a rest and you've just said she needed one.'

'We're full of the back-chat this morning, aren't we?'

'No. I'm just being cheerful. So can I go out, please?'

'Oh, if you must! How long is he home for?'

'The usual five days.'

'And I suppose you'll want time off every day?'

'I will so, ma'am. Is there anything you want me to do before I go out?'

'No. I'm not in my dotage yet.'

'True for you,' Maddy muttered under her breath as she left, relieved there had been no direct questions asked.

Chapter Twenty-one

Martin was waiting as Maddy walked along Dale Street and crossed the road by the Town Hall.

'Maddy, you look lovelier by the day,' he told her appreciatively. 'How did things go at home?'

'I told Johanna but no one else.'

'Was she upset?'

'No, she wasn't. She actually said she was glad and that I deserved some happiness. She said not to worry about them, they'd find other jobs.'

'She sounds like a very sensible young woman.'

'Oh, she is. She's more of a sister than a sister-in-law.'

'Maybe she realises just how much they owe you.'

Maddy didn't reply.

'Will we go for a cup of tea or to a coffee-house?' he asked her.

'What about the business you had to attend to?'

'I have done it all except for one task, which can wait.'

'No, let's get it over with then we'll have the rest of the day to ourselves.'

'It's just a call into the bank over there. You're sure you don't mind waiting?'

'I'm sure.'

The bank was an old and respected one. Inside, it was dim and smelled dusty. There was a long counter of polished wood behind which frockcoated clerks worked.

'Sit over there, I won't be long.' Martin led her to a chair that was set into an alcove which effectively hid her from sight. Settling her skirts, she sniffed the air again and grinned. Maybe this was the smell of money! The place needed a strong blast of fresh air through it, but she could see that the tall windows were sealed with numerous coats of varnish. Relaxing, she allowed her mind to wander until a familiar voice brought her back to reality.

'Are you certain, Mr Kiernan, that Mrs Buckley has asked for an increase of twenty pounds a month?'

'I'm quite certain, Mr Robinson. She was most clear and insistent about it. Do you want me to bring in her request in writing?'

'No, that won't be necessary, Mr Kiernan. Mrs Buckley trusts you and that is all the proof I need. Will you wait for a moment while I enter this cheque?'

'Of course.'

Maddy sat open-mouthed in the alcove. It was Tom. It really *was* and he was asking for more money. She herself knew just how much the old lady had in her purse each week but he was asking for twenty pounds extra – obviously for himself. A whole twenty pounds! She felt herself grow hot and then cold, her anger increasing. Why was he stealing? Did he think he'd never be found out? He was despicable! Robbing an old lady who had been so very good to him. This must be his way of increasing his savings. Oh yes, he'd have quite a nice little nest-egg saved when the Mrs Buckley eventually died. Enough to defy Maddy when she inherited the estate, never knowing that she wouldn't inherit it now. He'd even have enough money saved when she announced that she was marrying Martin. Oh, she could kill him!

'I've just seen your brother. What is he doing here?' Martin asked, putting his wallet into his pocket.

'He collects money for the mistress once a month. They trust him, so does she, but . . .' She fell silent as Tom caught sight of Martin and stopped.

Then Maddy stepped forward and Tom retreated. Maddy! What the hell was *she* doing here?

'I see you've been collecting the household allowance,' she said coldly.

'Is there anything wrong about that?' Tom blustered. He hoped to God she hadn't heard him ask for the extra money.

'No. I was sitting here, waiting for Martin and I recognised your voice.' She wasn't going to make a scene here; she'd wait until they were at home. She didn't even want Martin to know, yet.

'I see,' Tom replied.

'Well, that's my business attended to,' Martin said pleasantly. 'Maddy and I are staying in town.'

'Good. I . . . I'll see you later, Maddy.'

'You will, you can be sure of that,' she said, giving him a steady look.

All the way back Tom was consumed with fear and anger. Why the hell had *she* had to be there at that precise moment? Had she heard anything? She'd seen him, but that didn't mean she'd heard him ask for the extra money. He could detect nothing in her voice. She'd been cold, but that was nothing new. Maybe she didn't know, but he'd have to wait until she returned to find out.

'What are you looking so worried about?' Johanna asked him when he returned home.

'I'll tell you what I'm worried about. Where's Carmel?'

'Upstairs, dusting.'

'I'm worried about us losing our jobs, being flung out of here with no references because my bloody sister has broken her promise!'

Johanna's hand went to her throat. 'How do you know?' she breathed.

'I heard you last night. I came down for a drink and heard it all. So, she's going to marry him when he's next home and you – my own wife – were glad for her! By God, Johanna, where do you think we'll end up? Back in the slum that we came from! Is that what you want? Do you want to see our children illiterate, dressed in rags?'

'That won't happen and you know it. We have savings and I can work, I always have done. It was so unfair of herself to make Maddy choose.'

'Oh, I see you're still taking Maddy's side. My sister is an interfering, hot-headed, arrogant little rossi and always has been!'

'How can you say that?' Johanna was distressed. 'We have her to thank for everything.'

'We've worked hard, too! She'd need more staff if we left but herself is too mean to pay for them. Why should she, when she's got us doing the work of three people?'

'Tom, that's not fair. She's *not* mean.'

'Never mind all that. You'd better make enquiries at that place you used to do sewing for. We'll need every penny we can lay our hands on over the next few months! Now, I'm going up to see her and when I come down, I'd like some dinner.'

Johanna's heart sank as he slammed out. He'd be unbearable from now on. He'd banked on getting his hands on those two ships and now his ambitions lay in tatters. She sighed heavily as she put the kettle on the range.

They were all silent at lunch and Carmel sensed that there had been an argument. She was surprised because Johanna seldom argued with Tom. She pushed her plate away; she ate little these days. Usually either Tom or Johanna or Maddy would remark on it but today no one seemed to notice. She wondered what Maddy was doing. She was so glad her sister had found someone to love. She knew what it was like to love and be loved, and she liked Martin Brennan. Of course, he would be away a lot, but Maddy didn't say too much about that.

'Oh, for Christ's sake! Can't a man have his meals in peace?' Tom exclaimed as the front door bell sounded.

'I'll go, Tom. Finish your meal,' Carmel said, getting to her feet. It wouldn't be Maddy, she would never use the front door. Maybe it was the vicar – no, it wasn't Sunday. Or maybe it was the solicitor. She knew he'd been sent for – she had posted the letter herself, though for what purpose she didn't know.

She was surprised to see a young man standing on the doorstep and he looked just as surprised at seeing her.

'Can I help you?' she asked, blushing as she always did when meeting a stranger.

'I hope so. I've come to see my Aunt Maud. Maud Buckley? She still lives here, I hope.' He'd never realised that the old lady employed someone as beautiful as this girl, even though she was pale and thin, and wore the uniform of a housemaid.

'Oh, yes she does. Come in, please.'

'I am Charles Murgatroyd. My father is Richard Murgatroyd, Aunt Maud's youngest brother. What's your name?'

'Carmel, sir. Carmel Kiernan.'

'A pretty name for a pretty girl. You're Irish?'

Carmel was blushing furiously now and she fixed her attention on the black and white marble squares that covered the floor of the hallway. 'I am so, sir. I . . . I'll go and tell her.'

'No need for that, Miss Carmel Kiernan, I'll go straight up. Give her a surprise. Do you think you could bring up some tea? I've hardly had time this morning to get any refreshments.'

'Of course. Will I bring some sandwiches too?'

'Now that would be nice,' he replied, smiling.

There was no doubt that he was handsome, with those twinkling brown eyes and dark hair, Carmel thought, and he was very well dressed, too, and full of compliments. It was nice to be flattered again. That's all it was, flattery. He could see she was shy, and was just being kind to her. She would never speculate on the feelings men might have for her. The memory of John was still strong. But he had been pleasant.

'Who was it?' Tom always had to know everything.

'Mr Charles Murgatroyd. The mistress is his aunt. He went straight up – he wouldn't let me announce him. He'd like some tea and sandwiches, he said. I don't think he's had any lunch.'

Tom was not pleased. 'You should have called me. You know what herself is like about etiquette. He should have been announced properly. She might not have wanted to see him. I've never heard her speak of him.'

'He's Mr Richard's son and I didn't really have time to stop him.'

'Never mind, Carmel. I'll make a fresh pot of tea and cut some sandwiches,' Johanna said firmly.

'Well, you can take them up, I'm not a housemaid!' Tom said testily.

'You'd better put on a clean cap and apron,' Johanna advised.

'Will it be expected?'

'Of course it will damned well be expected,' Tom replied, irritated.

Carmel was nervous as she carried the tray upstairs. She was still a little afraid of the old lady, especially when she shouted. Maddy, of course, had no trouble. She just yelled back.

'So, it was you who let this ruffian in?' the old lady said.

'It was so, ma'am.'

'You should have stopped him. He came bursting in here like an overgrown puppy, and gave me quite a start. He only comes to see me if he wants something.'

'I say, that's a bit steep,' Charles protested, smiling at Carmel.

'But it's the truth! What is it you want now, apart from ogling my staff, although I have to say she is a very pretty girl.'

Carmel ducked her head and her cheeks flamed. Oh, it was awful being talked about like this.

'She's more than pretty, Aunt Maud. She's a real beauty.'

'Stop talking about the girl as if she weren't in the room. Didn't your parents teach you any manners?'

Mrs Buckley was quarrelsome, and sure the devil in the wild woods wouldn't content her in this mood, Carmel thought, fidgeting and wondering how soon she could get away.

'Carmel, child, leave those things. My nephew can pour the tea. It will give him something to do. I doubt he does anything at home.'

Carmel was glad to get out, but Charles Murgatroyd managed to give her another smile before she turned away.

'Oh, she's as cross as a bag of cats today!' she said when she went back into the kitchen.

'She's getting worse,' Johanna agreed.

'And wouldn't you be, with people barging into your room and demanding tea and sandwiches at all hours?' Tom snapped.

'She says he only comes when he wants something.'

'There could be some truth in that. He's never been here before.' Tom was speculative. Had the lad heard about the old lady wanting to change her Will? Well, that didn't matter much now.

'He said some very nice things about me, but I was so embarrassed.'

'What kind of things?' Johanna asked.

'Oh, that I had a pretty name for a pretty girl, and when herself called me pretty, he said I was more than that, I was beautiful, but I'm sure he didn't mean anything by it.'

'I hope not. He's very forward,' Johanna frowned.

Tom said nothing. With Maddy giving up all the money, when the old lady died it would be divided between her three brothers – and Charles was the only son of one of them. An idea was forming in his mind. He'd show the young fellow out and get the lie of the land with regard to Carmel. It was very unusual for a girl of Carmel's rank to marry someone like Charles Murgatroyd, but it did happen.

Fifteen minutes later the old lady bellowed that her visitor was leaving.

Tom got to his feet. 'I'll go and see him out.'

Carmel nodded thankfully.

309

He was a good-looking lad of about twenty-one or two, Tom thought as he took Charles's hat from the hallstand where Carmel had placed it.

'Oh, I hoped it would be little Carmel who would be waiting for me.' There was a note of disappointment in the young man's voice.

Tom smiled. 'Mrs Buckley likes things to be done properly and Carmel is quite overcome.'

'Is she? Really?' He looked hopeful.

'Oh, indeed. I'm her brother, also her guardian.' Tom smiled ingratiatingly.

'Parents dead?'

'Long ago.'

'She *is* very beautiful, you know.'

'I do so, sir. But thank God she's neither vain nor bold. She's very quiet and shy and biddable.'

'I thought there were three of you. Aunt mentioned "Maddy".'

'Maddy is my other sister and not in the least like Carmel. Not as pretty and she's stubborn and strong-willed and at present is courting a seaman.' The last word was uttered with a sneer.

'I might be popping round to see the old dear more frequently in the future,' Charles said casually.

'I'm sure you'll be most welcome, sir,' Tom said, opening the front door. 'She gets few visitors.'

'I'm not surprised,' Charles said drily. 'Hello – who on earth is this?' They both turned their attention to the cab that had just stopped outside the door.

Damn! Tom cursed to himself. 'I think it might be Mr Hatfield, the solicitor,' he said aloud.

The smile vanished from Charles's face and was replaced with a look full of suspicion.

'You don't know why he's here, I suppose, Kiernan?'

'Only that Mrs Buckley sent for him. I know nothing else.'

'She hasn't mentioned anything about her Will?'

'No, sir, she hasn't.'

Charles still looked suspicious as he went down the front steps and raised his hat to the elderly man who was giving instructions to the cab driver. He'd gone to see the old lady at his father's request, to check on her state of health and also to see if he could wheedle some money out of her. Charlie had always been her favourite, even though she loathed his father and his two uncles. His father wasn't very generous concerning the allowance he gave him each month, Charles thought moodily. But he would go back and see the old lady again; it might help him in the matter of the Will and also he'd be able to see Carmel again. If what her brother said about her being shy and biddable was true, then who knew what delights the future held.

Once again Maddy had had a wonderful day. She had pushed all thoughts of her brother to the back of her mind but as Martin kissed her and wished her a good night, she knew it had to be faced.

'You don't look very happy, Maddy,' Johanna remarked as Maddy took off her bonnet.

'I'm not. Oh, I had a wonderful day, but—'

'You're not thinking about him going away yet, surely?' Johanna pressed.

'No. No, I'm trying to dismiss that from my mind. It'll come soon enough.'

'Then what?'

Maddy looked at her brother. 'Jo, dear, will you go and see to herself?' she said quietly. 'You know how useless Carmel is with her.'

Johanna looked confused. 'Very well,' she said. Then: 'We had a visit today from that fine bucko of a nephew, Charles Murgatroyd. He was very taken with Carmel and was full of flattery. Poor girl, she was quite overwhelmed. You know what she's like.'

'Then it's even more useful if you go and put herself to bed. I'm not in the mood for any of her tantrums,' Maddy pleaded.

When her sister-in-law had left the room she turned on her brother.

'You thieving, lying, ungrateful sod, Thomas Kiernan! Twenty pounds! What do you want twenty pounds for so badly? You're a disgrace! It's glad I am that Mam and Da aren't here to see how you've turned out!'

'I wouldn't need to take her money but for you!'

'For me?'

'Yes. Thanks to you we'll all be turned out on the road without a penny when she finds out that you've broken your promise and will marry Brennan after all!'

'How do you know that? Did Johanna tell you?'

'No, she didn't. I overheard you, last night. You don't care about us, about our children. They'll get nothing from life now except whatever kind of a wage I can earn. You're a selfish, conniving, lying, hard-faced bitch!'

'At least I never stole from her. That's despicable.'

'And it's despicable to let your family go without, and Johanna not so far to her time! And what about Carmel? You know she's not strong – what will happen to her? She can't live with us, I won't be able to feed another mouth. You've abandoned her too!'

'Carmel will live with us, don't worry about that. I would never turn her out on the road, as you put it. You're exaggerating. You'll get a good position, and I know you have savings.'

'Don't try and fool me, Maddy. How long do you think the bit of money I have saved will last? I shall tell Mrs Buckley that you've broken your promise. I've nothing to lose now.' Tom looked at her cunningly, knowing he'd caught her in a trap.

Maddy fumed inwardly. 'I won't tell her about you drawing out the extra money if you don't tell her that I'm going to marry Martin. It will give you time to look for another job and another place to live, and I'll help out as much as I can – with money, I mean.'

He was somewhat relieved. Maddy would never change her mind about marrying Martin Brennan, so he had a couple of months in which to make plans. He still intended to draw out the extra money. Maddy would never know and when the old lady died he'd be well away from here so there would be no chance of her brothers finding out.

'Right then, we both keep our mouths shut,' he agreed.

Maddy turned away. What had she done to deserve a brother like him? They were as different as chalk and cheese and he didn't get his badness from either Mam or Da. Where those traits came from would always be a mystery to her. Her parents would be turning in their Irish graves if they knew what a child they'd produced, they truly would.

Chapter Twenty-two

To everyone's surprise, two days later Charles Murgatroyd came to visit his Aunt Maud again. It was Maddy who opened the door to him, and from Johanna and Carmel's description she instantly recognised him.

'You're Charles Murgatroyd.'

'Right first time, and you must be Carmel's sister Maddy.'

'I am.'

'Well, you don't seem to be any of the things your brother said about you.'

'Indeed?' she answered dryly. 'Well, Tom and I have never really seen eye to eye.'

'Where is Carmel today?'

Maddy smiled. 'She's gone into town on some errands. I thought you'd come to see Mrs Buckley?'

'Oh, I have. I just thought . . .' He grinned.

'Maddy! Maddy, who is at the door?' Mrs Buckley's voice carried loudly down the stairwell.

'It's your nephew Charles, ma'am,' Maddy shouted back.

'Good grief! Does she never use the bell?' Charles winced.

'No, it's one of her peculiarities. You get used to it.'

'Now I know why it was me who had to ring to be ushered out.'

'What does he want now? He was only here the day before yesterday,' came the disembodied voice from above.

'I don't know, ma'am. I'll send him up and he can tell you himself,' went back the reply.

Charles chuckled. 'It must be like living in Bedlam!'

'As I said, you get used to it.'

'Do you think Carmel will be back before I leave?'

Maddy grinned. 'If you stay long enough, she's bound to be. You'd better go up before your aunt starts losing her temper.'

Back in the kitchen, Maddy told Johanna meaningfully, 'He wants to know, will Carmel be back before he leaves?'

'He must be keen.'

Maddy's smile faded. 'Jo, you know he's not one of us.'

'I know he's a gentleman, but sometimes it does happen and maybe it's what Carmel needs. Tom told me that he'd said to Charles that she was shy and biddable. A romance between them might work out, if she feels the same way, of course. Just think about it.'

Maddy nodded. She'd ask Martin for his advice when she saw him later on. His leave had been extended for three days as there was a hold-up on the cargo and they were both exultant about it.

'Well, he certainly means to stick it out,' Johanna said

three-quarters of an hour later when Charles still hadn't emerged from his aunt's room. 'I wonder what he finds to talk about to herself?'

'I've no idea, but here comes Carmel. Will I tell her or do you want to?' Maddy asked.

'You tell her.' They both giggled.

'Maddy, I couldn't get the cocoa you wanted, but I got the rest. Why are you looking at me like that?' Carmel asked, putting down her heavy basket.

'Charles Murgatroyd is here again.'

'To see herself,' Johanna added.

'But we all know it's you he's really come to see. All right, don't get upset, you don't have to see him if you don't want to,' Maddy added quickly, seeing her sister's expression change to one of panic.

'Are you quite sure it *is* me?'

'Johanna and I are. Do you like him?'

'I've only met him once. He was very nice and he said some lovely things to me.'

'She will never realise just how beautiful she is,' Johanna said to Maddy. Maddy nodded, chewing her lip anxiously, and Carmel looked confused.

'He's been up there for ages, waiting until you came back. I'll see if they want more tea.' She went out to the hallway and cleared her throat.

'Ma'am, do you wish for more tea? Carmel is back with those special biscuits you like,' she bawled.

Almost immediately Charles's head appeared over the banister rail.

'I was just leaving but now I'll stay for more tea.'

Maddy nodded, unsurprised.

'Go on, take up the tray when it's ready,' she said to her sister and Carmel blushed. It was a nice feeling, knowing that someone like Charles Murgatroyd, a real gentleman, thought you were pretty and interesting. But she was a little afraid that she wouldn't be able to hold a proper conversation with him. She didn't want to make a fool of herself.

'Is he still here and is she back?' Tom asked, coming into the kitchen with a scuttle full of coal for the range.

'It's yes to both. We sent her up with the fresh pot of tea and biscuits.'

Tom nodded. It was all going well but he wished Carmel had a bit more go about her. Then he looked at Maddy and was glad his younger sister wasn't like her.

'I'm worried about young Murgatroyd's intentions,' Maddy said to Johanna as she took the flat-iron off the stove and began on a pile of ironing. 'I don't want Carmel to get hurt again. And even if he is sincere, what would his father and mother think and say, if he wanted to take her to meet them? She's only a maid of all work, after all. And she's well under-age – barely sixteen.'

'Ah, but he's past the age of consent. He can do what he likes,' Tom joined in.

'Not entirely. I don't think he actually works much and his father could put pressure on him, financially.'

'You mean disown him?' Tom asked thoughtfully.

'Yes.'

'Well, I don't know why we're talking about things like that. They hardly even know each other,' Johanna interrupted. She was shaking out the linen and sprinkling cold water on it to make the ironing easier for Maddy.

'You're right. Let's not get carried away,' Maddy said, pressing down hard on a damp pillowcase, which bloomed with steam.

When Carmel returned, her cheeks were pink.

'Well?' Tom asked.

'Well what?'

'What did he say to you?'

'Nothing, apart from "Hello", and, "It's nice to see you again, Carmel".'

'Didn't he ask where you'd been or anything like that?'

'No, but herself asked had I got the cocoa and I said I had not and then he said he couldn't understand how anyone could like the stuff and then I could see herself getting cross, so I came out.'

Johanna smiled and raised her eyes to the ceiling, whilst Maddy carried on with the ironing, wondering, with more than a little trepidation, where all this would lead.

Half an hour later, when Charles Murgatroyd rang down to be shown out, Tom made sure he was the one to do so. He was determined to show Charles Murgatroyd he knew the value of his sister. There was no way this young lad was going to get something for nothing.

'Sir, could I make so bold as to ask you a rather delicate question?' Tom said smoothly.

Lyn Andrews

'I wish to God you'd stop calling me "sir". You sound as though you're addressing my father. Call me by my name.'

'Oh, I couldn't do that,' Tom protested, yet it was encouraging. The lad wanted to get on the right side of him.

'Then call me Mr Murgatroyd if you must. What's your name?'

'Thomas or Tom.'

'Right, Tom, what was it you wanted to ask me?'

'Do you have any kind of interest in my sister Carmel?'

Charles looked taken aback but quickly became serious. 'As a matter of fact I do, Tom. I know it's not usual, but then *she's* not usual. She's very beautiful and she is shy and demure. In fact I'd like to ask your permission to court her, if she's willing to. My father isn't as wealthy as my aunt, and won't be until she dies, but we're not badly off and I'd apply myself more, get a real job and be able to provide for her. The truth is, I fell in love with Carmel when I first set eyes on her, but obviously, that is taking things a bit too fast. Have I your permission to ask her out?'

Tom smiled. 'Of course you do. We all realise that it's an unusual situation but I don't think you'll have any complaints from Carmel or even Maddy. She does care very much about Carmel's future and happiness.'

Charles was beaming. Every word he'd said was true. He knew there would be the most unholy row at home when he took Carmel there, but he didn't care. This angelic young girl was his ideal woman. He felt protective and wanted to take care of her. His parents would soon get used to her. She

320

wasn't cheap or brassy; she would be guided by his mother and there would be no rows between them.

'Then may I call for her tomorrow?' Charles asked.

'Of course. What time will I tell her?'

'About three.' Charles took Tom's hand and shook it warmly. 'Thanks, Tom. Now can you call me Charlie? Everyone else does. Except Mother and Aunt Maud.'

Tom was full of suppressed excitement. It had all gone far better than he'd envisaged. Now, with Charlie on his side it didn't matter what Maddy and Martin Brennan did. With Carmel as a daughter-in-law Richard Murgatroyd wouldn't scorn her brother and he could easily manipulate Charlie. The future looked rosy again. All he had to do now was persuade Carmel to marry Charlie, though that might be harder to achieve. He'd have to tread carefully, especially with Maddy.

Later on that afternoon, he cornered his younger sister as she was putting the freshly ironed items of linen back in the big airing cupboard on the rear landing. 'Carmel, I want to talk to you,' he said.

'What about?' she asked a little fearfully.

'Nothing bad, in fact it's very good news. Charles Murgatroyd asked my permission to court you. Of course I said yes, so he's coming tomorrow afternoon at three to take you out. You do like him, don't you? I wouldn't want you to feel as though I'm pushing you into anything. He's a very decent young man and he thinks very highly of you. We both agreed that it's out of the ordinary, but it's entirely up to you.'

Carmel looked from her brother to her sister, who was helping her with the linen.

'It's all a bit sudden,' Maddy said doubtfully.

'I know, but if it's meant to be . . .'

'Do you want to go out with him, Carmel?'

Carmel's cheeks blushed pink again and she kept her eyes downcast as she gave a brief nod of her head.

Tom breathed an inward sigh of relief.

'Then you go and enjoy yourself,' Tom said expansively. 'He does seem to be a very genuine lad.'

That evening, when Maddy was alone with Martin, she voiced her fears to him. 'If I didn't know better I'd say Tom was just using her to get at any money Charles Murgatroyd will inherit. But Charles doesn't know about the promise so he can't be just playing with Carmel, can he?'

'What about Carmel herself?'

'She seems happy enough to go out with him but I won't let Tom force her into anything. We scarcely know the man.'

Martin deliberated. 'Your brother can't be that bad.'

'He can. Have you forgotten that he stole from an old lady?'

'I had. You're probably right to worry. Just keep an eye on him. Remember, you'll soon have me to help you.'

'I know and it will be wonderful to have a shoulder to cry on.'

'Maddy, I hope there will never be tears.'

'Only those of happiness,' she replied, reaching up and gently touching his lips with her fingertips.

* * *

322

When Maddy returned she was surprised to see so many lights burning.

'Why does the house look like a Christmas tree?' she asked.

Johanna looked worried. 'It's herself. She's not well, Maddy. She took a turn while I was reading to her, but she won't have the doctor out.'

'Where's Tom?'

'He went out for a drink and to think, he said. It's all to do with Carmel.'

'Oh Maddy, I don't want to cause any trouble,' Carmel cried.

'You're not. I'll go up and see her.'

She was shocked by the old lady's appearance. She'd only been out for a few hours, but in that short time, Maud Buckley seemed to have shrivelled and shrunk.

'Ma'am, are you asleep?'

The old lady opened her eyes. 'No, and there's no need to be creeping about and whispering.'

'Johanna said you had some kind of a turn but you won't have the doctor. Well, I'm going to send for him. You don't look well at all and I'm having no nonsense.'

'The reason I don't look well is because I'm dying, and the doctor has no cure or remedy for that!' came the flat reply.

Maddy was astounded. 'No! No, you can't be dying, it's just a little turn.'

'Maddy Kiernan, I *know* I'm dying! And don't you dare try to stop me. I'm tired of this life, and I want some peace.

I want to see my parents and my husband again. I've struggled on all these years, now I just want contentment.'

Maddy's eyes filled with tears. She knew now that what the old lady said was true. She'd finally lost the will and the reason to live.

She took one skeletal hand in her own. 'Oh ma'am, please . . . is there anything I can do? Anything at all?'

'There are four things you can do for me.'

'Anything, ma'am.'

'For the first and last time, will you call me Maud? You have been like a daughter to me, Maddy. You remind me of myself when I was your age. Now, enough sentimentality. I want you to send for Mr Hatfield, the Reverend Owens, your own priest and that young man of yours. Will that be possible? He hasn't sailed yet, has he?'

'No, Martin is still here, but please, Maud, why all those people?'

'Don't question me, just do as I ask and get them here quickly. I'll not last the night. While you see to all that, send Johanna up to me. She's a sensible, compassionate young woman. I know you'll look after her, but your brother isn't an honourable man, Maddy. Old age makes you a good judge of character. She's a good wife and mother. I would have liked to have seen the new baby . . .'

'You will, you really will.' Maddy choked on the words but she got to her feet and raced down to the kitchen. She had a lot to do now. The old lady's breathing was growing more laboured by the minute.

'She *is* dying!' she burst out as she hurried through the green baize door. 'Johanna, she wants you to sit with her while I carry out her last wishes.'

'Oh Maddy, no! We'll get the doctor!'

'No, she doesn't want that. She's resigned to it, Jo. Where's Freddy?'

'In bed.'

'I'll get him up and send him first for Reverend Owens, then Father Molloy, then Martin – but I've no idea how to get in touch with Mr Hatfield.'

'What does she want them all for? And Father Molloy? Are you sure she said him?'

'Yes. Oh Jo, I hardly know what I'm doing!'

'Tell Martin to go for Mr Hatfield. Herself has his home address, it's in her little diary. I know where she keeps it,' Carmel said, bustling about.

'I'll go for Martin myself,' Maddy said.

'Oh, I wish Tom was here. He's no use to us stuck in some tavern or walking the streets to think!' Joanna said despairingly, then she went upstairs to sit with Mrs Buckley. Maddy flicked quickly through the pages of the diary until she found what she was looking for.

'Maddy, can I help, please?' Carmel asked. She was upset for she knew Maddy spoke the truth. Their beloved Mrs Buckley was dying.

'Carmel, do you think you could find your way to the Reverend Owens's house?'

'Yes. I know where it is. Johanna pointed it out to me one day when we were passing. I'll hurry.'

'Get your jacket while I write him a note.' Maddy scribbled a few words on a piece of paper; thank God he didn't live too far away. 'Here, take this while I go and get Freddy. I'll wait here until you come back. Freddy can go to fetch Martin.'

When they'd both gone, Freddy looking half asleep but understanding the importance of his errand and the need for speed, Maddy sat down at the table and dropped her head in her hands. She had no idea why her mistress had sent for Martin and Father Molloy; but at least she didn't now need to tell her of her intention to break the promise she'd made – and for that she thanked God.

Carmel was first back with a concerned Reverend Owens just behind her.

'Oh sir, thank God you've come. She's . . . she's dying. My sister-in-law is with her.'

'Then I'll go straight up. There's no need to accompany me, Miss Kiernan.'

She nodded and sat down shakily. Carmel caught her hand. 'Do you think we should tell Charles and his father?'

Maddy shook her head. 'She didn't mention either of them. We'd better wait.'

Johanna came downstairs and eased herself into a chair. 'I've left him with her. I thought there might be private things she wanted to say to him. Sort of make her Confession, if they have Confession at all.'

'They must have something,' Maddy answered.

'Will I make us some tea?' Carmel asked. She was really

trying to be of some use to them and she hadn't felt at all afraid as she'd run through the dark streets.

'That would be nice,' Johanna said gratefully.

The kettle had just boiled when Freddy arrived back with Martin.

Maddy jumped to her feet and threw her arms around him.

'Maddy, is she dying?' he asked seriously.

'Yes, the vicar is with her. What about Father Molloy and Mr Hatfield?'

'Both on their way. I went to see Mr Hatfield in case he wouldn't believe Freddy. Sit down, my dear, you look distraught.'

'Oh Martin, I am! She's been so good to me, to all of us, and she said I was like a daughter to her, and asked me to call her Maud.'

'Did you?'

'Just the once. It was so hard to do.'

'What does she want myself and Father Molloy for?'

'Maybe she's going to ask him to bless us or something.'

'You didn't tell her you'd changed your mind?'

'No. I was waiting for the right time.'

'It doesn't matter now, love.' He released her and gently pushed her down onto a chair while he stood by the range, his hands deep in his pockets.

After what seemed to Maddy to be an age, they heard the sound of horses' hooves on the cobbles of the square.

'That'll be Mr Hatfield. I'll go and let him in,' Martin said quietly.

As he left there was a tap on the back door and the priest let himself in.

'Oh Father, thank you for coming so quickly!'

'She's not of our faith, is she?'

'No, her vicar is with her, but she definitely asked for you to come. Martin is letting Mr Hatfield, her solicitor, in through the front door. She asked for all four of you.'

They all went into the hall, apart from Carmel who couldn't face up to the ordeal but promised to send Tom up the minute he came home. Johanna was now getting annoyed by his prolonged absence.

Maddy then ushered them upstairs. Even though it was a big room, it seemed to be crowded Maddy thought as she closed the bedroom door behind her.

'Everyone is here now,' Reverend Owens said.

The old lady opened her eyes. She'd made her peace with God in the presence of her vicar.

'Then I want you, Father, to marry these two now, before I go.' Maud turned her frail head on the pillow to look at Maddy. 'Maddy, it wasn't right of me to demand that promise and I did intend to release you from it the next time your young man was home. You're a good girl.' Her gaze travelled to Martin. 'Mind you look after her or you'll have me to answer to when your time comes to face the Grim Reaper.' A smile crossed her weary face.

'I promise I will, ma'am.'

'Mr Hatfield . . . Edward . . . you've been a faithful coun-sellor to me; you are also a witness to this union, as is Reverend Owens.' The sick woman's voice grew fainter, then she rallied. 'When they are married I want you to read out my new Will. Mrs Johanna Kiernan will be a witness too.'

'That's all right and proper, Maud. You need have no worries on that score,' Mr Hatfield replied with a catch in his voice. He'd been her friend and solicitor for many, many years.

'Get on with it, Father, I might not last much longer,' Maud then said, attempting to raise her hand to make a gesture to hurry him along but she didn't even have strength enough for that.

Instinct had made the priest bring his scapula and he took it out, kissed it and placed it around his neck.

'In the name of the Father, the Son and the Holy Ghost. We are gathered here to see this man and this woman joined in Holy Matrimony . . .' he began.

Johanna tried to kneel but the priest shook his head and Reverend Owens helped her to a chair as the most bizzare wedding ceremony he had ever seen took its course.

It was over so quickly, Johanna thought, watching the love and joy that shone in Maddy's eyes gradually dim as she remembered just where she was. It was very irregular but Reverend Owens had acted as a witness for Martin; she herself as Maddy's witness.

'Give me a kiss, Mrs Brennan, then I'll go happily.'

There were tears on Maddy's cheeks as she bent and kissed the withered cheek. Martin took the old lady's hand gently.

'Thank you, Mrs Buckley. Maddy and I will always remember you.'

'See that you do,' the old lady replied with a flash of her usual high-handed manner, 'on your anniversary.'

Next Johanna kissed her mistress and held onto her hand while Mr Hatfield cleared his throat and began to read out the Will which left Mrs Maud Buckley's estate, apart from a bequest of three hundred pounds to Reverend Owens, to Mrs Magdalene Brennan.

'You see, Maddy, I intended to see you married long before I died.'

'But I was going to break my promise! We . . . we were going to get married . . .' Maddy broke down; it was all too much for her. She didn't care about the money.

'Of course you were. I've never been a fool, Maddy. Just take care of . . . of everyone.' And then Maud fell silent as though asleep, as if the ordeal had been too much for her.

'I'm afraid she's gone, God rest her,' Reverend Owens said, holding the limp wrist that no longer had a pulse of life left.

Maddy turned to Martin and buried her face in his jacket and he held his new wife to him. 'God rest her, may she be at peace,' he said quietly.

'I'll go and send for the undertaker,' Johanna said, going to the door.

'I think all our work is finished now,' Mr Hatfield said shakily. 'Good night, reverend gentlemen.'

Johanna was halfway down the stairs when she heard Tom's voice. Oh, about time too!

'Johanna, what's going on? I can't get any sense out of Carmel. Why is the house full of people? Is herself ill?'

'She's dead, Tom. If you'd have come home sooner, you would have been some help!'

'I needed to think. How was I to know she was that ill?'

'Well, she was! She sent for the vicar, Mr Hatfield, Father Molloy and Martin Brennan.'

'What the hell for?'

'She was entitled to leave this world in her own faith. Father Molloy married Maddy and Martin, and Mr Hatfield read out her Will. She left everything to Maddy, apart from a bequest to the Church of England.'

Tom was struck dumb.

'Well, aren't you going to say anything?'

He still couldn't speak but anger started to smoulder inside him. All the plans he'd made this night were as nothing now. The old lady had left everything, *everything* to Maddy and her new husband. There would be no money and no ships for himself from Maddy and Martin.

Chapter Twenty-three

The next day, Martin made it his business to send word to the old lady's brothers and they, and their wives, arrived mid-morning.

Maddy didn't like any of them, but she particularly disliked Richard's wife, Elizabeth. A cold-looking woman with iron-grey hair and a sour expression on her face, she was accompanied by her son Charles. Her two daughters had been left at home. Maddy was relieved to leave all the explanations to Martin.

'We should have been summoned last night!' Richard Murgatroyd said.

'I realised that, sir, but as she had passed away, we thought it best to leave informing you until today.'

'Oh, did you indeed, and why did you think you were a fit person to make that decision?' Harold Murgatroyd demanded.

'Because everyone was upset and needed a night's sleep. It was a terrible shock for the household.'

'That was very presumptuous of you!'

'I think Mr Brennan was just being thoughtful, Father,' Charles interrupted.

'When I want your opinion, Charlie, I'll ask for it,' his father snapped.

'I don't think there's call for such comments, it's neither the time nor the place for an argument,' his wife interrupted coldly. Charles was her only son and therefore she held him dear; she certainly wasn't going to have him humiliated before family and servants.

'Mrs Buckley left specific instructions for her funeral in her Will. Reverend Owens will take care of all that,' Martin informed the visitors, a reproving note in his voice.

'Does Mr Hatfield have her Will? When does he intend to read it?' Edmund Murgatroyd asked as Carmel brought in the tea tray.

Charles looked at her with sympathy. 'Are you all right, Carmel?' he managed to whisper as she placed the plate of shortbread biscuits and decanter of sherry at his elbow.

She blushed, but gave a brief smile and nod, neither of which escaped his mother.

'He read it last night, sir, in the company of myself, my wife Maddy, my sister-in-law Mrs Johanna Kiernan, the Reverend Owens and Father Molloy.'

'A priest! A Roman Catholic priest! Just what was he doing here?' Rose Murgatroyd, Harold's wife, demanded angrily.

'He married me and Maddy, at Mrs Buckley's request.'

'But what about the will?' Edmund pressed. He wanted

to hear no nonsense about marriages and dying requests.

'Apart from a three-hundred-pound bequest to Reverend Owens's church, everything has been left to my wife, Magdalene Brennan.'

There was total silence. Edmund's wife upset her teacup but paid no heed to the stain that was seeping into her skirt.

'Did I hear you correctly?' Richard gasped.

'You did indeed, sir.'

'She can't do this! She can't set us all aside and leave everything to . . . to . . . servants! We'll contest it!' His face was purple, while his son's had gone a deathly white.

'You are quite free to do so, sir, but Mr Hatfield assured us that it was within the law, correctly drawn up, signed and witnessed. No one here was a witness, so no one knew the contents. Mrs Buckley asked a neighbour to come in to do that, I believe. I'm sorry, but you'll have to accept her wishes.'

'Like hell we will!' Elizabeth fumed. 'Never mind the sherry, we're leaving. We intend to go to see Mr Hatfield immediately.'

All three brothers and their wives stared at Maddy, furious that this slip of an Irish servant who'd only been here a matter of a year or so was now wealthy beyond her wildest dreams, while they had nothing.

'I'll try to come and see you, Carmel, when tempers have cooled,' Charlie whispered. He was feeling upset about his aunt's death and needed to come to terms with her decision to leave him out of her Will. Carmel nodded; she hated rows of any kind.

'They can rant and rave as much as they like, but it won't do them any good at all,' Martin said as they returned to the kitchen. As far as he was concerned, the bequest was Maddy's. Mrs Buckley's wishes were final.

Maddy automatically began to make tea.

He knew how they felt, Tom thought. Maddy was quite at ease letting her husband take over. His only chance of advancement now was to see that Carmel married Charlie – but under the circumstances, and from the look on his mother's face as she'd taken his part, it didn't bode well.

They all went to the funeral; the other mourners were few, but everything was beautifully done. They stayed at the back of the church in a little group, which included young Freddy and Ronan. The family, clothed entirely in black and inwardly fuming, sat at the front.

'Well, at least they came,' Maddy said when they got home.

'She had everything of the best and Charlie did seem upset,' Carmel added a little tearfully.

'He was the only one of that lot who was,' Johanna said. 'All they were interested in was her money. They weren't upset – they never visited her.'

'Except Charlie,' Carmel put in.

'And he'd only come to touch her for a loan, the first time, I'm sure of it,' Johanna said ruefully. 'The second time, he came to see *you*.'

'But he got on well with her,' Carmel defended him.

At least that was a good sign, Tom thought.

'I suppose you are all wondering what happens now?'

Martin said as they all sat around the table. He was due to sail on the evening tide and didn't want Maddy to have to face all the arguments alone. They had spent their wedding night locked in each other's arms, but the presence of the old lady's body in the bedroom next door had hung over them. Since then they'd had little time to talk privately.

'Tom, of course you will go on living here and attend to any important things that crop up. When I get home next time, we will have a long discussion over the future.'

'Will we indeed?' Tom answered acidly.

Johanna looked at him, her glance counselling him not to lose his temper.

'Things will go on as normal, except that we will all be able to choose bedrooms and even employ staff.'

'Us, employ people? I wouldn't know where to start,' Johanna said, becoming flustered.

'You don't have to do anything you don't want to do, Johanna.'

She reconsidered. 'I could certainly do with *some* help.'

'We'll get someone in to do the heavy housework, I'll cook and Carmel will carry on as before. Is that all right, Carmel?' Maddy asked.

'Oh yes. I enjoy doing it.'

'She should take things easy, she's never been strong. Get her out more, Maddy – order her some new clothes,' Tom suggested. He didn't want Charles to go on thinking of Carmel as a servant.

'She'll have all that,' Maddy promised, smiling at her sister. 'I'll take her into town myself, after Martin's sailed.'

* * *

It was a tearful farewell, that took place in Martin's cabin. The Mate had made himself scarce and as Maddy was now Martin's wife, there were no objections to her going aboard.

'Oh, there's so much to talk about and I'm going to miss you so much, I really am.'

'And I'll miss you, Maddy. You'll be in my thoughts day and night. Are you sure you can cope with Tom if he gets out of hand?'

'I can so. I've had years of practice.'

'Try not to have too many arguments.'

She smiled up at him. 'Let's forget Tom and everyone else. I only have a few minutes,' she murmured, drawing his lips down towards her own.

She stood on the dockside for an hour, watching as the ship under full sail moved slowly upriver. She felt desolate, yet she should be happy. She had everything in the world she wished for now, and Martin's next trip would be as Master of his own ship, for everything she had was to be shared with him.

When she got back, the kitchen was empty but there were lights burning in the drawing room and two of the bedrooms. She smiled to herself as she climbed the stairs. Tom hadn't lost any time in making himself at home in the rooms Mrs Buckley had lived in.

Her brother was reading the evening paper, sitting before the ornate fireplace in an armchair covered with faded rose-coloured brocade. Johanna was sitting on the long sofa but she looked uncomfortable.

'Has he gone?' Johanna asked.

'Yes. I watched the ship go out for as long as I could. Will I make us some tea? Give me a chance to use the best china,' she smiled warmly.

'That would be nice, Maddy, but . . .' Johanna's last words were cut off as a pain ran through her.

'Oh God! Is it starting, Jo?' Maddy cried and Tom put down his paper.

'I think so.' Johanna looked scared.

'Where's Carmel?' Maddy asked.

'Sorting through her things – she's chosen the blue bedroom. Aah!' Another contraction made Johanna cry out.

'Fetch her, please, Tom. Tell her to go for the midwife now.'

Tom got up. 'Oh, she'll be no use. I'll go.'

'At least she can boil the water. Tell her she's plenty of time to move her things.'

Three hours had passed since the midwife's arrival. Maddy made endless cups of tea and Tom paced the floor.

'You'll have the pattern worn off that carpet,' Maddy told him. 'Sit down, for God's sake, and try to read your paper.'

Tom tried, but every time Johanna screamed, he put it down, got to his feet and started pacing again.

'Oh, I can't stand this,' Maddy burst out. 'I don't care what that woman said about other people bringing in disease – I'm going in. She's got some funny ideas, has that one.

339

Clean sheets and towels, spotless aprons and cuffs, plenty of strong soap! The woman's a fanatic!'

'But she might be right, Maddy. A lot of babies die and she said it was the dirt of the rooms and beds that killed them,' Carmel said, trying to calm her sister.

'Well, spotless aprons and cuffs she'll have! I'm going to the kitchen for them before I go in,' Maddy said grimly.

With her hair clinging in damp wisps to her perspiration-covered face, Johanna finally gave birth to a daughter at half past midnight.

'Oh, she's beautiful, Jo! I do envy you.'

Johanna smiled at Maddy tiredly. 'You'll have one of your own one day.'

Maddy nodded. Yes, she would. 'What are you going to call her?'

'Aideen. Tom and I both like it.'

'It's pretty, just as she's going to be.'

'So, everything's all right then?' Tom asked as he came in.

'Everything is just grand, Tom. Look, take her.' Johanna handed the baby over.

'Aideen Kiernan. My little princess,' he said fondly, as Johanna and Maddy exchanged surprised glances.

In the days and weeks that followed, both mother and baby thrived. Maddy had taken on two girls, one to do the heavy housework and an older, more experienced girl to help with the cooking and shopping. Maddy and Carmel went into town and spent what Maddy considered to be a small fortune on clothes for them all, Ronan and Aideen included.

'Oh Maddy, I just can't believe that all these things are for me! They'll fill a wardrobe entirely! I've never had so much underwear, or stockings – and so many pairs of boots and shoes that I'll never wear them out!'

'It's not the object to wear them out, Carmel. They're to match your dresses and coats.'

'It was all terribly expensive,' Carmel said, holding up a pale blue dress of fine wool, trimmed with rows of black braid around the hem, cuffs and collar. Autumn was on them now and winter wouldn't be far behind, but instead of feeling depressed at the thought of the miserable days ahead, Carmel felt excited. Oh, she had so much now. A beautiful bedroom of her own, access to the drawing room, the dining room, the comfortable, cosy breakfast room, the luxury of a bathroom and so many other rooms besides, all furnished beautifully.

'I suppose this time last year we would have said it *was* terribly expensive, ruinously expensive, but now . . . Carmel, we'll never want for anything, ever again.' Maddy had invested Maud's money wisely, so the bank manager told Martin, and there were the two ships. Even if they wanted to sell them – which they didn't – they would bring in a fortune.

Carmel impulsively hugged her sister. 'We've come a long, long way from Rahan, have we not?'

'We have so, but the most important thing in my life is being married to Martin.'

Carmel drew away. 'I'm glad you're happy, Maddy, and I think Johanna is happy, for most of the time.'

'And you? What about you?'

Carmel shrugged. 'I just told you how lucky I am.'

Maddy became serious. 'Do you think you could love Charlie, enough to marry him? Enough to spend the rest of your life with him?'

Carmel shook her head. 'I don't know, Maddy. Sometimes I think I do, that I can do all that. And other times I don't think I can.'

'I'm not going to force you to do anything, Carmel. There's no rush, you are very young. I don't want you to make decisions you might well regret later on in life.'

'I know, but what if Charlie doesn't understand?'

'I'll make him understand. I promise,' Maddy said determinedly.

Charlie was equally determined in his plans to go and see Carmel. His parents had fumed and fought, threatened and even cajoled, but to no avail. The Will was valid, that was final, Mr Hatfield had stated. Since then, Richard Murgatroyd had been in a constant state of near-apoplexy.

'Are you still intent on this stupid idea of seeing that girl?' his mother demanded as Charlie came to tell her he was going out for the evening.

'I am.'

'Charles, how could you?' she pleaded. 'She's a servant, she's a common little upstart!'

'She's not, Mama. She's no longer a servant, she was never an upstart, she's shy and she's *not* common!'

'I don't care what you say, I refuse to believe that she's

anything else. I feel that she's not so much quiet and shy as quiet and *sly*! Even with all of that malicious, vindictive old woman's money, she'd have a hard time catching herself a decent husband! She can't even speak correctly, and I dread to think what her manners are like, *and* she's a Catholic. You can't be serious!'

'I am, Mother. You don't know her the way I do.'

Elizabeth laughed cuttingly. 'The way *you* do? All you've had are a few brief conversations, nothing more than a couple of sentences. Unless of course there are things you haven't told us?'

'There are not!' Charlie said, angry at the implication, and he slammed out.

Richard had been quiet during this altercation, but now he spoke.

'Elizabeth, have you no sense at all? Don't you see, we now have some claim on Maud's money. If Charlie were to marry this Carmel person, whatever her sister settled on her, Charlie would be entitled to. By all accounts, Mrs Brennan is very fond of her sister, and the girl doesn't look as if she'll make old bones. She doesn't appear to be very bright, either. It would be easy for Charlie to persuade her to do any number of things that would enrich us.'

'You can't expect me to condone Charles *marrying* the girl?'

'If you want to go on living in comparative luxury then you'll have to put up with her, won't you?'

'Oh, I hope that old bitch is roasting in hell!' Elizabeth shouted suddenly. 'Your father was mad, completely mad to leave everything to her in the first place, and now . . .'

'We'll never have a hope of getting our hands on any of the money, the property and the more expensive pieces of furniture unless we encourage Charlie in his courtship of this girl. It's the only chance we have, my dear.'

'I do wish you wouldn't call our son Charlie. It sounds so horribly vulgar,' his wife sighed, knowing that what her husband said was true. But she hated the situation. Well, if the girl was to be forced on her, she'd make sure her life was a misery. At least she still had the power to do *that*.

Chapter Twenty-four

'Oh Maddy, I'm so nervous,' Carmel whispered. 'Do I look nice?'

'You look more than just nice. You look absolutely gorgeous altogether. He'll be delighted with you,' Maddy promised.

'Really?'

'Really.'

Carmel felt so nervous about this outing. She liked Charlie, but who wouldn't? She had thought about John Shannahan these last couple of nights. She *had* loved him and she would never forget him, but Charlie was so different. As Maddy had often said, she couldn't live out the rest of her life grieving for John, and she was sure that he wouldn't want her to.

'Well, at least he's punctual,' Maddy said as Tom and Charlie came into the room.

'Oh Carmel, you look stunning!' Charlie cried. He meant it. She was dressed entirely in pale pink and in the height of fashion. She would turn everyone's head and he was proud to think that he was her escort.

'Take her away, Charlie, before she drives us all mad!' Maddy laughed, as he took Carmel's hand and led her into the hall.

They were going for a walk in the park. Carmel grinned to herself as she remembered the mix-up with Johnnie Fearon, David Evans and the Palm House.

'You look very pleased with yourself,' Charlie commented, seeing the smile hovering on her lips.

'Oh, I didn't mean to look smug,' she said hastily. 'It's just that once I was asked out to see the Palm House but I never got there.'

'Who asked you?'

'Oh, no one important. No one for you to worry about.'

'I'm amazed that I haven't had to fight off a whole horde of suitors.'

'Oh, I've never been like that.' Carmel looked horrified. 'I would hate to have more than one man in my life.'

'Really?'

She nodded.

Charlie held her hand tightly as he helped her into the cab. He was certain now that he loved her and wanted to marry her. Yes, she was not of his own kind, but she was like no other girl he'd ever known, and he couldn't get her out of his mind. Day or night.

'Charlie, I'm not . . .' she faltered, 'bold – very forward,' she explained. 'I don't like meeting people – other men.'

'I'm glad.' He smiled down at her. She wasn't forward and he *was* glad of it. 'Carmel, do you think you could like me? Really like me?'

She dropped her gaze. 'Oh Charlie, I do already like you a lot. I'm very fond of you. You're so different from anyone I've ever met before.'

'You know what I mean, Carmel.'

'I do so, but . . .'

He put his arm around her shoulders and drew her to him and she made no protest.

'Carmel, I love you, I really do. I know it's crazy, I haven't known you very long at all and we'll have difficulties, but I don't care.'

Her heart began to race and she turned towards him. 'Oh Charlie!'

He gently cupped her chin in his hand and brushed her lips with his. He didn't want to frighten her. 'My little dove, you are so sweet!'

She felt decidedly dizzy, as though she were drifting on a cloud. She'd thought she would never feel like this again. She'd been so sure that she'd buried her heart with John Shannahan, but she hadn't. Everything Maddy had told her was true.

'Do you know, Charlie,' she said in wonderment, 'I think I may love you too.'

Again he kissed her gently. 'Carmel, you've made me so happy. I'll come and take you out as often as I can.'

'I don't need to go out all the time,' she teased him, 'and I'm sure Maddy won't mind you coming to the house as often as you like. We can stay in – get to know each other better.'

'Of course we can. I want to see you every single day. I want to hold you and kiss you every single day too.'

She was very relieved by his words. She *did* hate going amongst strangers. Carmel was happiest at home with people she knew and trusted and loved.

'You will take care of me, Charlie?' she whispered.

'I will, I promise. I'll take the best care of you I can. No one is going to upset you. No one at all!' he answered vehemently.

It had been a wonderful afternoon. There were other people in the warm humid glass-house where all manner of tropical plants and trees grew, but she was quite content to let Charlie guide her around, holding her hand tightly as he explained what each exotic plant and flower was called. They'd got a cab home too and he'd kissed her again, promising to see her the next day. She liked him kissing her; he was very gentle and she felt safe and secure when she was with him. He wouldn't let anything unpleasant happen to her.

'I'll come again tomorrow, my love. Is the same time convenient, or would you like me to come in the evening?' he asked as she pressed the door bell.

'The same time will be fine, Charlie, and thank you. I've had a lovely time and I'll really look forward to tomorrow, I mean it.'

'I'm so glad. In fact, you don't know just how glad I am.'

'I do know, Charlie, I really do.'

He held her hand to his lips before turning away and retracing his steps.

It was Maddy who opened the door to him the following day.

'I've come to see Carmel, if I may?' he said.

'Of course you may.'

'I brought these, one for you and one for Carmel.' He handed Maddy a large bunch of flowers.

They must have cost a pretty penny, Maddy thought, especially at this time of year.

'Could I have a word with you first?' she said quietly.

'Of course.' Charlie thought he knew what she was going to ask.

'It takes some getting used to actually living in these rooms, but it's what your aunt would have wanted,' Maddy said, ushering him into the drawing room.

'I suppose it does.'

Maddy sat down and indicated that he do the same.

'I think you've probably got some idea of what I'm going to say, but I'll say it anyway,' Maddy began. 'The fact is, I worry about Carmel. She's very unworldly. She's very trusting and sometimes that can be a bad thing. Has she told you about John Shannahan?'

'No, she's never mentioned anyone, except for family.'

'When we first came to Liverpool, before we found Tom and Johanna, we lived in a very downtrodden area. Carmel fell in love with a neighbour's son and he with her. It was a very happy time for them both. Then there was trouble with a girl at work. She became so jealous of Carmel that one day, she and her two sisters set about her, leaving my sister in a desperate state.' She paused. Charlie was giving the story his full attention.

Maddy's voice trembled a little as she continued.

'Of course, John and his father went to see these girls, but they came from a very rough family and their male relatives attacked the two men. They were both severely beaten up. John was paralysed and died, not long ago. Carmel blamed herself and was completely overcome with grief. So, you can see why I worry about her. She mustn't be hurt again. Are your intentions serious, Charlie?'

'They are. I love her and want to marry her. I'll look after her, I promise.'

'I don't want her pressured, Charlie. I don't want her pushed into something she'll regret and you'll regret.'

'Oh, I won't do anything like that. I had hoped to ask her to marry me today, but if you think it's too soon . . .'

'I do. You hardly know each other.' His gaze settled on her wedding ring and she smiled. 'Yes, it's true – Martin and I fell in love at first sight, but I'm not like Carmel. I know my own mind and I'm confident now. Your Aunt Maud taught me a lot. I'd like you to wait, Charlie – for a few weeks, anyway.'

He was disappointed, but he nodded his agreement.

'Now, what about your parents?' Maddy continued briskly. 'They can't be very happy about all this. Do they know what's going on?'

'Yes, they do and you're right, Maddy – they are not a bit

happy about it. However, I think Father will relent in time and as for Mother, well, no one would ever be good enough for her only son. Sometimes I feel as though she's suffocating me. I keep hoping that once she talks to Carmel and gets to know her, she'll see what a lovely, gentle-natured girl she is.'

Maddy nodded and stood up. 'Then that's all right.' She smiled at him. 'I think Carmel is in the kitchen but I don't intend to summon her in the way your Aunt used to.'

He grinned as she crossed to the bell-pull.

'Charlie's here – and look at the beautiful flowers he's brought us,' Maddy said when her sister came into the room. 'Right, I'll leave you two alone. I promised Johanna I'd take Ronan out, to give her a bit of peace.'

Carmel sat down on the sofa and Charlie sat opposite her.

'The flowers are lovely, Charlie, thank you. I've never been given flowers before.'

'I thought they might brighten up the days,' he replied, glancing through the window and noticing that the leaves on the trees in the little park were turning yellow and red.

'Carmel, would you like to go out again?' he asked. 'The weather's fine – we could take a walk in the park again and then go somewhere for lunch.'

'I'd like to go for a walk, Charlie, but I'm not sure about lunch. I've never been out to lunch anywhere. I'd show you up.'

He leaned forward and reached for her hand. 'Carmel, you will never "show me up" as you say. Everyone will be

351

falling over themselves to know who the beautiful girl is that I'm lunching with.'

'Oh dear – I wouldn't like that at all.' She looked alarmed.

'All right, we could do something else instead, or would you like to stay in?'

'I'd like to stay in, please.'

Charlie smiled with relief; for a moment he had thought she just might refuse. Now he could see what Maddy was talking about; Carmel was really very shy indeed, and totally unaware of how lovely she was. He was a bit disappointed not to be able to show her off, but he wouldn't rush her.

When Maddy went into the kitchen, Tom was there.

'I hear he's come to ask her out again,' he said.

'He has. He seems to be quite serious about her. He wants to marry her, in fact – that's why he came today, to propose. I asked him to wait, though, to be patient. You know how delicate she is.'

At his sister's first words Tom was genuinely pleased. Things were going well, but now he was irritated.

'For God's sake, Maddy, why make them wait?'

'I want Carmel to know what she's doing, to know her own mind.'

'She'll never know her own mind,' he scoffed unkindly. 'Half the time I think she hasn't got one at all! She'll never grow up, Maddy, unless she's given a bit of a push.'

'A bit of a push? There's no one going to "push" her into anything she doesn't want to do, not while I'm here!'

'Then she'll keep the poor wee feller dangling on a string

for ever or until he gets fed up. He's not a bad lad. A cut above us to be sure, but from a decent family.'

'Decent family! They were all waiting like vultures for herself to die so they could get their hands on her money.'

'Maddy, she'll not get any offer of marriage just sitting around the house, hiding from the rest of the world.' Tom was exasperated. Sometimes he thought that his younger sister was walking the fine line between sanity and simple-mindedness, but he would try to get her to agree with his thinking. She shouldn't let Maddy run her life.

His opportunity came the next afternoon. Maddy had gone to post a letter to Martin and had taken Ronan and Aideen with her for some fresh air. Johanna was resting and Charlie was coming again after dinner.

'Carmel, I hear young Charlie was here yesterday?'

'He was so.'

'Do you like him – really like him, I mean?'

'I do, Tom.'

'Enough to marry him? He's a nice lad, from a good background. Quite a catch for any girl from a family like ours.'

'I know he's nice and he comes from a good family and I do like him.'

'Do you love him?'

'I think I do. That's what I said when he asked me.'

'Then will you marry him?'

'I really don't know, Tom. I don't want to hurt him, but . . . it's different. He's different from John.'

Tom became impatient. 'Carmel, grow up! You were far

too young then; Maddy should have put a stop to it. I know you're not much older now, but you can't compare John Shannahan to Charlie Murgatroyd. You refuse to go out so you won't meet anyone. If you're not careful, you'll end up an old maid; that young feller won't wait for ever. He'll find someone else. Is that what you want, to be living with either Maddy or myself, looking after our children but never having any of your own?'

There were tears in Carmel's eyes now.

'I'm only concerned about your happiness,' he said gruffly.

'I know that, Tom.'

'Then just think about it. Will you promise?'

She nodded her head.

'I don't want you to tell Maddy about this conversation. There are times when our dear sister can't see what's under her nose.'

'I won't.'

'So, when you go out with Charlie, enjoy yourself and think about what I've said.'

Carmel thought about it. She didn't want to be an old maid, left on the shelf. Charlie was a good catch and maybe he wouldn't wait for ever; she was fond of him – but was that enough? She instinctively knew he would look after her, but she didn't want to live the kind of life he lived, mixing with people who were well off, educated, and who had all the social graces. If she married him, she would want to live a quiet life, and when children came along she would care for them and she would be happy. She would so love to have children of her own. Very well, she decided. If Charlie proposed, then she would consent. She didn't want to die childless and a spinster.

Charlie came most evenings. He was working hard now, he told Maddy and Tom. Yes, he'd wasted his time since he left Cambridge but now he was planning to be a solicitor and was training under a friend of his father's. The more Maddy saw of him, the more certain she became about entrusting her sister to him. He was a decent young man, no matter how unpleasant his parents were, and from the bits and pieces he let slip, they appeared to be terrible snobs. His mother in particular was a fearful snob, and he was having a rough time of it at home.

Maddy had recently had two very long meetings with her bank manager, and had remarked to Tom that when Martin came home, they were going to change some things. This kind of talk didn't bode well, Tom thought, and he was determined that he wasn't going to live on hand-outs from Maddy. They had moved up in the world, but not high enough, as far as he was concerned. The sooner he could get Carmel married to Charlie, the better. He'd make sure he was indispensable to the inexperienced young man and, with access to his money, he'd be able to have things the way he wanted them, and to hell with Maddy!

Charlie too felt he'd waited long enough, and the next evening when they sat by the fire in the breakfast room, he brought up the subject.

'Carmel, I can't stand it any more, although I promised

Maddy I wouldn't press you. I love you and want to take care of you. Will you marry me?'

'I . . . I will so, Charlie, but I'd like to live a quiet life. I'm not much good at conversations with people I don't know.'

He took her in his arms. 'I promise we'll have a quiet life. No lunch or dinner parties. No musical soirées.'

'Oh Charlie, that sounds grand.' She was so relieved.

'What about your religion – and mine, come to that?' Charlie said.

'Maddy says that Father Molloy won't marry us. He can't. Things are very strict.'

'Does that upset you?'

'Yes and no. Yes because I've always followed the teachings of the Church and no, because I want to marry you.'

She leaned her head on his shoulder.

'The Reverend Owens will marry us,' he told her gently. 'We are all High Church and I believe there's not much difference between that and the Catholic Church. We have Confessionals and Communion and Confirmation and nuns too.'

'I didn't know all that.'

'So, will we tell them the good news?'

'Yes. I hope they'll all be delighted.'

'Why wouldn't they?' Charlie asked with a smile.

'Of course we're thrilled for you both,' Tom said, shaking his future brother-in-law's hand. 'We'll have to have some kind of celebration, won't we, Maddy?'

She ignored him, turning instead to her sister. 'Carmel, are you sure?' she asked in a low voice.

'Oh, I am, Maddy. I really am.'

'Then we will have a celebration. Just the two families,' she added hastily, seeing a shadow cross her sister's face.

'That might prove a bit difficult,' Charlie said, thinking of his mother's reaction at having dinner served up to her here, surrounded by all the beautiful antiques that she had coveted for years.

'Oh, I'm sure you will be able to persuade them, and your sisters too,' Maddy said airily.

She hadn't known about Charlie's sisters, but upon questioning her brother she learned there were two of them. Caroline was Maddy's own age and Christine was thirteen and still at school.

The proposed marriage and dinner party had caused Charlie a lot of grief. His mother had flatly refused to go anywhere near Carmel and her family, nor would she attend the ceremony, whenever it might be. Caroline was highly indignant, taking her cue from her mother. Christine said nothing. Her opinion wouldn't count for anything. His father had been more amenable and had told him to go ahead with all the plans for the party and that he would have a serious talk with Elizabeth and try to win her round.

'I'm sorry I invited them now,' Maddy said to Johanna as she looked at the array of glasses and silver cutlery Tom had set out on the sideboard.

'Why? Things will be a bit strained but we'll cope.'

'What am I going to give them to eat? They'll expect something fancy.'

Johanna looked thoughtful. 'Why don't we hire a job cook from an agency?'

'What's a job cook?'

'Someone who is a very good cook but prefers not to be tied to a single family for one reason or another.'

'Will she have any ideas? I don't want to look a fool.'

'I should think so. We can also hire a couple of maids to wait, or even a butler or a footman for the evening.'

'Oh, I couldn't cope with that!'

Johanna laughed. 'You'll cope with anything! Look, why don't you ask Carmel to write out formal invitations? Her handwriting is beautiful and it will give her something to do, apart from being in a state about what to wear.'

'Jo, I just hope this isn't going to be a huge mistake. She swore she'd never love anyone after John died and maybe we're being a bit too ambitious. We're only working people, when all's said and done.'

'Maddy, she says she loves him and wants to marry him. I know she's your flesh and blood, but no one knows any other person inside out. She might be happy, she can't grieve for ever. He seems to really care for her; if I didn't like him I'd soon tell you, but I do. Everyone does.'

'You're right. I'm just getting in a state about this flaming dinner. Where is the agency where these wonderful people can be found?'

'In Whitechapel. Go and see them – and make sure the girls you hire know how to set a table properly.'

Carmel was instructed to write out the invitations on some thick, expensive writing paper Maddy had found in Mrs Buckley's bureau, and Maddy went down to the Staff Employment Agency.

It was really only a small room set out as an office in one of the large houses, and she was greeted by a rather prim woman who had the disconcerting habit of looking over her lorgnettes at people.

Nervously, Maddy explained what she thought she needed, explaining frankly how little she knew about what was expected on such an occasion. If the woman was surprised she didn't show it.

'That is no problem, Mrs . . .?'

'Mrs Brennan,' Maddy supplied.

'Just have a word with Mrs Beale the cook, she'll discuss the menu with you, and I'll send you two experienced girls and maybe a butler? He would be very useful for ushering in your guests, serving the wine and port and brandy – and of course it would look infinitely better to those being entertained. I have a highly experienced, semi-retired butler who would be pleased to assist.'

'That would be just perfect, thank you.' Maddy was tremendously relieved.

'Good, then I will send both Mrs Beale and Mr Morrison to you the day before, to discuss things and view the facilities. Be so good as to give me your address, Mrs Brennan.'

'Twenty-two Faulkner Square.'

'Thank you, Mrs Brennan.' The little woman removed

her lorgnettes and gave Maddy a warm and encouraging smile.

'I've a job cook, two girls and a butler coming on Thursday,' Maddy announced when she got home.

'Well, that should do the trick!' Tom said with some gratification. He, too, wanted to impress the future in-laws.

'I suppose then I'll have to go out early on Friday morning to order all the food.'

'And I'll have to go down into the cellar to see what wine there is.'

'I never knew there was a cellar just for wine,' Carmel said, thinking of their cellar home in Gillings Entry.

'Well, there is. Mind you, I've never been down there. Never had a reason to. Herself only ever drank the occasional glass of sherry.'

'Do you think we should have flowers on the table?' Maddy asked.

'I don't know, but I think there is supposed to be something in the middle, beside the candlesticks,' Carmel said dubiously.

'Something else to ask advice on. Oh, I wish I'd never mentioned this! It's going to be a terrible strain on everyone.' Maddy sank down into a chair, wringing her hands.

'Don't think like that, Maddy. We don't want them to suspect that we're in awe of them,' Tom said rallyingly. 'We're as good as they are, any day.'

'I suppose you're right,' she sighed, but her heart was full of dread.

* * *

It was a hectic week. They all worked hard, cleaning, polishing and sweeping the rooms that would be used. Maddy dragged furniture out to clean behind it. Rugs and carpets were taken up, thrown over the washing line and given a good beating. All ornaments were either washed or polished.

'Hope they appreciate all this,' Maddy gasped, wiping the perspiration from her forehead as she dragged a valuable Persian rug back into the dining room.

Mrs Beale and Mr Morrison arrived on the Friday morning, together with two girls, one about twenty-two, the other nearly thirty, and Maddy and Johanna found them all very helpful.

'Oh, you've taken a load off my shoulders, Mrs Beale, so you have!' Maddy exclaimed after the woman had guided her through an elaborate menu written in French.

'It's no trouble, madam. It's what I get paid for. I much prefer working like this.'

'It's great for us that you do. The lot that are coming would terrify you.'

Mrs Beale smiled. 'We'll give them a real eye-opener then, shall we?'

Just then, Tom walked into the kitchen, followed by Mr Morrison.

'Your former employer left you a fine cellar, madam,' the butler said gravely. 'We've chosen a light, refreshing white wine to accompany the hors d'oeuvres, an excellent claret for the main course, a fine dessert wine to follow and a prime French brandy and a bottle of tawny port of considerable age for the gentlemen.' He beamed at her. 'If your guests are used to good living – and Mr Kiernan here has told me that they are – they cannot help but be delighted. Now I'll just run through some things with the girls, if you'll excuse me?'

'Oh Maddy, this is going to be a night to remember,' Johanna said excitedly. 'They are all so confident and experienced that I don't think we'll have anything to worry about – except what we're going to wear.'

'I wouldn't be too sure of that, Jo,' Maddy sighed. 'That mother of Charlie's has a face that would stop a clock, and don't forget – they'll not be too delighted at drinking wine that they thought would be theirs!'

'Well, Tom seems very pleased. I reckon my husband thinks *he's* entertaining them, acting the gentleman. I heard him ask Mr Morrison about the way he should address them.'

Maddy laughed. 'Well, that will give you a bit of peace.'

'What are we going to wear?' Carmel asked, being carried along with the tide of excitement.

'I'm wearing my black bombazine, the one with the long sleeves. It can be cold in that dining room,' Johanna said. 'I have a pretty locket and a cameo brooch to brighten it up.'

'I remember Mrs Mitchell having a dress of black bombazine,' Maddy recalled. 'Don't worry, Jo, black suits you, though it looked terrible on her.' She grinned at the memory of the plump, plain Canal Agent's wife.

'What about you, Maddy?' Jo asked.

'I'll wear my wine-coloured velvet. After all, I am a

married woman so I have to look sedate and steady.'

'You're only a girl!' Johanna laughed.

'Still, I'll not have remarks passed.'

'Will you wear the old lady's jewellery?'

Maddy had been overcome when the jewellery box was opened and she realised that everything in it was hers.

'Yes, I will, in her honour. I think I'll wear that pearl necklace and earrings. Carmel, you can wear the sapphire and diamond necklace, earrings and bracelet.'

'Oh, can I, Maddy? They're gorgeous! I'm going to wear my pale blue organza and taffeta dress, with the low neck and short puffed sleeves. I've got a lovely white shawl I can use if I get chilly.'

'You'll look wonderful. His sisters will be green with envy,' Maddy said with satisfaction. Everything was perfect; if only Martin could have been here.

The house looked wonderful, Maddy thought as she made a final tour of inspection on Saturday evening. In the kitchen was the most sumptuous meal she'd ever seen and Elsie, the older of their parlourmaids, had done a first-class job of setting the dining table, supervised by Mr Morrison. She had also arranged seasonal flowers and fruit in an ornate bowl in the centre of the table. Maddy had seen Tom, in his first dinner suit and looking well in it, being given instructions by the butler as to the right order in which he should escort his guests into the dining room, after the sherry had been served in the drawing room.

'Oh Maddy, I'm so nervous,' Carmel fretted as she looked at all the trappings of wealth that surrounded them.

'Don't worry, they'll all be impressed, especially Charlie – and that's all that matters. Go in and join Johanna and Tom, I'm coming in a minute.'

Maddy observed her sister with pride. No man could fail to be struck dumb by the sight of her. Then she looked at herself in the hall mirror. A dark-haired young woman, full of confidence, looked steadily back at her. She didn't come anywhere near Carmel in the beauty stakes, but she didn't look bad. Again she wished Martin was with her. 'Well, he's not, so you'd better get on with it,' she told herself.

The Murgatroyds, when they arrived, were all rather stunned. Elizabeth looked around quickly, but there was nothing she could fault. The place looked far better than she'd ever seen it. The Kiernans had got themselves a butler and there were at least two maids in black silk dresses and fancy white aprons and caps to wait on them. The woman had to admit that they all looked exceedingly well dressed, but her eyes widened and she caught her breath when Carmel stood up. Now she knew what Charles saw in her; Carmel was the most beautiful girl she'd ever seen in her entire life. She heard Caroline gasp too. Beside Carmel, her eldest daughter looked drab and plain. To Elizabeth's annoyance, Richard seemed to have fallen under the girl's spell as well as Charles. He was actually kissing the chit's hand!

'May I offer you a glass of sherry, madam?' Morrison was faultless.

'Thank you,' Elizabeth replied, taking a glass from the silver tray he held.

All the ladies, except for Christine, had glasses of sherry.

Tom, Charlie and his father had crystal tumblers of whiskey and Johanna stared pointedly at her husband, reminding him not to drink too much and thereby make a show of them all.

'The house looks well, don't you think, Mrs Murgatroyd?' Johanna broke the ice.

'It does. In fact, it looks different. Have things been changed?'

'No, just cleaned.'

Elizabeth sniffed.

'I do hope you like chicken fricassée?' Maddy said sweetly.

'One of my favourite dishes, Mrs Brennan.' Richard smiled ingratiatingly and his wife stiffened.

Charlie grinned at his father. He was sitting as close to Carmel as he could within the bounds of propriety; he was completely smitten, dazed that someone as beautiful as she was his alone.

Maddy tried to engage Caroline in conversation but the girl was not cooperative; she just stared enviously at Carmel and answered in monosyllables. Maddy then turned her attention on young Christine, who was more forthcoming. Tom and Richard seemed to be getting on well, she thought, as Morrison appeared and informed them that dinner was served.

Tom offered his arm to Elizabeth and Richard offered his to Johanna. Charlie was forced to escort Maddy while Carmel and Caroline followed, and Christine brought up the rear.

Maddy exchanged a triumphant glance with Johanna as everyone exclaimed at the magnificently set table.

Inside, however, Elizabeth was raging. Some of this should have been hers! There was far more silver and crystal than she had imagined that Maud had owned, and the sight of the turquoise and gold Spode dinner service made her suck in her lips with the outrage of it all. It was like strewing pearls before swine! What were they, but jumped-up, ignorant Irish peasants who had had the good fortune to be taken on by old Maud Buckley who, she was certain, had not been possessed of her wits. There was nothing she could do about it now, Elizabeth thought bitterly, except suffer it and be thankful that by Charles marrying the girl, some influence could be brought to bear to claw back some of the money that should rightfully have been split between her husband and his two brothers, Harold and Edmund.

The food and wines could not be faulted, and Maddy resolved to pay Mrs Beale and Mr Morrison and the two maids double what the agency paid them. When Johanna rose and said, 'I think it's time for the gentlemen to have their port and cigars,' Maddy was so proud of her. You would have thought Johanna was an experienced Society hostess, not a young wife and mother who had only that afternoon learned what was expected of her.

'I know what they'll be talking about – business, if Papa has anything to do with it,' Caroline said flatly. She was bored now and wanted to go home.

'It's no concern of ours what they talk about, Caroline,' her mother rebuked her. 'That is why we leave them.'

'I suppose we should really talk about the wedding,' Johanna said pleasantly.

'I suppose so.' Elizabeth's tone was curt.

'How many of your relations do you think will attend?' Maddy asked.

'Not many.' Elizabeth's mouth snapped shut like a trap.

'There will only be immediate family on our side too. Myself and my husband, Martin. Johanna and Tom – and that's it, really. I think Carmel would like Caroline and Christine to be her bridesmaids. Have you any objection, Mrs Murgatroyd?'

Caroline glared at her mother but Elizabeth ignored her. With a very bad grace she agreed.

'Tom will give her away and Martin will be Best Man. Charlie was quite happy with that arrangement.'

'I'm sure he was.' At least he wasn't going to ask one of his friends. Elizabeth would die of mortification if it got round that Charles had married a beautiful but empty-headed, ignorant Irish servant girl.

When the men finally appeared, both Maddy and Johanna were relieved. Elizabeth rose; she too had had enough and wished to prevent further conversations.

'Richard, will you please ring for our coats?' she ordered.

'So soon?'

'Yes, indeed. We are all tired,' his wife answered through gritted teeth, as she made her thanks and farewells with the greatest possible speed. In no time at all, the visitors had been despatched and the Kiernans were left alone, apart from the staff who were still clearing away in the kitchen.

'Oh, thank God for that!' Maddy cried, collapsing in a chair. 'I never want to spend another evening like that again! I'm exhausted!'

'Neither do I,' Johanna agreed, 'but it went very well. Very well indeed.'

'Now can I have a proper drink?' Tom demanded. He'd found Richard Murgatroyd very interesting, and even affable.

'You can drink a whole bottle if you like,' Johanna laughed.

'Ah, Mr Morrison . . .' Maddy exclaimed as the butler knocked on the door and entered.

'Just Morrison, madam. Was everything to your satisfaction?'

'Oh yes, indeed. Everything was *perfect*.'

'Excellent. Then I'll tell Mrs Beale and the girls they can go. I believe you ordered a hansom cab to collect us here at midnight?'

Maddy got up. 'Yes, but please wait. I want you to have an extra payment. We would have been completely lost regarding etiquette and the like without all of you, but especially you, Morrison. I'll come downstairs with you.'

'It's very kind of you, madam, but the Agency doesn't encourage it.'

'I suppose they take a share of what you earn?'

'That is how it works, madam.'

'Well, what they don't see won't hurt them. We all know what it's like to work one's fingers to the bone and be exhausted at the end of the day. Please – I insist.'

'And so do I,' Tom added, already on his second large whiskey.

Johanna couldn't suppress a smile and neither could Maddy.

Chapter Twenty-five

Even though the weather had become really cold, with heavy frosts alternating with gale-force winds and lashing, ice-cold rain, Maddy didn't care. In two days Martin would be home. These days she bought the *Journal of Commerce* fortnightly to try to gauge just where he was, as his letters were very erratic in their arrival from foreign ports. She and Carmel had employed some workmen to decorate the house. Johanna had helped to choose the paint and wallpaper. Although Johanna supervised the two girls they'd employed, it was still a full-time job looking after a lively pair of youngsters.

Carmel grew ever more excited as the wedding plans were made and both Maddy and Johanna were delighted with the change in her.

'Just think, Maddy,' her sister said dreamily. 'Next year I'll be married and might be having a baby. I'd love that. I'd be so happy.'

'Indeed you might. You're really looking forward to the wedding, aren't you?'

'I am. It will be a wonderful Christmas.'

'It will so, for all of us. Do you remember our first Christmas in Liverpool? It was a nightmare. Sleeping on the floor in what was little better than a house of fallen women.'

'Oh Maddy, don't tell Charlie that!' Carmel looked alarmed. 'I wouldn't want him to know that we were so desperately poor.'

'I won't if it upsets you.'

'The memory does upset me – it was horrible.' Carmel shuddered and then resumed making a list of everything she had to do. The young couple were being married on the second day of the New Year, 1849. It would be a new life and a very different one, Carmel knew, and she wished that she wasn't so afraid of Charlie's mother and his eldest sister. She would be thrown on their mercy as she and Charlie were planning to live with his family for the first year of their marriage. She pushed that thought to the back of her mind. She wasn't going to let it spoil this Christmas.

Maddy hugged her coat closer to her as she stood on the waterfront watching the tiny speck that had just appeared on the waters of the estuary. It came nearer and nearer until, with sails billowing and bow cutting a white wave in the dark grey waters of the Mersey, Martin's ship came home.

It seemed an endless wait for them to come alongside, drop anchor, tie up and the dockers start unloading her cargo. Maddy was cold, she could hardly feel her feet, but she didn't care. She was impatient now. Why was her husband being so slow? He has to sign off, you eejit, she told herself.

His was a responsible job; the crew would be paid off first.

At last her patience was rewarded. She watched him come onto the poop deck, shake hands with two older men and sling his seabag over his shoulder then make his way to the gangway.

'Oh Martin, I've missed you so much,' she sighed.

He took her in his arms. 'Maddy, my love, there have been times when missing you was an unbearable ache.'

When they finally drew apart, an action hastened by the whistles and cat-calls of the dockers, he took her hand.

'How are things at home, Mrs Brennan? I did get most of your letters but obviously not all.'

'Oh, and I wrote so many.'

'I know.' He squeezed her hand.

'Carmel is going to marry Charlie Murgatroyd on the second day of the New Year.'

'You're happy about that?'

'I am. You should see the change in her. It's as though someone has lit a candle behind her eyes. She sort of glows.'

'That's a relief.'

'It is, so. I told Tom not to push her but he did. I was annoyed with him at the time but I have to admit that it was what she needed.'

'So she will be going to live with him and the rest of his family? I did get your letter about his mother and sisters.'

'I don't like them at all. Carmel certainly can't stand up to them and that worries me, but I'm hoping Charlie will do something about that sooner rather than later.'

Martin frowned. 'He seems a bit of a dandy.'

'I know what you mean, but he's working in his father's friend's law firm and is doing reasonably well. He *is* making an effort. He has no money of his own to speak of, but I'll make sure Carmel doesn't suffer because of it.'

'Do you think it would be better if we were to buy them a house of their own?'

Maddy deliberated on this. It was something she'd thought about too. 'If we do that for Carmel, Tom will expect the same, and while I'm very fond of Johanna and the children, I've not forgotten how he stole from Mrs Buckley. Given the chance and opportunity, he'd steal from us too.'

'How?'

'Oh, he'd probably let the house to another family or something like that, and I don't want any rows. If Carmel really can't stand living with them, then I think we should talk about it again, don't you?'

'You know your family best, Maddy. Oh, but it's great to be home, it really is,' he said meaningfully as he handed his blushing wife into a cab.

It was the best Christmas any of them had ever had. The rooms looked bright and cheerful, huge fires burned in the fireplaces, and in the dining room the table positively groaned under the weight of the food set upon it. There were gifts for everyone, and the children were mesmerised.

'They're really too young to appreciate it all. Wait until next year,' Johanna said, removing a cut-glass bon-bon dish from her son's chubby grasp before any danger befell both the child and the dish of sweets.

'There might be others on the way by then,' Carmel said bashfully.

'True for you, Carmel,' Tom said kindly. He was quite content for the moment. They had everything now, he thought, looking around. The scene was like a picture from a book, something with 'A Happy Family Christmas' written under it. He'd had a few stiff whiskies and had mellowed. In this mood, he didn't even mind his brother-in-law.

Charlie was coming to tea and arrived two hours early.

'I couldn't wait. I *had* to see Carmel and give her her gift.' He kissed her gently on the cheek as he handed her a small parcel. 'Go on, open it,' he urged and everyone gathered around.

Carmel tore off the paper. Inside was a jewellery box in soft cream leather with a pattern of acanthus leaves picked out in gold.

'Oh, Charlie!'

'Open it,' he repeated.

'Oh look!' she cried. Inside, on a bed of red velvet, was a golden locket in the shape of a heart on a slender gold chain.

'It's beautiful,' Johanna said.

'It really is, Charlie,' Maddy agreed.

Carmel was dismayed. 'I haven't anything like this for you! Oh, I feel so mean!'

'My darling, I didn't expect anything,' he told her tenderly. 'I have your love and very soon I'll have *you* – and that's enough to make any man happy.' He kissed her again while everyone clapped and Carmel, as usual, blushed to the roots of her hair and buried her face in Charlie's jacket.

As the New Year approached, the final details and arrangements for the wedding were made. They were to have the reception, small as it was, at the bride's home. Johanna had already gone to the Agency and booked the services of Mrs Beale, Morrison, Elsie and Jane. The flowers had been ordered and the girl from the shop was to come and arrange them in the hall, drawing room and dining room.

The Reverend Owens was marrying the young couple, since Father Molloy had refused to do so. Maddy had had an argument with him about it when she'd gone with Carmel to see him.

'I *can't* Maddy. It's as simple as that,' he told them both. 'In the eyes of Holy Mother Church they can't be married, unless he becomes a convert.'

'It's a very hard rule, Father, and I'm sure he won't want to convert. It's a big thing to ask.' She was certain about that. It would be the last straw for his family.

'But a very necessary one. Catholic souls are very precious to God and we must make sure they stay that way. If there were mixed marriages taking place all the time, what would happen?'

'With respect, Father, I don't think that would damage anyone's faith, as long as they still believed and went to Mass and took part in the Sacraments, and surely it wouldn't be what God wants – someone who would change religion just to get married?'

'Maddy, I know how generous you've been to this parish and I thank you for it, but that's a very serious, almost blasphemous thing to say.'

'I can't understand why, Father.'

The priest's face became set in hard lines and Maddy had taken Carmel's arm. 'I think we'd better go home before anything more is said.'

The Reverend Owens was a little doubtful, too, but knowing Maddy and Carmel, and the fact that the groom and his family were Church of England helped him to make his decision.

'Maddy, er, Mrs Brennan, you're quite sure about this?'

'I am so, sir. The marriage will be recognised as such by the law, won't it?'

'Oh, indeed.'

'Then I would be very grateful if you would marry Carmel and Charlie Murgatroyd. You gave a lovely sermon when old Mrs Buckley died.'

'I'm quite sure we can make it a very special day for Carmel,' he'd answered pleasantly.

Caroline had flatly refused to be a bridesmaid and nothing her brother or father could say would change her mind. Her mother remained silent but it was a silence of conspiracy. All Elizabeth wanted was to get this charade over and done with. She could cope with Carmel once she was living under her roof, she thought grimly. The woman was well aware that Maddy had opened a bank account for her sister and had lodged the enormous amount of five thousand pounds in it.

'Don't get upset, Carmel. Christine has agreed and I'll be your Matron of Honour, if you like,' Johanna offered.

'Will you, really?' Carmel begged. Caroline didn't like her at all and it made her nervous.

'Of course. You can have Maddy too. She's just as much entitled as I am – in fact, more so. Why don't you ask her?'

'Can you have two Matrons-of-Honour?'

'I think you can have as many as you like.'

'Could I just have you and Maddy?'

'You could, but don't upset little Christine. There may well come a time when you'll need her friendship.' Johanna too was worried about Carmel going to live with her in-laws.

In the end she, Maddy and young Christine were to attend Carmel. Christine, who though fearful of her mother and sister, had determined to have a bridesmaid's dress and wear flowers in her hair.

'You'll have the eyes out of the head of all of them!' Maddy exclaimed when she had finished getting a very nervous and agitated Carmel into her wedding dress.

The bridal gown was of cream silk trimmed with pale blue bows, with ruffles around the hem and sleeves. Her bonnet was also of cream silk with pin tucking and wide blue ribbons to fasten it. She would carry a small posy of seasonal flowers and foliage.

'I'm so nervous, Maddy,' she fretted. 'I hope I won't make a fool of myself.'

'How could you? Just think that it's really only Charlie who matters, no one else, and concentrate on that. Now sit there until I see if Johanna is ready.'

Johanna was. She was just fastening the buttons on Ronan's new coat.

'Maddy, you look lovely.'

'Do I really, Jo? I know it's Carmel's day, but I didn't have a new dress of any kind when Martin and I got married. Not that I'm complaining.'

'You look lovely. I mean it, and Martin will be bowled over by the sight of you.' She meant what she said. The sapphire-blue velvet suited Maddy far more than it suited herself, as did the white satin bonnet decorated with small clusters of white flowers on the underside of the brim.

'Do you think the children will be all right with Julia?' Maddy asked. The parlourmaid was going to look after Ronan and Aideen in the church.

'I think so, but if they do start to become restless or start wailing, then she's to take them out until the service is over. I'm not having Carmel's future mother-in-law looking down her nose at us more than she already does.'

'Well, I know it's only a small wedding, but everything is of the best that money can buy. I hope that satisfied the old dragon! Now – are we ready?'

'We are. Tom will bring the carriage around to the front. I just hope young Freddy's going to be able to drive it without any accidents.'

'He's been practising all week. Maddy, stop worrying. Everything will go like clockwork,' Johanna said firmly.

Freddy, in a black overcoat and sporting a top hat for the occasion, managed to get them to the church without mishap.

'Well done, lad. Here.' Martin passed him a coin. Tom

raised his eyebrows. The lad had already been paid, why waste more money?

'Maddy, you look beautiful,' Martin whispered, kissing her quickly on the cheek.

'I see they're all here,' Johanna remarked, peering through the glass doors of the church's vestibule.

'Is Charlie here?' Carmel asked, hanging tightly on to Tom's arm.

'Of course he is. Now I'd better get inside. I *am* the Best Man when all's said and done.' Martin grinned and pushed open the door.

'Now, Carmel, take a deep breath and hold Tom's arm lightly. Christine, you walk behind them and we'll follow,' Johanna instructed.

Maddy thought how quickly the service seemed to go. A Nuptial Mass took much longer, but it was a wedding service and that was all that mattered. Carmel looked radiant, there was no other word for it, she thought and her young husband obviously thought so too, for he gazed at her adoringly. At last she felt a sense of relief. Carmel, so frail, so painfully shy, so sensitive, would from now on be Charlie's responsibility.

Back at Faulkner Square, the conversation was a little stilted. Both Richard and Elizabeth Murgatroyd kissed Carmel politely on the cheek, and Caroline was prompted to do the same by a fierce glance from her mother. Young Christine needed no prompting. She liked Carmel and thought her elder sister was being horrid.

'So, how does it feel to be Mrs Murgatroyd?' Maddy asked, holding both her sister's hands.

'There are three Mrs Murgatroyds already,' Elizabeth remarked dryly.

'And now there are four,' Maddy said sweetly, but her gaze was icy.

'Well, never mind about all that. The wedding breakfast looks wonderful and I for one am ravenous,' Richard said, trying to lighten the atmosphere. He thought Carmel was a charming little thing. Charlie had done well for himself there, he thought. He'd be more than able to get his hands on the five thousand pounds that now belonged to his wife. All he had to do was hint and Carmel would do anything he said. Dear, dear, Elizabeth was a fool at times. Richard belched discreetly. This damned indigestion! He'd not felt too well when he'd got up that morning but put it down to too many celebratory glasses with Charlie last night. A good meal and a 'hair of the dog' would do wonders; it always did.

There was enough food here to feed a small army, he thought appreciatively as he took the glass of whiskey Morrison offered him.

'It's definitely going to be a "them" and "us" do,' Martin whispered to Maddy.

'No, it isn't. Morrison set out the place cards in strict order. They'll *have* to talk to us.'

'She looks a real tartar.' Martin indicated with his head to where Elizabeth stood with her daughters. 'A smile would crack her face.'

'Oh Martin, I'm beginning to feel really worried about Carmel. However will she manage?'

'Maddy, my love, you worry far too much about Carmel. She's a married woman now and Charlie will see she's well treated. It's not as if they were going to live abroad or even move to another town. You'll be able to see her and she'll be able to come here.'

'You're right – and Charlie does love her.'

'Besotted, I'd say. Just as I am with my wife.'

'Oh, Martin Brennan!' Maddy laughed as he squeezed her hand.

The meal was served and eaten, the toasts – such as they were – were made and the small party moved into the drawing room. Tom, Charlie, Martin and Richard were making inroads on the decanters of whiskey, port and brandy and were all smoking cigars. The women clutched crystal flutes filled with the most expensive champagne, although none of them really liked it.

Carmel sat on the long sofa with Maddy and Johanna, and young Christine managed to squeeze in on the end.

'You wait, Christine, one day you'll have a beautiful wedding dress and a handsome husband,' Johanna said, smiling at the child.

'That will be a long time in the future,' Elizabeth, who was not happy at her younger daughter's flouting of her instructions, said icily.

'Maybe, but surely you have someone in mind for Caroline? She's the same age as Maddy, I believe, and not even betrothed.' Johanna's tone was soft but it carried a barb.

'I'd thank you to leave discussions of that nature to myself and my husband.'

Johanna smiled and looked pointedly at Caroline, whose face was red with anger.

Elizabeth had had quite enough. It had been a dreadful day. 'Richard! Richard, I really do think we should be going. After all, Carmel will need time to be with Charles.'

Richard, now on his fifth glass of whiskey, didn't share her intentions. 'We can't go yet, dear, it's bad manners et cetera. Tom and I are having a great discussion.'

Elizabeth sat down. Oh, what wouldn't she say to him when she got him home, providing he was sober enough to understand, of course.

Morrison brought in more champagne but everyone refused it. Christine had pulled a face and had whispered to Carmel, 'It's got up my nose!' Carmel had giggled. At least Christine liked her.

The talk from the corner in which the men were gathered grew louder.

'Jo, I think we'd better do something before they all become incapable,' Maddy said anxiously. 'Richard looks particularly unsteady and his face has gone puce.'

'I agree. Martin and Charlie don't look too bad, but Tom and Richard . . . Oh, God!'

They all jumped to their feet as Richard suddenly slid to the floor, his glass falling on the carpet.

'Oh, Martin! Why did you get him into a state like this?' Maddy cried.

'I didn't, Tom did, but—'

'Thomas Kiernan, you're a living disgrace!' Johanna said angrily. 'How could you ruin Carmel's day?'

'I . . . I . . . haven't ru . . .' Tom's words were slurred.

'Will someone please get the carriage this minute!' Elizabeth raged. Oh, how humiliating! 'Charles, I'll never forgive you for this! Your father is drunk! The disgrace of it!' Her cheeks were red with fury.

Martin was still bending over Richard, trying to get him on his feet. Maddy could see that her husband looked very concerned.

'Martin, what's the matter?'

'He's not drunk, he's ill. Very ill, I think. Maddy, will you take Carmel and the two girls upstairs for a few minutes, please.'

'But if—'

'Maddy, *please*!'

Subdued and puzzled she ushered them out, ignoring Caroline's protests.

'Martin, how ill is he?' Johanna asked, leaning over her brother-in-law's shoulder.

'I'm sure he will be better when I get him home and send for the doctor,' Elizabeth said curtly. Oh, would this day never end? How much more could she be expected to stand?

'I'm afraid he won't, Elizabeth. Your husband is dead. I am so very sorry. Johanna, fetch her a chair, will you?'

'Oh, my God! He *can't* be!' Tom exclaimed, sobering up quickly.

'I'm afraid he is. I thought he didn't look well in the

church but put it down to "the morning after". It must have been his heart,' Martin said quietly.

Elizabeth's hand went to her throat and all the colour drained from her face.

Johanna, who was also very shocked, took the situation in hand.

'Here, Elizabeth, sit down. Martin, pour her a small glass of brandy, and you'd better send Freddy for Dr Prosser.'

Charlie looked ghastly. 'Father can't be dead! He *can't* be!'

'Pull yourself together, man. Your mother and sisters and your wife will need you,' Martin said firmly.

'Merciful God, what a way to end the day,' Johanna said quietly.

'And what a dreadful start to a marriage,' Martin agreed sombrely.

Chapter Twenty-six

Everyone sat shocked and numbed. Maddy couldn't believe it. The man had been enjoying himself just a few feet away from her, and now he was dead! Martin sat on the arm of her chair, his arm around her, as stunned as everyone else. Carmel was crying softly, her head on Charlie's shoulder. Charlie himself was still deathly white and Tom had insisted that he should have a glass of brandy too.

Elizabeth sat on the sofa, her daughters either side of her. Christine was crying but Caroline and her mother just sat staring into space. Tom stood in front of the fireplace, his hands in his pockets, a frown on his forehead.

Johanna broke the silence. 'I think I'll go and wait for the doctor in the hall. Freddy shouldn't be too long now, I told him to run all the way.'

'A good idea. Under the circumstances, perhaps we should all go back into the dining room,' Tom suggested quietly. Although Johanna had covered Richard's body with a white sheet, his very presence was disturbing.

'No. I'll wait here.' Elizabeth was firm.

'As you wish, Elizabeth,' Maddy said.

'Girls, go into the dining room with everyone else,' Elizabeth instructed her daughters.

'No! I don't want to have anything to do with any of *them*!' Caroline answered vehemently.

'It would be best to do as your mother tells you.' The girl was unpleasant but Johanna felt sorry for her.

'No, I won't! It's all their fault, Mama!' Caroline got up, her fists clenched, her eyes burning with grief and anger, and she turned on Maddy. 'This would never have happened if you hadn't been left the money. It wasn't yours! You came in here and took it all away from Father and his brothers. You know how angry he was. It was their money and stupid old Aunt Maud goes and leaves it to the likes of you! I hate you!'

Maddy sat white-faced and mute at this onslaught but Martin got to his feet and faced the girl.

'Caroline, I don't think it is very appropriate for you to be shouting abuse and your father not even cold and in the same room. Maddy never wanted anything. She came here to work, that's all. She had given up all claim to the money by choosing to marry me. You didn't know that, did you? Old Mrs Buckley gave her a choice. Stay unmarried for ten years or until after she died, whichever was the soonest, and she could have everything. Maddy decided to marry me, thereby breaking her promise and giving up her right to inherit. But the old lady relented, as she had always intended to do, and saw to it that Maddy and I were married before she died. Everything that has happened was at her behest.'

'Do you think I care about all that?' the girl's sneering voice rose an octave.

'Caroline, that will be enough!' Elizabeth ordered her daughter.

'Mama, I hate them!'

'CAROLINE! Do as I tell you, this minute!'

The girl hesitated, looking around. 'Well, *she'll* never be happy,' she said, glaring at Carmel. 'She's got Charlie, but she won't ever be happy. Don't you see, Mother, this is a bad omen for her.'

Carmel uttered a frightened cry and clung to her new husband. She believed Caroline was right.

'That's quite enough of that nonsense!' Martin thundered. 'You – go into the dining room and stay there until your mother has decided what will be the best course of action to take. And I don't want to hear any more abuse hurled at either Maddy or Carmel!'

The girl stared him out for a few seconds, then dropped her gaze and went into the dining room, followed by her sister, Maddy and Carmel.

'I'll ask Mother what I should do, then I'll come and tell you,' Charlie told Carmel, torn between his wife and mother and shocked by his sister's vindictive outburst.

'Well, Mother, what would be best?' he asked of the woman who had seen her son wed and her husband dead in one day.

'When the doctor has been and the . . . arrangements have been made, I will go home and take the girls with me.'

'And what do you want me to do?' Charlie asked.

'I'd like you to come home, as planned, but . . .'

'Without Carmel.' It wasn't a question.

'Yes.'

'Mother, how can I leave her? It's our wedding night!'

'And your poor father is lying over there in the corner. Is it too much to ask?'

At this point Martin intervened. He understood both their positions. 'Charlie, I know it is hard on you, but don't you think you could go with your mother and sisters? You've your whole life ahead of you, you and Carmel, and I don't really think she'll mind for one night. She'll have Maddy and Johanna to comfort her.'

Reluctantly Charlie nodded his agreement.

After a couple of protests Carmel was persuaded by Maddy and Johanna that it would be best for her to stay.

'Charlie's family are very upset and shocked. I know Elizabeth looks to be very calm but she must be in a terrible state underneath – near breaking point. She just manages to hide it well, that's all. Let's get this night over with,' Maddy appealed and reluctantly Carmel agreed.

The arrangements were made for the funeral to take place in three days. They were all going to attend.

It was a bleak affair. Harold and Edmund and their wives and children remained dry-eyed throughout. Elizabeth and her daughters also bore it well. Both Caroline and Christine were red-eyed, but Elizabeth showed no visible signs of grief or loss.

Carmel had objected to staying at Faulkner Square until the day of the funeral.

'I just want to be with Charlie!' she'd cried, disappointedly.

'I know you do, but Charlie has so much to do at the moment, and think how desperate it would be to be there all day with Elizabeth and Caroline so . . . upset,' Maddy had counselled. Neither she nor Johanna wanted Carmel's first few days of marriage made even worse by temper tantrums from Caroline.

'It's only two more nights,' Johanna said soothingly.

The funeral tea was held in Richard's house. When the mourners had departed in dribs and drabs only Charlie, Tom and Elizabeth remained in the drawing room. The food had barely been touched by anyone, and in an atmosphere you could have cut with a knife, Christine and Caroline went to bed.

'Why don't you go up too, Mother? It's been a long and harrowing day,' Charlie urged.

'I think I will. Thank you, dear, for everything you've done to help me get through it. Good night.' Elizabeth kissed her son on the cheek, then turned to Tom. Her tone changed. 'Good night, Mr Kiernan,' she said frostily.

Tom just nodded his acknowledgement.

'Well, there's just you and me. How about another drink?' Charlie asked.

'I think that's a good idea. What a day!'

'I know, but I thought we all bore up well, including

Carmel. She's dreadfully upset, Tom, keeps talking about it being a bad omen.' He sighed.

'Ah, take no notice of all that nonsense, Charlie. It's women all over. Now, there's something important I want to discuss with you.'

'What?'

'What are we going to do?'

Charlie looked mystified. 'About what?'

'Your father's estate. I've given this a lot of thought, and if we pull together we can build up the business together.'

'I . . . I don't know anything about commerce,' Charlie told him. 'I deal with the law.'

'Ah, sure commerce isn't hard to fathom at all. It's all investment and speculation. If we could borrow some money, we could perhaps buy a cargo ship of our own. It would be a start.'

Charlie was confused. 'A cargo ship? Where would we get that kind of money?'

'From Maddy or Carmel. I know Maddy has settled a large amount on her.'

'Oh, I wouldn't want to upset Carmel about money.'

'She won't be upset, not if I talk to her. She has no sense at all about money. She's never had any of her own, she wouldn't know what to do with it. Maddy's always given her everything.'

'No, leave her out of it for now,' Charlie said firmly. Carmel had had enough to contend with over the past week. His poor wife was in a terrible state of nerves.

'Then we'll go and ask Maddy,' Tom replied. He didn't

want to, but if he had a chance to make even more money than Maddy had in the long term, he'd do it. Basically Charlie was weak. A decent young man who genuinely cared for Carmel, but weak in terms of the cut and thrust of the world of business.

A still unsure Charlie accompanied Tom to see Maddy the following day. He didn't want to go but Tom insisted. 'If you stay there with all those women, it will drive you mad,' he'd said.

'Charlie and I want to talk about something important, Maddy,' Tom announced, which immediately aroused her suspicions.

'How are things at home, Charlie?' she asked as she carried the tea tray upstairs herself. Johanna had taken the children into town and Martin had gone to see his Bank Manager.

'Tense. Caroline is still angry with Carmel and everyone here. I do hope she'll get over it. It's the shock, and she was always Father's favourite. I hope when Carmel comes home with me tonight there won't be trouble.'

'Nothing you can't handle, Charlie. Right – what is this important matter you wish to discuss?' Maddy asked as she poured the tea.

'Charlie and I were talking things over last night and we've decided to invest everything in a joint business.'

'What kind of a business?' Maddy began to wish Martin were there.

'Commerce, but we need some extra capital. We thought that if we could use Carmel's money—'

'Oh no, you don't, Thomas Kiernan! That money is for her security, her peace of mind and a certain independence.'

'But Charlie's her husband. In law he's entitled to use it,' Tom protested. He'd expected some kind of argument.

'That's as maybe, but I took advice from Mr Hatfield, the old lady's solicitor, and invested it in such a way that only she can draw on it. It's a gift from me to her,' Maddy said pointedly. 'Nothing at all to do with either husbands or brothers.'

'Maddy, if it's going to cause so much trouble, then forget about it. I don't want Carmel to be worried,' Charlie intervened.

Maddy smiled at him. Tom had obviously talked him into this.

'Charlie, I've told you, it won't upset her!' Tom pressed determinedly.

'At least someone cares about her,' Maddy replied.

'Let's forget Carmel.' Tom was losing his temper.

'How can you forget Carmel?' Maddy shot back. 'Just what is this commerce venture anyway?'

'Shipping. Cargo and vessels.'

Maddy leaned back in her chair and nodded slowly. 'Oh, now I see what this is all about. You want to buy a ship, start up your own shipping line.'

'And what's wrong with that? You've got two ships already.'

'I inherited them, along with the staff who have run the business successfully for years. I wouldn't know what to do with the damned things if I didn't have them. And remember – I didn't ask to be left anything, let alone two ships!'

She lowered her voice. 'Tom, why can't you be content with what you've got? I know you have savings put aside, and there was that other matter before Mrs Buckley died. You've a splendid roof over your head, we all live well, you have money in your pocket, good clothes, a rising position – what more do you want?'

Tom had grown angrier and angrier. 'I want my own bloody business, Maddy! I don't want to be under any obligation to you or Martin. You didn't earn that money, Maddy, and by rights it should have gone to Richard and his brothers, until you wheedled it out of herself.'

Maddy was on her feet. 'I did no such thing! You know damn well I didn't! Well, you'll get no money out of me. You'll never be satisfied, Tom. You're greedy through and through.'

'Oh, isn't that great coming from you? Who was it that wouldn't be content to stay in Ireland? The pair of youse should have stayed there!' he yelled.

'Who was it who thought he could marry the likes of Florence Mitchell and have the job as Canal Agent handed to him on a plate?' she shouted back.

Charlie intervened. 'For heaven's sake, will the pair of you stop this!' He knew they didn't get on well together but he'd never witnessed a full-blown row like the one that was now brewing.

'Charlie, he's not to touch a penny of Carmel's money!' Maddy said hotly. 'I know him. He'll keep on and on at her until she's so confused she won't know what she's doing and I won't stand for it!'

Tom's face was now puce. All his life his sister had thwarted him, sneered at his ambitions – well, no more.

'I'll not let it go, Maddy. I'll not stay under this roof another night. When Johanna comes back, we'll pack up and go.'

'Go where?'

'To live with Charlie. I'd sooner have his mother sneering at me than you. I'll work, I'll save.'

At his words, Charlie looked first startled, then dismayed, but brother and sister were too fired up to notice his reaction.

Maddy was scathing. 'The same way you "saved" when Mrs Buckley was alive?' she shot back at him.

He gritted his teeth. He should have thought of drawing extra money long before he had done so.

'I don't suppose Johanna will have any say in this?'

'She's a good wife. She'll obey me as she promised when we were married. Come on, Charlie, I'm not wasting any more time here.'

Looking completely out of his depth, the younger man followed Tom out of the room after first casting Maddy an imploring glance.

'Maddy, what's the matter?' Johanna said, finding her sitting in the kitchen. She handed Ronan and Aideen over to Julia. 'Come on upstairs and tell me,' she urged. 'Where's Martin?'

'At the bank and I wished he wasn't,' Maddy answered with sincerity.

'So, what is it?' Johanna asked, sitting down in an easy chair in the drawing room.

'Tom came around with Charlie and we had a huge row. Not Charlie, Tom and me.'

Johanna sighed. 'What over now? I thought how well you two were getting along.'

'I know, so did I until this morning. I'm sure he dragged Charlie along. He seemed confused as well he might, having only buried his father yesterday.'

'Oh, honestly! Tom has no tact or sensitivity.'

'He never has had. They came to ask me to more or less give them a free hand with Carmel's money.'

'What for?'

'To go into "commerce" as Tom called it. They want to buy a ship. A cargo ship like those Mrs Buckley left me. I said no, that that money was for Carmel's security and comfort. Then Tom really got going. I told him it was a gift and he had no right to it, so the outcome was . . . that he's gone.'

Johanna looked concerned. 'Gone where?'

'To live with Charlie – and you and the children are to go as well.'

'What?' Johanna was astounded.

'Oh, I told him he was too ambitious, but it only made him worse.'

'But we've got everything here. I don't *want* to go and live with Charlie and his frosty-faced mother and that little madam, Caroline.'

'He said you had no choice, that you will obey and

stand by your marriage vows. Oh Jo, you'll *have* to go!'

'No. I'll speak to him. Make him come home.'

'I don't want him saying I broke up his family, Jo.'

Johanna didn't answer. Maddy was right. If she refused to obey her husband and stayed on here with the children, the family would be torn apart. She'd thought his obsession with success had lessened of late. He'd seemed content living here, ostensibly as the head of the family. Then she remembered that that was before Martin had come back and he and Maddy ran the household. She sighed.

'You're right, Maddy. I have no choice. In time, when he's got over it, I might be able to persuade him to come back. He might hate living in that house. I know I will.'

'He might but yet again, he's a much stronger person than Charlie. He'll be ruling the roost before long.'

'I can't see that happening, Maddy, not with Elizabeth. She's a very strong, domineering woman.'

'I know, and I'm afraid for Carmel. She's already upset and she's no match for either Elizabeth or Caroline.'

'At least I'll be able to keep an eye on her, Maddy, and I can stand up to those two.'

'That's a comfort. She's had a terrible start to her marriage.'

'I can't remedy that but I'll make sure she's not put upon. Charlie idolises her so I don't think there will be any trouble from him.'

'Oh Jo. Just when things were beginning to settle down and look good.'

'Never mind. Tom can't stop me from visiting you and I will.'

Maddy smiled. 'Thanks, Jo. You really are a comfort to me.'

'Good. Now I suppose I'd better go and start the packing.'

Chapter Twenty-seven

Carmel gazed out of the bedroom window. It was June and the weather was beautiful. The sky was forget-me-not blue, with here and there a wisp of white cloud. The quiet tree-lined road was dappled with sunlight. It was a day when she should have been outside in the fresh air but she was listless and depressed. Turning away from the window, she sat on the low slipper chair and leaned her arms on the windowsill. She'd been married for six months and she'd never been so miserable in her life.

No one had told her about the dreadful things Charlie would want to do to her when they were in bed. She would never forget that first time. It had frightened her and it had hurt. She'd begged Charlie to stop but he'd said he couldn't. Now she could barely stand it when he touched her. She cried out, she turned away from him and he got upset and said he felt guilty but he loved her so much that he couldn't help himself.

Christine knocked quietly and opened the door. She had

become very fond of Carmel, even though her mother and sister said she should keep her distance, remain aloof. She felt so sorry for her young sister-in-law. If it hadn't been for Johanna, poor Carmel's life would have been a misery. Christine admired Johanna. She was the only person she knew who could stand up to her mother. It had been awful when they had first moved in. There were arguments all the time. It had been very distressing and that's when she had become close to Carmel. They were both so sensitive that the rows frightened them and they sought comfort from each other.

'Carmel? Can I come in?'

Carmel turned and smiled. 'Of course you can, but shouldn't you be at school?'

'We finished early. It was the last day today. Just think, three whole months without lessons, although Caroline said I should have a tutor until school starts again. She's hateful!'

'She can be at times,' Carmel agreed, thinking of all the occasions when the girl had managed to make her look and feel a complete eejit.

'Is Charlie going to take you on a holiday?' Christine asked, sitting at the end of the bed.

'I don't think so. He is working very hard at the moment.' It was the truth; he did work hard, and no matter how often she begged him to use the money Maddy had given her, he refused. She knew there had been words between Tom and Charlie over the matter, and Maddy had told her that on no account must she give anything to Tom.

'We always used to go to Llandudno, in Wales, for three

weeks. That was when Father was alive,' the child finished wistfully.

'Well, why can't you go this year? I don't mind staying here and I'll pay for your holiday. I can give your mother the money. No one can object to that.'

Christine's face lit up. 'Oh, would you, Carmel?'

'I will. Go and tell your mother now.'

The girl kissed Carmel on the cheek and ran off excitedly.

It would be worth the expense, Carmel thought, just to have the house more or less to themselves. Charlie was out all day and so was Tom. Her husband now worked as a senior clerk in the offices of the Charteris Line. It didn't pay a fortune, but they managed. She wished Maddy hadn't given her all that money. It had caused so much trouble.

Carmel got up and looked at herself in the mirror. She looked dull and listless, no wonder Charlie stayed at work so late in the evenings. Oh, why had everything gone wrong? She turned as Christine came back into the room, her face flushed.

'What's the matter?'

'Mother said . . . she said she wants to see you immediately.'

It was seldom that Carmel received such a summons and she knew Johanna was out with the children.

'What for?'

Christine shook her head and went out. Carmel followed with trepidation.

Elizabeth Murgatroyd was sitting at a writing desk in the corner of the drawing room.

'You wanted to see me?' Carmel asked timorously.

Elizabeth stood up, her face set in harsh lines. She hated this girl and her entire family; her brother, his wife and the two brats had foisted themselves upon her without even consulting her at all. They had just moved in and Charles had let them. In fact, he had been insistent that they stay. She found Johanna the hardest to deal with, for the young woman was not in the least bit in awe of her as her daughter-in-law was.

'I hear that you told Christine to inform me that you would pay for a three-week holiday?'

'I did so. She was saying that normally you all went every year and so I thought . . .'

Elizabeth stood up. 'Well, you can think again. I will not take charity from the likes of you! I hold you responsible for all the trouble and anguish that has befallen my family. What Charles ever saw in you I don't know, but I have the distinct feeling that you can manipulate him for your own or your brother's ends.'

The tears welled in Carmel's eyes. Oh, she wished Johanna were here or that she could stand up to her formidable mother-in-law.

'I . . . I'm sorry,' she muttered.

'And you can turn off the tears! Crocodile tears won't wash with me! You have ruined this family. With Richard gone, how am I to hold out any hope of finding a respectable husband for Caroline? Who on earth would want to be connected to a family who has a pack of Irish peasants amongst their members. Oh, your brother can dress himself like a gentleman, but he's still "a smart Mick on the make" as Richard always called him. We don't *want* your holiday, we don't *need* your holiday. Now get out of my sight!'

Carmel turned and ran from the room, tears pouring down her cheeks. Oh, how she hated it here. How she hated Elizabeth and Caroline. Charlie usually stood up for her, but only yesterday he hadn't been as enthusiastic as he'd once been. They must have been talking to him.

She flung herself on the bed and sobbed into the coverlet. Oh, everything was such a mess. Nothing had gone right since she'd married Charlie.

Johanna found her still sobbing when she returned to a very quiet house over which a tense atmosphere hung.

'Carmel! What on earth is wrong? You're dreadfully upset.'

'Oh Jo, I didn't mean any harm. I just wanted to help.' Between sobs, Carmel explained what had happened.

Johanna was furious. The nasty, bitter, bullying old bitch! She wasn't going to get away with this. She stormed downstairs but could find no one. Back upstairs, she banged hard on Elizabeth's bedroom door but there was no reply. Nor could she get a reply from Caroline or Christine's rooms. Well, they might go out but they weren't getting away with upsetting Carmel like this. She'd sort them out at dinner. She went back to see if Carmel had calmed down.

'Your dear mother-in-law has gone out and I think she's taken the two girls with her.' Jo paused and looked at Carmel. There was something troubling her. She had been very quiet the last couple of days; Johanna had put it down to the heat but it was more than that. 'Is everything all right, Carmel? Apart from that lot?'

Carmel shook her head. 'Oh Jo, it's Charlie and me,' she blurted out. She *had* to talk to someone.

'What about you?'

'I don't like being married.'

'Why on earth not? You were so happy. What's happened?'

'I was happy at first and I tried to be good to Charlie. I just wanted to be a good wife and mother. You know I love babies and children, but . . .'

'But what?'

'But I don't like what you have to do, what Charlie has to do, for us to have a baby. I can't help it, but now I can't bear him to touch me. I hate myself because he's so kind to me. I *do* love him, it's just . . .'

'Oh Carmel, didn't you know? Did Maddy never tell you?'

Carmel shook her head.

Johanna took her hands. 'There's nothing bad about it,' she said gently. 'It's something you should enjoy, both of you. It's a way of showing how much you love each other.'

'I can't do it,' the other girl burst out. 'It makes me feel sick.'

'Oh pet, come here and I'll try and explain.' She took the girl into her arms. No wonder she didn't enjoy the physical side of marriage if she'd never been told what to expect. Johanna had no way of knowing how hard or how often Charlie pressed his attentions on his young wife, and in the same way she had no knowledge of how long he would put up with Carmel's attitude before he went elsewhere. She'd have to have a word with Maddy over it. It was very worrying.

She was still concerned and disturbed when Tom came home, but when she broached the subject he was in no humour to listen to more of his childlike sister's woes.

'In the name of God, she's a married woman! It's time she grew up!' he said heatedly.

Johanna sighed. She wasn't going to tell him about Carmel's biggest problem and one, after talking to the girl for over an hour, that she didn't think could ever be resolved. She felt guilty, too; she hadn't thought there *was* a problem.

'She spends too much time with that Christine. She has more in common with that child than she does with anyone else, her husband included. I'm not going to get involved in any more arguments tonight, Johanna. I've had a hard day!'

'And you're a hard man at times, Thomas Kiernan,' Johanna replied through gritted teeth.

Neither Carmel nor Christine appeared for dinner. Carmel said she couldn't eat a thing and she couldn't face her mother-in-law either.

'I might have something, when Charlie gets in,' she'd said to Johanna.

At the table Caroline, ignoring Tom and Johanna, turned to her mother. 'Do you think we should wait for Charlie, Mother?'

'I think that would be an excellent idea, Caroline. Then we can all hear what kind of an explanation your mother has for the way she treated Carmel this afternoon,' Johanna said firmly, holding Elizabeth's gaze without wavering.

'Perhaps we might wait,' Elizabeth conceded.

'Well, I'm not waiting. I've been working hard all day and I want my dinner,' Tom declared impatiently.

'And since when have *you* had the right to decide matters in this house?' Elizabeth said angrily.

'Does it matter? Just eat your bloody dinner, woman!' Tom shouted.

Elizabeth's cheeks became bright red but her eyes were like two pieces of flint. 'How dare you speak to me like that! Never once in our married life did Richard swear at me, but I don't suppose we can expect anything less from a jumped-up, bog-Irish manservant.'

Johanna froze. Tom also had a terrible Irish temper. He got to his feet slowly. 'Maybe it would have been better if your sainted bloody Richard had sworn at you and maybe given you the odd swipe. You'd have been the better for it, you brass-faced old bitch!'

Elizabeth rose to her feet, knocking over her glass. 'Caroline, stand up! We are going out to dine. Fetch your sister!'

'What the hell is going on here?' Charlie shouted from the doorway, still wearing his hat and coat.

'Charles, I insist that you throw these people out at once! He used foul language to me! That low, common, dirty Irishman said your father should have sworn at me and struck me.'

'She deserved it!' Tom sneered. 'All the airs and graces

out of the sour-faced old besom. I bet she led your father a right dance.'

Before anyone else could start, Johanna got to her feet.

'I want this sorted out now,' she said, her voice low but carrying. 'Charlie, out of the goodness of her heart and with no thought in her head except for your mother's and sisters' happiness, Carmel offered to pay for them to have a good holiday in a very nice hotel as they used to before your father died. Your mother called her down here and insulted and browbeat her. I came in and found her in a terrible state.' She glared at Elizabeth. 'But this one wasn't brave enough to face me. Oh no. She went out, leaving Carmel heartbroken. Now all this nonsense started because she insisted we wait for you to come home until we had dinner and Tom wanted, deserved, to have his meal. He's been working all day, as you have.'

'God Almighty! I'm sick to death of all this!' Charlie exploded. 'Mother, can't you keep a civil tongue in your head and Tom, I'll not have you swearing at her or anyone else! Where is Carmel?'

'Upstairs, probably in tears,' Johanna answered grimly.

'Again! Is she ever anything else?' Tom fumed. 'She's nothing but an eejit – soft in the head. She's a huge disappointment to me. *I* can't get a penny out of her to help start up a business, but she's quite prepared to pay for a holiday for those three!'

'We want nothing from her,' Elizabeth raged. 'She has brought only trouble on this house! In the name of God, Charles, why did you ever marry her?'

Charlie looked around at them all. He was sick of them and he was getting sick of Carmel. She was more than just childlike, she *was* still a child. She cried and moaned and squirmed away from him whenever he tried to touch her, and it made him feel guilty and then angry. There were times when he thought she almost looked vacant, unaware of what was going on around her, uncaring too; deep in a world of her own and one into which he couldn't seem to gain entry. He felt as though he'd lost her but didn't know or understand why. Was there some trait of madness in the Kiernan family? It was a question he'd begun to ask himself.

'For better or for worse, I did marry her, Mother,' he said steadily.

'For worse. You said it, Charles, not me,' Elizabeth shot back at him.

'You can't blame Carmel. She doesn't understand and she has a certain problem she's going to have to overcome,' Johanna said, looking directly at Charlie. Surely he wasn't going to turn against the girl?

'So she told you,' he said flatly, as if there were no other people in the room.

'Yes, and she's very upset about it. Someone should have told her what to expect.'

'It's a bit late now.'

'Oh, surely not?'

Charlie became flustered. 'She's like a child and yet she wants a child of her own. But the way we're going, there's little chance of that.' His voice was bitter with frustration. 'I don't think we'll ever have children.'

'You've only been married a short time; there are years ahead of you yet.'

'I told you, Johanna,' Tom interrupted. 'It's about time Carmel grew up and realised that she *is* married, and at least tried to act like an adult. Now can we please just get on with our dinner. Charlie, sit down, man, for God's sake.' Tom made a mental note to speak very strongly to Johanna later. Charlie took off his coat and hat and threw them on a chair.

'Sit down, Mother. I don't want any more arguments, do you hear?' Elizabeth had never heard him use this tone before.

With a very bad grace everyone sat down and there was no more discussion on anything. The food, which stuck in everyone's throats, was eaten in silence.

Outside, in the hallway, Carmel leaned her forehead against the wall. She'd made a huge effort to put in an appearance at dinner. She'd washed her face, changed her dress and re-done her hair only to come down and hear her husband's terrible words. He thought of her as a failure. Believed she would never give him children. She felt cold, so cold that she was shivering. She was a disappointment to her brother, a worry and a burden to both Maddy and Johanna. She was the cause of John Shannahan's death, Richard Murgatroyd's death too, and had brought only discord into the home of his wife and daughters.

She would never have a baby of her own because she could never endure what it entailed to conceive one. Slowly she turned and went back upstairs.

Chapter Twenty-eight

Elizabeth and her daughters had gone to bed. As soon as the meal was over they had left the table in silence. Johanna was seeing to the children, and Charlie and Tom sat in the drawing room. Tom had poured them both a generous measure of whiskey.

'We're going to have to do something about Carmel and your mother,' Tom said seriously.

'What do you suggest?'

'You heard her. There'll be no peace in this house while she and Carmel are under one roof. Maybe Elizabeth would be better off in a place of her own.'

'This *is* her own. She's always lived here – are you suggesting I throw her out? And while we're on the subject, I won't have you swearing at her. No one has ever sworn at a woman in this house.'

'All right, all right, I just lost my temper, but you know how she feels about all of us.'

'Can you blame her?'

'For God's sake, Charlie, don't you start getting on your high horse. I was only trying to find a way around this problem. Maybe you and Carmel would be better off in a place of your own. Just the two of you.'

'Look, Tom, I'm not moving, we can't afford it.'

'You could damn well afford it if she didn't keep such a tight hold on that money.'

'I know you're disappointed that we can't get started in our own business, but I'm not asking her again. It's humiliating and besides, Carmel and I have a few problems to sort out.'

'Well, you can thank Maddy for the humiliating bit; what problems?'

'Personal ones.'

'Oh, I see. All that stuff Johanna was going on about?'

Charlie didn't answer but he poured himself another drink.

Tom held out his own glass to be refilled. 'I shouldn't, I've work in the morning, but ah, what the hell. I'll have one for the day that's in it!'

'A good sentiment, I'll drink to that,' Charlie agreed, knocking back his drink in one gulp. Being with Tom always made him more reckless. He knew that Kiernan was a bad influence, was only ever using him, but Charlie was drawn to his strength and confidence.

'You'll have to lay down some rules as far as Carmel's concerned. Maddy's always babied her, made excuses for her, but she'll have to understand that she's got to grow up. She knew what she was doing when she took her wedding vows and she was bloody happy to do so. You'll have to be firmer with her.'

'I don't think I can be, Tom. I think it's something in her nature.' Charlie paused. 'There's never been any trait of . . . eccentricity in your family, has there?'

'What the bloody hell does that mean? Do you think she's mad, out of her wits?'

'No! It's just that, well . . . since we got married, she's not . . . we've not . . .'

'She's refusing you your marital rights – is that it?'

Charlie nodded miserably. He hadn't intended to tell Tom but it had just slipped out.

'We can sort that out right away,' Tom said forcefully. 'I'll tell Johanna to speak to her. That's no way for a wife to carry on. No bloody wonder you're fed up. Have another one.' He refilled their glasses. 'At least that can be remedied.'

'I don't want to force her.'

'You won't have to, after Johanna has spelled it out. This is typical of bloody Maddy. She's the one who should have told her, but let's forget that and concentrate on how we can get her to part with that money. I don't want to be a bloody clerk all my life, and I bet you don't want to be a solicitor either.'

Charlie thought about it. He didn't enjoy his work at all; it was tedious and they were all so hide-bound in that office. Lately he'd begun to think longingly of the carefree days before his father had died and he'd met Carmel. These days they had to watch every penny just to keep up some semblance of the way they'd always lived. His father hadn't left a fortune.

'No, I can't say I enjoy my work, but we'll have to think of something that Carmel won't mind parting with some of her money for. Then, of course, there's explaining it away to Maddy.' He looked gloomy.

'You're right, we need a convincing reason – and as for Maddy, leave her to me.' Tom drained his glass and set it down decisively.

Johanna awoke from a shallow sleep. Tom hadn't come up yet and it must be past midnight. She got up and put on her dressing gown. There was a sliver of light showing beneath Charlie and Carmel's bedroom door but she didn't knock in case she disturbed them. She was halfway down the landing when she heard male voices coming from the drawing room. So Charlie wasn't in bed asleep, he was still down there with Tom. She hoped there would be no more arguments; she'd had enough for one day. She turned and made her way back. When she reached Carmel's bedroom she stopped. The light was still on. Was the poor girl waiting up for him? Was she going to try to make him understand how she felt, which was what Johanna had advised her to do? She knocked quietly but there was no reply.

'Carmel! Carmel, it's Johanna – are you all right?'

Again there was no response so she rapped harder. Something was wrong, she sensed it. Had Carmel overheard the row earlier on?

'Open the door!' she cried, but there was still no reply.

She tried the handle and it opened easily. Carmel was asleep, the covers pulled high around her chin. Johanna breathed a sigh of relief. Then her gaze strayed to the bedside table. Charlie's razor was lying there, open, and there was blood on it. She ran to the bed and dragged the covers away and her screams echoed through the silent house. The bed was soaked. The once crisp white sheets were stained scarlet, as was Carmel's nightdress. She ran to the door, shrieking for Tom and Charlie to come quickly.

Caroline opened her bedroom door and peered sleepily at her.

'Get back in your room,' Johanna told her. 'Get back *now*!'

Both Tom and Charlie were unsteady on their feet but as Johanna, now unable to utter a word, pointed into the room, Charlie's face drained of all colour and he uttered a strangled cry.

'Oh, Jesus, Mary and Joseph! What's she done? Johanna, what's she done?' Tom shouted.

'Her wrists . . . she's . . .' Johanna collapsed against his shoulder, shaking and crying.

Charlie was demented. He was sober now. Half sitting, half kneeling on the blood-soaked sheets, he held the limp form of his young wife in his arms, rocking her and calling her name over and over.

Elizabeth appeared in the doorway. 'Oh, Lord have mercy on us!' she exclaimed, glancing over Tom's shoulder and catching sight of her son, half covered in blood, with Carmel in his arms.

'Don't let those two girls anywhere near this door,' Tom commanded.

'Is she . . . is she . . .' the woman asked.

'I don't know! Johanna, pull yourself together,' he told his wife. 'I have to go for a doctor and someone will have to go to Faulkner Square for Maddy.'

Johanna made a huge effort. 'I'll go for both of them . . . You'll have to help, Charlie.'

'Get a cab. God, I wish there was someone like young Freddy here! Get dressed. Will you be all right?'

'I think so.' She must concentrate now on getting the doctor and Maddy. She must push to the back of her mind the sight of her poor sister-in-law and that dreadful scene.

'Charlie, are there any towels? Anything to stop her losing more blood?' Tom asked.

Charlie couldn't speak. She was dead. He'd lost her for good now. His beautiful, sweet-natured little wife was dead.

It was Elizabeth who snatched two towels from the wash-stand and handed them to Tom.

'Bind them as tightly as you can,' she instructed. Although visibly shaken she was in control of herself. If the girl was still alive, they had to try to save her. She had to pry Carmel's arms from her son.

'Give me some help while I strip off these sheets. Charles, *Charles* – get off the bed. Come on, son, sit in the chair with her.' Elizabeth thought how like a beautiful lifeless doll Carmel was. In fact, that was just what she had been – a pretty, shallow, empty-headed doll. It was so hard to tell whether she was alive or dead. But the bleeding seemed to have stopped.

Tom helped Charlie into the chair and Elizabeth hastily stripped off the bloody sheets and bundled them into a corner. The mattress was soaked, but that couldn't be helped. Then she went and found clean sheets and blankets and remade the bed. It would do until the doctor had been.

Charlie wouldn't relinquish his pathetic little burden.

'Lay her on the bed, man. Let us make her decent for the doctor,' Tom urged.

Charlie looked up at him with wild eyes. 'No! No! I drove her to this! You'll not take her off me.'

'Charles, no one is trying to take her off you. Sit by her on the bed. Just let us make her more comfortable.' Elizabeth closed Carmel's eyes. The girl had never been comfortable in this house. She and Caroline had seen to that.

Between them they managed to get Charlie to release her. Weeping, he helped his mother to remove the blood-soaked nightgown and pull another gently over her head. Then they laid her on the bed and drew the clean top sheet up over her.

'Don't cover her face, Mother! Please don't cover her beautiful face!' Charlie begged.

'No, we'll not do that, my boy,' his mother said heavily. 'The doctor should be here soon.'

Elizabeth washed her hands in the bowl on the wash-stand and then went to inform her daughters of the tragedy. Tom stood with his arms folded, watching Charlie. What had possessed his sister to do this terrible thing? *Was* there some taint of madness in her? Had she heard the argument? He'd never expected her to do anything like this, not in a million years. Like all Catholics, Carmel knew that self-slaughter was a mortal sin. And in killing herself, she had killed all of his chances of ever getting enough money to achieve his ambition.

The tick of the clock on the mantelpiece seemed very loud and he was relieved when Elizabeth came back, dressed and composed. Shortly afterwards, they heard the front door bell.

'I'll go. That will be the doctor,' Tom said, thankful to leave that awful room.

'How long ago did she do this?' the doctor asked as he followed Tom upstairs.

'We don't know. It could have been half an hour or two hours ago.'

'Did you feel for a pulse?'

'No, no. Her husband wouldn't let us anywhere near her. He's in a terrible state.'

'As would be quite natural in the circumstances,' came the curt reply.

Dr Prosser nodded to Elizabeth before he approached the bed, his gaze straying to the heap of bloodied sheets in the corner. He took Carmel's hands and turned them over. Then he felt her neck for a pulse and shook his head.

'Whenever she did it, she lost too much blood. She's dead, I'm afraid.'

Charlie moaned and slumped onto the bed.

'God have mercy on her soul. I should have sent for the priest,' Tom said quietly.

'Too late now for any of that,' Elizabeth murmured.

'You do realise that suicide is a crime? I will have to report it to the police.'

'Oh, is that really necessary? Oh, to think of the shame,' Elizabeth moaned.

Charlie raised his head. 'Is that all you care about, Mother, the bloody shame of it?'

'Now, young man, that's no way to speak to your mother,' Dr Prosser told him. 'I know you're all in a state of shock and I'll prescribe something for all of you, but let's have no arguments, please.' The doctor's calm but stern tones seemed to bring Charlie some measure of peace.

Maddy sat silently in the cab beside her husband and sister-in-law. As their horses trotted through the silent night-time streets, she tried to make sense of what Johanna had told her. At first she couldn't believe it. Johanna had been in a terrible state and could only gasp that Carmel was dead and by her own hand.

Martin had taken charge immediately, instructing Maddy to get dressed and getting Julia out of bed to make Johanna a cup of strong, sweet tea. Maddy had been worried about Carmel lately, commenting on how much quieter than usual she seemed. She had only that afternoon said she would go and see if Carmel would talk to her.

Martin had been so busy lately; both ships had been overhauled and were almost ready to sail again. He had contacted all the merchants who used to send all their cargoes to Buckley's for transportation. Although the business was well run, the old lady had let things slide a little and Martin was trying to expand with old and new clients. He'd also taken his Master's ticket so he could captain one ship, and he was looking for a good, reliable Captain for the other. It had all taken time, Maddy acknowledged to herself. But she should have made time for Carmel and her problems; they both should have done.

'Jo, I can't believe it. I just *can't*!' she said.

'Neither can I, Maddy. I should have gone and checked that she was all right, after the row.'

'What row?' Maddy asked listlessly. Oh, how she wished she'd visited her sister more often. What on earth could have happened, to make Carmel do such a thing?

'Oh, between Tom and Elizabeth and then Charlie. I *have* to talk to you, Maddy, but not here and not yet.'

'What about? Did you know anything, Jo? Anything at all?'

'Not now, Maddy, please.'

'Calm down, love,' Martin said, cuddling her. 'Johanna knows best. She was there.'

'And I wasn't. Oh Martin!'

'Now don't start blaming yourself,' he said compassionately. 'How could anyone have known?'

It was a relief when they finally pulled up outside the door. Martin paid the driver while both girls ran up the steps and into the hall.

Maddy was the first to reach the bedroom but as she

entered she clutched the door frame for support. Carmel was lying on her back with the sheet pulled up to her chest, her arms out of sight. Even in death she looked beautiful.

'No! No! Please God, Carmel, no!' She crossed to the bed and fell to her knees, tears pouring unheeded down her cheeks. She reached out for Carmel's hand but Martin stopped her.

'No, my love, better not. Leave her at peace now.' He gently pulled a stricken Maddy to her feet.

Johanna had buried her head on Tom's shoulder and was sobbing quietly. Charlie was sitting stroking Carmel's forehead and his shoulders shook with the force of his emotions.

'When? When, Charlie? And why? For the love of God, will someone tell me why?' Maddy begged.

'It was my fault. I'll never, ever forgive myself,' he answered.

'How was it your fault?'

'Maddy, please, not now,' Martin begged.

'Martin, I *have* to know!'

Johanna detached herself from Tom's arms. 'Come with me and I'll tell you.'

'That's right, go with Jo,' Martin said, and reluctantly she followed Johanna to her bedroom.

Johanna closed the door and pushed her sister-in-law gently into a chair.

'Why, Jo? What happened?'

Johanna knelt beside her. 'I think she might have overheard the row that took place here tonight. Tom lost his temper with Elizabeth over when they should eat, Charlie came in and it got worse. Tom said Carmel should grow up. She was willing to pay for her husband's family to go on a holiday, he said, but she wouldn't give him a penny for their business. He said she was a big disappointment to him and Charlie more or less said the same. Charlie said he was afraid they would never have children because . . .' She stopped, unable to go on. It was too sad and awful.

'Because what?' Maddy whispered.

'Because Carmel hated that side of marriage so much that she couldn't bear Charlie to even touch her. She just didn't know what was expected of her.'

Maddy looked horrified. 'Oh God! It's my fault! I never told her. I . . . I thought she loved Charlie so much that it would just follow naturally. If only she'd come to me.'

'Maddy, you mustn't blame yourself. You weren't to know it would end like this. Tom has to take some blame and so must Elizabeth and that spiteful daughter of hers. Carmel must have kept all this bottled up for ages. She only told me something of it this afternoon. I advised her to try to talk to Charlie about it, but she died before she could do so.'

'And it's too late now.' Maddy stared straight ahead, her eyes swollen with grief. 'I protected her so much – too much. I never let her take responsibility for anything and I should have.'

'I don't think she ever would have grown up, Maddy,' Johanna consoled her. 'There was always something . . .

missing. She and Christine were close and Christine is only thirteen.'

'Oh, Holy Mother of God, forgive me!' Maddy cried. 'We'll have to send for the priest.'

Johanna stood up and braced herself to deliver the next blow. 'No priest will minister to her, Maddy, and they won't bury her in sanctified ground either. She took her own life, remember – and that's a mortal sin.'

Maddy groaned in anguish. She'd forgotten all about that. It was an added burden for them all.

'May I go back to her now?' she asked.

Johanna nodded.

Martin was standing in the bedroom doorway.

'Let me see her again,' she pleaded with him.

'Maddy, come down with me and we'll have a drop of medicinal brandy.'

'Please, Martin. Let me see my sister just once more.'

He stepped aside and she went in. She looked at the pale, almost translucent face of her beautiful sister then bent and kissed her cheek. 'Carmel, I'm sorry. I'm so sorry for all your pain,' she whispered.

Martin put his arm around her waist and led her out.

Down in the kitchen, Elizabeth had made some tea. Johanna sat at the table, her head in her hands. As Maddy sank onto a chair next to her, Jo reached out and touched her.

'Tom has some sleeping powders the doctor left for us,' she murmured.

Maddy nodded.

Elizabeth placed a cup and saucer in front of Maddy. 'Here, drink this,' she said brusquely. 'It might help, though I doubt it.'

Maddy looked up at the older woman and anger began to burn in her. One way or another they had all contributed to Carmel's despair, but this woman had deliberately set out to make her poor sister's life a misery.

'I suppose you're happy now?' she ground out. 'You can have the house to yourself, Johanna won't want to stay here any longer. You hated Carmel. You tried to humiliate her, dominate her from the day she first set foot over this door.'

'I won't deny that I disliked the girl.'

'Dislike! Was it your "dislike" that drove her to do this? She offered to pay for a holiday for you – and all she got was abuse!'

'No one could have predicted that she would go and do this. No, I never wanted her here. I never wanted *any* of you here.'

'Don't worry, Elizabeth, you won't have to put up with us any longer,' Johanna interrupted tiredly.

'You can have this house to yourselves, but you'll never get any peace here,' Maddy warned her. 'That room will always be there to remind you of her. Of your cruelty to her. Of how she despaired, how she died . . .'

Elizabeth was about to reply but Tom and Martin came into the kitchen.

'Charlie won't leave her. We've tried but he's adamant,' Martin said, placing his hand on Maddy's shoulder.

'I couldn't care less what he does now. He is at fault too,' Maddy said bitterly.

'You can't blame him. He was a good husband,' Elizabeth fired up.

Maddy rounded on her. 'Was he? We're all responsible! You because you hated her and you showed it, as did Caroline. Charlie because he wasn't patient with her, me because I protected her too much but not when I should have, and you, Tom, because you thought of nothing but getting that money out of her for your own selfish ends! I'll never forgive myself but I'll never forgive you either. You're no brother of mine. I wish to God we'd never found you.'

'And I wish to God that you'd never left Ireland! You're an interfering, stubborn girl, Maddy, and I want nothing more to do with you.'

'Tom, Maddy, please! For the love of God, she's dead, let there be no more rows between you,' Johanna intervened. 'Yes, we're all guilty in one way or another, but fighting won't bring her back. And where, Tom, do you expect us to live?'

'I'll not live here and I'll not live with *her*! We'll get a house of our own.'

'With all the money you must have saved, no doubt you can afford one,' Maddy snapped. 'Oh Jo, I don't want to fall out with you.'

'You won't, and I intend to see you often,' Johanna said quietly but firmly. 'We *do* have enough money, and Tom has a decent job . . .'

Maddy shook her head. 'But he'll never be happy, Jo.'

'No, I bloody won't! It's fine for her to sit there with all her property and money—'

'And ships! That's all you want, isn't it? To see your name at the top of a letterhead. Owner of a shipping line!'

'So what if it is? I've worked and saved, you've done neither.' Their voices had risen and they glared at each other.

Elizabeth was outraged. They were arguing about her late mother-in-law's money, which should, by rights, have gone to Maud Buckley's next-of-kin, not this unspeakable family. 'If this is the way you carry on, I'll be glad to leave you to it,' she said coldly, picking up her cup and saucer and leaving.

'She's right,' Martin said. 'Carmel is dead because of all the hostility toward her. Let there be an end to it. Tom, I can understand ambition. It's what drove me on.' He clasped Maddy's hand and squeezed it before he went on: 'Find a place of your own and Buckley's will stake your first cargo. When you sell at a profit, we can work something out for the future. Trade is booming, Liverpool is growing, there's plenty of room for new businesses. What do you say? Let's be partners, not enemies. There's a lesson to be learned from tonight's tragedy.'

Johanna held her breath and prayed Tom wouldn't turn the offer down.

Maddy looked astonished. She was still furious but she trusted Martin's decisions. She was hot-headed, while he was always more clear-sighted. He didn't want the family torn apart.

Finally Tom nodded. The offer was better than nothing.

Chapter Twenty-nine

The funeral of Carmel Kiernan, was a very quiet affair. Maddy had bought a piece of land next to the small local cemetery and Reverend Owens had agreed to conduct a brief service. Her own Church had turned its back on Carmel but Maddy was determined that her sister should have some kind of Christian burial. Father Molloy had wept for the destruction of the gentle girl and had promised to pray for her soul.

In the days that followed Carmel's death, there had been so many things to do but everything had a dreamlike quality to it. Tom and Johanna and the children had moved back into the house in Faulkner Square. Tom and Martin had been closeted for hours, discussing all their futures. They had seen nothing of Charlie, even though Maddy had sent Freddy around with a list of items she would like returned. They were small things, bits and pieces that would remind her for ever of her sister. A day or so later, they had been neatly parcelled up and delivered, but there was no note with them.

The day of the funeral was thundery. Clouds hung in threatening dark grey banks and it was hot and humid. Everyone was uncomfortable in their mourning clothes. Maddy, holding tightly to Martin's hand, looked across the yawning black hole at her feet to where Charlie, his mother and sisters stood with bent heads. She knew that she would never see any of them again. That period in their lives had passed.

Johanna stood with her arm linked through Tom's and he patted her hand. She was so thankful that at last there seemed to be some peace and security ahead. It wasn't an ideal situation as far as Tom was concerned, but it was better than the option of being a clerk all his life. He seemed to have come to respect his brother-in-law, who had been very fair with him, she thought. There had been no need for Martin to make such an offer, but thank God he had. She dabbed away a tear. Carmel's short life had not been very happy. She had lost her parents, she had lost John Shannahan, her physical beauty had been a curse and Johanna was privately convinced that the girl had been mentally unstable. It was a theory Martin agreed with, which helped to make everything more bearable for Maddy who blamed herself so much. For herself, Jo would be glad when today was over and they could all start again. Together. As a family.

The Reverend Owens cleared his throat and read the Twenty-third Psalm in a well-modulated voice. One by one they all joined him as the men Martin had hired, lowered the coffin into the ground.

Both Maddy and Johanna refused the handful of earth, substituting roses in its place.

'She's at rest now, my love. We must all remember her the way she was, not like the last time we saw her,' Martin said soberly.

'I'll always remember how she looked on her wedding day,' his wife said tearfully.

'Beauty like hers, like that of the roses, never stands the test of time. It fades quickly, Maddy.'

She nodded, and after thanking the vicar, they turned away. There was to be no wake. It didn't feel appropriate.

'There's something I want to show you, Maddy,' Martin said as they approached the waiting carriages.

She looked puzzled. 'What?'

'Wait and see. It's a surprise.'

'I'll be glad to get home. I've a headache. I think it's the weather,' Johanna said. 'You can tell us all about this surprise later.'

Tom gripped Martin by the shoulder in a gesture of thanks and solidarity before directing his wife to their carriage.

'Why are we heading for the docks?' Maddy asked, fanning herself with the small ivory fan she had brought in her purse.

'I told you, it's a surprise.'

'Does Tom know about it? I thought he looked a bit smug.'

'He does. And I'm not answering another question, Maddy.'

She smiled to herself. She had a surprise for him too.

As usual the docks were very busy and some of the odours on the quayside were far from pleasant.

'Oh, I'd forgotten how they stink!'

'Not far now.' He took her hand and hastened their steps. Then he stopped and lifted her up on to a bale of cotton.

'Why have you put me up here?'

'So you can get a clear view.'

'What of?'

'Of that.'

She followed his pointed finger. Two square-rigged sailing ships were tied up. Their hulls were resplendent with new paint and varnish. Their new white canvas sails were furled.

'Don't they look grand, Martin?'

'They do, but look at their names, Maddy.'

She read the black lettering. *Brennan's Pride* and *Brennan's Promise*. 'Oh, Martin!'

'You are my pride,' he said tenderly, 'and my promise is that I'll always take care of you.'

She smiled back. 'Us. You'll always take care of *us*.'

He frowned, then his brow cleared. 'Does that mean what I think it means?'

'It does. In six months there will be three of us!'

He gathered her into his arms and swung her around. 'Then what will we call the next ship?'

'The next ship?'

'Well, you know your brother, Maddy. We won't stop at just two.'

'Then we'll have to wait and see if it's a boy or a girl!'

'And until then you'll have to take care of yourself.'

'I will, Martin Brennan, I promise. After all, we'll need an heir or heiress for the Brennan Line.'

We hope you enjoyed reading LOVE AND A PROMISE.

Read on for an extract of Lyn Andrews'
new novel . . .

Liverpool Sisters

Available now in paperback.

HEADLINE

Chapter One

1907

'It's like closing the door on our old life, isn't it, Mam?' Olivia Goodwin remarked, smiling at her mother as they stood on the worn stone doorstep of their terraced house. There was a note of wistfulness in her voice, however, for it was no longer *their* house.

Edith smiled back ruefully at her eldest daughter, thinking how at sixteen Livvie – as she'd been called from babyhood – resembled herself at that age. The same thick, light chestnut hair which waved naturally, the clear grey eyes and fair complexion, the same slender build – although her height she'd inherited from her father. And Livvie was right; they *were* closing the door on their old life. Number 11 Minerva Street off Everton Brow had been her home for most of her married life. The houses were old, early-Victorian terraced villas with a yard at the back and were far from what could be termed spacious, having only a kitchen, scullery and a parlour downstairs and two bedrooms upstairs. They were not the easiest to keep clean either for they opened directly on to the street, but it had been 'home'.

She reached up to the brass door knocker, highly polished as usual, and gave it a slight push to ensure the door was firmly shut, before turning away. A frisson of regret washed over her at this final moment of departure. When they'd first come to live here they hadn't had much, just the very basic necessities really, but gradually over the years they'd acquired more and better quality furniture for her husband Thomas's efforts to raise their standard of living had been nothing short of superhuman. Now he'd decreed that this house – and indeed this area – was no longer at all suitable for their status and income and she'd been given little choice but to agree, but she was sad to leave this house behind for another family to move into for she was leaving so many memories behind too.

Both Livvie and her younger sister Amy had been born here, and here too she'd suffered the loss of her baby boys, both stillborn. Two boys whose tragic loss Thomas had bitterly regretted and railed against, while she had mourned them silently and stoically, knowing these things all too often happened.

'I suppose it *is* like leaving our old life, Livvie, but we should look on it as a new beginning – a blessing, in fact. Your pa's worked so hard so that we can all enjoy a better, a more comfortable life.' Her gaze took in the smartly tailored pale grey three-quarter-length coat edged with black braid that Livvie wore over a matching skirt that reached to her ankles, revealing black leather buttoned boots, and the large-brimmed, elegant hat that covered her daughter's upswept hair. At sixteen Livvie was classed as 'grown up' and was now dressed accordingly, but she, Edith, had never had such clothes at her daughter's age; she'd possessed a jacket for Sunday best but she'd had to make do with a shawl for everyday use. Yes, thanks to Tom's efforts they'd definitely come up in the world.

Livvie took her mother's arm as they stepped on to the pavement, slowly nodding her agreement. She knew she should be delighted, excited even – after all, they were moving to a much nicer area and a much bigger and grander house – but she wasn't. She felt very apprehensive. She knew all their neighbours here and she'd grown up with all of the kids; would they fit in in the new neighbourhood? Would they be welcomed and accepted or would they be looked down on and shunned? Despite her mother's optimistic cheerfulness she knew that Edith was feeling apprehensive too and was also suffering the wrench of having to leave friends and neighbours of many years standing.

She glanced down the street for the last time, seeing a couple of women standing on their doorsteps despite the raw cold of the October morning. Most of their farewells had taken place yesterday but those few stalwarts were watching the proceedings with avid curiosity for the Goodwins' furniture and possessions had all been loaded into the removal van her father had hired at some expense. He'd said it wouldn't be at all seemly or dignified for them to arrive in the new neighbourhood with everything piled haphazardly on to the back of a horse-drawn cart. These days her pa seemed to set great store on what he considered 'dignified', she thought. In the past when people had come into or left Minerva Street their possessions had been transported on a cart or, if they had virtually nothing, moved on a hand cart.

Her father was urging her mother and sister into the hired hackney which was to transport them to their new home.

'Livvie, stop dawdling! We don't have all day!' Thomas Goodwin's tone had a sharp note of irritability.

'Coming, Pa,' Livvie replied, casting a last glance over her former home and raising a hand to wave goodbye to the watching neighbours, before hurrying across to the hackney and climbing in, settling herself beside her sister, who appeared to be quite excited.

'Well, that's goodbye to Everton Brow and I can't say I'm sorry to be leaving all those narrow, dirty old streets behind,' Thomas stated with some satisfaction as the vehicle moved slowly off.

Edith managed a smile. 'Oh, I wouldn't say that, Tom. We had some happy times there.'

'And some that were not so happy either, Edith. No, life for us all will be far better from now on.' He brushed an imaginary speck of dust from the sleeve of his coat. 'I've achieved what I set out to do, what I always *intended* to do. Make my way in the world – in society – have my own business and a home in a respectable, affluent area.'

Edith nodded slowly. Yes, that had always been his ambition in life; he'd grasped every opportunity that had presented itself and had worked long hours, never sparing himself in his efforts to achieve that goal. Middle-aged though he now undoubtedly was, he was still what she considered to be a handsome man. He'd not put on weight, his bearing was still upright and almost military and even the fact that his once dark hair was now turning grey suited him. It made him look distinguished, she thought. His suit was of a good quality woollen cloth and his dark overcoat well cut, his bowler hat brushed to sleekness. In all he was the picture of a successful man, she mused with some pride. Oh, he wasn't the easiest of men to live with these days; she had to admit that. As he'd grown older he'd been spurred on by ambition and he'd become acutely aware of his shortcomings and strove to overcome them, developing a profound sense of 'decorum' which she thought sometimes bordered on the obsessional. At times he could be dictatorial and overbearing and he'd never been a very demonstrative man but she'd learned to accept all that. He was a good husband and father.

Lyn Andrews

'An outstanding storyteller' *Woman's Weekly*

Now you can buy any of these books from your bookshop
or direct from Lyn's publisher.

To order simply call this number: **01235 827 702**
Or visit our website: **www.headline.co.uk**